Calamity Rayne Gets a Life

CALAMITY RAYNE
BOOK ONE

LYDIA MICHAELS

Calamity Rayne Gets A Life

Print ISBN: 978-1-957573-28-1

Romantic Comedy

Dedication

This book was written for Briana, a dorky hypochondriac who traded her chalk for a quill and discovered her calling by trusting a long line of accidental events. You jumped with a half-ass parachute, but what a blast the fall has been. Bring on the calamities.

Somehow I'm Thirty

1

S ometimes adults do reckless things to prove they aren't old. I might be approaching one of those moments. As a courtesy to myself, I rejected terms that started with *mid-life* anything, because those labels were for old guys with little dicks, buying flashy sports cars and investing in hair clubs.

I wasn't old. Nope. I was a wobbling little calf fresh from the womb. I was veal—a rather aged, thirty-year-old veal—but still veal.

My twenties weren't overly challenging, and I loved having the authority to decide my life, but as I entered this new decade of adulthood there came an unexpected and immense pressure to accomplish something. I, of course, had no clue what that something might be, so I was scared shitless about my future. This was a first.

I stared at my flickering birthday candle, wondering if other thirty-year olds still put this much thought into wishes at this stage of the game—or even blew out candles for that matter. Not that I cared what other people did, but everything I was, and planned to be, seemed to hang in the balance of this one little wish, so I needed to make it count.

Give me a sign, something that tells me what I should be doing with my life...

Breathing in, I held it for a moment then released the breath. A trail of smoke slithered from the cooling wick.

"Welcome to your thirties!" Elle cheered.

Coffee houses were our mecca, so I was ringing in this birthday with my best friend and a glorious chocolate muffin I intended to annihilate—guilt free—because there were no such things as calories on birthdays.

I plucked the candle out of my muffin and sucked off the crumbs. "Thanks."

"You're gonna have a great year, Rayne. I can feel it."

Unlike me, Elle seemed to accept our aging with resigned grace that retained her sex appeal. I had no sex appeal. That wasn't an age thing. It was a me thing.

Studying my friend, I broke off a piece of the muffin, a pinch of envy for her self-assuredness teasing my celebratory mood. My envy had nothing to do with the fact that she was prettier than me or had her career in order, but everything to do with her irrefutable happiness. It radiated from her in waves.

I'd never been overly content with my life. I sort of just floated on the cusp of acceptable behavior. Elle's confidence was borne of milestones I'd yet to experience, and a big part of me feared I'd never again have the opportunity to make up for everything I skipped over in my twenties.

I was clearly being irrational and stupid. Thirty was just a number. So why did this number carry more weight than all the others? Bullshit concerns bogged down my everyday thinking. Would my boobs noticeably droop by next year, before I ever got the chance to use them as weapons of mass persuasion? Dumb crap like that was all I could think about now.

"You're stressing. I can read you like a book," Elle commented, well used to my irrational thought process.

"Doesn't it get to you?"

"What, being thirty?" She laughed. "No. For all we know this could be the best decade of our lives. Stop acting like the crypt keeper and eat your muffin."

Most days, I was easy like Sunday morning and as redundant as a slinky. My lack of major accomplishments didn't typically faze me, being that I'd been living with myself for thirty-freaking years. But three decades was a long time and realizing so much time had passed made me wonder if I was doing something wrong with my life.

Here I was, living life as I always had, then—*boom*—I was suddenly squinting through what was once twenty-twenty vision trying to figure out how the fuck a rogue hair grew out of my neck overnight. Shit like that really pissed me off, because deep down I still felt young, but my age was proving otherwise.

"I don't like it. Maybe I'll just be twenty-nine again. Women do that, right?"

"Rayne," Elle said with patience borne of a lifetime of knowing me. "You will continue to be you. Our age doesn't mean anything."

But it did. It meant everything was perhaps halfway over, and I had nothing to show for that first half of my life. "Maybe I'm depressed."

"You're not depressed."

"I could be. The rest of the world is."

Elle rolled her eyes. "You're a hypochondriac, and you need to get over yourself and stay away from medical websites."

Women in their thirties wore "mom jeans" and talked about grocery coupons. I'd live off dairy products if I could. *I'm probably eating too much cheese.*

I never quite mastered "adulting". While all my friends discovered their purpose in their early twenties, I avoided any hint to mine, lacking that elusive focus factor that gave them the diligence to follow through. There was a very high chance my mother forgot to fill out the paperwork diagnosing me with some sort of attention deficit disorder because my focus never stuck on one goal for too long. That included things like relationships, possessing my own shelter, or having a savings account.

"You need a boyfriend," Elle reiterated for the ten thousandth time.

As always, I treated her statement as a rhetorical one. There was nothing wrong with me. I could be girlfriend material. But boyfriends weren't *my* material. They didn't do for me what they apparently did for the rest of the heterosexual, female population.

A backdated issue of *Rolling Stone* was wedged between the bench and the window of the booth. Pulling it out of the crease, I tossed it on the table and paged through. My attention snagged on an advertisement for tequila. A sunny beach and a dewy shot of liquor filled the page as an unrequited longing to escape my life took hold.

Sighing, I bit into my muffin. "I need a vacation."

Elle glanced at the magazine. "So take one."

I snorted. "Oh, okay. Where did I leave my trimming sheers for the money tree?" Waitressing was a paycheck-to-paycheck job.

Elle turned the magazine and gave the advertisement a second glance. "You could book a flight and spend a weekend at a resort for under a thousand dollars. Don't act like it's impossible."

Maybe finding a boyfriend would be easier. Two women walked by our booth holding hands, laughing and looking totally at ease. "Do you think lesbians have it easier than straight women? I could be gay."

"You're not gay. You just sleep with the wrong men."

"Yeah. I'm not gonna do that anymore."

She laughed. "You haven't done anything in *two* years."

Rolling my eyes, I once again wondered if I'd ever view sex the way my friends did. Elle loved *the sex*. Me not so much. Maybe I was non-sexual. Was there an acronym for that? It really didn't matter.

This was the pointless shit my life had whittled down to, worries about my nonexistent sex life I had no interest in resurrecting.

I swallowed the last of my muffin. "I think I could date a woman. People act like dicks are the main event. I could go without. No one even noticed when I gave up penises for Lent."

Elle sipped her coffee and silently chuckled. "You're not Catholic."

"I still support the cause."

She shook her head. "You're an idiot. You just need to find the right guy, someone to distract you from the monotony of life."

"Blah. Who am I going to date? We see the same people all the time." That was a definite drawback of living in a small town. "And I don't feel like worrying what someone else thinks."

Elle folded her arms on the table. "Rayne, you know I love you, but you've been in this funk for a month. I want to see you happy, but *you're* the only person in charge of your happiness. Sometimes you have to face your fears to reap the rewards. You need to switch things up in your life."

"I think I'm just overdue for a vacation. I need to figure out my finances."

"Good." Elle nodded. "Start planning and make it happen."

Digging my phone out of my pocket, I signed into my bank account app. "Ugh, someone definitely forgot to water the money tree. Jesus, my finances are pathetic. We should be at a bar." I flashed the screen to Elle and she grimaced.

"You can't afford drinks," she joked. "You just

have to think outside of the box. Maybe you could get a summer job near water or something."

"Like as a camp counselor?" Visions of swatting away mosquitos and children screaming filled my head.

She shrugged. "Or maybe working for someone rich who would let you stay in their big, fancy guest house."

My brow quirked. "Like a personal assistant?"

I'd never thought of doing that for a living, and I'd thought of many different careers over the years. Waiting on people or following directions wasn't something I excelled at, but I did like money and being the personal assistant to the right person could pay off in more than cash, especially if that person was rich and wanted to put me up in a nice bungalow overlooking a golf course or a beautifully landscaped heated pool. Totally unrealistic, but that fantasy was much more pleasant than the camp counselor scenario.

My smile grew as I imagined basking in golden rays of sunshine while an oiled up pool boy fanned me with a palm leaf, but the vision shifted, and *I* was suddenly holding the palm leaf, my arms tired, an annoying bead of sweat working its way down the center of my back as a the soft buzz of cicadas grew to an overwhelming roar. *Erase.*

Living with my mom and waitressing at the same place since college didn't scream big prospects. I definitely had financial limits. I guess you could say I was ordinary, living one week to the next.

My degree in education loomed in the back of my mind like an unclaimed opportunity to make a decent living, but it turned out I wasn't a huge fan of teaching. I was more of an office supply hoarder who got turned on by Sharpies in every color and various sized sticky notes. But my quasi-organization skills had to be worth something.

"You should think about it," Elle pushed. "Dust off your resume and see what's out there. A change would be good for you."

"I'll think about it."

When I got home that night, I figured what the hell. I updated my resume, put it out on a few of those nifty job search sites, and left the filters pretty wide open. Two days later my inbox was overflowing.

"Holy shit," I muttered, scrolling down the page of emails. Did I accidentally lie about my qualifications? This was going to be easier than I thought.

Or not. As I clicked open the first few messages I was disappointed to find they were not for resorts, but cubicles—otherwise known as soul sucking death traps. The starting pay was barely above minimum wage. The rest were spam.

And why were so many emails offering me Viagra? "Damn it. I don't have a penis, people!"

After sending half the emails to spam, I scrutinized the remaining job offers. There were no positions overlooking the coast of Greece or boasting sandy beaches and cerulean seas. So unfair. Stupid adulthood.

The erectile dysfunction spam kept coming, along with several invitations to online dating sites. Giving Elle's dating advice some consideration, I uploaded a picture of myself to one of the match sites and made a very generic profile. My information came down the next day after a member sent me a close up picture of his penis.

I nearly ruined my laptop when I spit coffee all over the screen. What the fuck was wrong with people? It seemed like everyone was trying to shove a metaphorical dick down my throat. No, thank you.

I wasn't some miraculous thirty-year-old virgin on anything so dramatic. That shit only happened in romance novels. I had *the sex*. It was unremarkable. Elle said I did it wrong, and I probably did the first time because all I remembered was the guy's crushing weight and things slipping around. But my partner seemed to enjoy it, so I had the sex again.

I made sure guy number two rounded all the necessary bases. He felt me up, got his hand down my pants, and even did some things that almost felt good, but switched gears too fast for any true pleasure to register. Then I was being stuffed like a Thanksgiving turkey, and it was over. Leaving me, once again, wondering why the fuck people were so obsessed with sex.

Me and *the sex* simply didn't mix. And I was fine with that. If donuts tasted like dog shit, I wouldn't eat them just because they had the reputation of being donuts. Sex had a reputation of being this incredible thing, but it wasn't. A big part of me assumed most females were lying about how good it was as part of some women's lib aftermath.

So after the online dating penis pic fiasco, I took dating back off the table and invited Elle over to help with my ongoing job search. Something was wrong with my resume because I was only getting spam and offers for telemarketing positions.

Sitting on my couch with a notebook and wine, we brainstormed. "Maybe I could volunteer for some research professor who's studying in the Congo."

Elle tipped her head, not ruling out the possibility. "If you could find something like that, but do you really want to risk catching some funky flesh eating bacteria or waking up with spiders in your tent?"

I shivered and gagged. "You're right. Screw that."

"Don't rule out personal assistant yet. I'm sure we can find someone looking for a live in. Maybe you could be an au pair. Your education degree would definitely help with that."

"Blah, taking care of a kid twenty-four seven? I don't think so. If I ever saw a beach, I'd be lugging a hundred pounds of sand toys and sunblock. And there would be no tequila on the job." Plus, kids made me nervous.

"So we need to find a rich adult looking for an assistant—preferably one with a guesthouse who lives somewhere exotic."

I pointed at her with my pen. "Yes. That is what I want. Now, where does one find such a job?"

"I dunno." She shrugged.

I carefully wrote the words *Assist Rich Person* on the center of my page that had penises doodled in the margin and a pretty decent sketch of Snoopy.

My obsession with doodling dicks was probably part of the reason I couldn't take sex seriously.

Penises were funny, especially when one doodled mustaches and hats on them.

I tapped my pen on the spine of my notebook. "I wish there was a special classified section for jobs like that."

The chances of me getting on Oprah's payroll were unrealistic, but maybe I could find a fresh, rich person to hire me. I wasn't rich, so I knew nothing about the places such people hung out or what sort of activities they might need assistance doing.

We wasted a great deal of time searching the Internet for Leonardo Dicaprio's address. He wasn't listed. After calling it a night I debated if I should stop chasing clouds and start living with both feet on the ground—maybe even put in for a teaching job.

In the days that followed I didn't remove my resume from the Internet, nor did I apply for any jobs in classrooms. I just sort of stayed exactly where I was, because making no decision was always easier than making a difficult one.

I stayed stuck in that stagnant place for days, falling into my ordinary routine of working and passing time after my shifts with our friend Tyler who frequented the bar.

I'd come to accept I'd likely retire at that bar after another thirty years slipped by, and somehow I told myself that didn't sting. But it did, so I stole Tyler's fries and consoled myself with food. Food was my drug, my sexual pleasure, my... I just really liked food.

Elle barreled into my work with a shit-eating

grin on her face and bustled over to our usual area. "I have the best news!"

She stole my cup and finished my draft as I frowned. That beer and Tyler's fries were all I had going for me in my life at the moment.

"You're buying the next round?" I asked. I'd wanted that last sip.

"Nope. Remington Davenport had a heart attack!"

Remington Davenport was an old silver fox that had more money than Midas. He was always being interviewed on television and getting politicians to bend to his will. Not the sort of celebrity Elle typically kept on her radar.

"Where did you hear that?"

"I was at the gym, working out behind Cute Butt Guy who happened to be watching CNN. See how much I love you? I actually interrupted my hot ass fantasy to change channels on my machine and do a little investigating. I don't really know who Davenport is, aside from being crazy rich, but I like the jewelry his daughter designs and his one son is hot—the other one is okay. Anyhoo, apparently, he had a heart attack at his estate in New Jersey and took a nasty fall down the steps."

"Get to the point," our friend Tyler griped, finishing his beer.

"Shut up," Elle snapped and turned her excited expression back to me. "So they were interviewing his son, you know, the serious one who's always with him—not the cute one with the man bun. The *other* one. He said his dad's recovering from the attack but he's going to be off his feet for the next few months because when he fell he also broke his leg or something. Isn't that great?"

"That he's recovering? Sure."

"No," she shook her head. "Don't you see, Rayne, they're going to need additional help!"

My brain finally made the connection and I gasped. "Oh my God!"

Tyler rolled his eyes. "Puh-lease. You think you're going to get a job working for the Davenports? You? They aren't going to hire just anyone. They're probably looking for a Harvard graduate and likely have an arsenal of interns salivating at the opportunity. You'd be lucky if someone even glanced at your resume before sending it off to spam."

Elle waved over a waitress and ordered another round. Turning back to Tyler she barked, "You don't talk anymore."

My heart was beating faster than usual as my mind started a mental checklist. I needed to act quickly since the story already broke on CNN. Would email be the best approach? Maybe something on paper would be better. Or perhaps a phone call if we could find a contact number. Remington Davenport was *huge,* and he had homes across the country. There had to be a phone number somewhere.

Elle's fingers snapped in front of my face. "Rayne, are you listening?"

I distractedly looked at her. "Hmm?"

"I said my boss used to do Naomi Davenport's hair when she worked in New York."

Connection! "Do they still talk?"

"No, but she might have her number."

Tyler shook his head. "I'm sure going through Remington's *ex*-wife is just the way to get in his good graces."

Rather than respond, Elle tapped the bottom of her beer bottle to the mouth of Tyler's freshly opened one, which caused the carbonation to erupt and forced him to plug his bottle with his lips and chug it down before it overflowed all over the table.

"You don't talk anymore," she snapped.

When she looked back at me, I whispered, "Will you ask her to call Naomi?"

Elle held up her phone. "I'll text her now."

It's really amazing when alcohol gets involved in life altering decisions. Logic fades and risks shrink from hurdles to hopscotch until nothing stands in your way. Then, on the tails of a hangover, you wake up in your childhood bedroom—not at all luxurious—and sobriety sets in hard.

After draining my first cup of coffee, I stared at my cell phone in shock. I had a voicemail from none other than Naomi Davenport, first wife to one of the wealthiest men in the world.

My fingers shook as I listened to her message a second time and I immediately had stomach pains. I don't know why, but I've always gotten cramps whenever faced with new opportunities like job interviews, car purchases, or the last pair of leather boots on sale just before winter. All of these things landed me in the bathroom. So it was no surprise that I was calling my BFF in a panic from the toilet the moment my brain kicked on and my coffee kicked in.

"She called! Naomi Davenport actually called *my* cell phone!"

"That's awesome, Ray!"

"Awesome? It is so much more than awesome. It's fucking amazaballs!"

"Did you call her back?"

"No, I'm waiting for my nerves to settle and trying to figure out what the hell to say to a woman like Naomi Davenport."

"Well, first, take some Pepto and pull it together. Second, stop using both her names. It's creepy and puts you below her. You gotta fake it 'til you make it, and that means acting like you're on the same level."

"But I'm not."

"Who says? They're just people with money and fancy cars and way nicer houses than us. You could play that role."

I honestly believed I could imitate "good enough"—at least for a short time. I could do anything I put my mind to temporarily, but duration was my Achilles heel.

I was the type to invest in expensive sneakers, run two miles, and never looked at a treadmill again. Some people had big eyes when it came to eating. I had enormous eyes when it came to life, but also the attention span of a squirrel on crack when it boiled down to following through. Which was why I owned about twenty beautiful journals with three pages written in each one, a diary for each year starting with a promise to write every day.

"Rayne! Focus!"

I stood and washed my hands, wedging my

phone between my shoulder and my ear. "I *am* focused. How long does a broken leg last?"

"I don't know. Five weeks? Two months?"

That seemed doable, but I was jumping ahead. "I guess I should call and see if she can give me a contact before I start thinking of the cons."

"Yes. You need to call her back before they find someone else for the position. According to the interview I saw yesterday, he's in the hospital for the next couple of days, but once he's out his family will have hired someone. You have to jump on this quickly, so stick a tampon up your ass and take a sedative to calm your nerves and make the call."

I smiled, because Elle truly knew me better than anyone else in the world. "Do you really think I have a shot at being Remington Davenport's assistant?"

"I think talking to one of his ex-wives is the closest you've come in your hunt for Occupation Luxury, so you better make the call before she forgets about the favor. Call her back. Call me when you're done."

I winced as my nerves continued to knot painfully in my stomach. "Okay. Thanks, Elle."

"You got this. I'm hanging up now."

I took a calming breath and glanced at the toilet. "Pull it together, Calamity Rayne." Backing out of the bathroom, I grabbed a notebook and turned to a blank page.

I replayed Naomi's message one last time and broke into a sweat. Maybe I had a glandular problem. The temptation to look up symptoms for sweating was resisted because I knew those websites only led to extreme hypochondria. But seriously, women were not supposed to sweat this much.

Ignoring the distraction, I saved the contact in my address book and hit the call button.

That Awkward Moment Called My Life

2

The call to Naomi was over in less than four minutes. She complimented my ambition, offered some sage advice on developing a thick skin if I planned to enter the vicinity of her ex-husband's ego, and concluded with a friendly laugh that bordered on patronizing.

As I stared at the number to reach her son, Hale Davenport, or the one Elle liked to refer to as "the other one", my skin broke out in a fresh sweat. Hale was Remington's eldest child and usually filled the background of any press conference that included his father. He had one expression—and it was very close to the kind of face a stoic man would make while receiving an enema.

To better prepare myself, I Googled the Davenports and beefed up my background information. There was another son, but I could never remember his name. He had long hair and Elle referred to him as "the hot one". He was younger and had that effortless, cool air about him. The only reason anyone knew he existed was because he sometimes showed up in family portraits whenever the media got a peek inside one of the Davenport's homes. And he was gorgeous.

Naomi, Hale's mother, was someone Remington had been married to for a New York minute. Seraphina, the youngest heir to the Davenport throne, came from Remington's third marriage. There weren't any kids from the fourth marriage, which actually seemed like it might last, but that wife passed away a little under a year ago, and there had been no news of future wives since.

Remington Davenport was attractive in a rugged, wealthy manner, sort of like a beat up one hundred dollar bill—quite valuable, but also well used. His silver hair and leathered complexion was shadowed by an intangible essence of authority. His wives—all four of them—were decades younger than him and clearly in it for more than his looks.

I wasn't saying someone couldn't love him for more than his money, but let's be honest. Remington Davenport didn't get to where he was by being easy. He was a demanding bastard with an ego the size of Texas. It made him a cutthroat businessman who exacted preciseness.

Basically, he was scary as fuck, but I totally wanted to work for him.

Assuming I might somehow manage to finagle my way into this man's life, I'd probably have the interview shits twenty-four seven, but working for the Davenports would be the experience of a lifetime, and I wanted the opportunity regardless.

Desperate to see how the other half lived, to have a minute to pretend I knew what it felt like to wipe my mouth on a linen napkin I didn't have to stain treat, I envisioned my success like *The Secret* had taught me. The fluffiness of their towels pressed into my skin and the affluent scent of their air filled my lungs. Yes, I wanted all of those luxuries. But without the price tag, of course.

Money took work. I couldn't imagine the amount of work it took to accumulate the sort of wealth Remington Davenport had, especially being that his parents were basic middle-class citizens at some point. It seemed reasonable for him to be a short-tempered grump. All the man did was work. I didn't want that sort of life. I just wanted a glimpse of the benefits. Who wouldn't?

After another long trip to the bathroom, I had my thoughts somewhat organized. One had to take chances to make changes, but I liked to have a bit of science backing all big decisions.

First, I decided I would call from the kitchen because my living room had a dead zone that sometimes dropped calls. Second, I would use my Marilyn Monroe voice because when I got excited, I sometimes spoke way too loud. The Marilyn kept me at a tolerable decibel without too much shifting from my natural dialect. It would be easy to phase out should I actually meet these people in person.

And third, I would finish up the call with an epic freeze frame jump and air punch, because hey, I was putting myself on the line here and might be making a total ass out of myself. Then I would have some ice cream because it was rude to leave half a pint in the freezer for more than a day.

Laying out my notepad I wrote down the words *thank you* and underlined them next to Hale Davenport's name. I was a fairly polite person, but sometimes I forgot to express my appreciation and gave the impression of having no manners.

Taking a deep breath, I dialed and hit send. The phone rang twice, and then my heart imploded, and all the air in my lungs evaporated.

"Davenport."

I liked to talk. I talked all the time. I even talked in my sleep. Ask me the time and I'd build you a watch. I didn't even need a conversation topic, and sometimes I talked about three totally unrelated things at once. So the fact that I was now sitting at the kitchen table like a brain dead mute shocked the shit out of me. For the first time in my life, I was utterly speechless.

"Hello?" the thick voice spoke into the phone again.

Say something. Say anything. Talk! Just fucking make a sound instead of sitting there. Jesus fucking Christ you're blowing it—

"Are you..." *Oh God.* "...happy with your current cell service?"

Annnnnnnnnd the line went dead. I was a total twat-faced tit. Tossing my phone on the table I dropped my head into my palms and groaned. "Great."

I blew it. What the hell was wrong with me? The severity of what just happened hit hard. All this searching and hoping was for nothing because now my number was probably blocked like a goddamn telemarketer.

Reaching blindly for my phone I dialed Elle while pressing my face to the surface of the table.

"Did you call?" she answered.

"Yeah," I moaned, still not lifting my face off the table. Why bother? I was going to live here forever.

She tsked. "Oh, that doesn't sound good. But hey, at least you called. You took a chance."

"You didn't hear my side yet."

After explaining what happened, Elle was silent for a minute. "So call him back."

"I can't. He probably blocked my number, and now he thinks I'm a telemarketer, or worse, a crazy person who impersonates telemarketers. Who does that?"

"You're not the first."

"Prank calls went out with the fourth grade, Elle. I ruined it."

"No, you didn't. You just need to call from a different number. And this time *talk!*"

"I don't know what happened. I've never been speechless in my life. He answered and suddenly I broke out in a cold sweat, and I couldn't think."

"Maybe it wasn't even a Davenport. Did it sound like The Other One?"

"Well, Naomi gave me his number, and he answered by just saying Davenport. His name's Hale by the way."

"I don't know if I've ever heard him talk. How was his voice? If he was a Davenport he'd probably have a stern voice."

I frowned at the phone. "I don't know. He said

two words and hung up. Can we please focus on the fact that I totally screwed up what might have been the chance of a lifetime?"

"Relax, Rayne, it was a phone call. Do the number block thing and call back once you get your big girl panties on."

"Can you call?"

"No. For God's sake, be a grownup!"

I huffed. "Fine."

That was a lie. I wasn't going to call back.

"I mean it, Ray. Call him back or you really will have blown your chance and I'm not going to pity drink with you when strapping on a pair and using words could've avoided this. Stop making such a big deal out of nothing."

"Fine," I gritted with a little more conviction. "But I expect some sympathy when I call you back in two minutes."

"Deal, but you have to call him first. Goodbye." The line went dead.

"God, she's such a bitch," I muttered as I punched in the code to block my number and dialed again. "This is so stupid."

It was now abundantly clear how farfetched this entire plan was from the beginning. The chances of more than a phone call were nonexistent, which really made me an idiot for being afraid. Admitting this was a one and done deal made everything a lot easier to face.

Send.

The phone rang only once this time. "Davenport."

I cleared my throat and winced at how bad that

probably sounded as a greeting. "Hi, I'm looking for Hale Davenport."

I'll tell him who I am and then this will all be over. I'm totally getting drunk tonight.

"Speaking."

Apparently, rich people only spoke in one-word sentences.

"Hi. My name's Rayne Meyers. Your mother gave me your number."

"My mother?"

Ah, two words. Progress.

"Yes. You see, I'm calling about your father. I'm sorry, by the way, and I'm glad to hear he's recovering. I heard he might be in the market for an assistant, and I was interested in the position—of assisting your dad on his road to recovery that is. I'd like to help out." God, I really should have rehearsed this.

"Are you calling from a company?"

"Um, no company. Just me here at Rayne Meyers and Associates." I silently laughed, certain I was self-sabotaging any chances. But let's be real. This was not how the rich and famous hired the help.

He didn't seem amused. "Are you a nurse?"

Feeling like I was back in the principal's office and half my age, making light of the situation didn't seem the most mature decision I'd made that day. I was clearly wasting this man's time. "No, sir."

"Have you ever worked for one of our companies?"

Now he was using lots of words and not blowing me off, which cranked my fear back up to full throttle. I pressed a hand to my stomach and shut my eyes, willing the nervous cramps not to return.

"No. Honestly, I heard your father was sick and might need some assistance. It sounded like an interesting opportunity and—"

"The position requires traveling and would be no less than six months. Is relocating an issue?"

Okay, now I was really scared because he was actually acting like this might be possible. "I...I can relocate."

"I'm sorry. Can I put you on hold for a minute? I need to take this call."

"S—sure." The line silenced and I stared at my kitchen searching for hidden cameras. When a minute passed, I started doodling penises. Big penises, little penises, hairy ball penises—

"Ms. Meyers?"

The pencil flew out of my hand as my palm covered the erotic graffiti on my page. "I'm still here."

"If you'd like to email me your resume I'll take a look. We need to fill the position by tomorrow, so you should hear back from someone within a few hours."

"Oh. Okay." What the hell was happening?

He rattled off his email, and I scrambled for my pencil, quickly jotting his contact info down in between dicks. When the call ended I wasn't sure if it was all a dream or what? It couldn't possibly be that simple.

Drumming my fingers on the surface of the table I considered calling Elle, but I knew she'd just yell at me for not sending the email first. So I pulled out my laptop, opened my resume and gave it a quick onceover before attaching it to an email.

Being that I forgot to say thank you on the phone, I made sure to slip my gratitude into the body of my email. Then I hit send.

I called Elle, and the waiting game began. I didn't know why the initial phone call made me so nervous, but once it was done I was fine. I was proud of myself for taking a chance. It was pretty badass to say I almost worked for the Davenports once. No part of me ever expected a response, so when the email came that night, I suspiciously wondered if someone was fucking with me.

They wanted to fly me out for an interview—all expenses covered. I would be meeting Remington Davenport in the flesh, along with two other candidates, and the selected person for the job would be staying on and starting the position immediately.

Big decisions required big cocktails so off to the bar I went to meet Tyler and Elle. Once I summed up the outcome of my day, they both stared at me like I had assholes for eye sockets.

"Say something," I begged because at the moment I felt trapped in a dream or a pretty wild acid trip. This situation was totally surreal.

"It's like a game show," Tyler muttered, with a starry gaze in his eyes.

Elle was still reading over the email I'd printed out. "They're going to pay for everything. Even if you don't get the job, you get a trip out of it."

Tyler snapped out of his gaze. "Can you afford to miss two days of work?"

The printed page smacked down on the table

with Elle's palm. "Why do you have to be so negative about everything? She could get the job and then she'll be living it up in a mansion, sending your sorry ass postcards for the next six months."

He scoffed. "What year are you living in? They don't even make postcards anymore. And I'm not being negative. I'm being realistic. This is going to wind up *costing* her money regardless. I'm just saying maybe we should look at this realistically. What are the chances they'll actually hire someone with no experience as a personal assistant?"

He was right. Missing two days of work would pinch. But I didn't come this far to chicken out. I swiped the email off the table and forced my lips into a nervous grin.

"I'm going. I mean, what's the harm? I'd only have to miss one shift if it doesn't work out. I could get a flight back within a few hours." Missing one day's pay was less of a hardship than missing two. "I want to at least say I tried."

"Atta girl!" Elle cheered.

Tyler's support was cautious. "I hope you get it. I just don't want you to be crushed if you don't."

"I never expected to get this far, so I have to see it through." Seeing things through was a new thing I was trying since turning thirty.

Shoving off the stool, I folded the email into my purse. "I gotta go. I have twelve hours to pack and figure out my flight arrangements."

Sliding my spare key off my keychain I held it out. "On the off chance that they hire me, who wants to get my car from the airport?" I could afford to park it there overnight, but anything longer would break the bank.

"I'll get it for you," Tyler said, taking my key and hooking it onto his set.

Standing, Elle gave me an affectionate hug. "You got this. Don't get too tan when you're visiting one of their private islands and try to text me at least once a day with pictures of weird rich people shit."

My arms squeezed tighter, hoping with every optimistic ounce of my being that I might have the chance to do just that. I faced Tyler and held out my arms.

Reluctantly, he stood and hugged me, patting my back twice. "Try to avoid calamities, Rayne."

I snorted. "Like that's possible."

Shoving off, I smiled. "This is cool, right? I mean, this puts me up there with that chick from high school that ditched reality for a year to ride elephants and meet monkeys, doesn't it?"

Elle nodded. "This is cool."

Blowing out a breath, Tyler smirked. "If you actually meet Remington Davenport for even a minute that's pretty awesome."

"Aw, look at you finding the good in a situation." I lovingly punched him in the arm. "You're growing."

There was a strange energy tucked in that moment, as I looked at my two closest friends, feeling like an era was ending and a new chapter of my life was about to open.

I smiled and blew them each a kiss. "I love you guys. Make sure—if I get the job—you only talk about me in your best Robin Leach voice. I'm off to spy on the rich and famous!"

Look out world, here I come! Cue *Mary Tyler More* theme song.

Ahoy! And Other Boat Words...

3

Crossing the threshold of the plane to the aerobridge, my stomach plunged into my feet. I made it. Everything familiar was back in Oregon, which was invigoratingly frightening, like an orgasm in a public theater with people eating popcorn in the next row. Not that anything like that ever happened to me, but once I was on a date at the movies and the guy started kissing my neck. We had to stop because I couldn't quit giggling.

Looking out at the bustling sea of travelers, I couldn't recall the last time I felt so delightfully uncertain. Maybe during my first substitute teacher job, but that didn't end so well. I really hoped this situation wouldn't conclude with the same *oh shit, I've made a huge mistake* epiphany.

No. I wasn't even going to entertain such thoughts. This was me taking a chance and discovering something great. New Jersey might be my mecca, my utopia, my final landing place that made all the immature voices in my head turn into grown up voices with big ol' balls that faced the world head on. Yes, that was the spirit!

I was *Sex in the City's* Carrie Bradshaw, hungry for a fast paced, high-energy world to set on fire with my feminine wiles. The travel clothes and flip-flops would be removed as soon as my wardrobe arrived. Once I located my luggage and a bathroom, I'd switch into my perfect *don't you want to hire me* ensemble and embrace my new, sexy self.

Clopping along with the stampede of disembarking passengers, I flowed with the current to baggage claim and smiled brightly as the belt crowded with suitcases. There was no going back now and soon enough I'd be sitting in front of Remington Davenport, or one of his very important underlings.

A man shouldered to the front of the mob, and I shifted out of his way. *Okay, buddy, we all have places to be.*

Rather than fight for a spot closest to the action, I held back and let the more aggressive passengers claim their luggage while I sent a text to Elle and my mother letting them know I'd arrived safely.

Elle responded with a,

Go get 'em, tiger!

Dots bounced on my mother's text for a good three and a half minutes. Finally, her message came through.

Wonderful! Call me when you can.

Followed by about twelve emojis.

Chucking my phone into my carry-on, I braved the conveyer belt again, which only had a few pieces left on the strip. Suitcases circled through the rubber curtain and back down the little slope. I couldn't wait to change and march out to a cab doing my best *shlemiel, schlemazel, hasenpfeffer incorporated* skip toward making my dreams come true. In my fantasies I was Shirley, but in reality, I was a total Laverne.

Now, where the hell was my suitcase? A new load flowed through the little car wash strips, and another swarm of hasty passengers crowded the luggage-go-round. A robust man blabbering into his cellphone trampled my toes and pain exploded in my foot. Practically swallowing my tongue as a throbbing ache shot up my leg, I hobbled back a step.

Son of a bitch! Annie Wilkes from *Misery* could have done less damage with a sledgehammer.

Limping out of the madness, I decided to wait by the mouth of the hatch and watch the suitcases roll onto the conveyer belt. As the second crowd thinned, I regrettably accepted that my luggage wasn't there, but that was okay. I'd give my name to baggage claim, and they'd find it soon enough.

Weaving through the mob, I scanned for a directory. Limping toward the sign that said BAGGAGE CLAIM, I passed time counting mustaches, wondering when they'd come back in style.

"May I help you?" the irritated attendant greeted without a grin.

I met his moodiness with abrasive cheer. "Hello, I didn't see my luggage on the belt."

He slid a laminated sheet across the counter with pictures of various types of suitcases. "What kind of bag was it?"

Scanning the selection, I found one that seemed similar to my suitcase. "I guess this one's closest, but it's a leopard print." That should make it easy to find.

The man's brows lifted, but his expression remained blank as he typed information into a computer. "Contact phone number?"

After rattling off my number I asked, "Do you know how long it'll take to locate my stuff?" I was sure they had an overflowing cart somewhere with a lonesome leopard bag waiting for me on it.

He rolled his eyes. "Could be anywhere between two hours and two days *if* they locate it."

"If?"

No, no. *If* wasn't an option. I had to pack for anywhere from six hours to six months in one bag, so I carefully chose all my favorite things. There could be no losing those items.

"I don't understand. Where could it have gone?"

He shrugged. "Sign the screen."

What exactly was I signing? Scanning the small print advising me of my rights to file a claim against the airline after seven days and asking me to list the value of my luggage's contents, I recalled what I packed, certain it was every priceless piece of clothing that could fit within the seventy-pound weight limit.

How does one put a numeric value on her favorite sweater—a sweater I bought back in high school from a store that no longer existed and therefore could never be replaced? Tapping the four-hundred-dollar option I slid the stylus back in the holder. They'd find it. No sense it worrying.

"Should I just wait on that bench while you look?"

Moody baggage claim guy had no sympathy for my loss. "I'd advise you to keep your phone on and wait for the airport to call. If you don't hear from anyone in a few days, call the number at the bottom of your paperwork." He printed out a receipt and slid it over the counter. "Have a nice day."

Did stuff like this happen to Carrie Bradshaw?

Stepping aside so the next person could file their claim I glanced down at my outfit. Dear God, what was wrong with me?

Plenty of well-dressed thirty-somethings wheeled their suitcases out of the airport, most of them clothed appropriately for any setting. Yet here I stood, rocking a faded T-shirt under an old cardigan. And what the hell was on my pants? Jesus, was that glue? When had I used paste? This was the perfect example of how I missed a few chapters in the *Being A Grown Up* handbook.

Spotting a gift shop, I headed in that direction. If I could grab a sundress or maybe a nicer shirt that might help, but they only had men's polo shirts and things that said New Jersey on the chest—and holy shit! Was that *forty* as in *dollars*? For a crappy airport shirt? Who was paying that? Certainly not this girl.

Working my way through the automatic doors, I came face to face with a clusterfuck of gridlock weaving around a parade of idling cabs and hostile drivers. Horn honkers were the worst. I never hailed a cab and was pretty sure I couldn't do one of those fancy whistles without slobbering all over my fingers, but I gave it my best effort.

Nope. Definitely didn't possess any hidden whistling talents.

Wiping the drool from my fingers onto my stained pants, I tried waving a taxi down.

"Hellooooo," I sang, hoping someone might notice me.

"Miss Meyers?"

Turning at the sound of my name, I frowned at the sleekly dressed chauffeur holding a sign that read *Rayne Meyers.* That was my name, but...

"Are you Rayne Meyers?" He glanced at a Blackberry and back at me with a frown.

"Yes, that's me." No one said anything about transportation.

He must have a copy of the headshot I was asked to send, which really wasn't an honest telling of anything, being that it was eight years old and from my cousin's wedding, one of the few times I actually wore makeup in the past decade.

"Do you have luggage?"

"They lost it. Are you with the Davenports?"

"Yes, ma'am. Mr. Davenport's awaiting you at the marina. He's anxious to be on his way."

"On his way?" Where the hell was he was going with a broken leg so soon after a heart attack?

"If this is all you have we should be going. The others are waiting." He ushered me to the sleek limousine and opened the door.

"Others?" I slid into the seat and the door

quickly shut. That was when I saw the other prospective caretakers sitting inside the limo.

Competition. "Hi. I'm Rayne." I gave a nervous finger wave.

Both were dressed to impress. The other woman, although she might actually be younger than me, seemed high strung, sparing only a glance and a partial smile before she went back to her iPad where she scanned some sort of text with her finger.

Oh, come on. No one read that fast.

"Are you interviewing for the assistant position?" the guy asked, dressed in a serious business suit, and seeming rather glad to meet me.

"Sure am." My answer made his grin double. No doubt he was sizing up the competition and found my presence non-threatening. "My, uh, luggage was lost. I planned on wearing something nicer."

The woman briefly glanced up from her iPad again, and I could swear she snickered. The guy held out his hand as the limo eased into traffic. "I'm Miles Pendleton. I'm from Davenport Communications, the page division. Are you from the intern program as well?"

Nervous laughter sort of clunked out of me. "No. I'm just a waitress."

Now, the girl gave me a full inspection. "Have you ever worked for Davenport before?"

"Nope, but there's a first for everything."

She closed the cover of her iPad and slid it into a black leather briefcase resting by her feet. She had the same shoes my grade school librarian wore. "Where did you go to college?"

"Oregon State."

Her brow lifted beneath her slicked back, blonde hair. "You're an undergraduate?"

"No, I graduated."

"What was your major?" she asked.

I didn't realize there would be an interview before the interview. "Education. What did you major in?"

"Business."

"I'm getting my MBA," Miles chimed in. "I won the legacy scholarship last spring."

"What's the legacy scholarship?" I asked and immediately wished I hadn't.

The girl's snicker was unmistakable this time. "It's a Davenport grant."

Okay, these people were a little more informed than I was about the whole Davenport enterprise. That was fair. They'd obviously done their homework and *not* lost their luggage.

"You don't honestly expect a man like Remington Davenport to hire a waitress as his liaison over the next six months."

"Um..." I shrugged, but the feisty chick in my head was getting ready to cage fight this twat mite for assuming she was better than me after two seconds of knowing me. "Why not?"

She laughed. "The fact that you can't answer that on your own shows how unqualified you are to even be in this car." She glanced at Miles. "Looks like the competition just decreased."

Oh, I'd cut a bitch. "I'm sorry. What did you say your name was?"

"I'm Cadence Thorndale, and I graduated second in my class from Yale."

I tipped my head empathetically, clicking my tongue to the roof of my mouth as I pouted. "Harvard wouldn't take you?"

Miles's mouth parted in a smile as Cadence gaped at me in horror. "I do hope they can send your luggage back to your home address. No doubt you'll be there before they locate your belongings."

"We'll see," I challenged, my gaze narrowing until she glanced away and withdrew her iPad. She didn't make eye contact for the rest of the drive, but neither did Miles.

Now, I really wanted the job. But another part of me admitted I was highly under qualified. If anyone deserved it, it was probably Miles. I mean, he put on a tie.

Slightly nervous, I texted Elle.

> Competition is fierce. I'm up against Sheldon from Big Bang and that moody chick from Erin Brockovich.

My phone vibrated.

> Who? Julia Roberts?

. . .

> No, the one who asked Julia
> how she contacted so many
> people and Julia made some
> snarky comment about blowing
> all of Hinkley.

> I'm sure you can give a better
> blowjob than that girl. Chin up.
> You got this.

I PURSED MY LIPS, WHICH HAD NEVER touched a dick, but I was pretty sure the sophisticated Cadence of Yale wasn't keen on sucking cock either, so the playing field was slightly level in that department. Neither of us were getting hired based on sex appeal.

As we rode to the marina, I organized my carry-on and took inventory of the few items I had on hand. If I stayed, I'd need necessities like deodorant, a toothbrush, and some snacks.

I tried to imagine the interview process, but being that we were going to a marina my imagination was stymied. Maybe I wouldn't even make it to meeting Remington. Chances were one of his toadies would narrow down the odds and make a choice for the man in charge.

Miles was the right choice. Cadence, on the other hand, had saber claws and the personality of chalk. I could probably outrank her with my glowing personality, but she had professionalism in spades. Me not so much.

I felt a little bad about going up against Miles. He seemed nice enough. Maybe it was part of the Davenport strategy to put us all together before the interview started. Shit. I was starting to sweat.

As a waitress, I had some people skills, but Remington Devonport wasn't people. He was more along the lines of an alien life form women fawned over, but I wasn't that sort of woman either, being that the opposite sex and I didn't exactly mesh when it came to fancy flirting or vagina tricks. My vagina had no tricks. It was just sort of there, part of me like an ear or an elbow. I needed it, but had no control over how well it worked. Anyway, yuck. I could never flirt with some old guy to get a job, no matter how cushy that job might be.

The limo pulled into a posh marina, and the other passengers shifted, stowing away their devices and adjusting their cuffs. I gave my hair clip a tug and licked my thumb before rubbing it over the stain on my pants. Nope, wasn't coming off. Seriously, when did I use glue?

"That's the *Lady Parr,*" Miles said as he pointed to the largest ship glimmering in the harbor.

Holy crap. It was like the boat from *Overboard* but bigger. I immediately wanted to see if the closets looked like the ones Kurt Russell built Goldie Hawn.

"Why is it called *Lady Parr*?"

Ten bucks said Miles had the answer.

Before he could answer, Cadence said, "Lady Parr was Henry VIII's first wife."

Everything she said struck me as irritating, so I acted like she didn't speak at all. Thankfully, Miles expounded.

"He buys a yacht every time he gets a divorce. It's part of his divorce-moon. When his first wife left, he named the yacht *Lady Parr*. When he and Barrett Devonport's mom split, he bought *Catherine Two*. After divorcing Seraphina's mother he bought *Anne of Cleves* and when his last wife passed away he got *Jane Seymour*, but he's never sailed in that one. I think it's because he loved her most."

"Jane Seymour was King Henry's favorite wife," I added, pleased I could keep up with the conversation.

I should have been disgusted that Davenport named boats after six queens, which left him the option for two more failed marriages, but I thought it was somewhat romantic, especially since he couldn't sail the one he loved most.

"You should ask him about it," Cadence suggested, as she slid her leather briefcase onto her lap.

I, too, shifted my discount Old Navy shoulder bag, treating it with the level of respect Armani luggage deserved. "Maybe I will."

We parked alongside a dock that crept over the bay. The door opened, and I exited first. The thick air was so different here, wafting with strange odors of sea life and the nearby marsh.

We followed the chauffeur down the weathered

planks to the enormous ship. Surely only rich people needed toys this big and shiny. How much did it cost to fill the gas tank of a monstrosity like this? I didn't have a clue, but I was pretty certain Mr. Davenport's dick was tiny if he needed four yachts this size.

The moment I stepped onto the plank—or whatever one called the bridge thing that went from dock to boat—I walked out of my comfort zone and trespassed into someone else's lap of luxury.

Grateful that my sunglasses were one of the few possessions I maintained during my travels, I placed them over my face as the late afternoon sun beamed off the gleaming exterior. A tall silhouette caught my eye as a man watched from above, but he was too far away to make out any features.

The fine hairs on my arms stiffened with a chill despite the heat of the day. No one else seemed to notice his presence, but as I stared up at him he seemed to look directly at me—

"Watch it," Cadence snapped, as I missed a step and my flip-flop tripped me. Who put steps on a boat? Gah!

I glanced back to the upper deck, but the man was gone.

"Mr. Davenport is awaiting you at the main deck dining area," the chauffeur announced.

I didn't do nautical terms, but I could manage a pretty decent pirate dialect when drunk. "And the main deck is...?"

"You're standing on it," Miles whispered helpfully.

"Gotchya."

Following the driver down a narrow corridor, the coast was on our left and frosted windows brightly reflecting the sun to our right. I tried to take in as much detail as I could, but everything struck me as clean, white, and shiny.

The bay air wasn't briny, but there was definitely a sense of being on a boat as large bells clanked in the distance and the slight rocking of the craft caused waves to lap at the sides. The faintest scent of diesel coated the marshy air.

Stepping through a glass door, the chauffeur cleared his throat. "The Davenports prefer no shoes touch the carpets."

Staring down at the pristine ivory rug I understood why. I slipped off my sandals and placed them next to Miles's polished dress shoes, feeling bad that he had to wear his nice suit with socks. We followed our chaperone through a few narrow passageways, around a bend, past a spiral staircase that led to places unknown and landed in an open common area.

"Welcome."

Ripping my attention from the polished marble tabletops, I glanced at Remington Davenport. He wasn't wearing his usual power suit, but his thick black brows against his tanned, weathered face and silver hair were unmistakable.

"It's a pleasure to meet you, Mr. Davenport." Kudos to me for being the first to speak.

Cadence and Miles topped me by doing the mature thing and shaking hands with him. Bastards. I should have thought of that.

"Have a seat." Wiping his mouth on a linen napkin, he tossed it over a plate of pasta and waved a hand, which immediately triggered a maid to collect the dish and carry it away. Someone was feeding him pasta? Shouldn't he be on a strict diet after a heart attack?

The three of us filled in the long edge of the polished table directly across from Remington. Reaching to the seat next to him, he produced three files, each one labeled with our individual names.

"Let's begin. Which one of you is Ms. Thorndale?"

"I am, sir," Lady McTwatface said.

He tipped his head, as he paged through the files and tossed them aside. "We'll start with you, Mr. Pendleton. Why should I hire you?"

Miles rattled off what sounded like a well-practiced and logical explanation for his services. At the end of his elevator pitch, I was convinced we all needed a Miles in our lives. He was clearly overqualified for the job.

"And you, Ms. Thorndale?"

"As you can see by my extensive resume—"

"Let me stop you right there," Remington interrupted, and I'd be lying if I denied getting a mild jolt of pleasure seeing her focus jostled right out of the gate. "I've read your resume and my memory's fairly decent. I don't need your stats regurgitated. Tell me what makes you better than the people sitting to your left and your right."

Cadence drew in a slow breath but didn't break a sweat. "Fair enough. I'm dependable, not easily sidetracked, and prepared to be the best option, no matter what that entails."

He raised a dark brow. "I praise your confidence and determination." His gaze shifted to me. "Ms. Meyers?"

There were probably tons of wise things I could have said, but let's face it, this man didn't need another person kissing his ass. Shrugging, I simply said, "I want the job more than them."

"And why is that?"

"Because I was looking for it before the position even became available. You fit my needs before I fit yours."

He glanced at the files and lifted the cover of mine. "You're the one who called Hale." It wasn't a question, but I nodded anyway. "And how is it you, with no prior experience with my companies, found out about the job opening?"

"Um, my friend saw your son on CNN. She knew I was looking for a similar position, and she told me you were in need of a personal assistant."

"You're a teacher?"

"Waitress...sir." I'd never naturally called a man sir in my entire life, but the others did, so I copied.

"And—I'm sorry, what exactly are you wearing?"

Pulling the lapels of my cardigan over my shirt I narrowed my eyes at Cadence who seemed to be fighting a smirk. "My luggage was lost."

He cocked his head. "Yet you arrived in that. You left your home, went out in public, and boarded a plane wearing a hand me down sweater and leggings, never once thinking something else might be more appropriate?"

A nasty little snicker slipped from Cadence's

direction. It wasn't like I left the house wearing footy pajamas. I mean, I'd be the best dressed in a *People of WalMart* video, but he had a point. I looked like a Women's Studies major on a three-day coffee bender gearing up for finals, not someone out to get a job from one of the wealthiest men in the world.

"An oversight, sir."

He turned his attention back to Miles, investigating his references and what he planned to do about his MBA classes should he be hired for the job. Similar questions were asked of Cadence, who had good answers for all of them, but when he got back to me, his eyes narrowed.

"Ms. Meyers."

"Yes, sir."

"Your mother assures me you're a nice young lady."

Who else was I going to give as a reference? I simply smiled.

"And Elle Tuttle tells me you always keep your appointments."

Fuck. He actually called *all* my references?

"Could you describe your professional association with Ms. Tuttle?"

"She's my, um, hairdresser."

"I see." His gaze lifted to my hair clip. I had a stylist for a reason. Ponytails and clips were as far as my expertise went. "Perhaps you should schedule another consultation soon."

"I'll do that." I'd probably have the opportunity tomorrow when my ass was sent home.

"Please take a piece of paper from the tray and a

pencil." Just as I was about to ask what tray, a woman appeared holding said tray. Once we had our paper and pencils in hand, Remington continued.

"Draw a circle with three lines in the center and three lines outside of the circle. Inside the circle, list three qualities all of you possess. Do that now."

Ah, shit. I drew vertical lines. Turning my page, I stared at the blank spaces. Well, Cadence was a competitive biotch. Miles was smart. And I didn't belong here. Realizing I had started to doodle while thinking, I quickly erased the start of a thick penis shaft.

Cadence put down her pencil and folded her hands. Miles had also finished writing. Damn it. I quickly jotted down the first qualities I could think of off the top of my head.

"Mr. Pendleton, what did you write?"

"Ambition, college degrees, and knowledge of the man interviewing us."

Damn. Good answers.

"And Ms. Thorndale?"

"Autonomous, resourceful, and perceptive."

He arched a brow. "Perceptive indeed, if you gathered all that about the competition during a short car ride. Ms. Meyers, what did you write?"

Ah, crap. "We're not wearing shoes, we're on a boat, and we all want to work for you."

Every set of eyes, even the woman who had delivered the tray of papers, shifted to me. Slowly, Remington's mouth turned up in an almost disbelieving, but amused smirk.

"I'd have to say you came up with the most indisputable answers, though I'm not sure you grasped the purpose of the task. On the three lines outside of the circle, I want each of you to write qualities that set you apart from the others and only you possess. If you match another person's answers, consider it a mark against you. Begin."

The rasp of pencils scratching over paper occupied the silence. Once I finished filling in my answers, I put down my pencil and looked up. Miles said he was earning his MBA, was trained by the page program designed by Davenport himself, and had memorized every detail of Remington's Wikipedia page and the pages of each of his companies.

Cadence referenced her knowledge of the stock market, the fact that she spoke five languages fluently, and her degree from Yale. It was getting a little pretentious. *We get it. You're smart.*

"And Ms. Meyers, let's hear your responses."

"Well, I have people skills, because I'm a waitress, so I interact with hundreds of strangers daily. I don't have any facts about you memorized because I'd rather learn from the source, and I'm not looking at this job as a means to an end, but more so an experience in itself. I just really think it would be neat to work for you for the next few months."

He nodded. "Eric will escort you above deck, and I'll call you back one by one. Miles, you may stay."

This was like a game show. I must have done something wrong to be put on the penalty deck with Cadence. We did each other a favor and didn't talk while we waited. I practically forgot she was there once we settled in on the foam bench bolted to the floor of the deck.

Holy shit, this place was totally nuts. There was a pool—a mother fucking pool—sunk into the floor not twenty feet away. I needed the chance to swim in that thing.

"Ms. Thorndale," the chauffeur, Eric, called.

Cadence rose and paused. Facing me one last time, she smirked. "It was interesting meeting you, Ms. Meyers. Have a safe trip home."

Oh ... that girl. Why were people nasty like that? What had I ever done to her? Sure, I was probably going home, but wasn't that enough? I mean, why rub my nose in it? I should—

My thoughts were distracted by the sudden sense that I wasn't alone. Glancing at the pool, I saw it was empty. My gaze wandered over the vacant deck, but no one was there. It was hot in the direct sun, but I shivered, the hairs on my arms lifting much like they had when I first arrived.

Shading my eyes, I gazed overhead and spotted a familiar silhouette, only this time I could make out his broad shoulders and the way the wind caught wisps of hair by his ears. He was wearing dark glasses, but there was something familiar about him. My attention zeroed in on his jaw, the slight shadow, and strong line. He wore a dress shirt open at the collar. Everything inside of me wanted him to turn—

"Ms. Meyers?"

I jerked my attention to Eric, who waited by the door leading inside. Glancing back to the upper deck, the man stepped out of view. Maybe it was Davenport's son, *The Other One*. He was usually in the same vicinity as Remington.

Eric led me back inside, and I was surprised to find Miles and Cadence absent. Where were they? Was this like some *Hunger Games* shit where people kept disappearing? Ah, they're in the study with Colonel Mustard and the candlestick! I really knew very little about fancy living, but I assumed even houseboats had all the elements of *Clue*.

"Have a seat, Ms. Meyers."

I dropped into the chair like a well-trained collie and looked for any signs of the others.

"They're gone."

Gone as in waiting in another room, or off the ship?

"Do you like waitressing, Ms. Meyers?"

"Not particularly."

"Then why do it?"

"Money."

"I assume you make something just above the poverty line."

Dick. "Roughly."

"Why not teach?"

"I didn't like teaching as much as I thought I would."

"So you won't do something you dislike that pays a sustainable income, but you'll do something you don't like for less than minimum wage."

I shrugged. He had a point. "The most I can mess up is an order of fries at the bar. I'd feel pretty bad about screwing up someone's child."

"Good point. Why is it you want to be my assistant?"

"I think it would be interesting."

"The job, not me. If you were interested in me,

you would have started with Davenport, but you started with a job search. What was it you hoped to find?"

"A change of scenery, mostly. I'm not really sure. I just thought it would be different."

He nodded. "I'll expect you to be at my beck and call. If I need something in the middle of the night your phone will ring, and I don't like to wait."

Wait, did this mean I had the job? "Are you offering me the position?"

"I do hope you'll become a bit more intuitive by the end of your six months, Meyers. Yes, I'm offering you the position."

"Er—why? I mean, Miles was perfect—"

"Should we call him back?"

"No, but..."

"Let me explain the basics of any investment. A decent businessman will always understand the return. You, a thirty-year-old waitress from Oregon, prove the most affordable investment, but we must also consider the risks. A woman like Ms. Thorndale will rebound quickly. Don't be foolish enough to assume this was her only opportunity. And Mr. Pendleton will do well to finish his masters and start at a higher paying entry position. You, however, have no other options, am I right?"

"Well, I could go back to waitressing."

"Thrilling, I'm sure, but I think *this* is your only opportunity for the change of pace you desire. That tells me you were being honest when you claimed you wanted the job more than the others." He tapped a finger to the surface of the table and pointed at me. "That's hunger, Meyers. I like working with people who are hungry for more. And, I like that you don't seem to sugarcoat situations even when it sheds an unflattering light on your own circumstances. Your clothes for example."

"The airport probably called by now—"

"Regardless, I think you're capable of hard work. Why else would you be on your feet all day when you could be sitting on a carpet reading stories to impressionable children?"

Dick again! The tiny teacher part of me that still remained took great offense. Teaching was hard as hell. If someone had told me that, I probably would have picked a different major.

"So you see, I can pay you less than I would have paid Thorndale and Pendleton, because it will still be more than you're used to earning, and I don't have to compete with someone else's philosophies when it comes to how I conduct business. You're used to taking orders. I like giving orders. Do you follow or am I moving too fast for you? Let me know now, before the others make it back to the airport."

And he knocks it out of the park! The crowd is on their feet and going wild. There's no denying it now, folks. Remington Davenport is a *total* dick sack.

"I see."

"Do you? Perhaps if you had dressed yourself like a professional, a different impression could have been achieved. The irony is, while you don't seem to hide your cards you aren't transparent either. You walk in here with cotton clothes and unkempt hair, giving the impression you don't know any better, yet somehow you managed to be sitting here all the same. Do you know how many resumes my staff reviewed for this position, Meyers?"

"Ten?" Why I guessed that number I have no idea.

"Three hundred and eight-two."

"Oh."

"Tell me, how did you manage to stand out above the rest?"

I have no fucking clue.

Maybe it was the call to Naomi that led me to Hale Davenport. Perhaps he was some sort of momma's boy who felt pressured by the mere reference to his mother. Or maybe he took the mention of her name as some sort of endorsement.

"I don't know, sir."

"Your resume draws no attention. There has to be something, perhaps a cover letter that was misplaced?"

"I didn't send a cover letter." All I'd sent was an email that said *Thanks for taking my call* with my resume attached.

"And so the mystery continues. Very well. We'll be leaving in two hours. Eric's driving the others to the airport, but my son will drive you into town to get a few personal items, seeing as your luggage is missing."

Reeling, I sat back and let it all sink in. I got the job. I must have been in shock because that didn't seem right. "Your son's on the boat?"

"He's upstairs. You can help me to my room then go find him and get the essentials you'll need for the next few days at sea."

Thank God, because I seriously needed some stomach medicine—and non-cotton clothing apparently. "Thank you, sir."

"Call me Remington."

I smiled, thinking he wasn't too bad. "Can I call you Remy?"

"Not if you expect an answer."

4

I helped Remington to his room on his nifty little scooter, which the doctors insisted he use for the next six weeks while his strength returned. He grumbled a lot about the inconvenience of having a broken foot—the reports were wrong when they said it was his leg—but he didn't say much about the heart attack. Being betrayed by mortality really pissed a man like Remington Davenport off, so I talked to him about other subjects.

He complained about the chill in the air, which I didn't feel, so I suggested he get a Snuggie, but he'd never heard of such a thing.

"It's a blanket with sleeves, sort of like a backwards robe, but longer. I love my Snuggie." Helping him ease onto his bed I situated the pillows so he'd be more comfortable.

Winded, he rested against the headboard. "That's the most asinine thing I've ever heard."

"You say that because you've never tried it.

Snuggies are great. They free up your hands so you can still hold ice cream, but your body stays warm."

His gunmetal eyes met mine and held for a moment. "I'll hold off while my dignity holds out. Hand me that laptop."

"This is nice," I said, passing him the device. He didn't comment. "Do you need anything else?"

"There's a pill bottle next to the sink in my bathroom. The blue pills, not the white ones. I need one of them and some water."

"Sure."

The bathroom was no joke. It was hard to believe I was actually on a boat because this was nicer than any room in my mom's house. Filling a glass with tap water, I returned to the master suite with Remington's pill.

"Here you go."

"Not that shit. Get me a bottle of water from the mini-fridge."

Turning, I scanned the room but didn't see a fridge.

"The nightstand."

"Ah." Popping open the wooden cabinet I found a mini refrigerator stocked with bottles. "What brand is this?"

He unscrewed the bottle and leveled me with an assessing stare, giving the impression that he was second-guessing his decision to hire me. "You really don't have a clue who you work for, do you, Meyers?"

It was still sinking in that I got the job, so I shrugged.

"Everesence is Davenport water. At least do a general Google search tonight, will you?"

Figures he'd own his own water. The man had rights to almost all the necessities of the free-living world; water, petroleum, agriculture. What else was there? "I will. Anything else?"

"That's it. Be back in two hours and we'll go over your duties before dinner. Hale's probably on the sky deck."

Right. I'd just mosey on up there and give good old Hale a shout. Sure. He had nothing better to do than taking the help shopping.

I'd offer to take a cab, but I didn't have a clue where I was or where I should go to get clothes and toothpaste and such. Plus, my funds were limited, so I had to spend wisely. Cabs were out.

"Okeydokey then."

"Meyers."

"Yes."

"Grown women don't say okeydokey."

"Right. I'll see you in two hours."

Finding one's way around a boat wasn't so easy when the boat was the size of a laser tag arena. I kept circling the same rooms and returning to the deck, but I couldn't find my way to the sky deck.

"What the effin' hell? How do I get out of here?"

"Lost?"

As if a ghost ran a finger down my spine I stiffened, spun, and gasped. Thank God it wasn't a sea ghost and was just Remington's son. As I stared up at Hale Davenport's eyes, I had a hundred realizations in the span of a millisecond.

He was like a cross between The Professor from

Gilligan's Island and John Travolta, all young and delicious in *Grease*, but with lighter hair and Ralph Lauren clothes. And what in all that was holy was that delicious smell? It was like an aphrodisiac for ovaries. I wanted Ben and Jerry to make ice cream in that flavor so I could eat it. Women could catch a pregnancy just by looking at this guy. And finally, television really did him a disservice.

He cleared his throat, drawing my out-of-body feminine rant to a halt, but once again words failed me. Twice, this man had rendered me speechless, and I had no clue why. This linguistic collapse was a new ailment and one I really feared might have been brought on by a secret stroke, the sort that happened when a person slept, and they don't know it happened, but suddenly couldn't remember common words like cereal or light bulb.

"Cereal," I muttered, just to be sure.

"Pardon?"

Shaking off my psychotic hypochondria, I pretended I was normal. "Sorry. I didn't think anyone was in here. I was talking to myself." Which happened a lot, but he wouldn't know that, because my words didn't work around him.

We had a bit of a staring contest, which made me want to make funny faces so he'd blink first, but I couldn't move. Why was he looking at me like that? And why did he look so different in person? It was definitely Remington's older son because he was doing that stoic enema face again, but man, he was a thousand times more attractive—and intimidating—in person. He probably stole the show in a game of Hold 'em. That was a serious poker face.

"And you are?"

What was my name again? "I'm Rayne, your dad's new assistant."

Without tipping his head, his gaze did a quick once-over of my outfit. "Of course you are. The crew quarters are through the galley. Shove past that door and you'll find your way."

I'd never truly watched a man speak, but when he spoke it was as if his lips caressed each syllable, made love to the nouns and did extremely naughty things to verbs like *shove*. Mmm... I bet he shoved real nice. I wanted him to say all sorts of dirty words like pull, tug, lick, and thrust. What the hell was wrong with me?

I continued staring. Words would help. "That's some fancy ship talk there, matey. What's a galley?"

Still no expression. Amazing. "It's the service kitchen."

His skin was literally flawless, nice natural tan, shadows of hair in all the right places. Did he wax or were his eyebrows naturally that perfect? *Focus!*

"Good to know about the kitchen, but I was actually looking for you. Remington said you could take me into town before we leave. My luggage was lost and I need a few things, but I don't know where I'm going."

"Already on a first name basis."

His disapproving mumble jolted my brainwaves in the opposite direction as I got the slight impression this handsome, poker faced prep might not like me for some reason. "Pardon?"

"Nothing." He glanced at his watch, which was

nicer than all of my jewelry put together. "You don't have much time."

"I'll be quick. I really appreciate you taking me."

"It's what I'm here for apparently." He turned, and I followed him through the narrow halls. Pocket doors! Duh!

Hale knew his way around the yacht like someone who'd spent many days aboard. I tried to memorize every turn, but it was damn confusing. As big as it looked on the outside, it was a Mary Poppins purse on the inside. If I ever wanted to learn my way around I'd need to leave lipstick marks around this place like that chick in the movie *Labyrinth*.

Once we were on the open deck, he picked up the pace. Being that Hale was a good foot taller than me, it took some work to keep up. By the time we reached the marina parking lot, I was huffing and puffing like an asthmatic woman in a child birthing class.

A car alarm chirped and lights flashed. "That's me."

"Wow. What kind of car is that?"

"It's a Wraith."

Never heard of it. "Oh. Right. I considered getting one of them, but my Honda's so good on gas, I figured it's better to stick with what I know."

His eyes, gunmetal gray just like his dad's, appraised me for a moment as he stared over the roof of his coupe from the driver side door, but he didn't smile. This one would be a tough nut to crack.

The windows of the car opened and I jumped back as the little signature hood ornament erected on the front of the car. Whoa, space car.

"Get in."

He disappeared, sliding behind the wheel while I was left staring at a door with no handle. "Um…"

Reaching across the seat, he popped open the door, but it was backward. Freaking suicide doors. I didn't know they still made them. While I didn't know what a Wraith was, there was no mistaking the double R stitched into the headrest.

Oh my Gawd! I was getting into a Rolls Royce! I could almost hear Robin Leach narrating my every move.

> Today on Lifestyles of the Rich and Famous, Oregon transplant, Rayne Meyers, embarks on a bright new world full of yachting and day trips along the coast of the Jersey shore. Hale Davenport, son of business billionaire, Remington Davenport, is escorting her in his six-figure Rolls Royce coupe to get tampons and deodorant. She's setting up for a luxurious few months at sea!

Okay, this was definitely the nicest car I ever sat in. Everything was polished wood and buttery white leather. It turned on with barely a vibration. Hale slid sunglasses over his eyes and suddenly we were moving. The ride was so smooth it was as if we were floating on steel rails.

"How fast does this car go?"

"Are you worried we won't be back in time?" His mouth remained unmoved and his eyes were once again hidden behind the lenses of his glasses, so it was really tough getting a bead on his personality.

I couldn't tell if he was being sarcastic or just one of those dry people that didn't know how to unclench. "Was that you making a joke?"

His brow rose, but he made no comment.

Easing onto the main road, his fingers flexed over the stitching of the leather wheel and my body sank a little deeper into the upholstery as the sleek vehicle picked up speed. Memories of riding the Gravitron at the county fair flashed through my mind as I reached for the seatbelt. My gaze skittered from the flash of road to the speedometer as the g-force actually pressed me into my seat.

"Shit. Slow down."

"We're barely moving."

The speedometer needle glided effortlessly over seventy as wind channeled through the strange windows. "Your ass, we're barely moving. You're going to get us killed!"

"You asked how fast she could go."

"She? Your car's a she?" The gauge passed one hundred and steadily continued climbing. "Oh, God, please slow down." My fingers curled into the seat as he glanced at me while taking the car swiftly around a bend. "Don't look at me! Look at the road!" This was how I was going to die.

His attention turned back to the road and the car immediately slowed. Great. Now I was sweating, and my hair was officially destroyed just so Richie

Rich over here could have his jollies. My fucking heart was going to explode.

He glanced at me again and dropped down to the actual speed limit. "It's okay.

I wouldn't have let anything happen."

I scoffed at the sheer stupidity of that sentence. "Oh, okay then. Hey, since you're God and all, could you let Mary know that I said hi?"

He laughed and shook his head. "*You're* who my dad hired?"

"What's that supposed to mean?"

Terrifying a woman made him laugh, but the rest of the time he looked like he had a club up his ass. He was clearly a sadist.

"I just assumed he'd go with someone a little more ... seasoned."

"What am I, a steak? What's seasoned mean?"

"If you were seasoned you'd know."

Now I was really starting to dislike him. "How about we don't talk anymore?"

"Fine." He shrugged with indifference.

"Good." Shutting my eyes, I willed my heart rate to settle and my muscles to unclench.

When I wasn't frightened for my life, the ride was actually quite luxurious. Trying to be sly, I angled my phone toward my feet and snapped a shot of the carpet with the double R sewn into the mat.

"Did you just take a picture?"

"No." I hit send.

"Yes, you did. I saw the flash."

"If I did, it was an accident."

His jaw muscle twitched, but he made no further comment. Stupid flash! Silencing the phone, I sent a text to Elle.

> Guess what kind of car I'm in!!!

MY PHONE BUZZED A FEW SECONDS LATER.

> Did you get the job?!? And are you in a Rolls??? BTW you desperately need a pedicure. Seriously, ew, Ray. Take that polish off TONIGHT! It's from St. Patrick's Day!

I FORGOT I STILL HAD THAT POLISH ON. I sent a quick text back.

> Got job. The Other One is trying to kill me. More later…

SHUTTING OFF MY PHONE, I TUCKED IT IN my bag as the deathtrap rolled into a parking lot outside of a posh looking strip mall. Okay, where was Target?

"You should be able to get everything you need here." He exited the car and took me off guard as he rounded the front and opened my door.

"Thanks." Giving the door a quick glance, I still didn't see the handle. I sized up my shopping options. "I'll start at the pharmacy."

I hadn't expected him to stick by my side the whole time, but apparently, that's where he was sticking. As I wheeled the cart down the aisles, I stocked up on buffer items to camouflage my personal things. I stuffed a box of tampons under the Oreos and made a mountain of shampoo, conditioner, and body wash around the Midol and Pepto-Bismol. After grabbing a few hair ties and a bottle of moisturizer, I was set. We waited in line at the register, still not talking, which was fine.

My gaze roamed over the counter as I debated picking up some chocolate when the tabloids stacked in front of the register caught my eye. I snorted, and Hale glanced down at me.

"Your dad's looking at us."

His brow creased in question, and I pointed at the cover of *The Wall Street Journal*. He rolled his eyes. Seriously, I'd never met someone with such impenetrable indifference.

Wincing as the cashier totaled up my items, I swiped my card and mentally broke down my wardrobe necessities into the cheapest categories. When she slid the bags across the counter, I was left empty handed as Hale grabbed all three before I could get my hands on one.

Okay then. He was totally carrying my tampons.

After dropping the bags off at the car, we visited a clothing store that I was almost certain took full responsibility for Laura Bush's wardrobe. Nothing was denim and everything cost more than thirty dollars, including the neck scarves.

"Does the boat have a washer and dryer?" I asked, sifting through the well-organized clearance racks for anything under twenty bucks.

"The house crew handles that."

"They wash your clothes?" Even underwear? Shouldn't I offer dinner and a movie before we got that personal?

He nodded and I figured so long as there was some sort of laundry system in play I wouldn't need much, which was a bonus. I could wash my undies in the sink until I got to know the other employees better. Or maybe they only washed the Davenport's clothes and I was one of the help, therefore, I would be in charge of my own stuff. That was actually the more comforting option.

In order to be thrifty, I stuck with black items only. This allowed me to mix and match without looking too unprofessional: two pairs of black crop pants, three black polo shirts, one bra, and four pairs of panties. And there went my savings.

I prayed the entire time at the register that my account wouldn't be overdrawn in front of Hale. Luckily, everything went through.

"You're the woman who spoke to my mother," he said, breaking the silence on the drive back to the marina.

"Yeah. I didn't know how else to apply for the job."

"Why this job?"

Shifting, I tried to read him, but the sunglasses were back on, and his attention was devoted to the road. "What do you mean?"

"Is it him?"

"Who, Remington?"

He nodded. "Certain women will do anything they can to get close to him."

I chuckled. "I'm not that sort of woman. I'm only interested in the job."

"Are you sure?"

My brow lowered as I studied him. He'd been awfully polite while shopping, holding doors and carrying my bags, but I couldn't shake the sense that he didn't like me.

"Are you asking if I'm attracted to your dad?"

I supposed some women liked the whole older man thing, but Remington was older than my father. And now I was imagining what a decrepit old dick looked like. Thank God my imagination wasn't very vivid.

"Are you saying you'd turn him down if the offer were on the table?"

"Seriously?" I couldn't decide if I should be grossed out or insulted. Probably both. What if that was why he hired me? "If it ever came near the table I'd bolt. Your dad's fascinating, but I'm definitely not interested in him that way. Plus, he's my boss."

"Like that stops people."

Rather than dispute the unlikely chance of office affairs, which Remington Devonport probably had his fair share of, I turned the focus on him. "Why did you pass along my resume?"

"I trust my mom's opinion."

"Did you speak to her about me?"

"No, but if she didn't like you, she wouldn't have given you my number."

I'd only spoken to his mother for a few minutes, so his reasoning wasn't very sound. "Do you like working for him?"

"I don't work for him. I work with him."

"Oh. My mistake. Do you like working *with* him?"

"I don't believe in doing anything long term that isn't personally satisfying on some level."

How very Steve Jobs. "So that's a yes?"

"Yes," he clarified, and then tacked on, "for the most part."

"He seems to be recovering well. I mean, I'm no nurse, but aside from the foot he looks like he's doing all right."

His lips compressed, but he made no comment.

Cutting through a residential area of the shore town, I admired the pretty Victorian houses as the events of the last two days started to catch up with me. Hale slowed as the brake lights of several cars lit up in front of us.

"What's this?" he mumbled.

"Traffic?" It seemed pretty standard, but Hale didn't appear to think so as he lifted his sunglasses and frowned.

Cars weaved around some commotion at the side of the road and slowly moved on, but as we spotted two older women standing on the grass and staring at the curb Hale pulled over.

He rolled down the window and a duck squawked rapidly at the women. "Are you ladies all right?"

His concern threw me for a loop. As far as judging a book by the cover went, he didn't seem the type to play the Good Samaritan. But what did I know?

The women approached my window, both wearing looks of concern. "There are ducklings trapped in the storm drain."

My breath sucked in as I looked to Hale. His expression was blank, his eyes briefly glancing at his watch. I sensed he was worried about the time so I quickly suggested, "Can we call animal control or something?"

His brow creased. "Let me pull out of the way and see what I have in the trunk."

Pleased, I smiled as he moved his car to the shoulder of the road. "I love ducks." Not that this was essential information in a rescue, but I wanted him to know I was glad he decided to help, even though there wasn't much we could do aside from call someone.

I followed him out of the car and around to the trunk. "Why do you have so many buckets?" His trunk was immaculate, but there was a stack of five gallon buckets and some other tools.

"They're left over from a project I was working on."

They looked brand new. "What sort of project?"

"Just some landscaping." He grabbed a pair of

leather gloves and I tried to picture a man like Hale Davenport cutting his own lawn. It didn't compute.

I followed him to the storm drain where we assessed the situation. The mother duck squawked frantically as she paced by the curb, slowing traffic. The peeps of several ducklings echoed from below.

"They've been down there for a while. We called the fire department, but no one's been here yet," one of the woman explained.

"Poor babies." I squatted close to the ground and used the light on my phone to count them. "I see six of them."

Hale rested his hands on the hips of his dress slacks and pursed his lips. The mother duck continued to quack ceaselessly, clearly concerned for her babies.

Hale sighed. "We'll have to get the grate off." Giving his sleeves a shove, he bent and lifted the heavy iron cover off the hole tossing it onto the grass.

Buttons. Were. Pushed.

Dear God the man packed some strength under those fancy clothes. I'd never seen a guy outfitted in a designer dress shirt and worn leather gloves, but it was totally doing it for me. And all for the sake of some fuzzy little ducklings. This was scoring points all over the place with my girlie parts.

The momma duck marched over in a panic, quacking belligerently at Hale's ankles.

"I think she's telling you off," I informed, incase he didn't speak duck.

"She doesn't seem pleased," the other woman observed.

The ducklings scurried along the edge of what appeared to be a wide drainpipe. "Do you have a net or a rope?" he asked the ladies.

"Rope? I likely do, but my house is on the other side of town."

Hale glanced at his watch again. I checked my phone and noted we only had about twenty minutes before my two hours were up. "What about one of those buckets in your trunk?"

He rubbed the back of his neck. "That won't reach."

"Maybe we should try the fire department again, Ethel," the first woman suggested.

"Don't worry," Hale said. "I'll get them out."

I stepped back as he dropped to the ground and lowered his legs into the storm drain. The women twittered nervously. "Oh dear, try not to step on them."

I watched, eyes wide, as a man dressed in what were likely two hundred dollar pants and a really nice button down, slithered into the sewer. Something happened to me in that moment. My heart raced, and my hearing started to buzz as I could hardly blink. Holy hotness, I hadn't been so impressed by a man in...

When was the last time a man gave me these squishy feelings? Huh. I couldn't recall. Maybe this was a first.

"Rayne," he called, and I shook off my shock, scooping the first fuzzy baby out of his gloved hands. "Put her on the grass so the mom sees she's safe."

My mouth made a soft and silent *awww* as I

cupped its little feathered butt in my hands. The momma duck quacked and followed me to the grass where I deposited the baby a safe distance away from the street. The older women followed, each carrying another duckling.

I returned and scooped the next one out of Hale's hands. The momma duck seemed to scold her returned runaways as she quaked and nudged each one, inspecting them with her beak. When the last two were reunited with the gaggle, she led them further away from the street.

I turned just as Hale was lifting himself out of the storm drain. His clothes were a mess, and his shirt was likely ruined, but he looked... *really* good. The women fawned over him, calling him a hero and praising him for a job well done. I took one last look at the ducklings and returned to his side.

"I can't believe you did that." My words came out a little breathless, but that had everything to do with the excitement and—I was sure—nothing to do with any sort of hero worship.

"That's a good man you have there, young lady. You hold onto him."

My eyes went wide at the older woman's misunderstanding. "Oh, we're not—"

"We have to get going," Hale interrupted, sending me a wink.

Who winked these days? Winking was reserved for men like Bing Crosby and Charlie Chaplin, yet somehow Hale pulled it off, and I was blushing from my roots to my metaphorical poodle skirt.

Blowing out a breath, I turned my attention to

the ladies. "Hopefully, they stay away from the drains."

Hale lifted the heavy metal grate and slid it back into place, brushing his gloves together to shed any loose dirt, but they were saturated with mud. The ladies waved goodbye as we walked back to the car.

"Your clothes are ruined."

"Well, the ducks are safe and the mother's happy." He opened my car door, and I stood frozen.

"What about your car?"

He paused, as if only now considering what a mess he was. "It's fine."

He moved to the other door as I stood in awe. Once he slid behind the wheel and leaned across the passenger seat, he looked up at me. "Time's up, Rayne."

Shit. I forgot about Remington. I clamored into the car and shut the door. "Here." I passed him a bottle of hand sanitizer from my purse.

"Thanks." He rubbed it into his arms, but he really needed soap and a sink. He sniffed his fingers. "Is that...?"

"Cotton candy. It's all I had."

"I like it." His mouth kicked up in a half grin, and I had to look away as my stomach tightened—not with cramps, but with something warm and heavy like chocolate fudge or warm cookie batter. I was obviously hungry since skipping lunch.

We were silent the rest of the ride back, and I kept my attention away from Hale. When we reached the marina again, he parked in a different spot, more removed from the other cars. "Are you leaving this car here for the next six months?"

"It'll be in Florida by Wednesday."

I laughed at such absurdity. He clearly had no concept of how strange that sounded, that a car could simply be shipped for his convenience as he yachted down the coast of the Atlantic.

"Is that where we're going, Florida?"

"To start." Once again he opened my door, but I wasn't sure if it was manners or because he wanted the leather carryon he removed from the backseat. He collected my bags, but I took two as well. I was the help after all.

"Have you ever spent the night on a yacht?" he asked as we walked the dock.

"Um, no. I probably should have grabbed some seasickness meds."

"You won't get sick. *The Lady Parr*'s smooth and the crew are accomplished."

"Good to know." Maybe he really did think he was God.

I still hadn't been shown my sleeping quarters, so I wasn't sure where to dump all my crap. "Do you know where I should unpack?" Once I stowed my stuff, I'd check on Remington. Later tonight I could settle in.

"Follow me."

"Crap. Our shoes."

He turned and frowned. "What?"

"Your dad doesn't like when people wear shoes inside—"

He laughed, catching me so off guard with the flash of straight, perfectly pearly teeth I stilled. There was a deep tug in my belly as I watched his full lips pull into a grin, the quick glimpse of his personality turning my insides to butter.

"Did he make you guys take off your shoes? Figures. It's a diversion tactic, sort of like putting the opposition in a smaller chair. It disarms the guest and immediately establishes the host's upper hand. Trust me, he doesn't care what's on your feet."

"Oh." I thought about poor Miles in his nice suit and socks. "Tricky."

He led me down a carpeted set of steps to an intersection of mirrored doors. The multiple reflections were a bit disorienting.

"Those state rooms have twin beds and this one has a double. Which do you prefer?"

Peeking into each option, I went with the room that looked the most inviting. "I'll take the double."

Nodding, he carried the bags inside and deposited them on the bed, which was dressed in deep navy with steel blue satin throw pillows. Wow. Everything was really nice.

"Your bathroom's through here."

"I get my own bathroom?"

"All the state rooms have private baths, so the other guests aren't disturbed."

Stepping into the bathroom, I was again impressed that this was on a boat. Modern *his and her* sinks filled the vanity, accented by polished chrome fixtures and plush sapphire hand towels.

It was all so lavish, nicer than any hotel I'd ever visited. The shower had floor to ceiling glass doors and a long bench against the wall. The tile was white porcelain, delicately flecked with gold.

My perusal halted as I looked in the wall-to-wall

vanity mirror. Hale watched me from the door, his mouth flat but his eyes missing nothing.

Finding his reflection just as intimidating as the real man, I waited for him to say or do something. Maybe he thought I had some sort of motive to get close to his family. We already established I wasn't after his father's golden shlong. Or maybe he thought I was trashy. I didn't know, but when he looked at me like that I felt nervous and unsure in a way I hadn't felt since ... ever.

Glancing down I broke the intense eye contact. "This is really nice."

He cleared his throat. "I'm in the room to your right, so if there's anything you need—"

"I'm sure I'll be fine." Ack! Blah! My words came out clipped and ungrateful. I wasn't being rude. I just didn't know how to read this guy, and he was making me beyond awkward. Maybe I was claustrophobic and boat cabins were a danger to my constitution.

"Very well. I'll leave you to get settled."

Thank him! My gratitude was on the tip of my tongue, but I couldn't get it out. Turning my back to the door, I shut my eyes and waited several seconds. When I opened them, he was gone.

It's Rude to Stare...

5

"Y ou're late."

My steps staggered to a halt as I entered the master suite and found Remington scowling from the bed. "Sorry. I was putting some things away."

"Where's Hale?"

I rolled the scooter closer to the bed, sensing he'd rested long enough. "I'm not sure." That man needed to stay far away from me until I got my senses in order.

Offering my arm to help Remington transfer from the bed to the scooter, he grumbled, "I need a minute of privacy. Don't go far."

"Yes, sir." Backing out of the room, I closed the door and waited, still on edge from earlier.

My attention lingered on the stairs leading down to the staterooms. If I listened close enough, I might hear the trickle of the shower where Hale rinsed off the grime from his heroic rescue. At first, I wasn't sure if his personality would match his unruffled persona, but now I was totally confused about what sort of man Hale Davenport actually was. I mean... he rescued ducklings! You can't be a prick and also rescue small, fluffy creatures. It's a rule.

Once Remington was finished in the bathroom, he called me back as if I should have anticipated the exact moment he'd be ready for me to enter the room again.

"Meyers."

"Yes, sir."

"I need the laptop, iPad, and that file there."

Scurrying to gather his items, I followed him out of the suite toward the common area of the ship at a snail's pace, my arms burdened with his requested items. "We should get you a bicycle basket for the front of your scooter."

"What the hell do I need that for when I have you?" So he was unpleasant after naps. Duly noted.

The dinner table had been set with centerfold worthy dishes and linens. Silver chargers cradled gold trimmed china and crystal glinted under the lit chandelier. I was so distracted by the gorgeous centerpiece that I crashed into Remington.

"Damn it, Meyers. Who's the one with a disability here, me or you?"

"Sorry, sir."

"Pull out a chair so I can sit."

Quickly withdrawing the heavy seat, I turned it so he could slide over. "You know, a simple please or thank you wouldn't hurt from time to time. You get more bees with honey, Remington."

He scowled at me, unimpressed. "Save the fortune cookie crap for someone who can only afford clichés. Pass me the laptop."

"Right."

He waved a hand at the chair next to him. "Have a seat."

Please... It was extremely tempting to prompt his manners, but I wasn't sure he had any. And you couldn't get blood from a stone. That was another fortune cookie cliché, but nonetheless true.

Sitting beside him, I watched as he slid the place setting out of his way and opened the laptop. A calendar filled the screen, showing barely any white as every date had abbreviated appointments scheduled.

Eric, the driver, returned, and a pang of guilt hit me. Where were Cadence and Miles? It seemed wrong that I was the one sitting here and they were likely waiting in an airport bar for a flight home.

"Did you get it?" Remington asked, and my attention returned to him as I prepared to ask what he was referring to, but Eric answered first.

"Yes, sir. It's all set up and synchronized."

"Good."

Eric handed Remington a bag, which he quickly opened, producing a very high tech smart phone.

"Pay attention, Meyers."

Where exactly should I focus? Already watching him, I forced my eyes as wide as they could open. "Yes, sir."

"This is a 360 Block Smart Phone. It's impossible to hack and it will be a part of you for the next six months. You're not to go anywhere without it."

He removed a small case from the box and snapped it into the bottom of the phone. "There are two batteries, so you'll never have to step away while it's charging. My itinerary's been synched and you'll have a bird's eye view of our location at all times with the GPS app installed. There's also a program that connects you with the crew and lets you read the knots we're traveling at any given time."

A touch overwhelmed, I nodded. Not only was I going to have to carry two phones, I was going to have to Google the term knots because I wasn't sure what one was. "Yes, sir."

"There's a Wi-Fi bar in each room, so if we're out of satellite reach you'll still be able to contact me via text or call. Even in an emergency, we'll be able to keep contact."

Excellent. Who needed 911 when there was Remington Davenport and his handy-dandy scooter to come to the rescue?

"My general contacts have been uploaded, but you'll only need to use them if I tell you to get in touch with someone. Eric handles most of my appointments, and he'll be the one to update my schedule on the main calendar drive."

I glanced at Eric who stood with his arms folded at his back. "You're not just the chauffeur?"

"No," he answered with a touch of insult. How was I supposed to know?

"Eric's been my PA for eleven years. He can answer your questions if I'm not available. Be sure to use his expertise in your favor, Meyers. He's still here because I like him. I don't like many people."

"Yes, sir." I couldn't figure out if I was on the like or don't like list yet, but something made him hire me. "Do you usually have two assistants?"

"I have several assistants, but Eric's my only personal one. However, I usually have two feet. You're here to compensate."

Great. I was a foot.

"Give it a test drive." Remington passed me the phone, which was larger than my other one and awkward to hold.

"What should I do?"

"Call someone. Call Hale."

"How about I call my—"

"Just call him so we can move on."

Fumbling through the apps I located the call program. Lo and behold, there was a short menu with three important numbers: Remington, Eric, and Hale. Swallowing thickly, my thumb tapped his name, and I brought the oversized phone to my ear.

"It's ringing," I whispered.

"Davenport."

Once again, I cleared my throat with the grace of a hyena. "It's Rayne."

There was a pause. "You have a different number."

"Your dad gave me a new phone."

"I see." Another long pause. "What do you need, Rayne?"

My eyes briefly closed as an image of him wrapped only in a damp towel flashed in my mind. There was something about his tone that sucker punched me in my equilibrium. He never spoke tersely, yet there was a touch of impatience beneath that thick, masculine voice that somehow traveled through my ears, around my belly, and down my legs.

"Does it work?" Remington asked, demanding my attention.

My eyes opened and turned to my boss. "Yes."

"Yes?" Hale asked through the phone, not realizing I was speaking to his father.

"Sir," I whispered reflexively, then shook my head. Wait, what? Yes, the phone worked, but no, I wasn't talking to Hale. I did just call him sir, though, which might have mixed up the whole caste system of the ship. I was a total disaster around these people.

Hale's voice lowered, making it all the more challenging for me to pretend I was normal. "Did you need something from me?"

My skin tingled as if his soft-spoken words were little caresses petting me in all the right places.

"Rayne?"

The slight rasp of my name eased my tension. I wanted to hum and shut my eyes again, wearing only a punch-drunk smile as he whispered in my ear. My breathing noticeably accelerated and I realized everyone was staring at me. This was bad.

"I have to go." I ended the call. There was seriously something wrong with me.

I was an utter catastrophe and if I didn't pull my head out of my ass and focus, I'd end up fired before the job even started. No more Hale thoughts!

Sliding the large tablet sized phone onto the table, I stared at it, sensing Remington still watching me. *Him* I could handle. Hale, on the other hand, was a freaking wild card that turned me into a puddle of awkward girl stereotypes I swore I'd never be.

Clearing my throat, I mumbled, "It works."

Satisfied, Remington went into a swift orientation of his schedule. I tried to focus as much as I could, but my brain was stuck on Hale. This was ridiculous. I never—*never*—got stupid around men.

First, I wasn't even sure I liked the guy. I sort of didn't until he went all *Wonder Pets* and saved the day for the little old ladies in distress. Sure, he held open my car door, which was incredibly old school debonair, like letting me touch the handle would be a crime against the last endangered gentleman of the world.

And yeah, he smelled like the mythical fruit that brought down the Garden of Eden. That stupid Hale scent tempted me to do all sorts of things that never crossed my mind. And third, I just missed everything my boss said. Fuck.

"So you never want to hit that command."

What command? I looked at the screen, but he was already minimizing the calendar and opening a new page. For all of Remington's instinct and success, he absolutely picked the wrong candidate for this job. Cadence certainly wouldn't be this clueless. I stared at the computer wishing he'd repeat his last warning, so I didn't accidentally blow up the ship.

"Are you clear, Meyers?"

"As a bell, sir." Elle had said to fake it until I made it, so that was exactly what I planned to do.

"Good. Eric, tell them we're ready to eat."

Eric disappeared after collecting the packaging from the phone, and Remington frowned at me.

"You sure you're up for this?"

"Yes, sir. I'm just tired from traveling." That had to be what was wrong with me.

He nodded but continued to study me. "You'll get the hang of everything soon enough."

The fine hairs at the back of my neck prickled and I sensed *his* presence without looking toward the doorway. My nose registered that indescribably smell, stronger now since his shower. How was I ever going to survive this man in such close quarters?

"Hale," his father greeted.

The air of the cabin charged with something heady and drew my gaze to Hale's silver eyes. He looked back and my throat was instantly dry. My stomach tightened—Oh God, I was getting cramps.

No smile. Not even half a grin, but I couldn't look away as his intense stare unapologetically took me in.

His hair was still slightly damp and his clothes were different. He must go through a bottle of starch a week with shirts that crisp. But he pulled it off with a just rumpled enough cuff at the elbow. He was the champagne of men, nothing like the guys I was used to seeing in Oregon.

Sweat gathered under my clothes as I tried to decide if he was challenging me or undressing me with his eyes. Outmatched, I gave up and broke the stare as the cool perspiration, lack of oxygen, and nerves bouncing around in my stomach made me want to suddenly hurl.

"Excuse me," I blurted, rising from the table. I needed a reprieve, a moment to get my game face on and knock all this senseless girlie crap out of my system.

In my haste to escape, I forgot my phone—the one that was supposed to be holstered to my person at all times. There was no way I was walking back in there until I had my shit together.

As I booked down the hall to the steps that led to my room, I didn't stop until I reached my sleeping quarters and clicked the lock on the door in place. I grabbed my personal phone and speed dialed Elle as I lowered myself to the bed.

"Hello?"

"I think I made a huge mistake," I hissed.

"Already? It hasn't even been a day."

"Crazy, I know. But I don't think I can do this, Elle. I'm pretty sure I'm in over my head."

The phone rustled and then her voice was a little clearer. "Catch me up. What happened?"

"We're on a yacht—not a houseboat. I'm talking something Oprah would own. There's a freaking pool on the deck. *A pool*, Elle. Apparently, we're going to Florida and—" My gaze shifted to the cabin windows. "Oh fuck. We're moving. We're fucking moving!"

"Slow down. You're sailing to Florida? That's awesome, Ray."

"It's more than I hoped for, but you know how I have a tendency to think I want something, invest a bunch of energy into preparations, and then I realize I was wrong?"

"Yeah."

"This might be one of those situations." I really hoped this wouldn't end like my teaching career, but I was only a few hours in and already having second thoughts—very reminiscent of my first day in the classroom.

"What's the problem? You're traveling. Focus on that part and just get through the rest. How hard could it be to freshen Davenport's mint julep and help him around a yacht? Give him a bell, put on a bathing suit, and go get a tan by the pool. I don't see the issue. Is he that bad?"

"No, it's not Remington. It's *The Other One*."

She laughed. "Who cares about him? You only need to keep Remington happy." She scoffed and I could sense her rolling her eyes. "Every time I see his son on television he looks like a prick with a secret. I bet he knows where Hoffa's buried."

"He's not a prick, but..." How to explain it? "I can't think around him. He watches me like I'm a kleptomaniac or something. And he tried to kill me in his Batmobile car then stopped to help sweet old ladies rescue ducklings."

"*Watches you* or *checks you out*? There's a difference."

"I think I'd know if someone was checking me out."

Elle snorted. "You'd think, but we all know better. Remember Jimmy Rice? He hit on you for years and then you went and sent him on a blind date with *me*. I've never seen someone less interested. You don't have good man radar."

"I don't want Remington's son checking me out!" I hissed. "He's old."

"Googling. Hold on." She tsked. "He is not old. He's thirty-three."

That couldn't be right. He came off way too mature. "Are you sure you're looking up the right one? I'm talking about Hale."

"Yes, Hale Davenport. Born in Avalon, New Jersey. Son of Remington Davenport and Naomi—"

"Okay, fine, none of that matters. How do I become functional again? Because I can't perform my job if I stowaway and hide in my room on the yacht."

"Just ignore him. Avoid him."

"We. Are. On. A. Boat. The halls are two feet wide!" There was a knock at the door. "Shit. Hold on." I lowered the phone and cracked open the door. Thankfully it was only Eric—another one that didn't smile. "Hey."

"They want to know if they should wait. Dinner's served."

My scalp was sweating. "You know, I'm not really feeling great. Tell them to go ahead and eat without me. I'll just grab something later. I think I'm going to call it a night."

His eyes narrowed and he held out my phone. "Mr. Davenport said to give you this."

"Thanks." I took the phone and he turned away. Shutting the door, I whispered, "No one likes me here and I don't know what I did wrong."

"Maybe they're just snobs. Who was that?"

"That was Eric, the other PA."

"Man, I want a PA. So unfair rich people get multiple assistants. How cool would that be?"

"Could you please focus? I'm freaking out."

Rummaging through my bags, I found the Oreos and tore open the package. Stuffing a whole cookie into my mouth, I garbled, "He gave me a phone the size of my Kindle and it's full of appointments and numbers. It has more options than the

Death Star. What if I accidentally delete his whole calendar?"

"Well, don't do that."

I groaned and devoured another cookie. "But you know me. I'm Calamity Rayne. I mess things up."

Elle switched to her serious voice. "Listen to me, Rayne. Taking this job was a good thing. It's even better that it's on a boat because that makes it impossible for you to jump ship when things get challenging. I know you're stressing and getting claustrophobic in the face of commitment, but I have faith in you. And as far as *The Other One*'s concerned, just tell him it's rude to stare and ignore him. Remington Davenport himself asked you to be there. If his son has a problem with your presence, he can take it up with Daddy Warbucks. Don't let yourself be intimidated."

Blowing out a breath I nodded. "Okay. You're right. I don't know why I'm spazzing out."

"You're spazzing out because this was all fun in theory, but now it's real, and anything real makes you run."

I frowned. "That's not one hundred percent accurate."

"Relationships. Careers. Mortgage. These things have you not, young Jedi."

"Fine."

"This is a commitment, Ray, but only a six-month one. You can do this."

Again, I looked out the windows. We were really moving now. I was stuck. "I feel like I'm going to be sick."

"Take some Pepto—"

"No." I turned away from the window and caught the wall with my hand. "Not that sort of sick. Oh, shit…" My stomach lurched, and I literally felt myself turning green. "I gotta go, Elle. Not good."

Tossing the phone on the bed, I bolted for the bathroom and crashed to my knees in front of the toilet just as my stomach locked and everything came rushing out.

Mother. Fucker.

Show Me the Money!

6

While *my* phone barely made a chirp, the Remington phone never shut the hell up. At six a.m. I got a text from Eric telling me Remington was showering and requested I join him for breakfast on the sky deck to go over his itinerary for the day. This would be fine if I hadn't been crawling back and forth all night from my bed to the toilet.

Stupid Hale and his *you'll be fine* speech could eat a dick. The next time we stopped, I was definitely picking up something for motion sickness. I'd finally passed out on the ceramic bathroom floor around four in the morning.

Treating myself like a breakable porcelain doll, I carefully showered and dressed for the day. Though I tried to avoid looking out all windows, when I reached the deck the view was inescapable. We were traveling down the coast, but there was no land in sight. We were just cruising through the sea and I had no clue when I might step foot on solid ground again.

The idea of breakfast made me ill, but the wind coming off the water helped settle my stomach. The mere thought of possibly heaving again made me queasy. Every muscle in my body was sore from tensing and I was pretty sure another night like my last would kill me.

"Meyers," Remington greeted, closing his laptop.

He sat under a canopy looking well rested and refreshed. The small table was dressed in crisp white linens. Crystal goblets held bright orange juice, which appeared remarkably steady for how fast we were moving. His plate was already picked over, but there was a basket of muffins and a covered dish at the empty seat I assumed was mine.

"Morning," I muttered.

"Rough night?"

"I feel like a hackysack after Woodstock."

Pushing my goblet closer, he said, "Have some juice. The vitamin C will do you well."

I took a small sip, afraid anything more might release the Kraken. "How's your foot?"

"In my way. You missed dinner last night. Eat and then we'll get started."

Passing over the eggs, I grabbed a muffin and nibbled slowly. "Do you always get up this early?"

"I'm most productive in the morning. I conquer the tedious tasks first, so they're out of the way. I get more accomplished before ten a.m. than most people do by happy hour."

"Interesting."

Being that I worked in a bar, I usually rolled out of bed around eleven. This was probably why Remingtons ruled the world and Raynes tackled smaller goals, like squeezing a whole season of *Game of Thrones* into one Saturday.

"Are you settling into your room?"

The small talk was unexpected but pleasant. "I don't have much to unpack, but the room's really nice. How much does a boat like this cost?"

He chuckled. "Asking a man how much he pays for his toys is a little like asking a woman her age, Meyers."

"I never got why that's offensive." Though, with my recent birthday I was starting to understand. "If a woman's in her fifties and someone has to ask, that should mean she's hiding it well. I'm thirty, by the way."

"And you look exactly that. What does that say about you?"

Squinting against the sun, I frowned at him. "Gee, thanks. I don't know. What does it say?"

"It says you aren't trying to look any younger and you're not getting enough exercise."

"I have a gym membership." I made donations there every month, because, hey, I'm a giver. I wasn't overweight, though I also wasn't fit. I'd probably pass out if I had to ride a bike uphill.

"If someone offered you a can of fruit versus the actual fruit, which would you choose?"

"The actual fruit."

"Exactly. A gym membership's a sucker's invest-ment. Call them today and cancel. The last thing you need is more time under fluorescent lights breathing in other people's body odor. The world's big, Meyers. Explore it. Experience the fresh air, travel until your bones know the true meaning of exhaustion, and make love until you collapse. That's the sort of exercise people enjoy."

I chuckled. "Is this the stuff you teach at your seminars?"

"I mention it, but those conferences focus more on investment tactics. I don't think you're interested in that."

"Your instincts are spot on."

He eased back, folding his arms over his chest, studying me as I finished my muffin and washed it down with more juice, which I was pretty sure was fresh squeezed because it was damn delicious.

"Do you have a boyfriend, Meyers?"

Placing the glass on the table, I smirked. "No, and that's by choice."

"Why is that?"

I shrugged. "I don't see the hype."

"Is it the freedom of being single?"

"Being that I've only left my home state a handful of times, I'd have to say no."

"Are you a lesbian?"

"Jesus, Remington!" It was one thing to talk about this stuff with my best friend. It was a totally different thing to discuss sexual orientation with my boss.

"It's a fair question."

"No, I'm not gay." Maybe I wasn't anything. "I'm just not into relationships."

"Have you ever been in one?"

"I don't see how this has anything to do with my job."

"It doesn't. But your boss is a nosy, eccentric

man who has limited company over the next few months and you're it."

"Once we get to our destination you'll have plenty of company, I'm sure. You seem like a man who enjoys his ... exercise."

He laughed. "I like you, Meyers. There's something about you that's not...carbon copied. You tell it like it is. Not enough women out there like that. Too many trying to play the part they think the world wants from them."

"I'm not real good at pleasing the world. Half the time I'm unclear about what *I* want. I can't worry about others' preferences."

A maid removed the dishes, and Remington sat forward, opening his computer and turning it so I could see the screen.

"This morning I'm going to teach you about how I made my first million. I may not know everything about you yet, Meyers, but I know you like money. What do you say we make some?"

"I say *giddy-up*."

Over the next hour, Remington took me through the basics of the stock market. I learned about the Dow Jones, NASDAQ, and the S&P. He showed me the world markets, the gainers, the losers, and ways to track a stock's performance. Once I had a basic understanding of the game—I called it a game because that's what it was, legal gambling for the wealthy—he convinced me to invest a one-hundred dollar pay advance on a commodity.

Gas and corn were down, but gold was up. That sounded simple enough, but Remington had other suggestions. Still, my attention kept returning to a company called *Hale Sterling & Gold*. Don't judge me. I saw the coincidence. But that's all it was, a coincidence.

Once we filled out a few online forms, Remington called his hedge fund accountant and introduced us. It was that easy.

As he ended the call, I smiled. "Maybe one day I'll be sitting on my boat telling someone how I started my empire."

My imagination painted an image of me swaying on a rusted dinghy as yachts bellowed their horns and rocked my little boat in their wake.

"You can follow it on your phone," he pointed out, showing me exactly how to do that.

"Cool. So, what else do we have to do?"

Footsteps sounded from the lower deck and I held my breath. I made a decision in the shower that morning not to get all twitterpated like some Disney character just because a halfway decent looking man was in my presence. No, sir. I was going to put all Hale issues out of my head and go about my business of getting Remington what he needed, and enjoying this adventure.

About to pass out from lack of oxygen I exhaled as Eric stepped onto the sky deck. Funny, I should have been relieved it wasn't Hale, but a tinge of disappointment struck. Eric's gaze immediately went to the cozy breakfast setting and laptop shared between Remington and me.

My smile turned a bit guarded, as I understood this buddy-buddy stuff might pose an issue for assistant number one. I wasn't trying to kiss the boss's ass or play favorites. Really, I was just happy not to have screwed up anything monumental in the last hour.

"Eric, I need to get ahold of Bradford. Smithfield emailed the schematics for the grass roots office, and the measurements are off in three of the four specs. If it isn't straightened out by the end of the day, I want you to get some feelers out for a new designer. I'm not cutting corners because my staff's incompetent. Get him on the phone and give him fair warning of my mood."

"Yes, sir."

As useful as an unnecessary piece of furniture, I sat there without making a peep. Remington threatened he was in a pissy mood, but he'd been pleasant all morning. It didn't seem fair that Eric was walking into a volatile atmosphere I'd been spared from. Feeling guilty, I shrunk a bit more into the backdrop, but that only worked for about a second.

"Meyers."

"Yes, sir." I promptly sat up, no longer playing statue.

"Go find Hale and tell him to bring me the thumb drive with the Hilton specs on it. He'll know what I'm talking about."

"Thumb drive. Hilton. Hale. Got it."

Happy to get away, it only registered that I was on my way to find Hale once I was below deck. Rather than worry about returning to the state of a blubbering idiot, I focused on the success of my morning. Remington seemed happy with his choice in assistant, and I believed there had been some mild bonding over breakfast. Plus—major bonus—I hadn't thrown up my muffin. Perhaps I was finding my sea legs after all.

I knew there was a crew aboard, but it freaked me out that I never saw them. Where did they go? So much of the internal yacht was taken up with posh living quarters, more spacious than one would imagine. I didn't think there was much room left to hide people. Were they all stacked up in dresser drawers, sleeping in some bunker below sea level?

"Hello...?"

Crickets.

No one was in the galley, or the living room, which was connected to the dining room. Remington's room was empty and I didn't see anyone on the lower deck. It was only nine o'clock. Maybe Hale wasn't awake yet.

Taking the carpeted steps to the staterooms, I heard the muffled rumble of his voice. Success. Target Located. I approached the cracked door and his tone made me hesitate before knocking.

"This is bullshit, Clayton. Why now? I'm telling you, this is all an attempt at exposure, and nothing to do with me. We've already signed off on the agreement and the period for further negotiation is over. It's a done deal."

I stepped back as he paced and I could see his reflection in the mirror on the wall. Dear God, he wasn't wearing a shirt.

Fascinated by the elastic waistband of his briefs peeking out from his pants and designer belt, my gaze traveled over each little divot carved into his tight abdomen. Six. He had six abs. Now that I had that covered, I counted his nipples. Two. Two fine, little chocolate nubs.

His hand dragged over the back of his neck and I caught sight of a soft tuft of hair under his arm. I couldn't recall ever being so fascinated by male anatomy. Maybe it was because Hale's body matched my definition of male perfection, something I used to believe only existed in literary porn.

I kept staring, searching for any flaws but found none. Even the little nick of a scar on his shoulder appeared purposeful and right.

A soothing calm settled over me as something tugged low in my belly. The forgotten familiarity of arousal hit like a cool rain, provoking the urge to bolt, but at the same time anchoring me to the ground.

It had been so long since a man caused any sort of reaction in me. It was ungrounded to have these feelings about someone I didn't know.

But looking at Hale, the way he carried himself, the flex of his muscles, the control of his words, and the smooth skin at his shoulders, I wanted to scale him like a girl scout earning a tree-climbing badge. My fingers twitched as I thought about digging my nails into that smooth skin and rubbing my lady bits all over his rigid body.

Problem was, he was the boss's son. Let us not forget that.

His words were muffled as he kept his voice low, but there was a serious note to his tone. I probably shouldn't be listening, but I wanted to know what exasperated a man like Hale who seemed to master remarkable calm in all situations. My mind couldn't piece together all these differing sides of him, and I really wanted to get the whole picture.

"Call me back once you get more information," he said, as he ended the call.

Facing the television, his back was just as sexy as the front. A news show played on mute. The host was so pretty it seemed unfair that she was also smart. That was the type of woman that would look perfect with Hale and that truth was enough to stifle my hormones for another frigid decade.

Afraid he'd catch me spying, I stepped back. If I could just convince myself that he was hideously un-attractive, life would be much easier.

His phone rang again and this time, his tone was completely different. "Hey, Barrett."

Barrett was his brother—*The Hot One* as Elle liked to call him. A soft laugh caught my ears, and I was moved by just how genuine and unguarded it sounded. In that moment, that split second laugh, I knew he and his brother were close.

"It should make for an interesting trip," Hale said. "He has a new assistant, so that's helping matters."

I grinned. I was *helping matters*.

He paused and sat on the bed then laughed again, but this time, the sound ended on a sigh as if he were emotionally drained from the past week. It had to be frightening almost losing a parent. That constant reaching for someone who isn't there... I wouldn't wish it on anyone.

"I know. I'm worried too. It puts a lot of things in perspective."

Stepping closer to the door, I studied his expression in the mirror, as there was a flash of something close to vulnerability in his eyes.

"I'm doing my best to let our issues go and not argue with him, but he doesn't make it easy." His brother must have said something funny because there was a brief curve to his lips. "Yeah. You too. I'll see you soon." He ended the call and the tension notably left his body as he stood.

Enough eavesdropping. Remington was probably getting impatient. "Knock-knock," I said as I tapped on the door.

He turned and took on his regular composed expression of indifference. In that moment I realized yesterday was a privilege. Hale didn't usually show his softer sides and something in his past taught him to always keep his guard up.

I wasn't sure what made him so guarded, but I suspected it had to do with his father and that made me sad because he really was likable when he let people see the softer sides of him.

"Rayne. Come in." He reached for a dress shirt and made quick work of covering himself.

I had a job to do and needed to keep my nose out of his private business. "Your dad wants you up on the sky deck with the thumb drive that has the Hampton specs."

He frowned. "Hilton?"

"Yeah, sorry."

He nodded then tipped his head. "Were you sick last night? I thought I heard you shuffling around."

Wonderful. Cue *Pomp and Circumstance.* I just graduated to a new level of sexy. "My sea legs were a bit delayed."

"Do you feel better today?"

His concern was, again, surprising, as I was never sure which side of him I should expect. I preferred the gentle, caring side, but there was also great appeal to his authoritative side. Especially after discovering he was only three years older than me.

He seemed so powerful at times, I wasn't sure how anyone in their thirties pulled off that sort of clout. I certainly couldn't.

I nodded. "I'm adjusting, I think."

His full lips twitched but only made it halfway to a smile, as if he caught the motion and intervened just in time. "Good."

My attention returned to the attractive newscaster on the TV and he followed my gaze and frowned. Reaching for the remote, he shut off the flat screen. "I'll get those files and be up in a few minutes."

"Okay." I didn't move because he wasn't moving either. Then I realized he was probably waiting for me to get out of his way. "Okay," I repeated.

"Do you like *The Lady Parr*?"

Relieved he asked a question that would keep the conversation going, I smiled, but had to think about what he was talking about. "The boat? Yes. It's really nice."

"Have you had a tour yet?"

"No." I chuckled. "Where does the crew hide?"

"There are quarters below. I could show you if you want a tour."

You'd think he'd offered me a trip to Paris for how eager my response came out. "I'd love that!"

The corner of his lips hooked in a half smirk. "Don't get too excited. The crew quarters are the least luxurious portion of the vessel."

Right. *Bring it down a notch, Rayne.* Sensing my overzealous grin, I forced my mouth into a resting position. "When did you want to do it?"

His brow lifted.

"The tour," I clarified my face heating with the heat of a thousand suns. "When did you want to give me a tour?"

"Now. I'll run this up top and we'll start there." He turned and reached for something in a leather bag. "Let's go."

I hesitated. "I'm working." It seemed wrong to go flitting off with Hale when I was here to assist Remington.

He waved a hand. "You need to know your way around the yacht. Eric's with him. He'll be fine."

Though he assumed the authority to make such decisions, I wasn't sure of the impression it would give my boss. If Remington objected I'd stay and take a tour later, but it would probably benefit me to learn my way around the ship as soon as possible.

As I followed him up the steps, I learned some things about myself. I was never an ass girl, but being on eye level with Hale's sexy ass as we climbed the stairs was straight up awesome. I couldn't help but study the way the seam of his pants fell perfectly over the crease of his cheeks and the bitable perfection that sloped into his legs.

Once we reached the main floor, I was eye level with his mid back and downwind from his yummy scent. He glanced back and my lips shifted into a weird smile. It was a fail. I totally bared my teeth like a growling ferret.

"Your new clothes fit okay?"

"What? Oh. Yeah. They're fine."

"They look nice." He held the door to the deck and I inwardly reveled in his praise.

The clothes were just overpriced capris and a polo shirt, but hey, if that's what did it for the trust fund type, I was game. I'd do it for him all night long.

Shaking my head, I mentally chastised myself. I seriously needed to slow my roll with the sexy talk, because even hearing it in my head was embarrassing.

The sea gods were smiling on me as we took another flight of steps to the sky deck. Hello again, Mr. Cute Bum.

Remington's voice rumbled, and as we crested the top floor, I saw he was on the phone. Eric had his nose buried in the laptop but looked up as we approached. Hale handed him something small, which I suspected was the thumb drive. Eric glanced at me, his eyes narrowing.

Seriously, we were on the same team. What was his problem?

Because I absolutely hated confrontation, I tried to be as friendly as possible. "How's it going, Eric?"

"It took you long enough."

My shoulders drew back and I casually glanced at Hale who was busy talking to his father as Remington held the phone away from his ear.

Looking back to Eric, I explained, "Hale was on the phone. I had to wait for him to get off."

His lips pursed. "Well, looks like he got off. You can sort through that stack of files over—"

"I'm going to show Rayne around," Hale announced, interrupting Eric's instructions.

I wasn't sure if I took direction from Remington's other assistant. Eric had seniority and knew a hell of a lot more than me, so maybe that was how this worked, but when Remington agreed a tour was a good idea, I didn't object. First and foremost I listened to Mr. Davenport.

"We shouldn't be long," I said, trying to keep the peace.

Remington waved me off, not seeming to care, but Eric's scrutiny weighed heavily on my back as we walked away.

As we approached the steps, Hale's father called, "While you have her, square away the paperwork, Hale."

Hale nodded and I sucked in a sharp breath when the weight of his hand rested on my lower back. We were touching? I didn't think we were there just yet, but as the heat of his palm warmed my shirt I found no reason to complain.

I needed a diversion before I giggled like a schoolgirl. It had really been far too long since I felt a man's hands on me. Needing a distraction, I waited until we were back on the lower deck and announced, "I don't think Eric's a fan of mine."

Hale's hand fell away as he stepped to my side and I drew in a deep breath. God, I was out of practice and for all I knew, this was just gentlemanly behavior. The opening of doors, bag carrying, and back touches could all be the result of a decent upbringing and totally unrelated to any sort of sexual tension.

He slipped on his sunglasses and faced me. "Why's that?"

"I don't know. He gave me the stink eye a minute ago and last night he seemed irritated when he delivered my phone. He never smiles and he always seems to scowl whenever he looks at me. Unless that's just his face, but he doesn't look at you guys that way."

"And so he shouldn't."

Hale wasn't being cocky, but the unruffled security he had in his authority triggered something in me. I wasn't usually around powerful men, but when he showed that assured side my woman parts became very alert.

It was that sort of authority that led to Lewinskys. I didn't know how to Lewinsky, because why would anyone want to do that? But there was a definite appeal to authority that made a girl rethink her stance on BJs.

"Don't worry about Eric. He's just not used to sharing my father's attention. In a day or two, I'm sure he'll appreciate your presence. My dad's a pain in the ass and his cast is only going to make him more demanding than usual. It's good you're here."

Relieved to hear him say that, I put my insecurities aside. "So...I'm ready to be awed by your nautical knowledge. Fair warning, I know absolutely nothing about boats, but I can do a mean pirate accent." Now that I wasn't as tongue tied in his presence talking wasn't so hard.

He chuckled, but the sound was abbreviated as if he didn't laugh often. "Is that so?"

"Aye. If you're a good guide, I'll tell you some of my pirate jokes."

Grinning, he turned, but shifted a little closer. "Then we should probably start here. *The Lady Parr* is what's called a tri-deck yacht."

Sliding open the glass door, he allowed me to step into the living quarters first.

"Everything was custom designed down to the finish of the furniture."

"So nothing from Ikea?"

He smirked. "The Swedes missed out on this one, I'm afraid."

The best part of Ikea was the names of their products. "We once had a chair from Ikea and I loved inviting people to sit on my *flärdfull.*"

He glanced over my shoulder. "It's a very nice *flärdfull.*"

What's that now?

Was that a joke? A sexy joke? I laughed nervously. He should see my *knubbigs.*

He smirked and continued on as if he hadn't just made a Swedish reference to my bum.

"The windows are customized with full height glazing to maximize the view without overpowering the room in glaring light." He pressed a button on the wall. "If you want to relax..."

My jaw unhinged as an enormous flat screen television rose from the bar between the seating area and the dining table. "Whoa. That's so James Bond!"

He nodded but didn't mimic my level of excitement. Once again, his guard was up. How did a person slip in an Ikea ass joke and jump right back into serious mode?

For being almost the same age, we seemed polar opposites as far as maturity went. When he did smile, it was brief and I never really heard him *laugh*-laugh. The little chuckles here and there were nice, though. Especially when I caught him at ease, like when speaking to his brother.

"While we're here we should go over your paperwork," he said, pulling a file from a drawer. He tossed it on the table and pulled out a chair. "Have a seat."

He managed to take control of situations so easily, I found myself eager to obey. "What sort of paperwork?" I slid into the chair he offered.

"Mostly tax stuff." He produced a pen and slid me a form. "You can start with this. And this one's for payroll."

Nodding, I read over the form and quickly filled in the information. "Do I use the address where we'll be staying or my home address?"

His gaze studied me. Was that a dumb question?

"I'd use your permanent address."

Why was he looking at me like that? Feeling like I had food on my face, I casually brushed my fingers over my cheeks and filled in the blank spaces.

Keeping my head down, I continued to catch him studying me from the next seat. When I faced him, my heart raced, and I couldn't take it anymore.

"You keep staring at me."

"Sorry." He glanced at my paper. "You have nice handwriting."

"Uh, thanks." My grade school teachers would be so proud.

His gaze didn't stay averted for long. This time when he looked at me there was a sort of resignation in his eyes. "You don't have to be nervous around me, Rayne. We'll be working with each other regularly."

That didn't calm my nerves—not one bit. So I fibbed. "I'm not nervous."

His hand settled over mine where my fingers were rapidly twiddling the pen. "You sure?"

Touching! I instantly stopped breathing. Was it hot in here? "Do you have anything else for me to fill out?"

He eased his hand back and studied me like a math problem. For the life of me I couldn't figure out what he saw. "Not right now. We should get on with our tour."

I stood, eager to put some space between us. "Lead the way."

He rose and walked through the narrow hall. "Down this hall, you have the master stateroom." He pointed to his father's suite.

"I've already been in there."

He glanced at me and his slight grin vanished. I didn't know what it would take to convince him I wasn't here to bone his dad, but if he didn't stop jumping to conclusions, I was going to start really messing with him.

Gesturing to the stairs that led to our sleeping quarters, he muttered, "You're familiar with the below deck quarters."

"How many people have you had stay onboard?"

"She sleeps ten guests comfortably, but there are a lot more onboard at any given time."

I really wanted to see where they were hiding the crew. We cut through the dining room and he slid open a door. The kitchen was pristine stainless steel with granite countertops.

"The galley is the hub of the yacht."

The stove had chrome channels around each burner. "I guess this keeps the pots and pans from sliding."

He nodded, his gaze neutral yet scrutinizing me. His voice softened in the small space. "There's commercial refrigeration, which is sea water cooled. We have enough freezer space to store food for a three-week voyage."

Although he was only describing the amenities, my attention zeroed in on his soft lips as they caressed each word.

"It's so professional," I murmured and swallowed. "Can I have a drink of water?" I was suddenly parched.

"Sure." He reached into one of the refrigerators and retrieved a bottle of Davenport water. Once he unscrewed the cap, he handed it to me. "You're probably dehydrated from last night. You might want to watch being out in the sun today."

I took a sip and nodded. That was probably what this was, just some simple dehydration.

I stilled as he pressed the backs of his knuckles to my forehead, our gazes holding for a split second that felt a decade too long. "You're a little warm."

My face felt like it was on fire. I took another sip as soon as his touch fell away. Shaking off my strange behavior, I returned my focus to the kitchen.

"After seeing this I'm a little upset I missed dinner last night."

"Our chef's one of the best. He's Creole. I highly recommend his beignets."

"What's a beignet?"

As his head tilted a thin strip of golden hair fell out of place. He was on the cusp of being a brunette, but the sun had definitely brought out his natural blond highlights. "You've never had one?"

"No, but I like all food."

"That's a shame. They're decadent, deep fried like a fritter and loaded with powdered sugar." His gaze dropped to my chest. "I wouldn't recommend eating one while wearing black."

My bra constricted as every breath pressed my breasts tighter against the material. His attention drifted to my mouth, lingered for a moment then shifted to my eyes.

"I'm sure we can have Laurent make a batch."

Captivated by the way his silver eyes looked almost blue, I whispered, "But I'm wearing black." Apparently I sucked at flirty banter.

He blinked and the eye contact was severed as he abruptly turned. I lost my balance as if his gaze were holding me up.

"We can tell him to go light on the sugar," he mumbled, moving on with the tour. "If you follow me upstairs I'll show you the captain's quarters."

Cursing myself for sounding dumber than usual I followed him out of the galley. Maybe I was totally misreading his signals and lingering glances. If that were the case I needed to clear things up, maybe remind him it wasn't polite to stare or turn women on with no intentions of following through.

"Hey," I called when we reached another narrow stairwell.

He paused and turned, but didn't seem the least bit aware of the mixed signals he was sending out. It was as if I'd imagined the whole thing. I didn't think I'd imagined the chemistry back there, but Elle was always teasing me about being terrible at reading men, so maybe I did.

He lifted his brows, waiting for me to say something.

"Um..."

Maybe I should just let it go. I was tired, dehydrated, and a little hungry now that my motion sickness had waned. All of that probably was having an affect on me. "Never mind."

He took a step down, putting us only a foot apart. "What were you going to say?"

"Nothing. I..." I shook my head. "It's nothing."

A shadow passed at the top of the steps and we both glanced in that direction. A female voice spoke to someone and I recognized the Spanish accent as the one belonging to the woman who served breakfast.

Hale looked back at me. "You sure?"

The only thing I was sure of in that moment was that this stairwell was too cramped for two people. "You just... seemed distracted. If you don't want to show me around anymore, I can find my way back."

For the briefest moment, his guarded expression

slipped again. It was like peeking behind the curtain of Oz and my breath caught every time I got a glimpse of the real him.

"I want to show you around."

I really wished Elle were here to interpret this situation. "Okay. I just didn't want you to feel obligated. I'm sure you have more important things to do."

"This is what I want to be doing."

Like that! Right there! Was that because of me or because he really liked playing tour guide?

To play it safe, I assumed the latter and put all my dirty thoughts away. I had no business having such thoughts anyway. "Okay then. Do I get to meet the captain?"

"I'll introduce you." Seeming satisfied, he turned and continued up the stairs.

I forced myself not to look at his butt this time, and I succeeded, for the most part. We entered another living room, this one completely surrounded by glass.

"Is this the captain's quarters?"

"No. This is where I usually am if you're ever looking for me."

"I guess I haven't been up here yet because of Remington's foot. How did he get to the sky deck this morning?"

"I helped him."

"Oh."

Being that I was the assistant, I should have been the one assisting him, but I couldn't imagine helping a man of Remington's size up a flight of stairs. Hale probably did it without breaking a sweat.

"The bar is there if you find yourself in need of a drink. Working for my father, I imagine you'll become quite familiar with our stock."

So far I hadn't had the impulse to hit the sauce, but it was good to know I had permission if the need arose. "Thanks. I'll keep that in mind."

Sliding open the glass door, we stepped onto another deck, but it wasn't the one I'd been on that morning. This one had a long dining table and was shaded by the sky deck overhead.

He pointed to the stairs. "They lead you back to the sky deck."

If I listened over the surf, I could hear the low rumble of Remington's voice above. I should probably get back.

Reaching in my pocket, I checked my phone and frowned. "I have a notification."

Hale waited as I navigated my way through the device.

"I don't know what this means," I mumbled. "He has so many apps on this phone I don't know what half of them do, and the damn thing's always pinging and alerting me of something."

He leaned closer, the intoxicating scent of his skin purifying the briny air. "Maybe I can help." Capturing my hand holding the phone, he angled the screen so he could see. "Your stock crashed."

"What?" I snapped. "I just bought it!"

Briefly glancing at me, he took the phone. "Did you—" His words cut off as he cleared his throat.

Facing me again, his voice lowered. "What made you buy that stock?"

Mortified that he might make some connection between the *Hale Sterling & Gold* stock and his name, I quickly justified, "Gold's up."

He laughed. "Gold's a defacto commodity. Our country's in debt and there's an election coming up. Whenever alarmists shake the faith in the American dollar, which is only as good as the solvent government that backs it, people fall back on global currencies. Hence gold going up. It fluctuates daily."

Whatever he just said was sexy as hell. Brains would always turn me on more than any other male organ.

"Well, that's just great. I should have invested in stupid corn."

"How much did you invest?"

"A hundred bucks. I'm going to punch your father."

Hale scowled. "Did he advise you to buy that stock?" He seemed more concerned that his dad might have fed me poor advice than he seemed worried I might punch the old man.

"No. He said something about the instability of gold and a bunch of economic mumbo jumbo, but I sort of stopped listening after the tenth *do you follow, Meyers.*"

Hale laughed. "Don't sweat it. It'll go back up by morning. When it does, pull your money and put it in something like E'say Marketplace."

"Really?" Assuming all wasn't lost brought huge relief.

"Yeah. By morning you'll be golden."

Hale Sterling & Gold, golden? Heh-heh. I'm so clever.

Leading us back inside, he showed me the server, which was like a little kitchenette on the upper deck. "We're just above the galley on the main deck," he said, opening a pantry. "In here is the dumbwaiter."

I peeked my head in the little cabinet. "How very *Clue*. Could a person fit in there?"

He laughed and this time, his smile reached his eyes. "Why?"

"I'm just saying, it might be a way to get Remington around."

"I'm almost positive he won't let you stuff him in the dumbwaiter."

I waved a finger. "But not one hundred percent positive."

He shrugged. "You do have a charming way about you." Turning, he exited the server and left me standing there.

I was *charming*? He thought *I* was *charming*?

Funny, all of my life I'd been told I was silly or cute or dorky in a good way or even pretty at times, but I couldn't remember anyone ever calling me charming. Charm was such a pride-worthy characteristic, being that it didn't stem from good genes and couldn't be faked. Hell, I wasn't even trying to be charming, but apparently, I'd done something to charm Hale.

Skipping after him I entered a room decked out in black leather and full of busy sounds, as the ocean rushed out before us.

"Rayne, this is Wyatt, the captain of *The Lady Parr*."

The captain turned in his seat and offered a wide, gap-toothed smile. "Pleasure."

Multiple computer monitors occupied the view just before the slanted windshield and I really didn't think we should distract the one person steering the ship.

Hale settled into the large leather seat beside Wyatt and flipped a couple of switches and rattled off some numbers. Wyatt immediately responded, speaking in the same sort of sea code. If Hale could actually captain a ship like this, my ovaries might just explode, because this was no small machine.

Doppler images scanned the ocean and I could almost make out the appearance of the coast, but for all I knew I might be looking at a pregnant woman's sonogram.

Oh, look, a penis and he has his daddy's eyes. Oops, never mind. That's just Nags Head, North Carolina.

"Do you want to try?"

My attention shifted from the computer screens to Hale. "Try what?"

"Driving her."

Eyes wide, I looked at him like he'd lost his mind. And now that I thought about it, his Kamikaze driving skills really shouldn't be behind the wheel of a vessel this size.

"No, thanks."

"Oh, come on." He stood and ushered me toward the leather seat, but my legs were too stiff to sit. "Relax, Rayne." He gave my shoulders a gentle press, and I dropped into the chair.

My hands folded tightly in my lap. If he had any

idea of my track record for calamities, he would not ask me to sit here. This was like the cockpit of that spacecraft Vader built after they destroyed the Death Star—The Super Duper Death Star.

"Put your hands on the wheel," Hale said from behind me. Having him lean over the chair far enough that his breath tickled my neck was not helping matters.

"I'm good. I think Wyatt has everything covered, don't you Wyatt?"

"It's all you," the Captain said, releasing the wheel.

Looking out the window with utter panic, my hands shot to the leather wheel, and both men laughed. "I don't know how to drive a boat!"

They laughed again and Hale leaned closer, adjusting my hands. "Relax. You aren't going to hit anything."

But Remington wouldn't tell me how much the yacht cost and I was pretty sure it was more than I could make in six lifetimes. And now my hands were sweating, which Hale probably realized, being that he was still touching me. And here came the cramps.

"Oh God."

All I could hear in my head were the voices of the characters from the movie *Titanic* yelling *Capitaine! Capitaine! Where do we go, Capitaine?* But I was pretty sure there weren't any icebergs on the east coast.

"It feels good having so much power at your fingertips, doesn't it?" Hale whispered, and I was almost certain my uterus imploded. Seriously, he should not be allowed to say things like that to me.

"Give her a little pull to the left."

Muscles tense, I turned the wheel with little resistance, but Hale's grip made sure I didn't spin us out of control. Could yachts capsize? When nothing really happened, I laughed out of sheer nervousness.

Hale reached for the controls and shifted a joystick between the captain chairs and my eyes widened. "What are you doing?"

"Just checking on things. You're doing great." His hand returned to mine and his thumb grazed my knuckle. Okay, that was definitely not my imagination.

My breath caught in my throat and I vaguely noticed Wyatt stepping away. "Where's he going?" I rasped.

"He'll be right back. Loosen your grip." He pried my fingers off the wheel and readjusted my hands, his touch incredibly soft and distracting.

"It's hard to concentrate when you're so close."

His head turned and I sensed him watching my face, but I was too afraid to take my eyes off the water. "Do you want me to back off?"

My gaze briefly skittered to his. That was a mistake. We were so close I could count his freckles. "Hale... if we crash... I'm blaming you."

He smirked. "Then you better keep your eyes ahead."

I cleared my throat and refocused, but he continued to guide my hands and lean over my seat. Strangely, as much as his nearness set me off balance it also put me at ease. While I had zero confidence in my captaining abilities, I trusted him to keep us safe.

"I remember the first time my dad let me drive.

It was right after my parents split up. I could barely see over the wheel. There's nothing quite as exhilarating as that first time."

I was never going to breathe normally again. "I don't think he'd approve of you letting me drive."

"I'm not one to wait for my dad's approval. Sometimes you just have to do what you want."

His hand gave mine a brief squeeze and then he eased back, hunching to my side, close enough to direct me. But it was actually pretty simple. There was no boat traffic and nothing but wide open ocean ahead.

I finally started to relax and let the experience sink in. "I'm driving a boat," I muttered and laughed. "I'm *driving* a boat. Me!"

He chuckled and glanced at me from the corner of his eye. The shadow of his short stubble matched the golden brown lashes around his eyes. My lips parted and I felt myself easing closer to him by fractions of a centimeter.

"You look good behind the wheel." His breath fanned over my cheek and I drew in a deep breath.

There was no mistaking that look—*I think* —maybe there was. Come to think of it, no one had ever looked at me quite like Hale was looking at me now.

I blinked several times, waiting for the haze to fade. But his eyes had super powers. "Why are you looking at me like that?"

This time, he didn't throw up his guard. "I don't know. I like watching you."

I couldn't hold his eye contact anymore. Licking

my dry lips, I looked down then glanced back to the water.

That was the first hint of confirmation that this tension wasn't one sided. It should have been enough to jolt me back to my senses, but it only made matters worse. I was suddenly entertaining a pretty intense fantasy of a shirtless Hale sitting in the captain's chair while I straddled him and dragged my tongue up his neck.

"We should let Wyatt get back to work."

Who the fuck was Wyatt and what did he have to do with my fantasy?

Hale stood to his full height and held out a hand. Oh, there was Wyatt. I hadn't heard him return. Seeing he had everything under control, I released the wheel and stood on shaky legs. I didn't dare take Hale's hand. I needed to get back to that bar for a shot or something.

Following him to the upper deck, Hale made some mention about the captain's cabin, but we didn't go inside. We took the stairs to the main deck and were once again on the floor with the dining room.

The moment we were out of the cramped hallway Hale seemed back to his usual self. His posture was reserved and the much-needed distance between us dispelled a good deal of my nerves.

"Did you still want to see the lower deck?"

"Is that where the crew sleeps?"

"Yes."

I nodded, and he led us down a stairwell paneled in sleek, polished wood, but that was where the luxury ended. The lower deck had its own kitchen and common area. The walls were made up of basic particleboard cabinets, so unlike the expensive carpentry on the upper decks of the boat.

The moment Hale entered the crew's domain, it was clear he didn't belong. A woman and man playing cards at the bench table paused and looked curiously at each other.

"How you doing?" Hale greeted them, and the other two nodded. "This is the crew mess," he said, and then pointed to a large monitor on the wall that showed similar images to the ones in the cockpit. "The crew has constant communication with the captain."

He turned and I offered an apologetic grin to the couple at the table. We were clearly barging in and interrupting their downtime. Hale didn't seem to notice.

"Back here are the sleeping quarters."

Each room had small bunks, with a personal reading light and a closed off port window. The beds were long, but stacked right on top of each other, which made me want to take a deep breath while I still could. I had yet to see a bathroom, but I assumed there was a communal one somewhere.

The cabin pressure made me very aware of swallowing and my hearing turned a bit muffled.

"How many stay down here?" I whispered.

"Quite a few. You have the engineers, the stewards, and chefs, the deckhands, the cook hands, the mates, the captain Tangiers or skipper, housekeeping, and of course one of the beds belongs to Eric."

"Eric sleeps down here?" My eyes went wide. No wonder he hated me.

I figured he had the same accommodations I did, but he was stuffed below deck breathing other people's carbon dioxide and sleeping on what was really a glorified shelf.

"I assumed you knew that."

Mortified, I glanced back at the couple patiently waiting for us to leave, and grabbed Hale's arm, pulling him back up the steps. Once we were in the hall and alone, I hissed, "No, I didn't know that. Why doesn't he have one of the rooms like ours?"

"There are only four staterooms, Rayne. Seraphina and Barrett might join us at some point. We couldn't put them with the crew."

No, the other Davenport children definitely wouldn't tolerate sleeping with the crew, but I was sure Eric would relocate if they showed up.

"But Eric's worked for your dad for eleven years."

"And he's quite accustomed to the sleeping arrangements. Why are you getting hyper?"

"I'm not hyper. If you think he's not pissed off he's sleeping down there after a decade of working for your family, especially when I breeze in yesterday and I'm sleeping upstairs, then you're not as smart as I thought you were. It's not fair, Hale."

He frowned. "Did you want to sleep down there?"

"No, but I should."

He took my hand and walked us briskly through the halls, towing me along as we turned and made our way to the intersection of stateroom doors. Ushering me inside my bedroom, he released my wrist and waved a hand at my bed, which someone had made.

"Go ahead, pack your stuff."

I pursed my lips. Well, I mean, I was already there, and my toothbrush was in the cup by the sink.

Shaking his head, he asked, "Do you really want to sleep in a cubby because it's *fair*? Come on, Rayne. Eric's a guy. He's slept there plenty of times. Don't make a big deal of it."

But it *was* a big deal. If I continued to stay in this luxurious room while he slept below deck with the crew, he'd never accept me and I had six months of dealing with him ahead.

Maybe I should suggest Eric relocate to the main deck unless Remington's other kids showed up, just for now. That might make Eric less cold toward me. I hated any sense of animosity between me and other people and I didn't want any issues with the other employees.

"If you think he wouldn't screw you over for a chance to sleep up here, you're out of your mind," Hale said and a bit of my charitable inclinations faded.

"I can't see him doing that."

"I guarantee he would, without a shred of concern for your comfort." Hale stepped closer and looked directly into my eyes. "As a matter of fact, if I went upstairs right now and said you were moving down with the crew to "be fair" and your room was open, I know he'd take it."

I scoffed. "Well, screw that."

"Exactly."

His voice softened. "I put you on this floor on purpose. No one's going to question whether or not you have the right to be here."

My brow lowered. "What do you mean?"

"I mean, it didn't seem appropriate to put you with the crew. You're new and this is your first time on a ship this size. You've already been sick once. This is the better room. Trust me."

"Oh." I'd sort of hoped it had something to do with his intentions to ravish me in my sleep, but with all the nocturnal seasickness, there really wasn't time for such nonsense. Maybe I was being ridiculous and should just let it go. "Well, thank you."

"You're welcome." He glanced at his watch. "We should probably get back. We've been gone for almost an hour."

I didn't dare take my gaze off him because directly to my right was a big bed begging to get messed up. Never before in my life did I suffer this impetuous urge to do something reckless, like slam the door and peg him to the wall so I could climb up his body and shove my fingers through his hair. This was bad—really bad.

Not only was I undeniably attracted to my boss's son. I didn't have a clue about his personal life. For all I knew, he could be engaged, or gay, but I really didn't think he was gay. At least I hoped. But above all, I needed to stop, because this was my job and I was starting to like it here, and I wasn't ready to go back to Oregon just yet. I needed to make back the money I lost in the stock market, and I really wanted to eat a beignet. So much ground to cover.

For a girl who never had much interest in sexual

encounters, I mourned the loss of my short-lived sexual awakening. Farewell, possibility of boat cockpit sex. So long likelihood of learning to Lewinsky. *Au revoir,* to butt bites and neck licks.

I sighed and took a step back, once again putting some distance between us. I'd never successfully establish boundaries if I didn't stop getting breathless every time he spoke to me. It was time to put on my professional pants.

"Okay. I'll be up in a minute. I just need to do a few things."

He nodded. "I'll see you up there."

Shutting the door behind him, I unplugged my personal phone from the charger on the wall and typed *Hale Davenport* into the search engine. Oh boy, there were so many pictures, but he really wasn't as photogenic as one would think. This was probably why everyone always thought Barrett was the cute one.

I searched for a few minutes, trying to find any mention of his personal life that might work as repellent, but there was nothing. Maybe I could get some repulsive details about Hale's private life from Remington. Or was that like asking how much a yacht cost?

I'd fish around and see what happened. The worst he could do was call me by my last name and not answer. Or he could fire me.

Doodles and Daydreams

7

"I want you to plan an event for the twelfth of July, Meyers."

My brows perked up as I'd been sitting in on Remington's phone calls for the past three hours. Reaching for my trusty notepad, I opened it to the first page. It was a brand new tablet and free of dick doodles. This was my professional, I'm a fancy PA notebook.

"What sort of event?"

"An intimate get-together. It's my daughter's twenty-third birthday, and she'll want something nice."

I wrote Seraphina's name at the top of the page and asked, "Do you have a theme in mind?"

"That's what you're here for. You're young. I'm sure you can come up with something."

I knew how to make Jungle Juice and buy plastic cups in bulk, but I had absolutely no knowl-edge about throwing soirées for girls like Seraphina

126

who already sat on their own little empire from a chic clothing line.

"What kind of stuff does she like? And is it a surprise?"

"Not a surprise, but this is something I'm doing for her, so I don't want her involved in the planning. Hale will probably be able to give you some ideas. You have Barrett in your contacts as well."

That was true. I also had other celebrity contacts, but I'd resisted the urge to call them so far. But the temptation was there.

"Will it be on the yacht?"

Remington rubbed his chin in consideration. "I hadn't thought of the *Lady Parr* as a possibility, but that might be nice. We can cruise down the Gulf and have everyone back sometime after midnight." He nodded. "Go with that, Meyers. I'll okay whatever you need to make it nice: music, catering, the whole deal. Figure on about fifty guests."

My eyes went wide. "Can *The Lady Parr* fit that many?"

"For a trip over the course of a few hours, sure. Ask Phina to email you a guest list. Her number's in your phone too." He looked at his watch. "Why don't you find a place to work with the iPad and start thinking up some ideas? Eric, I'm ready to go back to my room for a bit."

Gathering my notebook and iPad, I made my way down to the main deck and regretted not buying a bathing suit, but swim attire would have annihilated my budget, and it wasn't like I could wear it during regular work things. Taking a moment to mourn my adorable tankini lost somewhere in cargo-space, I made do by rolling my sleeves to my shoulders, so I didn't get too horrible of a farmer's tan.

No one had called from the airport about my luggage. Maybe I'd at least get a check for my lost items, but it wasn't like the Pony Express would be swimming out to sea so that money would be no help. Once I got paid I'd buy a swimsuit.

Settling on the foam-cushioned bench that wrapped around the pool, I kicked off my flip-flops and keyed on the iPad. The first thing I had to do was figure out what a girl like Seraphina Davenport would like, so I Googled her.

Hale's sister was really pretty. She had plump lips, a youthful glow, and her jewelry accented every outfit perfectly. I wondered what she was like in person, but was in no rush to meet her, at least not until I was more settled in my position as her father's assistant.

I wasn't sure what sort of theme I should go with, but I kept imagining rap videos and eccentric rich people doing lines of cocaine in the bathroom. I don't know. I was going off a mental montage of Crocodile Dundee, *Pretty Woman*, and Britney Spears videos. Apparently my experience with anything outside the realm of picnics and keggers was limited. I needed to get in touch with current pop culture.

As I perused images on the Internet, I mentally considered what my role would be at the party. I'd likely be sweating my ass off, limping around in fancy shoes, running cocktails back and forth to

Remington while Hale hit on some runway model that worked with his sister. Splendid.

Okay, so clearly I had a crush on the guy, which was weird because I hadn't had a crush on *anyone* since Jonathan Snipes let me use his glitter paint in second grade, and that was really more about the glitter than the guy.

My reference points for infatuation were all jacked up and out of date. I had no clue how adults handled these sorts of situations, situations I typically avoided. My mind was certain any sort of crush on the boss's son was bad news, but my body was in firm disagreement. Part of me wished he did have a girlfriend so all these distractions would go away.

"Gah!" I mumbled, reaching for my phone.

I opened up a text to Elle, but wasn't sure what to write. How do I get out of a crush? Is a guy coming onto you if he rubs your knuckle and likes looking at you?

I was an inexperienced idiot. I tossed the phone aside and put all Hale thoughts away. Picking up my notebook, I got down to business.

Okay, rule number one about rich-folk parties... stay in the shadows. Making a list was probably my best bet, so I started with that. The list grew pretty fast as I thought of things to ask the chef and realized the crew would likely be my greatest alliance in making sure things went smoothly. It was rather bizarre having an entire staff at my disposal, but if I pretended I was a young, hip Martha Stewart, there was a chance I could knock this party out of the park.

In my head, I also made a mental list, a partying

with rich people survival guide. It included things like don't get drunk, don't take the brown acid, remember escargot means snails, and dick jokes are not okay in this crowd.

"You look busy."

My pen stilled and all of my focus abandoned me as I looked up at Hale in a pair of swim shorts and no shirt. Oh, this was not a step in my *get over Hale* plan. As a matter of fact, this seemed more like stage two of my get *under* Hale plot that was sabotaging my *be the indispensable, always capable, totally sophisticated PA plan.*

What to do? What to do?

I shut the book and smiled. "I'm planning a birthday party for your sister. Any suggestions?" *How about you come over here and whisper them into my cleavage?*

He must not be a mind reader, because rather than join me on the lounge, he slithered into the pool and holy mother of biceps did his arms and shoulders look good wet. Dunking his head under the water, he broke the surface and did the male porn version of Ariel perching on the rock spraying wet hair everywhere. I could almost feel the tiny drips of water hitting me.

"Rayne?"

Shaking my head, I blinked. Or I just totally imagined all of that, because he was staring at me, wearing the same clothes he wore that morning, and his hair was bone dry.

Great. Now I was hallucinating. Note to self, WebMD hallucinations at the first opportunity.

"I'm sorry, what?"

"I said if the iPad gets low there's an outlet behind that cushion."

Reaching, I lifted the cushion. Oh, look at that. It was an outlet specifically made for an iPad adapter. Rich people were funny. "Thanks."

"What are you working on?"

Deja vu. Let's try speaking for real this time. "Your dad asked me to come up with ideas for Seraphina's birthday."

"What do you have so far?" He sat on the bench and scooted close enough to read my notes. Once I stared long enough to assure myself he was really there, I put my worry about vivid daydreams aside.

Flipping open the cover of the notebook—*penis!* I quickly scribbled over the doodle I must have drawn while I was brainstorming.

"Um..." My pen rapidly scratched out the drawing and I fell into acceptable dialogue to distract him. "I was going to ask the chef if he wanted to go with something inspired by the French Quarter."

Once the penis doodle was obscured I met his gaze and...yeah, he saw it.

Sighing, I confessed, "I doodle dicks. I don't know why, but they're the only thing I know how to draw aside from Snoopy."

"You doodle dicks," he repeated slowly.

My face was on fire. There would come a moment in time that these people would realize they should have hired one of the other candidates for the job, but the more I tried to divert them from that realization, the more I was reminded how much of a calamity I truly was.

So I came to terms with reality and told it like it was. "Yes. Big ones, little ones, some with faces. Once I drew one wearing a cape and an emblem with the letters SS. We called him Super Scrotum and hung him on the wall of our dorm. It's a problem, but I've been doing it since high school and sometimes I do it without even realizing it. Hence, the penis you just saw."

"That's quite a talent."

"Not really." I hadn't seen a living-breathing dick in so long, for all I knew the model changed and I was just drawing a bunch of snakes wearing helmets. "It's stupid. Anyway, your sister's party—"

"I can draw Woodstock."

I met his gaze and was relieved to see he was smiling. "You can?"

He nodded and took the notebook and pen. Turning to a fresh page, he quickly doodled Snoopy's partner in crime. It was perfect.

"Wow. I'm impressed."

"I also do dicks, but they're mostly self-portraits, and I'm going to assume we aren't there yet."

I snorted. A joke *and* a cock mention? Double whammy! Maybe dick jokes did mix in rich crowds. "You might need a bigger notebook." *Annnnd I just ruined it.*

His laughter took me by total surprise. "Definitely."

Parry and thrust. Gather around, children, we have ourselves a sparring of dirty minded wits. Giddy-up!

Trying to keep the banter going, I spaced my fingers about six inches apart. "A notebook this big?"

He shook his head and my hands moved a little further apart.

"Keep going," he rasped.

Labored breath passed my lips as I separated my hands a bit more and looked into his eyes. Glancing down at my palms, which were now over a foot apart, I dropped them into my lap. "Oh, come on!"

He laughed. "The world may never know."

Of course, he'd make a lollipop reference. I took my notebook back.

"Anyhoo, I'm planning this party for your sister, and I don't have a clue what she might like."

He eased back on the lounge and crossed his arms behind his head. "Phina? She's easy. She likes technology, gourmet pizza, shoes made out of hemp, ancient grains, the fashion industry, and selfie-sticks."

"Did you just generalize her into a Millennial?"

He frowned and tipped his chin. "Maybe, but she does like all those things."

"Do your dad."

He grinned at the challenge. "He doesn't use complicated sentences, he owns countless ties, but every single one is in the red family, he keeps a small spritz bottle of vermouth on him at all times in case of an emergency, and his prized possession is the horse he won in a bet against Eleanor Wicket."

Laughing, I asked, "What was the bet?"

"I don't know, but the stakes were pretty high and involved her being naked for the payoff. The horse was a mulligan and he loves holding it over her head."

Impressed, I said, "Do me."

His brow hitched and his lips curved into a half grin. "Hmm... I'm not sure I know you well enough yet."

"Come on. Please."

"Fine." He scratched his chin in thought. "You don't own a curling iron. You're a lot more popular than you realize. You're well educated but incredibly indecisive. You're curious, optimistic, yet strangely afraid to try. You doodle dogs, dicks, and do a mean pirate impression—which I haven't heard yet. And I'm guessing you have no problem indulging in dessert before dinner. How was that?"

I gaped at him. "How did you do that?"

His grin turned cocky. "I pay attention and have fairly decent instincts about people most of the time. And you still owe me a pirate joke."

"You'll get one. And I'm not 'afraid to try'."

I had to give him credit for accuracy on everything else, but the truth was I'd try anything once. What I sucked at was seeing things through. However, Hale had been the one to say he didn't believe in doing anything-long term that didn't bring some form of personal satisfaction, so maybe we had more in common than we realized.

Low lidded eyes watched me as his smile remained and he whispered, "Tell me a pirate joke."

My heart should not be beating this fast. "What's a pirate's favorite letter in the alphabet?" I rasped.

He smirked. "*Arrrr.*"

I slowly shook my head, unable to take my eyes off his mouth. Putting my pirate accent in place, I said, "You think it be *R*, but I'm in love with the *sea*."

He laughed silently and shook his head. "Terrible."

"I know." I shrugged, reorganizing the items on my lap.

"Your turn," he said.

"What?" Gah! Every time he looked at me like that my IQ reduced.

"What do you see when you look at me?"

Oh, so many pretty things. "I don't know how to generalize people." I was terribly unobservant.

"Just give it your best shot."

I sat up, licking my lips, and considered all I knew about Hale Davenport. Great ass, top shelf abs, glacier gray eyes, aphrodisiac pheromones. Knowing I couldn't say any of that, I stuck to the basics.

"You like your job on most days and love your dad enough to stick with it on the days you don't. You're tidy. You like fast vehicles and powerful machines. And you appreciate a good beignet."

"You forgot brunettes."

"What?"

"You forgot to say I like brunettes, especially short ones with green eyes."

Alert! Alert!

The air raid siren in my brain sounded, and all of my split personalities screamed in panic, spinning in circles and crashing into images of every guy from my past. I swear, every oddity running the show up there was ten times more awkward than the outside me. They should all be fired!

My smile fell away as I studied Hale, waiting for any sign that he might be playing some sort of twisted, fucked up, humiliate the new girl kind of joke. He wasn't smiling or frowning, but he watched me expectantly.

Crap. Where was Elle when I needed her to decipher tricky messages? I mean, I know he just named three qualities I had but was he talking about *me*? What if he didn't even realize my eyes were green and he was thinking about some bombshell he was currently fucking?

"Sorry." He glanced toward the pool. "I thought you picked up on that. I guess I was being a little presumptuous."

"Wait." I shook my head until all the little minions running amuck in my brain settled down and shut the hell up so I could think. "Um, if you're just joking around, now is the time to tell me, because I'm really bad at reading people, and you're not the easiest person to read anyway, with your poker face and reserved words and half smiles. I'm not making any sense right now, but could you just maybe go back and clarify what you just said? My eyes are green by the way. In case you didn't notice."

The look on Hale's face was a cross between intrigue and regret. If there were voices in his head, they were definitely yelling *abort!*

Now he probably realized the can of worms he'd poked was stuffed full of crazy lady. Good luck tidying up that mess. He clearly wasn't referring to *my* green eyes and brown hair.

I'm such an idiot.

His gaze shot to the cabin, and he rubbed the

back of his neck, looking anywhere but at me. Reaching into his pocket, he withdrew his phone and made a pretty convincing sound of disappointment.

"Damn. I have to take this call."

The screen lit, but I couldn't see what it said. Maybe he just pushed a button. "That's fine," I said, letting him off the hook.

Clearly, I'd taken his comment way too personally, and now he was desperate to escape. Quick and painless.

His mouth opened and I couldn't bear to hear him make up apologies because I was a jackass. Rushing his escape, I said, "I have work to do anyway. Take your call."

I did my best big girl smile and pretended no harm no foul. He had the phone to his ear before he was even off the deck. The sad part was, I doubted anyone was on the other line.

Shutting my eyes, I groaned and eased back on the lounge chair. Maybe if I pretended none of that happened it wouldn't exist anymore. Yes, that seemed like the best solution. I'd just will it right out of history and piece together my dignity once I made it back to my safe bubble of make believe.

It took effort, but I shoved all fantasies of Hale deep into the recesses of my subconscious where I hid other unfulfilled dreams like living in England, having my own home theater room, or meeting my dad.

Yeah, some of those aspirations were a little more complex than the others. But the truth of the matter was, all Hale would ever be was a fantasy, because he was well groomed and sophisticated and uber-successful while I was a train wreck.

138

8

That evening I endured a quiet dinner with Remington, Eric, and, I believe, Hale was there too. I couldn't be sure, as I forbade myself to look at him. But yeah, I'm pretty certain the scent of sexy male wafting across the table was all him.

After dinner, I helped Remington get settled and said goodnight.

"Meyers."

Pausing at the door, I hoped he didn't have any outlandish requests. Today had been busy, and my lack of sleep was catching up to me. I was exhausted and ready to call it a night.

"Yes, sir?"

"You're welcome to use the common areas of the ship. Treat yourself to a drink upstairs. You did good today."

My smile, although small, was perhaps the most authentic show of happiness I'd had since arriving. The jolt of satisfaction didn't have anything to do with my exotic surroundings or my nearness to an impressive man like Remington, or even my off axis nerves around his son. It was merely a compliment, a genuine one, from a man who reserved his praise for those who truly earned it.

"Thank you, Remington. That means a lot."

"Did you check your stocks?"

Tricky old bastard. He knew that stock was a bust, but he wanted me to learn the hard way.

"I saw it went down, but that's probably due to political climate. It'll be up again by morning. I think I'll move it into something more dependable. Maybe E'say Marketplace."

His brows lifted. "I'm impressed, Meyers. We'll take care of that over breakfast tomorrow morning. Seven-thirty."

I nodded. "I'll be there."

The unfortunate thing about losing one's luggage was that I completely forgot to buy pajamas. My skin was salty from the sea air, and my hair was a bit wiry, so I decided to shower. If I wasn't so tired, I might have visited the bar like Remington suggested, but it was probably best I stayed sober.

Thankfully there was a plush terrycloth robe in the bathroom. That made it a bit easier to get around without PJs.

I plugged in my phone and considered calling Elle, but that would require revisiting my screw-ups of the day, and I lacked the strength. I did text Tyler though to let him know I missed his grumpy ass.

Settling into bed, I reached for the tie of the robe and stilled, as there was a knock at the door. Closing my robe, I climbed out of bed and cracked the door.

"Hale."

"Can we talk?"

"Um, sure." I stepped back as he let himself in.

He glanced at the rumpled bed and dim room. "Shit, you were already in bed. Sorry."

"It's okay. I was up."

Noting my wet hair and lack of clothes, he turned and faced the wall. "I wanted to apologize for earlier."

Did something happen earlier? I'd completely blanked it out of my mind, or at least I was working toward doing so. Talking about it was a step in the wrong direction. "Please don't—"

"Let me say my piece."

"Okay."

I wasn't used to him cutting me off, but he seemed to have something to get off his chest. Though I didn't need it spelled out. Hopefully, his little rejection speech would be swift and only mildly excruciating.

He rubbed the back of his neck and paced in front of the bed. "That was a really important call I'd been waiting for."

"I'm sure. It's really fine, Hale. I understand."

He lifted a brow. "Do you?"

I gave up. "No, not really."

He sighed. "Do... Do you want to come upstairs and have a drink with me?"

Hesitating, because upstairs meant dragging this out, I tried to convince myself his offer was inviting trouble. Sort of like an evil mermaid seducing the captain of a ship to his doom. But, wow, it was tempting.

"I'm in a robe."

"Everyone's in bed."

My well-accomplished inner monologue about staying sober through the first week of my new job flew out the window. Fuck it. I wanted booze and I apparently had no willpower when it came to this man.

"One drink."

The ship was dark as I followed him quietly to the upper deck. He looked at home behind the bar as he filled a stainless steel martini shaker with ice. "What would you like?"

"I'll just have whatever you're having." I didn't think people like the Davenports kept the fridge stocked with Bud.

Nodding, he made what was probably the most flawless dirty martini I'd ever seen. Seriously, this was some James Bond shit. I wasn't a martini drinker per se, but there was something eloquent about having a perfectly composed cocktail made from liquor that came from crystal decanters.

"*Fan-shee*." I accepted the drink. One sip and my sinuses cleared. "Wow. That's a strong martini."

He raised his in a toast, which I probably should have waited for before I sipped. "It's actually a Manhattan."

"I knew that." No clue what the difference was —pretty sad for a girl who worked in a bar for the last decade.

Hale took a slow sip and sighed. When he didn't immediately jump into conversation I took another sip. Yowzers. This was pure alcohol.

When I made it halfway to the bottom of my

glass I set it aside, certain finishing one of those in fewer than five minutes was a little trashy. I really needed to work on my willpower if this was me not drinking. "So, what did you want to talk about?"

Again, he sighed. "You know the saying when it rains it pours?"

"Of course." His father would hate that cliché. Very fortune cookie.

"I'm in a deluge right now."

"Okay..."

"I'm very particular, Rayne. I like things a certain way and I don't like to justify why that is."

"Is someone questioning your methods?"

"Yes. Me."

"I'm not following." And part of my face was slightly numb from the potent drink.

Taking a long swallow of his Manhattan, he said, "There's a certain method to doing things. There's a Rayne method, a Remington Method, a guy working to feed his family method, a woman trying to get her degree method—"

"And the Hale method." I got the point.

"Right. Everyone has their own technique of what works for them. I like my method. It's never failed me." He shook his head and his brow creased. "But it's not working anymore."

His frustration was cute. Life being unfair was the first lesson in *Living 101*, but maybe rich people got a different syllabus.

"I didn't want to tell you this, Hale, but your whole omnipotence complex, you know, the one where you make guarantees like you're God, it was disproven the moment I got seasick. You promised I wouldn't. Sometimes we don't get to decide how things turn out. I'm afraid that includes you." I patted his knee. "Welcome to the school of mere mortals and hard knocks. Your next class will be Murphy's Law and after that we'll tackle things like the banana principle."

"It just seems—Wait, what's the banana principle?"

"It applies to grocery shopping." I couldn't picture him ever needing to use this. "If you buy a ripe banana, or an avocado for that matter, it'll be rotten before you get a chance to eat it. You have to buy them before they're ripe, but chances are while waiting for it to ripen, you forget you bought them and they go bad anyway. It's a wonder I get any fruit in my diet. Oranges are pretty dependable, though."

He frowned. "I'm not sure how we got on this topic."

Retrieving my drink, I waved my hand for him to continue. "Go back to what you were saying."

"I try to be a guy who goes out of his way to do the right thing, even when it's the most difficult option."

That was more than I could say about myself. I was a big fan of shortcuts and low drama.

"That's an admirable quality."

"Life shouldn't turn around and stick it to you when you apply yourself to accommodating others."

I snorted. "Why? Because Hale Davenport said so? Life isn't fair. Kids get sick, good people die; nepotism steals jobs, and I'll never be a size two. I find it best to accept what is and make the best out of it."

"What if I can't? What if the only honorable thing I can do appears to be the least honorable outcome, but it's the best for everyone involved?"

Trying to crack his code, I narrowed the possible source of his problems down to three options. "Is this about love, money, or loyalty?"

"None of the above. Maybe a little about money, but trust me, any profit isn't for my benefit."

"Are you being blackmailed?"

He stilled. "No."

But he wasn't opening up to me about it. That much was clear.

"Look, I'm happy to listen and give you my point of view, but I'm not really up to speed on the situation, and it's only fair that I warn you I'm a bit of a walking fustercluck." The Manhattan had struck. "Clusterfleck." *Damn it.* "Cluster. Fuck."

He chuckled and I felt myself leaning forward. "You okay?"

I waved a hand. "I'm also a bit of a lightweight. Probably should have told you that."

"Sorry. I'm used to making doubles. Do you want something else?"

Staring into his beautiful gray eyes I wondered how offended he'd be if I took a great big whiff of his shirt. And I was tipping out of my chair.

"Whoa." He caught my arms.

Yes, I'd definitely been leaning a little too much. "Sorry. I don't hold Manhattans well."

His grip loosened, keeping his hands on my

arms and sliding down to my wrists as I found my footing. We were really close and everything smelled like yummy Hale and Manhattans.

"I almost broke my rules today," he whispered, our mouths only a breath apart.

"Horseshoes and hand grenades, Hale." Wait, that wasn't right. "I mean, death and taxes."

He laughed softly, his warm breath caressing my cheek like a million tiny feathers. "You're not making any sense."

Irritated with my inebriated mind, I slurred, "I'm talking about almosts and guarantees. Almost only matters with horseshoes and hand grenades and the only guarantees we have in life are death and taxes."

"What does that have to do with what we were saying?"

"I'm saying screw the rules. Do what you want. That's how I got myself here on this fancy ship. You gotta take chances."

"Do what I want?"

I nodded. "Yes, that's what I meant to say." I thought I'd said that.

"Forget about the rules?" he muttered, and I swear we were getting even closer.

"You and me..." I waved a finger between us. "We're on the same page."

"How angry would you be if I kissed you right now?"

I blinked. Maybe we weren't on the same page —or were we? Was this another hallucination? "Me?"

His lip hooked in a half grin as he removed my

glass from my hand. "If we're throwing out rules for the moment, why fight it?"

"Oh, *I'm* against the rules," I whispered, getting what he was getting at.

His palm flattened on my lower back and pulled me forward. "Do you still think I should do what I want?" he murmured, tucking a strand of damp hair behind my ear.

I nodded slowly, because let's face it, I was beyond curious.

I'd do him. Maybe not well, but I'd do my best. Even if we only did some kissing, that would be more doing than I'd done in the past year. I was due for some doing, and I was definitely half past tipsy.

His finger traveled over the loose sleeve of my robe to the lapel, where it traced the slope of my breast. The moment his skin made contact with mine, shivers chased over my flesh, and my breasts turned into super sensitive beacons. My signals were waving his ship into harbor!

Wow. Davenports really zeroed in on a target when they saw something they wanted. I couldn't recall a man ever being so brazen, but I sort of liked it.

And it was all-good until I self-consciously giggled and whispered, "Your finger's on my boobie, Mr. Davenport."

He paused, looked into my eyes and back at his hand. "Should I move it?"

I snorted. "Not on my account."

His arms dropped between us as he hastily tugged the belt of my robe and muttered, "You're so fucking sexy. Just let me see you."

And then there was a cool breeze hitting my front from my navel to my nipples and I went utterly still. Yup, my robe was definitely open. Party hats and piñata on full display.

His breathing turned labored, a soft echo between us. "Tell me to stop," he murmured, the backs of his fingers trailing over my stomach.

"Um..." The words were there, but I didn't want to say them, not when he kept touching me and filling me with all sorts of erotic urges.

More importantly, were there condoms onboard? Someone had to have a condom. We only needed one, because this was going to end in a total letdown. Not on his part, but mine.

A warning seemed the polite thing to do. "I should probably tell you now, I'm not real experienced with ... *the sex*."

His gaze, which had been fastened to my chest, lifted and his brow creased. "You're not a virgin." He said this as if he'd already concluded as much and had the authority to inform me about my past exploits.

"No." There had been those three times. "I'm just not good at ... *the sex*."

A disbelieving chuckle rumbled in his chest. "You're not *good* at sex? Who told you that?"

"You mock me, but I know the truth. You'll see."

All laughter silenced and his expression turned serious. "Will I?"

If I had any instincts at all, this would probably be the point I started playing hard to get, but the whole cock tease thing eluded me. I clearly wanted to see him naked. But we were getting a little ahead of ourselves, and my front was getting cold.

Extricating myself from between his thighs, I tied the sash of my robe and reached for my drink, but it was empty. *Who drank that?*

He remained silently observant as I situated myself. Despite being a bit intoxicated, I was still sober enough to know fair was fair. I shouldn't show him mine until he showed me his. I returned to my stool.

"Maybe we should go back to sitting on separate chairs again." I lifted my body onto the seat and blew out a breath. "What's happening here, Hale? Is this like a 'you see my boobs and act like nothing happened' thing, or is this a 'that was an accident and you—"

"This is an 'I can't get you out of my mind, and I want you in my bed thing,' Rayne."

Oh. One of those. Sure, I was familiar with them. Had plenty. While I fed myself a load of bullshit, the real me broke into a sweat.

"I knew that."

Hale eased out of his seat and crossed the small space between us, obliterating the distance I'd just created. Without touching me, he leaned close until any which way I moved I'd touch him.

"I think you're sexy and funny and nothing like the women I usually date."

"You know, humans are creatures of habit, and maybe there's a reason you only—"

"If you're not attracted to me, I'd accept that, but I won't apologize for making my feelings known."

"You sure can be forward when you want to be."

He definitely wasn't guarding himself now. I nervously laughed and glanced at the floor, but he caught my chin, those silver eyes holding me still.

"Are you attracted to me, Rayne? I thought I picked up on some signals earlier today, but maybe I misread you. I'm not into mind games so I'd rather keep things as direct as possible between us."

Hello grown up conversation. My heart was racing so fast. "Attraction is a funny thing—"

"Rayne."

"Okay, fine. Yes. I think you're hot."

But Hale being hot and wanting to do whatever with me was sort of like giving an exotic car to someone without a license. There was a good chance the pretty car would end up totaled.

His smile was slow but full of male arrogance. Casually, he eased away from my seat and held out a hand. "I'm glad we clarified that. I'll walk you back to your room."

"What?" This was why men sucked. Here I was making car analogies and I'd apparently missed the moment of payout. "This makes no sense. I thought you didn't like games." And they called women the confusing gender?

"You're tipsy, Rayne. It isn't anything that won't keep. Trust me."

This was my punishment for holding my liquor like a leaky bucket. I was being sent to blue ball purgatory when all I wanted was to sniff him and kiss him and love him as hard as Lenny loved the rabbits in *Mice of Men*. I would hold him and pet him until I crushed this little infatuation to death. That wasn't too much to ask, but of course, I was drunk so who the hell knew what I was talking about?

Following him back to the staterooms I realized he'd actually done something pretty sexy by putting on the brakes. Props to Hale for being all kinds of honorable, because I totally would have been mid-drunk-cowgirling him—or whatever sex position was trending—had he not insisted we put a pin in it.

And realizing he'd protected my honor when I was too tipsy to recall I had any, made him all the more appealing. Dreamy Hale was promoted to chivalrous Hale.

Once outside of my room he cupped my cheek, but only gave it a little thumb graze. What the hell was that? Was this what the kids were into nowadays?

What happened to Frenching and copping a feel where it counted? Okay, there was a slight chance I overthought sex, which could very well be why I never enjoyed it.

"Goodnight, Rayne." He stepped back.

That little cheek caress was all I was going to get. Still, it was more action than I'd seen in the past two years, so I considered it a win.

I forced myself not to pout. "Goodnight, Hale."

Thank You, Sir. May I Please Have Another?

9

I t turned out I had a knack for party planning. Once I got Eric to show me, grudgingly, where he was getting the Post-Its, I found the utopia of office supplies and was like a happy whore in brothel paradise.

I started with a flowchart of various themes, narrowing each one down by resources and the growing list of characteristics I gathered from stalking Seraphina on social media.

I'd taken over the big table on the upper deck and was currently using teacups as paperweights to map out my plans. Remington was on the sky deck above, so if I had a question, I only had to climb the steps and ask. However, every time I asked him his opinion on a certain band or color scheme, I got the same answer.

Figure it out, Meyers. What am I paying you for?

So I started making my own decisions and figured the sky was the limit, which, in all reality, it was. If I gave Remington two options, one several thousands of dollars more than the other, he never batted an eye. It became clear money wasn't an issue, and his daughter's party demanded the best of the best. He obviously adored Seraphina, but didn't want to be bothered with the finite details of coordinating her birthday.

He did want all the applause, though. That was clear after the sixth *make it good, Meyers.* But that was fine. It was his event. I was merely planning it and having a damn good time doing so—for the most part. Eric was an occasional set back, one I was still trying to interpret.

There was definitely some sort of resentment between us, but I didn't understand why. This couldn't be just about sleeping arrangements. He seemed to talk down to me as if he wanted to establish some sort of hierarchy that set him above me. Maybe he just didn't like women? Yet he seemed fine with Marta, the maid.

Hale said I shouldn't worry about Eric, but every encounter made me more certain the man didn't care for me. As a matter of fact, I had the sense he was hoping I'd screw something up and get fired.

"Mr. Davenport wants you to see about getting the lunch menu changed. He has heartburn," Eric announced on his second trip past my table.

I was in the middle of reading an article about Seraphina, so his request took me off guard. "Um, okay. Do I talk to the chef about that?"

"No, you ask the Tangiers." He rolled his eyes. "What do you think?"

Comments like that made me certain he had a

problem with me, but, again, I didn't know why. "I was just asking."

He huffed and walked away. I put aside my work and went to the galley to find the chef, whom I had yet to meet. The kitchen was busy and full of delicious scents. A tall man with dark molasses skin chopped celery at the counter.

"Are you Laurent?"

"I am."

"I'm Rayne." I held out a hand and he brushed his on his chef jacket before shaking mine.

His smile was startlingly bright and put me at ease. "Good to meet you, Rayne. What can I do for you?"

"Remington's having a little heartburn today, so he wanted to keep the menu light."

"No problem."

That was easy enough. I spotted a basket of fruit on the counter and gestured toward a pear. "Can I have one of those?"

"Take whatever you like, bé."

I grinned and bit into the fruit. "What's bé?"

Laurent shrugged. "Honey."

Wasn't he cute? Mission accomplished, I nodded and returned to the deck.

Twenty minutes later Eric returned and interrupted me again. "Mr. Davenport wants a bloody Mary."

I frowned, wondering where his wait staff was. "I thought he had heartburn."

"Just do your job and make the drink."

I stiffened, unsure if making drinks was part of

my job and certain I didn't deserve his tone. "Is there a reason why you're speaking to me like that?"

His eyes narrowed, but he said nothing, just walked away.

As I put aside my work again, I went on a mission to find bloody Mary mix. I didn't realize this was something Laurent made from scratch, so it took several minutes to fill the order.

As I carried the cocktail up the stairs to the sky deck, the scent of fresh pureed tomatoes and spices made me rethink my stance on the mixers we used at the bar. Remington looked up and held out a hand, his attention divided between me and whomever he spoke to on the phone.

He took a sip and set it aside. Eric watched as if waiting for something to happen, but I didn't stick around. Maybe I could get through the next hour without another interruption.

When I returned to the lower deck Marta was waiting nearby. "Hi, Marta."

She smiled and approached the table. "You have work to do. Next time you need something from the galley, I'll get it."

"Oh, it's no problem."

She glanced at my notes. "You planning the party for Ms. Phina?"

"Trying."

She patted my shoulder. "You'll make it nice for her. Busy. Busy. I'll let you work."

I grinned, thinking she was rather nice and thoughtful, sort of like the maternal figure of the ship. It wasn't that I minded waiting on Remington. That was my job. But Eric never asked me for anything. He *told* me what to do. Maybe his seniority gave him the right, but I didn't see the need for the pissy comments whenever I asked a simple question.

Shoving the irritating thought of him aside, I got back to work. I might have overdone it with the theme, but after taking Hale's description of Seraphina into consideration and combining it with my socialite notes, I had some decent leads.

Those hemp shoes Seraphina liked, she didn't like them because they were fashionable. She liked them because the maker donated a large portion of its profits to putting shoes on impoverished children. But that wasn't the only charitable thing in this Davenport's world.

She also was an activist for no kill animal shelters and spoke out against animal testing, which painted a favorable picture of her in my mind. I hadn't realized her entire cosmetic line was based around cruelty-free products. Her father grumbled about how much money she spent doing things the "tree hugger" way, but I liked that she did things the right way—at least they were right to my way of thinking.

In the end, I settled on a Casino Royale theme, because rich people liked to play with money and I could slip in some silent auction items that would go toward some of Seraphina's favored charities. I was rather proud of myself for coming up with such a clever scheme for a girl I'd never met.

On top of a very productive day, my stocks were up, and my to-do list was full of items that added to my personal value and kept my mind off the other passengers. I saw Hale briefly after my breakfast slash stock market meeting with Remington that morning, but I didn't want his presence to derail my focus, so once I had my instructions, I said a quick hello-goodbye and relocated to the deck below.

Yes, I occasionally caught his voice and got a little tingle, but I was filling a role here, and that role was Awesome PA, not salivating, infatuated teeny-bopper. The longer I managed to phase out his presence the more entrenched I became in my work.

At the end of the day, long after Remington retired to his room for his pre-supper nap, I hurried to wrap up any loose ends. My bare feet rested on the table as I jotted down the figures being dictated to me over the phone in my little coastal office.

"And the roulette table?" I asked the vendor who worked for a franchise that rented pricey party props. "Does that include someone to run the table?"

The man gave me a list of options that included white-gloved service and some that only included the game tables. I knew immediately that we were going to order the full show, but it was in my nature to barter, so I got all the options first.

As a shadow passed over the table, I lost my train of thought and turned to find Hale standing behind my chair. My first concern was why hadn't I chipped away the nail polish on my toes? I'd looked for nail polish remover, but on a ship of mostly men, I didn't have much luck. My second thought was, boy, he's *pretty*. Tucking my feet under my chair I smiled and held up a finger.

"Okay, well, I'll look over the numbers with our

budget and be in touch. Thanks for all your help." I ended the call. "Hi."

"Hi." He glanced at the sticky notes all over the table. "You were busy today."

I gathered the Post-Its in strategic order. "Yeah. I think your sister's going to like what I have planned."

"Are you doing the New Orleans theme?"

I closed my notebook and stashed it with my iPad in a basket I stole from the galley. "No. I think I came up with something better."

"What is it?"

"You'll see when you get your invitation."

His mouth curved slightly and his eyes darkened with intensity as he moved a little closer. Because I wasn't ready to relinquish my common sense just yet, I took a step back.

He noted my retreat and paused, likely wondering why I was suddenly skittish. It probably had to do with the lack of alcohol and surplus of shame I suffered this morning when I recalled him looking at my boobs only to send me packing with a mediocre cheek brushing. Definitely not my best moment.

Hale glanced at his watch and, without seeing the time, I knew I had to check on Remington who was probably awake and waiting for me. On cue, my phone buzzed.

"The boss is calling."

"Will you be at dinner?" he asked.

I nodded, as a thousand minnow tails seemed to tickle my belly. Though Remington hadn't given me an explicit schedule, my workday seemed to exist between eight a.m. and five p.m. Dinner was strictly used for casual conversation and marked the start of my downtime. The only responsibility I had at night was getting my boss settled.

"I'll see you there," he said, and I collected my basket and left him staring after me. Yup, he was staring at me. *Me!*

Once I was outside of Remington's door, I had myself a silent victory dance. For once I hadn't been a basket case in Hale's presence.

Knocking on the door, I waited for Remington to invite me in.

"It's about time."

"Did you sleep well?" I pulled his scooter to the bed and retrieved a bottle of water.

"See about having the sheets changed on my bed, Meyers. I don't like the way my cast scratches against the ones on there now. Something with a higher thread count."

"Yes, sir." Where exactly would sheets like that come from on a boat? It wasn't like the crew was hiding a Macy's below deck.

After helping him onto his scooter, I remade the bed while he used the bathroom, then I gathered his phone and waited in the hall.

"You got some sun today," he commented, as he scooted past me to lead the way to the dining room.

"I forgot to buy sunblock when we went shopping."

"There's some around here. Ask Marta where she keeps it."

"I'll do that." Marta was married to one of the stewards, but I had yet to figure out which one was her husband.

"Are you making progress with the party?" He navigated his way to the common area.

"Yes. I should have all the arrangements firmed up by the end of the week."

"Good. You might want to ask Marta about finding you a sea band too. We have some south west winds coming at us and a hurricane watch ahead."

There went my newfound sense of security. "We might hit a hurricane? Will we pull over if we do?"

Remington laughed. "Where do you suggest we park? We're in the ocean, Meyers."

"But...maybe you should tell the captain to take us closer to the coast—just in case."

"Why don't we leave the navigation to Captain Wyatt and you worry about pulling out my chair."

I shifted the chair and helped him transfer from the scooter to the seat. "Are they bad?"

"What, hurricanes? They aren't pleasant. *You* can almost count on getting sick since you're a rookie. Just hope the rest of us do well enough, or you'll be holding your stomach helping me back and forth from the head."

All I could picture was the intro to *Gilligan's Island* and scenes from *Forrest Gump* after Lieutenant Dan went mad. I'd be puking over Remington's shoulder while everyone else powered through. This was not good.

"Maybe we'll beat the storm and make it to Florida before—"

"No way around it, Meyers. Get yourself one of those bracelets and hope for the best. We have at least eight more nights at sea."

Lovely. As soon as I saw Marta I was getting one of those band thingies.

Eric entered the dining room and took a seat at the table. I was done with his cold shoulder nonsense, so I forced him to converse politely with me.

"How was your day, Eric?"

Appearing startled by my congenial approach, he collected himself and unfolded a napkin on his lap. "My day was fine, thank you."

"Did you get a lot accomplished?"

His eyes narrowed and I could read his distrust. I was just making small talk. I wasn't trying to lure him to his death or anything.

"Well, I wasn't doing anything as globally instrumental as picking out a birthday cake, but I'd say I accomplished enough."

My brows shot up as his barb hit its target. "Oh, well then..."

It took me a moment to shift gears. I hadn't realized we weren't faking civility in front of the others anymore. I could play that game.

"Maybe tomorrow, if you can take time out of your busy schedule, you could show me how to use the invoice program on one of the laptops. We can meet in my room. It's on the main deck, just *above* the crew quarters." It was a total bitch shot, but I did way more than pick out birthday cake today.

Mental note, don't forget to order a birthday cake.

"I know where your room is."

"I'm sure you do." I held his gaze until Hale entered the dining room.

Picking up on the tension, he asked, "Am I interrupting something?"

Remington grumbled and poured himself a martini from the chilled shaker on the table. "Only a disturbing display of playground politics. If you two have something going, get it over with, and spare the rest of us the gory foreplay and juvenile banter."

Mortified that anything I said could be mistaken as some sort of flirting, my words locked up in my throat.

Stupid Eric. Why couldn't we just be civil? Every time I was in his presence, he made me feel like a pest, and I never asked him for anything more than to tell me where the office supplies were.

"The market did well today," Hale purposely changed the subject.

The food was brought out and the conversation shifted to small talk. I focused on eating my Cajun pasta because man alive was it scrumptious!

"I guess your heartburn's gone, Remington?" There was some serious heat to the pasta.

Remington frowned. "Who said I had heartburn?"

I paused, my next bite suspended an inch away from my mouth. Glancing at Eric, who was busy eating, I waited for any acknowledgement that he'd lied.

When he still wouldn't look at me, I said, "Oh, I thought you weren't feeling well. My mistake. I must have been misinformed."

When Eric excused himself, he took a lot of my tension with him, and I could finally enjoy my meal.

"What's in this sauce?" I asked, seriously making love to my dinner.

"It's probably the paprika you're tasting."

My fork stilled. "Paprika?"

So I might have a mild food allergy I should have mentioned to the chef.

Hale tilted his head in concern. "Is there something wrong with the pasta?"

"No." I cleared my throat, feeling like I'd swallowed a fistful of cobwebs. Putting down my fork, I inspected my face, but couldn't tell if it started to swell. "Are you thore ith papweekah?" *Ah, fuck.*

Hale's eyes widened. "Are you allergic?"

"Duth mildly. I haf antahithtameen in my purth. I'll go get it."

"Yeah, you probably should."

Rising from the table, I quickly worked my way down the stairs before my eyes swelled shut.

"Thit. Thit. Thit. Thit. Thit," I cursed as I dug through my purse.

When I found the little box, I popped a pill out of the foil and swallowed it before I even had water. As I entered the bathroom, I flinched at my reflection.

"Oh, Deethuth Chritht. I duth look thtunning." Hopefully the pill would kick in fast and this would clear up soon.

Once I drank a glass of water, I ran a washcloth under cool water and held it to my face as I sat on the toilet and waited for the swelling to go down.

"Rayne?"

Here was a perfect example of how life was unfair. I'd conducted my behavior perfectly today, not making an ass out of myself once that I could recall, and now I looked like a fight club reject who took a beehive to the face.

"I'm thitting in here."

Hale stepped into the bathroom and winced at the sight of me. "Jesus. Are you okay?"

"Yeth. Duth a little bit thwollen."

He crouched before the toilet and inspected my face. "You should've told us you have food allergies."

"I'm not uthed to having people cook for me."

He offered a sympathetic smile. "I still think you're pretty."

My brow pinched together, which told me the antihistamine was taking affect. "You're tho thweet for lying to me, but I thaw my reflecthon."

"Are you going to stay in here all night?"

"Well, I don't like walking around looking like Quathimodo, tho probably."

He laughed. "You don't look like Quasimodo."

Folding my hands around the washcloth I sighed. "I had high hopeth for tonight, but I gueth that thip thailed."

Now he really laughed. "Maybe avoid the letter S until the swelling goes down."

I sighed. "Calamity Rayne thtriketh again."

He chuckled. "You're not a calamity."

Oh, if he only knew the half of it.

"You left before I could show you the surprise I arranged."

My brows lifted. "You got me a thurprithe?"

He nodded and stood. "Why don't you come back upstairs and I'll show it to you?"

I hesitated. "I don't want to frighten the localth."

"Don't be silly. It's only my dad up there and he's watching the news. He won't pay you any mind."

Not used to getting surprises, I really wanted to see what it was. "Okay."

I followed Hale up the steps and made funny expressions behind him in an attempt to get my face back to normal. I probably looked like the victim of an exorcism.

Remington was on the couch exactly where Hale said he'd be, but he wasn't as preoccupied. "Christ, Meyers, you look terrible."

"Thuch a thweet talker, Remington."

He laughed. "Did you take a pill for that?"

"Yeth, thir."

"Good. I told Laurent no more paprika. Any other allergies he should know about?"

"That's it unleth he'th putting penithillin in the food."

"You need anything else, Dad? We're going up to the sky deck."

"I have my phone."

Hale nodded and I was extremely self-conscious as he rested his palm on my lower back right in front of his dad. Once we were outside, I said, "You probably thouldn't do that in front of your father."

"Do what?"

"Touch me like that."

He frowned. "I didn't touch you."

"You had your hand on my back."

Waving away my concern, he said, "That's not touching, Rayne. Trust me. You'll know when I'm touching you, and I'd never touch you in an inappropriate way in front of him."

Was that because of my position or because my boss was his father? Either way, it seemed awfully possessive of him. But who was I to argue, because that little domineering touch was perhaps one of the most erotic things I'd ever experienced.

"Thanks for clarifying."

"You got your S's back."

"Sssssss. Seashells, seashells by the seashore. Oh, thank God."

As we stepped onto the sky deck, I saw the table was draped in white linen, and a silver covered dish sat beside a bottle of wine. Smiling, I peeked at the bottle.

"I hope this wine isn't as strong as the Manhattan you made last night." I could not afford a repeat episode.

"It's port, and I'm not sure it's a good idea after you took an antihistamine." He tucked the bottle out of sight and pulled out a chair. "That's not the surprise, though. Have a seat."

Lowering into the chair, I smiled. "I'm not used to all this pampering. Holding doors, pulling out chairs, whatever would the suffragettes say?"

"They'd tell you those things are expected of any gentleman and you're thinking about the feminist movement which took place across the pond about fifty years after suffragettes were around."

"Well, I didn't realize I was speaking to someone so well versed in *her*story. Tell me more about women's lib."

He sat, looking completely at ease as he leaned

back and folded his hands over his flat stomach. "No bras were harmed during the 1968 Miss America Pageant. It's a myth. It was illegal to have a fire on the boardwalk, but women did bring bras to the protest the rigid, male imposed standards of beauty. The whole burning bras thing isn't accurate, though."

"Really?"

"Truth." He gave a nod. "But I'm not as rigid as my ancestors, so feel free to remove your bra at any time."

Impressed and amused, I laughed. "Only if you remove your undergarments first."

He arched a brow. "Is that how it works?"

I shrugged, unsure how any of this flirty stuff worked. "You tell me."

His gaze dropped to my chest and I was very aware of the ninety percent chance that he was imagining my boobs at that very minute. I wanted to cover myself and giggle, and furtively checked to make sure all my clothes were still in place. Yup, still good.

"What's under the tray?" I asked, trying to diffuse the sexual tension and get the focus off my body.

Grinning, he leaned forward and lifted the silver cover. The air mixed with the sweet scent of sugar. "I had beignets made for you."

My mouth opened as I stared at the pile of puffed squares doused in snowy powder. "Oh, boy. I should warn you now I have a problem with sweets."

"Another allergy?"

"More like an addiction."

I shopped at bakeries like some women shopped at Tiffany's. There were six, so that meant I had to give Hale at least three. Although I'd never eaten a beignet before, I'd also never met a dessert I didn't like.

Hale laid a linen napkin in front of me and placed a beignet on it. "Try one."

I laughed. "One? You know that plate's going to be gone in about ten minutes, right?"

"We'll see. They're very sweet."

That mattered not. I was eating all of them. Lifting the soft puffed pastry to my lips, I breathed in the sugary scent. Oh, yes... Biting into the fresh dough, I—*Have mercy*. It was like the queen of donuts if she were still warm and melting on my tongue.

"Holy crap," I mumbled over a mouthful of decadent heaven. My eyes closed as I savored the delicate flavor.

"Do you like it?"

"No talking. I'm in the middle of something over here." I took another bite and fell back in my chair. "Why do these taste so much better than donuts?"

"They're less dense because they don't have holes. I think that's why they taste less sweet, despite the powdered sugar piled on top."

His words were like ear porn as my tongue had one tiny orgasm after another. I stuffed the last bite into my mouth and hummed happily.

"Are you going to have some?"

His gaze turned heavy as his mouth slowly curved. "Truthfully, I'd rather watch you eat them."

I stilled as I sucked the sugar off my thumb and casually dropped my hands onto my lap. I had the table manners of a caveman. And all that sugar was now on my chest.

"I see what you mean about eating them while wearing black."

Trying to dust off the mess I only rubbed it in, making it worse.

"And this is why they call me Calamity Rayne. Please eat some, so I'm not the only one looking like a slob."

With a commiserating smirk, he broke a corner off a beignet and popped it in his mouth without dropping a single speck of sugar on his pressed shirt. Figures.

"Have some more," he coaxed, after swallowing his pesky bite.

Don't have to ask me twice.

Grabbing another, I used the napkin as a plate and broke this one into little morsels, so I looked like less of a pig. Hale's eyes followed my every move and grew darker each time I popped a piece in my mouth.

"Do you have some weird fetish about watching women eat?"

"Maybe. I like watching *you* eat."

"Well, then you're in luck because I love food, especially sweets."

"What's your favorite?"

"I'm thinking it might be beignets, but I'm also a big fan of anything chocolate."

"Good to know."

Once I finished the second one I was stuffed—
or so I told myself because I was supposed to be a
lady, of sorts. The other beignets still tempted, but I
decided I'd smuggle them back to my room and
gorge on them before bed. That was enough pigging
out in front of Hale for now.

"Thank you. They're delicious."

"You're welcome."

Easing back in my chair I frowned at my chest.
"I look like an extra in *Scarface*."

He laughed as I tried to puff out my shirt and
bounce the sugar off my chest.

"Come here."

Everything in me tensed as his request registered. A slow nervous laugh whispered past my lips.
"What?"

Sitting up, he scooted his chair back from the
table. "Come here."

Why, because he said so? Yeah, that worked.

I deliberately stood and stepped beside his chair.
This was awkward and outside of my wheelhouse.
My arms hung like dead weight at my sides as I
waited for further instruction.

His fingers caught mine and he gently rubbed
his thumb over my knuckles but didn't do anything
else. Still, it was enough to start my insides thrumming and get my women parts humming.

"Um..."

"Last night," he started softly. "When you said
you didn't have a lot of experience..."

Oh, that...

"How little are we talking, Rayne?"

Being that I was rapidly getting off from his

little finger massage, I'd say my experience was close to none. "There have been a few guys."

"But you're not involved with anyone now?"

"That would be a negative."

"Good." He pulled my hand until our knees brushed and then he reached for my hips and continued tugging.

I laughed, my motions lacking any level of grace. "What are you doing?"

"Sit down."

"On you?"

"Yes."

I tried to envision an elegant perch as he urged me to straddle his thighs. I achieved no such thing as I gawkily collapsed my weight onto his lap. "Well, I can't recall ever sitting on Santa this way."

He smirked and ran his finger under the collar of my shirt and my hair, sending chills down my neck.

"Okay, what are you doing?" I laughed again as my muscles convulsed in little shivers and my shoulders lifted. If he continued to touch me that way I'd lose all common sense.

He leaned forward and brushed his lips against mine, and I froze, my eyes going wide.

"You okay?" he whispered, that hand still caressing the hair that had fallen out of my ponytail.

I loved the way his breath teased my lips. Its warmth, the trace of his masculine scent, the all over affect it had on my lady bits. Jesus Christ, this was possibly the most turned on I'd ever been.

"Mm-hm." I didn't say too much, afraid he might take those lush lips away.

His mouth traced mine, and I hummed, sinking a little deeper into his hold as my eyes slowly closed. Oh, he had very nice lips, soft yet firm.

His head tilted and his palm curled around the back of my neck, pulling me closer and then I felt the caress of his tongue and sighed, giving him the chance to take things a little deeper.

My hands rested on his shoulders, making a slow climb to his ears, where my fingers could reach the soft hair at the back of his head. So soft. He deepened the kiss but kept it gentle. My breasts grew heavy as hands glided down my back and rested on my ass. It amazed me how perfectly my butt fit into hands as large as Hale's.

When he squeezed, I moaned into his mouth, and his grip tightened. Little thrills of excitement chased up my spine as I scooted closer, cupping his jaw and anchoring my body onto his. The friction of my clothes against my sex was divine as I slowly started to rock.

Why had I forgotten kisses could be this good? Maybe because it had never been this enjoyable with anyone else. I seriously didn't remember making out to ever be this satisfying. It wasn't like this with other kissers.

Maybe, like wine, kissing got better with age. Or maybe this was all Hale.

When his fingers brushed the skin of my back just under the hem of my shirt, I sucked in a breath. His palm slithered beneath the material and rode the line of my spine until it rested over the strap of my bra. The next thing I knew the hook was undone and he was rounding my ribs toward my chest.

I didn't care if we should slow things down or maybe take a breather, because I was too preoccupied with willing his fingers to my nipples. Cupping the weight of my breast, he grazed the tip with his thumb and I whimpered. The slightly rough pad of his fingers met the ruched tip like waves meet the shore, perfectly suited and meant to move against one another.

His lips worked to the corner of my mouth and down my throat as that tricky little thumb of his continued to tread over my sensitive nipple. Sweet Jesus, what was he doing to me? My head tipped back as he kissed my neck, but he never tried to remove my shirt or do more than gently fondle my breast.

For all of my distasteful memories about being poked and prodded in sexual encounters, my body was begging for him to do more. I wanted him to cup me, pull me, suck me, and maybe even bite me. I needed him to touch me lower, take my clothes off, and put something inside of me. I didn't care what it was. I just needed some form of relief.

When his mouth returned to mine, I was riding him like Sea Biscuit. Things were feeling really good until he winced and caught my hips.

Breaking the kiss, I saw the flash of pain in his eyes. "Oh my God, did I hurt you?"

"It's okay." He closed his eyes and shook it off then adjusted my position.

My eyes went wide when I noticed his erection pressing beneath his pants. *"That's a penis,"* I blurted and grimaced, not expecting to actually say the words out loud.

His chuckle wasn't at all self-conscious, but rather relaxed.

Ah, men and their penis pride. What would the world be like if women took as much pride in their vaginas as men took in their dicks? Would we walk around bragging about the size of our labia and boast about how deep things could go? That would be weird.

"You still with me?" His fingers brushed my heated cheek.

"I'm here. Just thinking."

His mouth curled in a half grin. "What are you thinking about?"

"Vagina bragging rights." Yeah, in hindsight I probably should've lied and said something a tad classier.

He laughed, maybe a bit nervously. "Excuse me?"

"You don't want to know the things that go through my head. Trust me, it's Crazyland up there."

His half-grin turned to a full smile. "I can only imagine."

A vibration shot down my hips and I shivered in pleasure until I realized the tremor wasn't coming from him. "Oh, crap. That's the bat phone."

"The what?"

"The bat phone."

I shifted, trying to wedge the oversized thing out of my pocket, and accidentally hit his sensitive parts again. Hale stiffened and winced.

"Sorry!" Sliding off his lap, I stood and removed the phone from my pocket. "See? Bat phone. This thing's way more sophisticated than my other phone. It's your dad." I held my finger to my lips. "Yes, Remington."

"Is anyone going to come get me or am I expected to sleep on the couch tonight? My show's been over for forty minutes."

"I'll be right down." I ended the call.

"Do you have to go?" Hale asked, standing.

I glanced at his pants and laughed. "Yeah, but you better stay here until you've come to an understanding with Prince Ever-hard."

He glanced at his waist then pegged me with a self-satisfied smirk, such cocky male ego in his gaze. "It was worth it."

Entranced by his handsomeness—*he was totally just making out with me*—I smiled. No one ever praised me for my sexy-time exploits, so hearing I didn't scare him off was great feedback.

"Thanks for *dessert*."

"My pleasure."

Look at me, making sexual innuendoes like a pro. As I walked downstairs, I entered the living room and found a frowning Remington. "Sorry."

"Left here to rot," he grumbled, as I wheeled over his scooter.

Honestly, he had every right to bitch. He was overdue for the pill that managed his pain, and he probably was feeling the aches of the day.

"I'll get your pill, then I'll get you settled."

I hurried ahead as he took the scooter down the hall. By the time he made it into the room, I had his bottle of water open and ready.

"Here you go."

Tossing back the pill and chasing it with some water, he frowned. "You're flushed, but your face looks better."

I'd totally forgotten about my allergic reaction. Peeking into the bathroom, I assessed my face. It was way better than the last time I saw my reflection, but not great. Luckily, I could blame the flush on the paprika and not the fact that I'd been making out with his son.

Sometimes Remington was like a cranky toddler, but he worried over the division of the GOP and occasionally smoked Black Russian cigarettes with little gold filters. Like any toddler, he was full steam ahead until he was ready to crash. Then he became a nightmare.

"Don't put the pillows there, Meyers. How do you expect me to see the damn TV?"

"I thought it might be nice for your foot to be elevated."

"Oh," he muttered, allowing me to slide the stack of pillows under his leg.

I realized in the short time I'd been working for Remington that Miles would have never made the cut. There was a distinct difference between the way Remington behaved in front of Eric and the way he carried on when he was alone with me. I partially suspected he hired a woman because he had a boo-boo and wanted a maternal touch. That would also explain why Cadence got the boot. She didn't have a very nurturing manner.

Drawing the blankets over his legs, I handed him the remote and dimmed the lights. "Can I get you anything else?"

"No." He pursed his lips then shocked the shit out of me with a mumbled, "Thank you."

Hiding a smirk, I left his phone by the bed and pulled the door shut. I celebrated the victory of my first *thank you* all the way down to my room, but my euphoria faded when I found Hale's door shut and the interior light on. I supposed our goodnight on the sky deck was all I was getting.

After I showered, I gathered up my laundry and left it beside the door. I was limited with clothing, so I needed to do some wash tomorrow.

Hale's muffled voice carried through the wall and I frowned. Who was he talking to at this hour? Although, he could be talking to someone in a different time zone.

I wanted to listen to his conversation, but I couldn't make out his words through the wall, and that just pissed me off, so I put music on the iPad and called Elle. I had people that wanted to talk to me too. I was *very* popular.

Elle answered the phone, proving just how much she'd missed my voice. "Hold on. I'm watching the finale of *Gilmore Girls*. Lorelei's trying to find Luke. She just talked to Sookie."

Yes, this was a show that ended many years ago and a series we watched countless times from beginning to end, but the whole storyline was one debacle after another that separated Lorelei and Luke. You didn't talk during a grand finale that took seven painful years to reach.

"*I just like to see you happy*," Elle quoted with Luke on screen and we both sighed.

Without watching, I knew the camera was panning away from their final kiss.

"So what's up, girl? How's life in the fast lane?"

"It's fast. I haven't stopped since morning, but I'm really starting to like it here."

"Aw. You need some *Annie* music to go with that positive attitude. I'm glad you're adjusting. Has *The Other One* stopped bothering you?"

"Not exactly."

"Seriously?" She scoffed. "What's his beef?"

"Well, it turns out you were right, and I was wrong. He *was* checking me out."

"Ha! I knew it! You are the absolute *worst* at reading men."

"The worst," I agreed with a laugh.

"So how did you figure this out, because we all know you wouldn't recognize a dick if it slapped you in the face."

"I'm not *that* bad." I pouted. "I picked up on it the moment he touched my boob."

"He touched your boob? Was there kissing or was he reaching for something and accidentally made contact? Because there's a difference, Ray."

"Trust me, it was intentional."

I spent the next thirty minutes catching Elle up to speed on all things Hale. The more I talked about him and reminisced about the way he kissed and touched me, the more my body ached for a repeat episode. I was a little terrified about how much energy I was investing in him, but Elle said I should see where things go and have fun.

Even if men like Hale Davenport didn't do serious, she thought I should see if he opened any doors for me. Not doors like opportunities to sleep with other men in his circle, but doors as far as my stunted sexuality was concerned.

"Just think, you might actually get an orgasm out of this," Elle announced, in total support of my sexual renaissance.

I snorted. "That would be impressive."

I didn't act like it was impossible, because whenever Hale touched me, it felt better than all the other touches from all the other men times infinity. So if anyone could make me come, I believed it was Hale.

Once we were caught up and my eyes were getting heavy, I said goodnight. I shut the music off and didn't hear anything from Hale's room, but that didn't stop me from imagining him in bed on the other side of the wall.

If I played my cards right, I might find out what that bed was like. For as uninterested in sex as I'd always been, sex with Hale opened up a whole new menu, and I wanted a taste of everything.

10

When I was fourteen, I had my first cannoli. Imagine what that does to a person. *Fourteen*, people. Fourteen. As that creamy filling first touched my tongue, I remember thinking, *where have you been all my life?* It was like I'd been robbed of a decade and a half of confectionery delight. Truly unfair.

My first experience with unspoken sexual tension was pretty much the same. I felt robbed. Why had I not realized it could be this exhilarating to like someone? Probably because I never liked someone the way I like Hale. Why, I had no clue. He just...did something to me other men didn't.

Every time Hale entered a room, my stomach got tight, and my heart raced. When he spoke I became hyper-focused on his lips and the sound of his voice, so much so, I didn't hear a single word he said, but nodded with unreserved agreement.

Sometimes he brushed a finger down my arm when no one was looking and other times he'd look into my eyes as if we shared the biggest secret in the world and no one else would ever have a secret as good as ours.

I felt totally ripped off that I was thirty freaking years old and just discovering such excitement could exist. My receptors to these little thrills were all hands on deck, so I was starting to think my sex problems of the past hadn't been about me, but, rather, the men I'd dated.

What a lousy batch of below the bar, pre-ejaculating, foreplay-rushing twats. I could have been having these feelings all along if they hadn't convinced me sex was uncomfortable and anticlimactic.

Of course, I wasn't actually having sex. I'd made out with Hale once. But look at the Pandora's Box that one-time opened. I said *look at it*!

My hormones were everywhere. My thoughts were in the gutter. My panties were wet and I was like a well-oiled fuse on a stick of dynamite ready to blow.

I mean, seriously, I'd even blow him. I'd made up my mind the moment I saw him watching me lick my sorbet spoon at lunch. I didn't think there was anything sexy about the way I ate my ice cream, but apparently I was wrong. Hale watched me take every last bite and by the time I was done he was breathing heavily, and his pupils were so big his eyes no longer passed as gray. Imagine what he'd look like if I replaced the spoon with his penis!

Late afternoon, I was called up to the sky deck. Remington wanted me to take notes as he made a conference call. I had no experience with shorthand, so this was the first assignment he'd given me that actually made me nervous.

"Just write down anything important and we'll decipher it later."

The call started before I was ready and by my eighth page of scribbled notes I was in a sweat and ready to shit myself. Three men were on the other line, and they all sounded the same, so I had no clue who was saying what.

When the call ended I let out a long breath as if I'd run a 5K. My hand was a deformed claw, and my penmanship would have earned a ruler whipping in a nun's eyes.

"Did you get all that, Meyers?" Remington asked.

I scoffed at the insanity as I tried to remember what my fingers used to feel like. "I got as much as I could, but I probably missed half."

"Take the laptop and type up what you did get. Email it to me when you're finished. Then you can be done for the day."

Wonderful. My typing skills were about as good as a chimp's. I'd be finishing up sometime around noon tomorrow.

An hour later and I was only on the third page.

"What are you working on?"

And there went my nipples, poking through my bra like two ballistic missiles. At this rate, I'd get no fun make out time.

Growling, I shoved the laptop away. "Typing up these stupid notes for your dad."

He frowned as he glanced at my notebook. "Who wrote this?"

"I did. There were four people talking at once."

He paged through the notes. "You have about twenty pages here."

"I know, and I can only read half of them. I'm going to be here all night."

"I think you're exaggerating."

"Really? I just spent four minutes searching for the letter Q. I'm convinced this laptop doesn't have one."

He reached over the laptop and pressed Q on the keyboard.

I pursed my lips. "Smart ass."

Sliding into the chair next to mine, he said, "How about you read and I'll type? We'll have it done in no time."

"Don't you have things to do?"

"Not really. I came to find you."

Smiling, because how freaking cute was that, I gave him a bump with my shoulder. I had the mating skills of a ram on the National Geographic channel, but he got the point.

"You're nice," I mumbled, just to make sure he didn't think I was trying to challenge him for a crack at alpha.

He shoulder bumped me back. "So are you."

"I really should do this myself. Remington asked me to do it."

"Does he know you can't type?"

In all fairness, I could text, but that was on a small screen using only my thumbs. This was different.

"Your father doesn't believe in the word *can't*. He'd just say something like, *Well, Meyers, how do you expect to learn if you don't try?"* My Remington voice was getting really good.

Hale laughed. "Probably. But in all fairness, if I told him a pretty lady blew me off because she had a deadline, he'd call me a short-sighted fool for not helping her so I could eventually have my way with her."

My heart went a bit spastic as he slipped in that compliment. Not to mention the insinuation that he hoped to have his way with me.

I twisted my lips. "Which one of us do you think he'd be more upset with?"

"Definitely me. My father loves a lot of things, but he never passes up a chance to have his way with a pretty lady."

That earned him another shoulder bump. "Say pretty lady again."

He shifted and tipped his face close to mine. "You're a very pretty lady, Rayne Meyers. And I want to have my way with you."

My cheeks heated as my insides trembled. "For that, I'll let you type my homework."

"Good."

Reading the notes was a hell of a lot easier than typing one word at a time, finding my place, and typing another word. With Hale helping, we had everything written up in about twenty minutes.

"That's it," I said, turning the last page.

"That's it?" He glanced up from the laptop. "What's he want you to do with them now?"

"He said to email them to him when—"

"Sent." He shut the laptop. "Now you're mine."

My breath hitched, as he stood. "Oh."

I'd been looking forward to Hale time since I woke up, but I suddenly felt very unprepared. As he slowly stalked around the table, I backed up until I was against the wall. "I should probably—"

His mouth closed over mine and whatever I'd been about to say flew right out of my head the second his tongue entered my mouth. Ten seconds of kissing Hale and my brain was completely scrambled.

Slowly, he pulled back and looked at me with half lidded eyes. "You were saying?"

Yeah, I had no idea. Launching myself at him I caught the back of his neck and pulled his mouth to mine. He groaned and grabbed onto my ass, which was perfect because I really needed to be in some sort of marsupial hold at the moment.

My feet left the ground as he cupped my butt and my legs wrapped around his hips. I grunted as he shoved me into the wall a little harder than expected.

"Sorry," he hissed.

No talking. More kissing! "I'll live."

He ground his body into mine, creating little pockets of heat that filled me with an urgent need to take off all my clothes. When his hand closed over my boob I arched and moaned into his mouth.

"Jesus, Rayne."

"I know. I'm not usually like this."

He toyed with my bra clasp through the back of my shirt and it suddenly loosened.

I gasped. "How do you do that?"

I'd been wearing bras for almost twenty years and even I couldn't open one as flawlessly as Hale.

His hand reached up my shirt as a door slid open and we both froze.

My eyes went wide as Marta entered the room with a dust cloth and began wiping down the end tables. Hale released my boob and held a finger to his lips telling me to keep quiet.

I bit down on my lips and held my breath. He pointed to his ear.

I shook my head, not understanding. Was this some sort of SWAT signal? He pointed to his ear again and I shook my head again trying to speak with my eyes.

Why the fuck do you keep pointing to your ear?

Keeping perfectly still, my body wedged between his and the wall, he rolled his eyes and tipped his head toward Marta then jabbed a finger toward his ear.

Oh. Headphones.

I gave him a thumbs-up, and he shook his head, silently laughing at me.

Carefully, he lowered my feet to the ground and stepped back. When I saw his erection poking through his pants I snorted, and he clapped a hand over my mouth, gesturing for me to be quiet. Catching my wrist, he bustled us into the hall where I broke into full out laughter.

"Did you want to get caught?" he muttered, adjusting himself.

"Oh, come on. That was freaking funny."

"I've known Marta since I was nine. She wouldn't think it was funny."

"I'm sure she knows you get erections, Hale."

He rolled his eyes and laughed. "You're incorrigible."

"Well, apparently that's a turn on for you."

He sighed and looked at his watch. "It's almost time for dinner. We better head down."

If anything, we took a bit of the edge off, but it would be really great if we could do some more kissing. "Do you want to come to my room later tonight?"

His brows lifted. "Are you sure that's an invitation you want to make?"

"Yeah." Did he think this was a one-sided thing?

"Sure. When?"

"I have to use the laundry room after dinner and get your dad settled, but any time after that. Say around nine?"

"I'll be there."

Dinner was rather bland compared to the night before, but Remington explained that was due to the oncoming storms. Being reminded of the possibility of hurricanes and rough seas terrified me. I thought it best not to eat at all, but the more experienced seamen said having something in my stomach was better than nothing.

Speaking of semen, I needed to find a condom.

After dinner, Marta gave me one of those seasick bands and showed me how to work the washer and dryer. Once my clothes were clean and back in my closet, I saw to Remington. He said the damp air was getting to him, so I took extra care setting up his pillows.

By the time I made it down to my room it was eight-thirty, leaving me just enough time to shower and get ready for Hale. At eight fifty-eight, I panicked and sniffed parts of my body that took a special sort of flexibility to reach, but everything seemed fresh.

At eight fifty-nine I started to sweat, which might have compromised my freshness a tad. By one minute past nine, I was convinced he wasn't coming. But at two minutes past nine there was a soft knock on the door.

Showtime.

11

"So this is my room." I shut the door behind him and winced. I was so lame. "Sorry. I don't really know how to do this."

He faced me, a gentle curve to his lips that immediately made me jealous. How was he so calm in these sorts of situations? I had no finesse.

Tipping his head, he asked, "Do what?"

Gah! I might not even be on the right page. What if he just wanted to talk?

"Um ... seduce a man in my *boudoir*. Or are we just hanging out? I don't know."

Laughing, he gave me a full smile. "I won't object to being seduced."

Okay. Good. That was good.

My hand rested on my hip as I toyed with various positions, none of them feeling sexy. "Does this work for you?" I posed, sort of like a clumsy model that had been roofied. "Or how about...?" Jesus, I was terrible at this.

He stepped close, invading my space and

making my skin come alive. Spreading a hand low on my back he pulled me to his front and whispered, "How about you stop trying to figure out what I'm hoping for and just be you?"

"Oh." That could be disastrous. I blinked and looked at his chest, my finger casually plucking at a button. "Well, this is how I do me." I let my hands drop and stood there like a lifeless mannequin, very Frankenstein before the whole come-to-life zap.

His fingers tipped up my chin until I was looking at him. "We don't have to do anything, Rayne."

But I wanted to do everything. Or I had. I wasn't sure what was going on now because it seemed like the flame had sort of flickered out.

When Hale did stuff I was revved up and ready to go, but when I tried to get the ball rolling everything stopped. I was not a pro-baller. I was a gutter ball heaver.

Oh my God, I was the girl version of a pre-ejaculator, all full steam ahead and then—*ptht*. Nothing.

"Why are you so nervous?"

Fidgeting out of his hold, I moved toward the bed but didn't dare touch it. "I'm an over thinker, Hale. Whenever I've been with a guy, it always starts out okay, but then I get lost in my head and start cataloguing every touch until the whole thing feels choreographed and fake and I'm just waiting for it to end so I can have my space back."

When he didn't say anything, I turned and found him studying me, his expression impossible to read. Knowing high maintenance had to be counter-balanced with something worthwhile, I muttered, "If this is too much work for you, I get it. I won't be mad if you leave."

"I'm not leaving."

His simple assurances caused the nerves knotting in my stomach to melt into tickling heat, which swirled in my belly and did nothing to help manage my anxiety.

"Are you sure?" He wouldn't be the first guy to walk away.

"Positive." Taking a step closer, he rested his hands on my shoulders and rubbed his fingers over the collar of my T-shirt. I was back in my yoga pants and travel clothes because they were the closest things I had to pajamas.

"Tell me what you imagined happening tonight."

"Um..." Always with the hard questions.

I'd imagined lots of things, but they were all segmented into little glimpses in my head. Fingers pressing into tight flesh, mouths licking, lips parting, bodies writhing. It was basically a montage of every hot movie scene I'd ever watched, including me falling on my ass like Jamie Lee Curtis in *True Lies*. I liked to keep things somewhat realistic.

"I don't have condoms," I blurted. Not what he asked, but still a fact he should be aware of.

"I'm not worried about that. I have condoms if we need them. I want to know what you were expecting."

"You have condoms," I mumbled, biting my lip, unsure why his preparedness irritated me. "Of course, you have condoms. What is it, like a twelve pack? How many do you have left? Nine? Six? Two?"

"What are you doing, Rayne?"

I growled and flung my body back on the bed. "I don't know. I suck at this. I don't even have condoms. That should tell you something about me. Single women have condoms, but I don't. You do, because, well, look at you. You probably buy them weekly. And I should be relieved you have them, but now I'm pissed off because I don't want a condom from the box you bought to be with someone else. See how irrational I am? You should really run while you can."

He pulled me into a seated position. "I'm not running and the box hasn't been opened yet."

"Oh. Well, that's a relief." I bit my thumbnail, mentally searching for another diversion.

While having protection was good, it also took away my biggest excuse for not sleeping with him. I wanted to have the sex with Hale, but deep down I think I was hoping to prolong things a bit. The problem was, we only had a few days until we reached Florida and once we got there I didn't know if he'd be staying in the same house.

"Do you have a house in Florida?"

"Yes."

"Is it by your dad's?"

"It's not far."

"So you won't be staying with him when we get there?"

He'd have his own place and his own schedule. Maybe that schedule included some late night entertainment and some chick's thighs wrapped around his face like an octopus. I'd see him in the mornings, just after he washed off the whore stench and he'd be all *Hey, Rayne. Remember when we had awkward, unsatisfying sex that time? That was weird. So glad we never did that again—*

"Rayne."

"Huh?" I glanced at him and debated if one and done was better than nothing at all. My attention dropped to his waist. "Okay. I'll have sex with you."

His brows shot up and he laughed. "Thanks, but I didn't come here just to do that."

Oh, he wanted to do other stuff too? Well, that was good. I liked when we made out and maybe—

"You really do overthink. I can see we'll have to pace ourselves. How about this? I'll give you the condoms and you decide when you want to open them. No pressure from my end."

"Look, if you want to open the box, I'm not going to stop you."

He smirked. "How about we leave the box closed tonight?"

"That's cool too."

My relief outweighed my disappointment. Clearly, I wasn't ready to get to *the sex*. Blowing out a breath, I relaxed and folded my hands in my lap.

He sat beside me and cupped my knee. "Feel better now?"

"Yes." I gave him a shoulder bump and he pressed his lips to my temple.

Keeping his lips against my hair, he gently massaged my knee. "My hand is traveling up your thigh."

I frowned as his fingers did just that.

"My other hand is approaching your ass."

An uncertain giggle slipped past my lips. "What are you doing?"

"Choreographing for you. But I think we'd have more fun if we just let it happen."

"You're making fun of me."

"Only because I think you're adorable."

Or crazy. "I don't do it on purpose. Trust me, I want to be distracted during sex, but my brain turns it into a math problem."

"Then we have to get you out of your head. That's all."

"Yeah, good luck with that."

He arched a brow and stood, holding out his hand. "Stand up."

Skeptical, I placed my hand in his, and he hoisted me to my feet. Looking in my eyes, he gently dragged his thumb over the crest of my cheek. As he traced the backs of his fingers along my jaw, I pressed into his touch like a cat trying to get fed.

"That feels nice."

Easing closer, he brushed his mouth over mine, hardly making contact, and I gradually leaned into the kiss. The longer he touched me, the more re-laxed I became.

Loosening the clip in my hair, he pulled the waves over my shoulders and fed his fingers through the mess. Shivers chased up my arms as he grazed my breast through my shirt and I moaned.

"You relaxed now?" he whispered, his fingertips lifting the hem of my shirt and trailing little circles over my stomach.

"Getting there," I sighed, wreathing my arms

over his shoulder and pulling him closer. Our lips gently brushed.

I couldn't recall a time when someone kissed me just to kiss me. Kissing was always a prerequisite to a questionable next step. I already told Hale I'd do the dirty with him, which included a few appetizers and sides, but he seemed in no rush to finish the first course, which was nice.

His hands traveled over my clothes, sometimes slipping under them, but never reaching too far. Every move was a slow tease, a temptation for more, and a promise that whatever was coming would not be rushed.

A sense of urgency bloomed in my belly, as deep longing and hungry desire had me gravitating closer to the bed. While Hale's hands remained over my clothing, I desperately wanted to get under his.

I tugged at his shirt breathing a little jaggedly, my fingers clenching in the starched material as my mind sent subliminal messages begging for more. Growing frustrated that he was still keeping things PG-13, I let out a frustrated breath.

"What's the matter?" he whispered, his mouth just below my ear where his breath did diabolical things to my senses.

"Nothing."

"Rayne."

Shivering at the playful warning in his tone, I sighed. "I want to be under here." My hand gave a subtle yank to the front of his shirt and he chuckled.

Stepping back, he watched me as his fingers traveled up the row of buttons and opened his shirt. *Come to Momma.*

He was easily the prettiest man I'd ever shared air with. Wow. Touching him made me nervous because all my life I'd been told pretty things were for eyes not hands. When I was in the third grade, we went to a museum on a field trip. The teacher gave a long speech about not touching the art because you don't touch a masterpiece. I wasn't planning on touching anything, but once they said we couldn't I really wanted to, so I snuck a touch, my unremarkable fingers with bitten down nails grazing the paint on the most masterful landscape I'd ever seen. And of course I got caught.

I had to stay by the teacher's side for the rest of the trip. My need to touch Hale was a million times stronger than my need had been that day, but I couldn't shake the sense that there would be repercussions.

"Wow. You have a really nice body," I muttered, a little heated and anxious.

He grinned but didn't make a big deal out of my compliment. Rather, he pulled me closer and kissed me again. My hands were literally shaking as they lifted to his chest. The moment I made contact, there was a sharp jolt of satisfaction that he didn't tell me to stop.

So much rigid muscle trapped under smooth skin. And he was warm like sunshine and fresh baked cookies and all things I liked. My fingertips mapped the geography of his chest, and my thumbs grazed his nipples, making him groan.

Breaking the kiss, he turned me and—oh, okay. My shirt was off. Wow. He was really good at removing women's clothing.

I faced the bed as he gathered my hair over one shoulder he pressed his lips to the back of my neck. I trembled as his mouth ghosted over the slope of my shoulder and he slid the straps of my bra down my arms.

My nipples hardened, and no matter how many times I inhaled I couldn't catch my breath. "Oh God."

"You okay?"

I nodded and there went the clasp. Bra gone. My chest rose with each breath as I stood before him, my bare back to his scorching stomach.

Staring at the bed, I sucked in a deep breath as he cupped my breast, rolling the nipple between his fingers while his mouth kissed down my spine.

Sweet Jesus, I could die like this and pass a happy woman. My head rolled back as pleasure knifed through me, cutting straight to my core.

"What is this magic you do?"

His chuckle was a slow roll of thunder in the distance, followed by a loud crack that ripped me out of my haze as something flashed.

"Oh my God. Is that the storm?"

My attention drilled into the window as another flash of lightening flickered, highlighting the choppy waves in the distance. Fuck. We were really going to die, just when things were getting wonderful.

"It's just a little storm. You wouldn't be able to stand still if it was anything serious." His hands continued to massage my breasts, but my focus was severed.

I closed my eyes, but they opened as another crash of thunder cracked in the distance. I bet all those other people believed it was just a little storm too. You know, the legendary ones like that Moby Dick guy and Geppetto. They all died, didn't they? I needed to brush up on my American literature.

Hale turned me and scooped an arm under my knees, lifting me off my feet, and I gasped, my head craning toward the window as he laid me on the bed. His fingers caught my chin and turned my face until I was looking at him.

"If you pay no attention to the storm, it won't bother you as much." His lips pressed to my mouth as his large body molded over mine, heated and heavy. I stretched out beneath him, trying to distract myself from the imminent death squalling outside.

I arched as his palm cupped my breast and then his mouth was closing over my nipple. My eyes closed as pleasure shot through my veins and my knees came up, trapping his hips. The hard ridge of his cock pressed into the crease of my pants, creating delicious friction between my legs every time he rocked over me.

Forgetting the storm, my fingers gripped his hair as his mouth did insane things to my nipples. "Holy shit."

He didn't acknowledge my mutterings as he continued to tease and suckle and—his hand was definitely in my pants.

His body lifted, putting a little space between us as he brushed his knuckle over my panties. He slowly rubbed and found my sweet spot. Then he slid a finger beneath the cotton and skirted my sex with the most delicate caress. He teased, finding a rhythm in less than a second, and I was making noises I never made before.

He was going to make me come! The mere thought jacked the bar of expectation so high I lost the slight quiver that made me believe it might be possible. Then he was just rubbing. Damn it. The noises stopped and the moment was gone.

It was disappointing that, just like all the others, Hale didn't notice that thin thread sever between my response to his touch and what could have been ecstasy. He just kept on doing his thing, and I was there, one moment loving it, the next totally indifferent.

"Can I take these off?" he whispered, running his other hand along the elastic band of my pants.

"Sure." What difference did it make? I was just a passenger at this point, but he seemed to be enjoying himself, and I didn't want to get in the way.

Stripping away my pants, he left the panties and placed a kiss over the fabric. I smiled, because politeness and sex seemed like they should go together.

His tongue traced my hip, and that was pleasant, but I was distracted from the pleasure as he pulled my underwear down my legs. As he kissed my knees, I feared he'd keep kissing until he was face to face with my vagina.

Dreading that possibility, I kept my thighs together. Why did people have oral sex? I didn't understand the gains on either side. There was nothing fun about having a penis jammed down your throat. I'd considered it earlier, but I was over the idea now.

And as far as having a guy go down on a woman, it was all rather embarrassing. I could never enjoy it because I was too worried about what I tasted like or smelled like and bodily functions and my lack of skill with a razor. It was way too much stress, and I'd much rather not have that sort of pressure in my life.

Warm hands pressed my knees apart, but I resisted, keeping them together. Hale looked up at me, brow lifted. "Everything okay?"

"I'm fine."

"Do you want to stop?"

His fingers were making a nice little swirly pattern in my knee pit, which made it hard to concentrate. "No."

His other hand rested on my belly, his thumb teasing the soft thatch of hair just below. "Are you going to let me in?"

I laughed nervously. Why was it so bright in here? I couldn't bring myself to tell him no, so I unclenched a centimeter, and he continued kissing up my thighs and my body locked up, clenching again. "You don't have to do all that."

He laughed. "What do you mean?"

My face felt like it was going to catch fire. "I'm okay."

"Rayne, what are you talking about?" he asked slowly, appearing to fight a laugh. "I want to."

"I know, but..."

He tipped his head and frowned. "You don't like it?"

Jesus, I was the unsexiest woman in the world. "I know a lot of men do it, but I don't need it." He was still frowning. "I'm not one of those women who ... require... all that."

He gave a disbelieving laugh. "I'm aware it's not a requirement."

"So we're clear then."

He sat back and studied me for a minute, and I was pretty sure I just killed the mood. No bringing this bitch back to life now. It was deader than Charlie Brown's Christmas tree.

I gasped as he yanked my body toward the edge of the bed and pulled my legs apart. "Wait—"

"Shut up and give it a chance." His mouth descended and my entire body tensed, but then came the soft tease of his tongue and a bit of my hesitation faded.

I eased up on my elbows. "I would have shaved if—"

He shoved me back down with a heavy hand on my abdomen. "Shh."

Okay then. Brow tense, I blinked at the ceiling as he pressed kisses to my folds and worked a finger inside of me. That was nice, but not enough to ease my self-consciousness. However, as he slowly pumped that gentle finger and closed his lips over my clit I found all my worries being pushed aside by the pleasant sensations.

His shoulders lowered, and he spread my legs wider, his mouth doing something really impressive and suddenly I was sucking in a deep breath and waiting for him to do it again. He did. And again. And then I boldly closed my eyes and sank into the bedding as another finger delved inside of me. If I kept my eyes closed, I could almost overlook the fact that this should be a humiliating situation.

"Sweet Jesus!" I gasped as he really struck a nerve.

His other hand traveled to my breast and found my nipple. Overwhelmed by everything he was doing, I tried to keep up, but he was sending so many sensations through me at once I couldn't keep track so I just fisted the blankets.

His rhythm increased, and I was panting as everything suddenly tightened, and I feared I was about to do something wholly embarrassing. "Wait, wait, wait, wait!"

But he kept sucking and feeding those fingers deep inside of me, and I couldn't hold on any longer. My body tensed and trembled as a rush of heat spread through me and he hummed as I sucked in a breath.

Mission Control, we have lift off!

My heart raced as I shivered under the hot pressure tingling under my skin. I writhed and moaned as my fingers gripped the bedding.

He never stopped following that thread of pleasure. As the pure euphoria shivered through me and a cool sweat coated my skin, I gasped, breathless and in total shock. "Well, holy... fuck."

He chuckled and lifted his body, covering mine as he pressed his mouth to my throat. "That wasn't so bad, was it?"

"I don't know what that was," I panted.

He laughed again and rolled me to my side, pulling my body into the curve of his. Stunned by what just happened, I played it back in my mind, but it was all a blur.

I, of course, masturbated. Sometimes, if I couldn't sleep, I'd duke it out and call it a night. But what I did and what Hale did were two very different things.

He kissed my shoulder and wrapped his arm around me, pulling the blankets over us. This was probably the moment I should bend down and repay the favor, but I was really tired and who was I kidding? I'd seen his penis through his pants. That thing would never fit in my mouth.

So I did what every shitty bed partner does. I fell asleep.

Girlie Feelings are a Pain in the Ass

12

I t took me a second to realize I was naked when I woke up, but the moment I recalled Hale's presence I tried to use my spidey senses to detect if he was still in my bed.

If he was behind me, I didn't want to wake him until I snuck out of bed and brushed my teeth. I had to figure out how to get from the bed to the bathroom—naked—without being seen. Maybe I should grab some clothes on the way because brushing my teeth naked seemed wrong, like it might be illegal in some backdoor town in the most obscure part of the south.

With absolute steadiness, I slowly shifted my arms and—I let out a breath. He was gone. Flopping to my back I stared at the ceiling and wondered if I should take offense that he'd snuck out in the middle of the night without saying goodbye.

After thinking about the countless unattractive things I could have done in my sleep, I got up and showered. The area between my vagina and my inner thighs was tender. I wasn't sure if they were tendons or muscles or what, but they ached like a motherfucker—a constant reminder that I'd done naughty things last night.

Were these secret orgasm muscles I'd never used before?

After my shower, I gathered my phone, slipped on my flip-flops, and thought about how the day might roll out. I'd have my usual breakfast meeting with Remington, tackle any tasks he had for me, work on the party plans, maybe sneak away around lunch for a nooner with Hale... Because really, how far could we stretch all this foreplay stuff before we got to the sex?

If we stretched it out too long, he might expect the presidential treatment, and that hype was just a lot of noise. Blowjobs sucked. Ha. I'm so clever.

Stepping out of my room, I—"*Penis!*"

Hale laughed, stepping out of his room at the same time. "Good morning to you too." He leaned in, calm as a summer wind, and my nerves jittered as he kissed me.

"Good morning. Sorry. You snuck up on me."

"Are you going up to the sky deck?"

"Yeah. Is your dad up?"

"He's having coffee."

"Oh. Good. Okay. Well, I better get up there then."

He smiled. "I'll join you."

But breakfast was my and Remington's time. Strange that I didn't want Hale to intrude. I wasn't sure if it was because Hale made me nervous or because I was actually coming to enjoy my private time with Remington.

Remington was the first older man I ever really talked to. I mean, I'd had professors in college I sometimes spoke to them after class, and my Uncle Rob tried to have inquisition conversations with me every Christmas when he visited, but other than that I had no other older men in my life.

I kept my mouth closed, worrying about why I cared so much as we took the stairs.

"Meyers," Remington greeted as I stepped onto the sky deck.

"Good morning, sir."

"Did you sleep well? Bit of a storm last night."

Funny, I hardly remembered the storm once Hale had distracted me. "I did fine."

"Good." He nodded. "You might finally be finding your sea legs. Hale, did you need something?"

Hale made himself at home at the table. "I figured I'd join you for breakfast."

Remington's brow twitched, but then he called for Marta to bring another setting. Their conversation moved to topics that didn't concern me, and I ate in silence. After thirty minutes of boring project talk and me silently eating as if I were invisible, I folded my napkin and stood.

"If you don't have any assignments for me this morning I'll go make some calls about Seraphina's party."

"That's fine, Meyers." Remington waved a hand and went back to what he was saying to Hale. I frowned and took the steps to the deck below where I worked yesterday.

Noon rolled around and I was preoccupied when Hale came to check on me.

"Did you want to join us for lunch?"

"No, thank you. I have to make a few more calls and then I have to lay out the menu with Laurent."

He came up behind me and brushed his hands down my arms. "Take a few minutes to relax," he whispered, pressing his lips to my temple.

I shouldered away from his kiss and avoided eye contact as I searched through my notes for nothing in particular. "I want to get this done."

"Hey. Are you upset with me or something?"

"No, I'm fine."

I wasn't fine. I was confused and having irrational feelings about my relationship with my boss. It didn't make sense for me to be so envious of Remington's attention, especially when he gave it to his son.

"I'm just busy."

His hand landed on the file I was paging through, shutting it. "Then why won't you look at me?"

I glanced up at his face, blanking my expression. "I'm looking at you."

I didn't want to act like a spoiled child, but I was on the verge of tears, and when I got like that I sometimes lashed out. Totally irrational, I know, but there were strange emotions happening.

"What's going on, Rayne?"

Maybe I was just stressing about trying to get the party perfect since it was my first big assignment.

It was a lot more involved than the rinky-dink little picnics my family threw.

"I'm sorry. I'm just in the middle of this, and I don't want to stop until I'm finished."

He frowned but pulled back his hand. "You sure you don't want to eat?"

"I'm sure."

And I was an idiot, because the moment his eyes shuttered with that impenetrable poker face, our connection severed.

"I'll see you later then." He turned and walked away and my mood plummeted even lower.

Ready to cry, because I was a girl and had all these stupid hormones running through my body and no experience communicating the irrational thoughts racing through my head, I blinked. I should go apologize but he was with Remington, and I didn't want anyone else to know I was this un-stable on the inside.

Trying to get over my issues, I buried myself in work and promised as soon as Hale was alone I'd apologize and explain that I have some insecure is-sues I'm still trying to figure out.

Over the next hour, every time their voices car-ried from the sky deck above, I suffered a little stab of uncertainty. Not only that, I was hungry. I could have gone up and joined them, but something held me back.

I didn't know how to read Hale when others were around. Of course, we weren't broadcasting our private business, but he hid it so well it stung. And Remington definitely couldn't know what we'd done, so when the three of us were together, the conversation turned to business, business that didn't concern me. I might as well just work through lunch—oh wait, I was.

I labored tirelessly until it was time to situate Remington for his nap. As I gave him his pill and positioned his pillows, he surprised me by asking, "What's the matter with you today, Meyers?"

"What do you mean?"

"You're not yourself. Usually, I can't shut you up. Today you haven't said more than three words."

"I'm fine—"

"Don't bullshit me. Is something going on?"

"No. I'm just a little off my game today I guess."

"Well, get back on it and go back to being your usual self. How are your stocks holding up?"

"They're fine." And he knew that, being that he checked the market every morning with a fine-toothed comb.

"How are the party plans coming along?"

"Laurent gave me a list for the menu and told me about a few helpful vendors by our port. He said I could set up the order ahead of time and then all we need to do is pick it up."

"Good. Have you talked to your parents since you've been onboard?"

"My parents?"

I could call my dad, but that would be awkward, him asking who I was and how I got his number. But Remington didn't need to know that, so I said, "I've texted my mom a few times."

His eyes were getting tired. "Maybe give her a call. You seem like you might be missing home."

His concern surprised me. I'd avoided calling

home so I wouldn't miss it, but maybe he was right. Sometimes moms made things better.

"I'll give her a call tonight."

"Good." He shut his eyes. "You do that, Meyers. I'll see you in two hours."

I quietly closed the curtains and saw myself out of his room. When I reached the steps, I paused.

I wasn't homesick. I was aggravated with the way I blew off Hale earlier, irritated with my inability to be an adult woman who handled her emotions rather than let her emotions run her.

The mature thing to do was to go find him and make things better. Staring up at the steps leading to the upper deck living room I heard the low rumble of his voice. I worried Eric might be with him, but as I turned the corner, I saw he was on the phone.

When he spotted me, he smiled, but it didn't reach his eyes. "Right," he mumbled softly into the phone.

I approached slowly.

As he listened to the person on the other line, his gaze moved across the table where he had a piece of paper. He flipped it over and I wondered if that was for my benefit. There was still so much I didn't know about him or the secrets he might keep. Whatever was on that paper held more meaning than I wanted it to, now that he'd hidden it.

"And what about the other issue?" he asked, holding up a finger, signaling me to stay. Or maybe asking me to be quiet. His brow creased. "Well, that's not true."

Standing, he pocketed the slip of paper and paced. Covering the phone, he whispered, "I'll be a just minute." Then he stepped onto the narrow side balcony and shut the door.

His posture was tense as he spoke freely, gesturing with his hands. Was this what angry Hale looked like? Or was this business shark Hale? I had at least thirty different personalities, but maybe other people only had a few.

After several minutes, the doors to the balcony slid open, and he pocketed his phone.

"Everything okay?" I asked, regretting that I disturbed him at all. I wasn't necessarily a private person, so I never knew how to take other people's evasiveness.

"Fine."

But he didn't look fine. Walking to the bar, he poured something from a decanter into a stout glass and swallowed it in one shot.

"Did you need something?"

Coming up here suddenly seemed like a bad decision. "No, I just wanted to see what you were up to."

"Are you finished your work for the day?"

I nodded.

He poured another drink and watched me as he sipped from the glass this time. "You seemed preoccupied today."

Feeling guilty for how I treated him earlier, I said, "I was a little bit of a bitch this afternoon. I don't know what was wrong with me."

He kept to the other side of the room, but his gaze went to the deck. I looked through the glass doors and realized there was a clear view from this table to the table where I worked.

"Interesting," he said quietly. "Sometimes what people say and what they show are two different things." He'd been able to see me all day, even the moments when I was freed up enough to tip my face back and catch a little sun.

"I really was busy today." Those moments of resting my eyes were for brain storming, that's all.

"I'm sure."

Whatever we were doing, I didn't want to do it anymore. He saw me naked. There shouldn't be this artificial politeness between us.

"I'm sorry," I confessed, using my genuine big girl panties. "I was upset."

"Why?"

My gaze fell to the carpet as I shrugged. "I don't know."

"You know."

Of course, I knew, but it was stupid and admitting it aloud was ridiculous. "Can we just start over?"

Once again he proved I'd never beat him in a staring contest. I shifted my gaze to the table and he waited me out until the silence was suffocating.

He could have guessed anything. He could have asked if I was upset that he left my bed before morning or if I regretted what we had done last night, but he didn't and I wasn't sure if that was because he was just that confident or if this was an issue of arrogance. Either way, he wasn't going to waste time guessing when he'd taken the time to ask point blank.

God, this was like being in the principal's office that time after Elle and I thought it would be a good idea to moon the lacrosse team from the bus. I growled in frustration. "Fine. I was mad at you."

"Why?"

Again with the why? "It's stupid and I'd rather not say."

His jaw twitched. "Clearly I did something to upset you. If you don't tell me what it was, how am I supposed to avoid doing it again?"

"That's the thing. You have every right to do it again. This isn't your problem, it's mine."

"Give me something here, Rayne. You blew me off earlier and you've been dodging me all day. When I tried to touch you, you shouldered me away. You owe me some explanation."

What did he have, a photographic memory? I huffed and mumbled in a rush, "I was mad about breakfast."

He frowned. "What about breakfast?"

"That's ... my time with Remington." His brows lifted and I blurted, "I hear how crazy that sounds. He's *your* dad. But our mornings are my favorite part of my job. He talks to me about things I have no idea about. Every day he teaches me something and today you were there and you both talked right over me about things I have no part of."

He chuckled and put down his glass. Rounding the table, he approached, and I felt so ridiculous, I couldn't look at him. He cupped my face and kissed my forehead. "I'm sorry."

"You don't have to apologize—"

"Yes, I do. That was rude of both of us, not including you in the conversation."

And there it was. He'd misunderstood and I

didn't have the balls to correct him. This wasn't about manners or including me in the conversation. It was about the pleasure I drew from getting fatherly advice from a man who wasn't my dad.

"Thanks," I whispered, because I really just wanted the whole matter put to rest. Pasting on a smile, I looked up at him. "Are you sure you're okay? That seemed like a pretty intense phone call."

Ah, it seemed we were all well versed in the fake smiles today.

He released my face and walked to the glass doors, showing me his back as he stared at the deck. He wasn't going to talk about it.

"Hale?"

"We should do something fun."

"Like what?" I was up for anything that got us out of this sudden funk. I wanted to reset the day and start over.

"Something exciting."

We were on a boat. There was only so much we could do. "Did you want to play cards or something? Flip cup? I'm pretty decent at beer pong."

Glancing over his shoulder, his smile finally reached his eyes. "I was thinking of something a little more exhilarating."

"What did you have in mind?"

He faced me and asked, "Do you have a bathing suit?"

I'll Punch a Predator Right in the Face

13

Hale found one of his sister's swimsuits I could borrow, a pure white bikini that I'd never dare try on at a store where my reflection was solely between me and my demons. As I stared in the mirror, I stretched the material over my boobs, but it wouldn't give, so I put my usual clothes on over top and went to find Hale.

After a few minutes of searching, I heard his and Eric's voices toward the back of the boat, but they weren't on the lower deck. "Hale?"

"Down here."

I peeked behind the pool on the back deck and spotted him and Eric screwing metal tracks onto a small platform. "What are you doing?"

"Come down here," Hale called and pointed to his right. "There are steps."

Lo and behold, there were stairs. The yacht wasn't moving, which had me worrying a propeller broke or something along those lines.

When I reached the small platform, both he and

Eric were ducked inside a sort of hooded door. "Is something wrong with the boat?"

Hale climbed out of the compartment. "Did the suit fit?"

"Yeah."

"Good. Put this on." He handed me a life vest.

This was it. The motor broke and we were all going to die. Or I'd end up on the news ten days from now found floating on a life raft, burnt to a crisp and dehydrated, speaking in tongues.

"That should do it. Guide her out, Eric."

Hale held a remote control attached to a curled cord, and suddenly a loud motor buzzed, but not loud enough to be the yacht motor. Then I caught sight of a lime green spoiler.

Curious, I stepped close to the platform and my eyes went wide. "You have a boat inside a boat."

Hale smirked. "It's a Jet Ski."

They literally had a garage and docking station right there on the yacht. "Is this why we're stopped?"

The small motor silenced once the Jet Ski was fully out of the little garage. "We'll be moving again soon. We're just taking a little intermission."

"We?"

"You better get that vest on if you want to come with me."

Decisions. Decisions.

If I put the life vest on I could go with him, possibly drown in the middle of the ocean, but have the chance to wrap my arms around his waist and cling to his body in broad daylight. If I stayed safely aboard *The Lady Parr* there was no risk of being eaten by sharks.

Deciding that touching him was worth a shark attack, I stripped down to my suit. As I was bent over to remove my pants, I heard Hale growl, "Eyes back in your head, Eric."

I quickly turned around and found Hale watching the other man carefully. Eric didn't look at me, but I assumed he'd been looking right at my money pit when I bent over. Ew. Self-conscious, I slid my arms into the life vest, and Hale stepped in front of me.

He snapped the three clips in place and whispered, "You want to make sure it's tight." As he cinched the straps, I sucked in a gulp of air, and my heartbeat skipped into a gallop. He turned and said, "Drop the dock, Eric."

The little slatted platform started to lower and Hale stripped off his shirt to slide on his life vest. Somehow the Jet Ski remained secure on the tracks until the dock was submerged and Hale guided it into the water.

Thankfully, the further south we traveled the warmer the weather. But the water, when I dipped my toe in, was frigid.

Hale straddled the Jet Ski, and the motor kicked on, the air briefly tinged with exhaust. Grinning, he held out a hand. "Your chariot awaits."

Taking his hand, I stepped ankle deep into the ocean and squeaked. "It's effing cold!" But Hale pulled me behind him and soon my feet were resting on the damp foot grips.

"Let her go, Eric."

Eric hit a button on the remote, and we backed off the platform, now free floating in the ocean. "Oh, God."

"Hold on tight." Hale did a quick little rev of the motor and then I was screaming in his ear as we sped across the surf leaving *The Lady Parr* far behind.

It was probably a fascinating sight, but my eyes were screwed shut so tight I missed it. My ass took a severe beating as we bounced over waves, the surf spraying my skin as the sun hung high above us.

My lips tasted salty, and I desperately wanted to see if Hale was racing us toward our death, but I was too chicken shit to peek. My heart thundered in my chest and my hands were permanently embedded in his life jacket.

The deathtrap suddenly slowed and my screaming cut off.

"Look," Hale yelled and it was hard to hear him over the pounding in my ears.

Forcing my eyes open, I stared ahead as we puttered toward the open horizon. "What am I looking at?"

"Dolphins."

My gaze searched the water and I gasped. Three, no four—five—dolphins swam beneath us, weaving in and out of the surf, cresting the water in our wake as we went.

"Oh, my God!"

"Beautiful, aren't they?"

More came and soon I lost count. Hale killed the motor and everything went silent aside from the gentle lapping at our feet.

I scanned the horizon for *The Lady Parr* and spotted her off in the distance, looking smaller than a rowboat. We sat in silence, watching the dolphins swim and then Hale sent our little craft rocking as he stood up.

"Come on."

"What? Where?"

He plunged into the ocean and I panicked.

"*Hale*! Shit!" I grabbed the handles and did a shaky downward-facing-dog type stand as I waited for him to resurface. The second he did, I screamed, "Are you out of your mind?"

"What? It's the ocean. People swim in it every day."

"On beaches! We're a million miles away from safety."

He bobbed and laughed, waving me to join him. "Come on. I'll protect you."

"How are you going to protect me from a shark?" I snapped. "Get back on the Jet Ski!"

"How are you going to give up the chance to swim with dolphins in the wide open Atlantic?"

He had a point, but what about the Shark Week montage playing in my head? Shutting my eyes, I sent a little prayer up to my guardian angel and held my nose, propelling my body into the deep.

The water was fucking freezing! Breaking the surface, I gasped and caught my breath, my teeth immediately chattering.

Hale reached into a compartment at the back of the Jet Ski. "Here. Put these on." He handed me a set of goggles and a snorkel and pulled out a set for himself.

Once I had them on, my legs pumping with every rolling swell, he smiled and popped the mouthpiece between his lips. When he took my hand underwater, I momentarily tensed, but then recognized the feel of his fingers entwining with mine. He gave my hand a tug and plunged his face under the surface.

I debated for a few seconds then dropped my face into the cool water, first checking if Jaws was lingering nearby. I watched a lot of nature shows and saw my fair share of deadly ocean encounters. Keeping my fingers laced with Hale's and my free hand balled into a fist, I reminded myself that the best thing to do was punch the shark right in the nose if it attacked. But Jaws was nowhere to be found.

The world silenced, muffled by the cool ocean at my ears as I stared into the depths of the sea. Hale kept hold of my hand and squeezed. An unexpected calm washed over me as I took in the vast view. The ground didn't exist and the coast was miles away. I never felt so alive and insignificant at the same time.

Here I was, floating like a speck in the deep, just one of the oceans on this vast planet, and nothing else existed for a moment—nothing but me, this, and Hale. I was suddenly a tiny part of the biggest thing I'd ever known. Life.

We floated for some time, the dolphins chirping around us as they curiously came close then drifted off again. There were no rules or politics here, only nature at its unrefined best. Sea plants and plankton floated in the water as we let the current hold us.

When we came up for air, the wind chilled my

face. He pulled his goggles down around his neck and I pushed mine up like a headband over my hair.

"It's indescribable, isn't it?" He bobbed closer, brushing the drops off his brow.

"I feel so small. I don't think I've ever been this far from civilization."

He glanced over his shoulder at the yacht in the far distance. When his gaze returned to mine, he whispered, "We're completely alone out here."

Weight and heat gathered in my center as I looked at him, unsure if this was one of those times I should be bold or let him take the lead. Thankfully, he hooked a finger into my life vest and tugged me across the distance separating us. "Come here."

My legs, slick under the water, wrapped around his hips as I clung to him. He kicked his legs slowly, keeping us upright in the rolling waves. His mouth gently closed over mine.

"What is it about you?" he asked, whispering against my lips.

His hand slipped into the bottom of my suit, softly squeezing my ass and I felt his body harden beneath mine. His erection bulged against my cleft and I instinctively wiggled closer as he groaned.

Pulling his mouth away, he whispered, "I'm usually much more reserved than this. But every time I see you I'm itching to touch you."

I giggled and squirmed. "You don't have to be reserved with me. I like seeing who you really are."

His gaze met mine and held for a short moment as I suspected he had something to say but held back. "I'm not a bad guy, Rayne, but... things might get a little complicated once we reach Florida."

That didn't sound great. "Why?"

He shook his head, mouth pursed. "Can we put a pin in that conversation for a few days? Let's see what this is between us first. If it's truly something, we'll get to all those talks, but right now I'm enjoying the simplicity of us."

Being that I didn't want to lay my soul bare in front of him just yet, I could respect his desire to take it slow with the personal stuff. In a week this whole little hook up might be over and done. No need to expose too much too soon. We were creating something easy and fun, which was really all I could manage. I didn't want to bog it down with unnecessary stress.

I pressed a soft kiss to his lips. "No worries. I do better taking things day by day anyway. Whatever this is, I like it, and I don't want to overcomplicate it."

"I don't think I've ever met a woman as straightforward as you. It's refreshing. Maybe I'm jumping the gun here, but I feel like I can trust you."

"You can."

He smiled and reluctance flashed in his eyes.

Clearly, Hale had some trust issues and a story to share. When he was ready—if he wanted to tell me about it—I'd listen, but I didn't need to know right now.

He glanced over his shoulder again. "We should get back."

Reluctantly, I disentangled my limbs from his. "This was fun."

"We can do it again. I can only take being onboard for a few days at a time."

The return ride to the yacht was smoother, but we were both chilly and wet.

We had a few minutes of quiet idling as we waited for Eric to come to the back and help us dock.

"Thank you for taking me," I whispered in Hale's ear, pressing a kiss to the damp, salty skin of his neck.

He turned and kissed my lips. My body immediately responded and I wished we had a little more time to ourselves. But when our lips parted we weren't alone. Eric stood on the platform watching us. His expression blank, but I knew he'd watched Hale kiss me.

I didn't know why Eric's judgment bothered me, but it did. I was a grown woman and allowed to kiss whomever I wanted, but for some reason, knowing Eric knew there was something going on between Hale and me, made me fearful. I didn't want him to tell Remington because I didn't want Remington to think poorly of me, like I was some gold digger trying to get in good with his son.

Hale jumped off first and helped me back onto the yacht. "Why don't you grab a shower? Your lips are blue."

I was shivering, so I nodded.

Hale remained below, working with Eric to get the Jet Ski back in the little boat garage. I grabbed a towel from beside the pool and dried off.

"Did you enjoy yourself?"

Startled, I pivoted, still ringing out my hair. "Remington. I thought you were napping."

"Couldn't sleep. That's probably a good sign, but I'm still tired."

I covered myself with the towel and got quiet, wondering if it was wrong that I'd used his Jet Ski.

"Don't cover yourself on my account, Meyers. I'm old, but I don't mind looking at pretty things from time to time."

Scrunching my nose, I gave him a rebuking look. "Then watch the sunset, because I'm not about being on display."

He chuckled. "Sit with me."

"Okay."

Settling in to the lounge chair beside his, I sighed. The sun heated my cool skin and removed the chill, but I still kept the towel wrapped around my body. We sat in comfortable silence.

"You like my son."

Comfortable silence over. "I like everyone."

"Don't bullshit me, Meyers."

I didn't know what to say so I said nothing. The truth was I did like Hale. Very much so.

"Hale's a good man," Remington commented quietly. "I'd take issue with the two of you if you hadn't told me you like being unattached. You're both young. There's no harm in enjoying yourselves."

My tongue was literally stuck to the roof of my mouth and I couldn't seem to blink.

Remington gave a raspy chuckle. "Don't look so petrified, Meyers. Your job's not in any jeopardy."

Well, that was good to know. If I hadn't told him I was opposed to serious relationships *would* he take issue with my interest in his son? No need to jump ahead.

"We're just having fun," I finally said.

"Is that all it is?"

I glanced at the rails and let out a slow breath. Was he fishing for reassurance? Trying to warn me off? Sending me a polite message that fun was fine, but anything more was not?

It didn't matter anyway because once we reached Florida I was sure we'd go our separate ways and that would be that. Hale and I both seemed in the market for something uncomplicated.

"It's nothing you need to worry about, sir."

The gears of the lower dock rising broke the peaceful quiet. When it stopped, Remington said, "Naomi was a tricky wife. I hardly think of her now, but when I do I still don't understand what it would have taken to make her happy. Hale's a lot like his mother in some ways. But he's also like me."

Footsteps carried as Eric and Hale crested the steps. Hale paused when he saw me sitting with his father and not in the shower.

"Good weather for a ride today," Remington said.

"The ocean's calm," Hale replied, and Eric just stood there glaring at me. Jesus, look somewhere else.

"I'm going to shower if you don't need anything, Remington."

"I'm fine for now. I'll see you at dinner."

Nodding, I gathered my clothes and took my leave.

The interior of the boat was air-conditioned and as soon as I stepped inside I shivered, my damp swimsuit still cold from the ocean. The glass doors slid open behind me and I turned as Hale came inside.

I grinned and paused at the top of the steps. "Are you following me?" I asked teasingly.

His gray eyes held a touch of mischief. "Yes. Keep going."

I took the stairs, glancing back every few seconds. His pursuit made me giddy and unsure in the best way. My hand glided over the railing as I made my way down to the staterooms.

When my fingers closed over the doorknob to my bedroom, he caught my wrist. I stilled and waited, my back to his front. Why was his body burning hot when I couldn't stop shivering?

"Are you going to shower?" he whispered, his breath teasing over my exposed shoulders.

My nipples pebbled under the damp material of my suit and I trembled, slowly nodding.

His hand pressed into mine, releasing the catch of the handle, and the door opened a crack. His fingers barely grazed my back, but suddenly my top was loose and the bikini strings dangled at my sides.

He stepped closer, his hot mouth pressing into my shoulder as he helped himself to my breast and my knees went weak.

"Let me come with you," he rasped, his lips working over that sensitive spot at the base of my neck.

His fingers pinched the tip of my nipple and I shivered. I'd never been around a man so domineering and assured. His confidence was incredibly sexy. It fed my curiosity and made it incredibly easy to give him more than I usually offered.

"Okay."

"Go inside."

Making my legs move was no easy task. I took a step and he walked with me, one hand under the skimpy top, another resting on my hip. The moment I crossed the threshold into my room, he spun me into the door and kissed me, his fingers working at the ties at the back of my neck.

The door snapped closed, and a fuse seemed to light between us, hot and urgent. "I want you," he rasped, peeling my top away and closing his mouth over the sharp point of my breast.

I gasped and pressed into the door as his soft lips sucked my flesh hard. My hands caught his shoulders as I breathed in the briny scent of his skin. His tongue dragged from one breast to the other as his fingers wedged beneath my damp bottoms and massaged the cool skin of my ass.

Somehow he always kept me teetering on the sharp edge of anticipation and when he pushed for more I was ready and willing, hardly giving our actions the consideration I usually did with other men.

Heart racing, I tried to keep up. He lifted me off the ground and my legs wrapped around his hips as his mouth found mine. He was hard beneath his swim trunks, his erection digging into my core.

As his palm cupped my breasts, almost bruising, he turned and tossed me onto the bed. His eyes were dark and wild, pinning me in place.

Without asking, he peeled my bottoms down

my legs and tossed them on the floor. When my knees knocked together, he yanked them apart and jerked me closer to him.

There was no time to prepare as his mouth descended on my sex, penetrating and licking me into a frenzied mess. My fingers tangled in his hair as he went at me. When my moans were unstoppable, I grabbed a pillow and shoved it over my face.

Arching and twisting beneath him, I tried to fight the overwhelming onslaught of pleasure, but he was a guru who knew exactly which buttons made me squeal. I came hard and fast, too soon to even track what he was doing to me.

He wasn't finished. Working his mouth up my body, he closed his lips over my breast and caught my hand, pulling it down to his hips. Somehow his shorts were gone. He thrust his cock into my palm, the heat of his body almost scalding my hand. Folding my fingers around what might as well be a drinking glass, my eyes went wide. He was so damn thick.

"Touch me," he rasped, working his mouth to my throat.

Jesus Christ, we could never have sex if this was the sort of heat he was packing. I blindly stroked him, trying to measure his length as I did some off the cuff science equations about the depth of my vagina and the mass of his dick.

I jerked to attention as his fingers brushed my sensitive clit and his other hand closed over mine, tightening my hold over his cock.

"You're really big down there," I said, hoping

his size might work as an excuse for my lack of finesse in the penis department.

He grunted and pumped his fingers with mine, using more pressure than I'd ever think to use on a man's most sensitive part. His forehead pressed into my shoulder as he used my hand to jerk him off, his breath beating against my chest. When he grunted again, his body tensed and sticky heat coated my stomach.

Come. He just came on me. Was that something normal people did without asking? Because I sort of thought that was reserved for pornography.

His grip loosened as he held himself over me and panted. I lay beneath him, worrying the mess might drip onto the comforter, wondering if Pinterest had any pins for removing come stains.

His lips found my thrumming pulse and pressed a kiss there. "You okay?"

Oh, I was just dandy. "Mm-hmm."

He eased back and kissed my lips briefly, before hauling me off the bed. Come was literally dripping down my belly.

I hitched a thumb over my shoulder. "I'm gonna grab that shower now." Without waiting for a response, I ducked into the bathroom and started the water.

As soon as the water warmed, I rinsed off and had another surprise as Hale opened the glass doors and stepped in behind me.

His arms closed over my waist as his lips rested on my shoulder. It was really hard to think of casual conversation after being ejaculated on.

"So...how about this weather?"

"Was that too much for you?" he asked gently, his arms loosening around my waist.

I couldn't possibly discuss what just happened because post-coital analytics were simply out of my repertoire. "Do you think we'll have any more storms?"

"I didn't expect to come at you like that, but you fucking turn me on, Rayne. I can't remember the last time I wanted someone with that sort of urgency."

And come at me he had. "Did you ever see a rainbow at sea?"

He turned me so I was facing him, but I couldn't meet his gaze. "Are you okay?"

I nodded, but I didn't want to make eye contact, so I shut my eyes.

"Rayne." His fingers brushed my cheek. "Why won't you look at me?"

"Because I have the maturity of a teenager and I'm naked." If I kept my eyes shut, I was invisible, right?

"Please look at me."

I forced my eyes open and blurted, "Your father knows about us."

His brow creased. "What?"

"He called me out on it upstairs."

"What did you say?"

I shrugged. "I told him we were friends and he told me not to bullshit him."

Kudos for Hale acting like this wasn't anything to worry about, but I still noticed the way his hands eased away from my body and he took a subtle step back. "Are you upset he knows?"

"Well, it isn't like he has all the details, but he is my boss, and you're his son, so it's a little awkward."

"And you're a grown woman."

I wouldn't be too sure. Currently, I couldn't think clearly because there was a penis in my shower.

"Can you pass me the shampoo?"

He chuckled. "Hey. We're talking."

"I'm not used to having naked conversations. I can be out in two seconds and then you can have the shower to yourself."

He made a strange face and laughed. "I'm not in any rush." He caught my hips and yanked my body flush to his. "You shouldn't be either."

"Okay there, soldier," I squirmed out of his hold. "I'm not used to all this... attention. You're going to have to be patient while I find my bearings."

Reaching behind him I snatched the shampoo off the shelf and turned around because it was easier to pretend I was alone if I wasn't looking directly at him.

"Why do you get so nervous around me?"

I never had such a hard time getting shampoo out of the bottle, but I was shaking, and now I had way too much in my palm.

"How am I supposed to act?" I shook the extra off and shoved my fingers in my hair.

"Don't you like when I touch you? I like when you touch me."

I vigorously scrubbed my scalp and rinsed. "I'm just not used to this."

"Rayne, please chill with the shampooing for a

second and talk to me."

Taking a deep breath, I lowered my hands and turned, my eyes pleading. "I don't know how to do this."

"Are we moving too fast?"

Maybe we were, but I didn't want to go any slower. It wasn't the sex stuff it was all the in between. "I suck at intimacy."

Voice calm, he said, "But you're not shy."

"I know I'm not."

He smirked. "And you're certainly not cold. I've watched you come."

"*Alrighty then.*" I quickly turned and he caught my arm.

"Hey. Talk to me, Rayne."

"About what? Orgasms? I don't know how to talk about that stuff. I'm totally freaking out about the fact that you're in the shower with me." I risked a look at his erection. *Dear God.*

He frowned. "You've never showered with a man before?"

"No. I've never even considered showering with another person. I'm a hot water hog and I'm totally uncomfortable when naked."

"Why? You're beautiful."

Now it was my turn to frown. "Thanks, but I have no grace. It's hard enough being around you in clothes. Forget being naked."

His mouth hooked in a half-grin as he brushed his thumb over my lower lip. "I happen to like being naked with you."

I fidgeted. "I like it too, sort of. But I just don't know what to do."

He laughed. "Just let it happen."

Letting it happen did help, especially when he took control, but when things slowed down, and reality set in, all my gawkiness came hurtling back. "Maybe we should have sex."

His brows shot up. "Now?"

"Well, not this very second, but soon."

He studied me for a long moment. "And what will that prove? That we can? I don't want to plan out our every move, Rayne. Don't get me wrong, I want to sleep with you, but if this is moving too fast for you, I have no problem slowing down."

"But we only have a few days left."

"What are you talking about, a few days?"

"Well, once we're in Florida, you'll be at your place, and I'll be with Remington and—"

"And nothing will change. Did you think this was some sort of travel fling?"

My hands waved out in frustration. "I don't know. Is it? I don't usually do this sort of thing and when we were in the ocean, you said you didn't want to overcomplicate maters."

Reaching behind me, he shut off the water and whispered, "I'm not looking for a one night stand. I like you, Rayne. I want to get to know you and spend time with you."

I had the hardest time accepting that a guy like this could actually like me. Maybe I was a little more damaged from my failed sexual exploits than I realized.

Closing my arms over my chest I murmured, "I like you too."

"If it's assurance you need, I'll give it to you. You

have my full interest and this is more than me just filling time."

I found great relief in his confession, but it bothered me that I couldn't match his confidence. "The truth is, I'm really inexperienced when it comes to relationships. Not just guys. People in general. I've sort of built my entire life around my mom and a few close friends."

His smile was gentle. "That's okay. My life's been in the shadow of my father's legacy for so long any bit of exposure comes with scrutiny. You can feel safe with me, Rayne. No one's judging us here. Talking is how people get to know each other. I'm interested in knowing the real you."

I never expected him to be so genuine, but he always seemed to surprise me with more incredible patience. "Okay. That helps. Just an FYI, I'm the sort of girl that needs things spelled out or I panic, especially when I'm in unfamiliar territory."

"Then I'll spell it out for you. I don't care who knows I'm interested in you. I wasn't necessarily hiding my feelings. To be honest, I'd prefer it if everyone knew. That way others won't feel so inclined to..." His words drifted off and he shook his head. "If it doesn't bother you, I'd rather not treat our relationship like a secret."

Chills chased up my spine as we stood there. "But I work for you."

"You work for my father. There's a difference."

"Is there? If you needed something, you wouldn't hesitate to make Eric get it for you, but you'll take me snorkeling with the dolphins."

"Eric's a grown boy. Let him worry about himself and you worry about you."

"He's my colleague and he's judging me."

"So? Let him. So long as he keeps his eyes where they belong, I don't care what he thinks."

I grimaced, recalling the way Hale snapped at him on the dock. "What did he do earlier that made you say something?"

"He was looking where he shouldn't."

And Hale corrected him. There was something really flattering about that—in a caveman sort of way.

Stepping close, he cupped my ass and whispered, "So long as we're doing this I don't want anyone else looking at your ass that way. Eric should know better."

The words *so long as we're doing this* snagged on something painful in my chest, but I shoved it aside. "He shouldn't know anything—"

"That's why I said something. He knows now. I catch him looking at your ass again and he'll have real problems."

Smirking, I rested my palms on his warm chest. "You're a little bit territorial, aren't you?"

"I'm a lot territorial." His hands slid to my waist where his fingers rested on my hips. "Consider your ass claimed."

"Do you have a flag? I feel like you should have a flag. Sort of like the moon landing."

He arched a brow. "Are you suggesting I find a suitable pole, too?"

Glancing between us, I muttered, "Maybe a verbal declaration's enough. I'm a little afraid of your penis."

He laughed. "That's a shame. I was hoping you two could be friends."

My mouth twisted. "I'm going to need a few trial play dates before I commit to anything."

He chuckled. "Fair enough. Let's find you a towel. You're shivering."

As I dressed, Hale returned to his room. He knocked just as I was slipping on my flip-flops.

Opening the door, I was suddenly breathless. It was a toss-up which Hale I preferred, the one in a dress shirt with cuffed sleeves or the bare chested one. They were both devastatingly handsome.

"You ready?"

Taking a deep breath, I nodded. Everything was normal as we walked to the dining room until we reached the end of the hall and Hale took my hand.

Stepping around the corner, both Remington and Eric looked up from their plates. If they missed the way Hale held my hand, there was no missing how he pulled out my chair and purposely sat by my side rather than by his father's like he usually did. Feeling their eyes on me, I cut into my chicken and kept my head down the entire meal.

Later that night, as I got Remington settled he watched me carefully. He'd been uncharacteristically quiet, which made me uneasy.

"Say what's on your mind, Remington."

"Why didn't you want to be a teacher, Meyers?"

I shrugged. "It just didn't fit."

"You'd rather take care of crabby old men?"

"You're not that old." I wouldn't debate his crabbiness. Handing him a water bottle, I went in the bathroom to get his pill.

When I returned, I said, "Besides, I'd rather be on a yacht than stuck in a classroom."

"Your job does have some perks, I suppose."

"A few."

He waved away the pill I offered. "I don't want that. My foot's not bothering me and I'd rather not take it if I don't need it."

I placed the pill on a tissue by the lamp. "I'll leave it here in case you change your mind."

"Hale said you were on the phone with your mother earlier."

I smirked. Nothing was secret for long on *The Lady Parr*. "I owed her a call. I think she's starting to miss me."

"Does your mother work?"

"Yes. She's in medical billing."

His brow lifted. "One of *them*."

I wasn't sure what that meant, but in his condition, I was certain he had some pretty hefty doctor bills. "Were you scared when you had the heart attack?"

"Not scared. Pissed."

"Why pissed?"

He looked so relaxed, leaning against the headboard in his navy blue pajama set that probably cost more than my prom dress. "I wasn't ready."

"Oh, I'm sure it was an oversight that God didn't clear His schedule with you."

He laughed. "It's too soon. It always seems too soon." His humor faded into something that looked like remorse.

I settled onto the edge of the bed. "Do you miss

your wife?" It didn't need clarifying, which one I was referencing.

"Rachel was young. My youngest bride yet, but the only one I ever lost." He shook his head. "Doesn't seem fair. Sometimes I think her death had more to do with me than it had to do with her."

"Why do you say that?"

He shrugged. "She was a good woman. She loved me even on my worst days. Her leaving this world was the greatest loss I've ever felt. Perhaps I'm being punished."

That was a little deep for me, so I focused on the parts I could handle. "You obviously loved her too."

"I loved all my wives, but there was something special about Rachel."

It was nice to know he hid a heart in there somewhere. I patted his knee through the covers. "Get some sleep."

"I'll see you at breakfast tomorrow," he said as I stood to leave.

"I'll be there."

"And Meyers." He waited until I turned to say, "It'll be just us tomorrow."

Despite being taken off-guard, I smiled. "Did Hale—"

"It's my decision. Don't worry about how I came to it. Enjoy the rest of your night."

"Goodnight, sir."

Little Pig, Little Pig...

14

Hale opened the door, and I smiled, waving the ice cream I'd stolen from the galley. "I was wondering if you liked chocolate or vanilla?"

Eyeing the two pints I held, he stepped back to let me into his room. It was pretty much a mirror image of my room, but his colors were slate gray and tusk.

"I'm not a vanilla guy." He shut the door and I handed him the chocolate and stuck the other pint on the dresser.

"Same." Reaching in my back pocket, I produced two spoons. "We'll have to share."

I sat on the bed with my legs folded under my bottom. He sat beside me and peeled back the lid, offering me the first bite.

Digging my spoon in, I took a decent scoop that would last a few licks and let my eyes drift around his room. "Whoa. That's some tux. Are you Batman?"

He glanced at the tuxedo hanging from the sconce on the wall. "It's for tomorrow night."

I frowned. "Tomorrow night? Are we having a theme dinner?"

He passed me the carton of ice cream. "Didn't my dad tell you about the dinner for Wes Sterling?"

"I have no idea who Wes Sterling is. Should I?"

"You will. He's planning to run for president in the next election."

My brows shot up. "Really? Is he coming on the yacht?"

"No, we're stopping for fuel and attending a fundraiser."

"So this is a political dinner?" I passed him the ice cream.

"It's a money dinner. Someone will make a speech, Wes will say a few words, and we make a donation to support his campaign."

"So you like this Wes fellow."

He shrugged. "He's not expected to interfere with our company's plans, so we back him."

"What if his opponent doesn't plan to interfere either?"

"Then we back him too."

Now I was really confused. "Isn't that a conflict of interest?"

"No, it's protecting our interests. Politicians need lobbyists."

That sounded a little slimy. "Is Remington planning to attend?"

"Of course. He orchestrated the event."

"He did?"

"He rents the venue, vets the guest list, and gets the right sponsors in the right place. Wes is then indebted to him and my father can take credit for any money collected."

I shook my head. "I miss the days when politicians would simply stand on soap boxes, say their piece, and move on to the next town."

"It's never been like that in our lifetime."

"I was talking about one of my past lives." I sucked the last bit of chocolate off my spoon. "They were simpler times back then."

"Politicians are a necessary evil."

I smirked, thinking Hale could definitely win some votes. He looked the part. "Did you ever think about running? Davenport's a pretty powerful name."

"God no. I'm not a fan of having my personal business plastered all over the media."

Leaning close, I whispered, "I hate to break it to you, but it already is."

He stilled. "What?"

I laughed. "Oh, come on, Hale. You're on the news every week. You're father's a legend."

"That's him. I have no interest letting the public into my home so they can see how I decorate or pick apart my family. My siblings are a little more open than I am when it comes to that."

I took the ice cream and scooped out another bite. "That only makes you more mysterious. What are you hiding?" I teased.

"Right now I'm hiding a beautiful woman in my room."

Being dramatic, I looked on the side of the bed. "Where is she?"

He caught my hand and took a swipe of my cold lips with his tongue. "You need to learn to take a compliment."

"It's on my to-do list."

He rolled me to my back, his body holding mine captive as he whispered, "Let's try to work on that."

I smiled, looking into his gray eyes. There was so much there and I the more I got to know him the more I liked what I saw.

"If you hate the public light so much, why do you do what you do?"

He sighed, breaking eye contact. "It's all I've ever known. It never used to bother me, but the older I get, the more disillusioned I become with the world. Sometimes I think about selling off my shares and moving somewhere no one can find me."

I knew about hiding from responsibility, but my daily pressures seemed like little nuances next to the Davenports. "Why don't you?"

"Because my dad needs me."

I smiled and caught his chin, drawing his attention back to me. "You're a good son."

Something flashed in his eyes, but he quickly disguised it before I could guess why my words might make him uneasy. His cold lips pressed against my mouth and I sensed he didn't want to discuss this further.

Softly, he whispered, "You taste sweet."

"So do you," I rasped, already breathless. "Hey. Give me back my spoon!"

He tucked the ice cream and spoons on the

dresser and pressed me into the bed, a devious smirk on his face. "No."

I laughed as his cold lips pushed to the underside of my jaw. "Your lips are freezing!"

"Are they?" He pulled up my shirt and had his cold mouth on my nipple in a second flat.

I squeaked and twisted, but he caught my wrist and pressed me into the bedding as he pinned my lower body with his legs. His mouth moved to my other breast, and I gave up. As far as torture went, this maltreatment wasn't so bad.

Pulling my bra down to my ribs, he lifted my shirt over my head and continued kissing my chest, but he wasn't just focused on my breasts. He kissed my shoulders, my nipples, my stomach...basically, every square inch he crossed got some lovin'.

When his fingers went to the snap of my pants, I lifted my bottom, and he had me naked a moment later. Fair was fair, so I gave his shirt a tug, and he sat up and quickly stripped it away. My hands roamed over his broad shoulders as we kissed, his fingers trailing to the heat between my legs and gently coaxing my thighs apart.

"Let me in."

It was becoming easier to bare myself the more we were together, but I still giggled and responded, "Little pig, little pig."

His finger sank between my folds and I moaned as my chest flushed with warmth. The weight of his body pressing into mine was perhaps the greatest feeling in the world. Slowly, he coaxed little sighs from my mouth into his as he touched me tenderly.

The press of his cock through his pants stole my

attention every time it nudged into my hip. Hooking my leg around the back of his thigh, I pulled him more on top of me and gripped his shoulders. I wanted to feel the pressure of his hard body directly at my core.

Shifting, he rocked into me, rubbing and gliding over my needy body until that wasn't enough. My kisses turned urgent as I mentally begged him to do more.

I wanted him to take me to the brink and send me over. I wanted his mouth back on my breasts. I wanted his lips on mine. I just...wanted everything.

"Now, Hale," I begged breathlessly between kisses. "I'm ready now."

I was certain he heard me, but he didn't stop to grab a condom or anything, so I reached for his pants, but he caught my wrist and pressed it to the pillows above my head. Why was he taking so long?

His palm slid down my arm to my side, as his mouth returned to my breasts. His fingers continued to pump in and out of me, but it wasn't enough. Maybe he didn't know how rare it was for me to actually request sex.

Using my other hand, I slid it down his arm and caressed his knuckles as they sank into me. "Please."

"Not yet."

What the fuck did he mean, not yet? I was ready. "But I want you."

His fingers, wet with my arousal, entwined with mine, and suddenly both of our fingers were inside of me. It was naughty, perhaps the naughtiest thing I'd ever done, fingering myself with another man. But goddamn it was hot.

I was no longer Rayne Meyers Personal Assistant Extraordinaire. I was now Rayne Meyers, Sex Goddess, concubine of Hale Big Dick Davenport.

Arching and breathing fast, I writhed against him as he slithered down my body and then his mouth was at my sex, licking over my wet fingers, pulling them into his mouth. We were both getting a first class ticket to hell because this couldn't be legal.

"Hale," I rasped as he touched me while sucking my finger deep in his hot mouth.

Peeking through my lashes, I watched him undo his pants and take himself in hand and something came over me. Reaching for his hips, I rolled him to his back and dragged my tongue over his side, taking a bite of his flesh.

He cupped a hand to the back of my head, angling my face toward his monster erection. Fuck. I hadn't thought this through.

Buying time, I kissed his other hip, licking up his side, but that thing never left my peripheral. Crap. I was going to have to bust out the metaphorical blue dress and give him the presidential treatment.

Collecting myself, I went through a few fast ground rules. One, no teeth raking. Two, anything past my molars and I'd gag. Three, something about humming to speed things up. And four, don't forget how that one guy flipped out when you stuck a finger up his ass.

I didn't think I'd ever stop hearing the echoed shrills of *That's not an entrance* as he rushed out of my dorm half-dressed. Exactly why fiction was not a reliable source for every day coupling. He totally overreacted, but still, guys got weird if you snuck in their backyard without permission.

Okay, time to get'er done. Get in and get out. This was DEFCON 5, and I wasn't taking any prisoners.

I crawled between his legs. My smile was full-on confidence and absolutely misleading. Stroking him with both hands—for the love of God, it was like a rolling pin—I started with a few kisses. That wasn't so bad.

Keeping my lashes low, I studied his expression for any signs of distress, surprised when his eyes rolled back at the mere brush of my lips. Okay, that was good. Maybe that's all he needed. My tongue teased up the side, and he hissed out a curse, his fingers tunneling into my hair.

As I continued to work my lips up, around, and over, he reached for my breast, which was disastrous, because I was highly focused and couldn't afford to be distracted. That was how someone wound up losing a testicle.

I turned, slyly putting my boobs out of reach, but that gave him better access to touch himself. He stroked his fist to my lips and added the slightest pressure to the back of my head.

Shit! I was going down! My lips stretched over him and the slightest hint that I might choke to death on his penis had me jerking back.

"You okay?" He ran a finger down my cheek with utter gentleness.

I nodded. "Yeah, sorry." Leaning back over him,

I attempted taking him again, but only managed a couple inches.

"Fuck, your mouth feels incredible."

Can I interest you in my vagina?

At least with good old missionary I just had to lie there. This was fucking work. I hummed because I seriously didn't know how anyone could do this for more than a couple of minutes.

"Do you have any idea how sexy you are?"

What's that now? My gaze met his and he groaned.

"You could make me come just by looking at me like that."

Of course I continued to stare because coming was the goal. But then he did the strangest thing and cupped my cheek. "You're so damn pretty, Rayne."

My mouth went slack, and I blinked at him, unsure if the feelings I was having were safe or lethal. No one had ever talked to me like that or looked at me like I disarmed them. I'd stopped blowing him, but he didn't seem to care, he just stared into my eyes and ran his fingers through my hair and grinned.

I swallowed and considered what all of these feelings meant in the grand scheme of things. "You probably say that to all the girls."

"No. It's you. Something about you."

My heart raced, as I suddenly wanted to do whatever possible to hold onto such adoration. What were we just standing around for, people? We had a job to do. I gave him a genuine smile and then I stopped pussyfooting around and set out to do my absolute best.

Apparently, I was better at this than I thought, because he nearly jackknifed off the bed and gasped in pleasure when my mouth returned to him. No one had ever given me the impression that I had any sort of sexual influence. It was incredibly empowering.

Every gasped breath and curse that slipped from his lips emboldened me. I played with various techniques, some got more response than others, but the more I experimented, the more I got into it.

I became a Nobel Prize winner of blowjobs, making academic advances for women everywhere. Or maybe I was the only person who didn't know blowjobs could fulfill a part of the giver the way this one was fulfilling me. It was definitely a learning experience.

The harder I worked the more I noticed. His body throbbed under my touch, swelling and twitching between my lips. The slightest taste of him met my tongue and I savored the flavor of male arousal. Everything about what we were doing was off the charts fucking hot.

"Enough," he gasped, pulling me back.

I groaned—*actually groaned*—because I wasn't ready to stop. I was solving world peace down there and—

The box of condoms came out of the drawer and as he ripped open the package, little packets flew everywhere. I never saw smooth, unshakable Hale in any sort of rush, so I laughed as he made a frantic grab for a condom.

Snatching one off the bed, he tore it open with his teeth. Mesmerized by the practiced way he slid it over his length, I hardly had time to consider that we were actually going to have *the sex*.

He pulled me beneath him and looked into my eyes. "Are you sure you're ready?"

I'd never been more ready in my life. Nodding, I parted my thighs. "I want you."

His lips brushed mine as he settled closer. "I want you too."

There was pressure—a lot of pressure. "Oh God."

His arms rested beside my head as he cupped my face and continued to look into my eyes. Proof that the blowjob had worked for both of us, I was very wet, but he was so damn big there was no way he was fitting.

His lips kissed along my jaw as he nudged forward. "You're small."

Yes, I apparently had a Keebler vagina, and he was on his way to shattering my tree house. Pulling my knees up to make more room, I silently grunted as he worked his way in and then my nails bit into his shoulder as I feared I couldn't take anymore.

No! I wanted to have the sex! I needed the good Hale sex!

This was so unfair. Just shoot me now, because if I couldn't have him inside of me, there was really no point to taking my next breath—

Oh... His mouth found that lucky spot on my neck and the tension in my body loosened and—he was in!

"You okay, baby?" he whispered, holding himself inside of me as I caught my breath.

Aw...he called me baby. I loved that. I never had

any sort of pet name before. I wasn't sure *baby* was one I would have chosen, but coming from his lips I loved it.

"Rayne?"

"Yes." I opened my eyes and found him studying me. "I think you're unusually big down there."

He laughed and kissed me, his hips rocking back slowly and pressing forward again. He didn't poke the shit out of me or even jackhammer his hips like past lovers had done. Rather, he continued to look into my eyes as he gradually moved in and out, figuring which way worked best for both of us.

I gasped as he struck a nerve and he read my response quickly, doing whatever he'd just done again. For once, I wasn't a pincushion for my partner. We were working like some sort of a team. Realizing this, I bravely lifted my hips to his, getting into the game.

He groaned and caught my ass in his palm, bringing me up against his body, as his mouth closed over mine. As we kissed, he ran his hands over my skin and things started to click.

My heart raced and my breathing labored as pleasure pinged from my breasts to my vagina and ricocheted around in my brain. Dear Lord, was he a mastermind at the multitasking! I just sort of hung on for dear life and let it happen, because it was happening better than it ever had before.

I sensed him getting closer as his pace increased. His hand fit between our bodies as he rubbed his fingers over me. My body tightened around him as the pleasure climbed and climbed until I was falling into a haze of euphoria where I could only chant his name and tremble in his arms.

I came so hard I was pretty sure he broke my eyelids because I couldn't summon them to open for the life of me. Warm lips coasted over my cheek as his sweet voice whispered words of praise. Praise!

I knew then that we were sexual soul mates, and I'd go Annie Wilkes on anyone who tried to come between my happy vagina and Hale's magical penis.

With a soft kiss, he withdrew, and I mumbled a slur of incoherent words. Just as I was trying to tell him I was cold, he pulled me to his side and the covers came over us. He rearranged my body so I fit in every nook and cranny of his much larger frame. I appreciated the assistance because my limbs were currently dead.

"You're incredible," he whispered, folding his thigh over mine and pinning me to him.

I *am* incredible, I thought, but that was all due to him and his generous skills. Flopping my hand limply over his forearm I gave him a pat.

"You killed me," I slurred, already drifting toward sleep.

He chuckled, warm and deep as his lips pressed to my shoulder. "Get some rest. I'm not letting you go until morning."

And that was just fine with me.

Pig Shrimp

15

"You're never going to be able to do that all night."

Remington glared at me under his dark brows. "A Davenport can do anything for a night, and when we do, we do it well."

"If there's some sort of innuendo buried in that comment, please refrain from making another one unless you want me to start spouting fortune cookie clichés again."

He rolled his eyes and hobbled on his crutches to the other end of the room, already winded.

"I don't understand why you won't take the scooter."

"It's undignified."

"No, it's not. You have a broken foot."

"Eric!" He called, ignoring my valid point. Assistant number one appeared and Remington barked, "Go get me some water."

Eric disappeared, and I said, "You have water in your fridge."

"Marta just filled it. I want something cold."

God forbid we drink from the tap. "Maybe you should take a break."

"Maybe you should go find something to wear tonight."

I snorted. "To play cards with the crew? I think what I'm wearing is fine."

Working his way back to the other side of the room he mumbled, "You're not playing cards with the crew. You're attending the party with us."

"No, no, no. I have nothing to do with this party."

"You have something to do with me, so you're going. It's not up for debate."

"I have nothing to wear, Remington."

"Where the hell is he with my water?"

Rolling my eyes, I uncapped a bottle from the fridge. "Here. A little tepid water won't kill you."

He took a long sip and caught his breath. This shuffling around couldn't be good for his heart, but he insisted on using crutches.

"Seraphina has dresses in her closet. Get something from there."

"I'm not wearing your daughter's clothes."

The bathing suit was one thing, but a dress was a different story. I'd probably end up spilling a blob of dip on the boob and ruining it. Plus, I wasn't a fancy party kind of girl, so I planned on abusing the shit out of any excuse to get out of going to one.

"Damn it, Meyers, if anything's going to kill me it'll be the tedious chore of bickering with you over putting on a dress. Act like a woman and wear something pretty."

I pursed my lips and mumbled, "You mean act like a woman and do what you say."

"That too. You do work for me, in case you've forgotten." Eric returned with the water and Remington grumbled, "It's about time. Forget it. Meyers already got me something to drink."

I earned a nice scowl for that. I smiled cheekily at Eric because I was seriously done with his moodiness. I wasn't interested in whatever competition was between us.

Eric left and Remington finally stopped and panted. His face was red and his hands were slightly trembling.

I pushed a chair to his side. "Take a rest. You can try again once you catch your breath."

He sat, but it took a chunk of his pride. "You're a pain in my ass."

"Then why do you keep me around? Eric could help you practice on the crutches."

He rolled his eyes. "You're a little thing, but if I went down, my money's on you getting me back up before him."

I laughed. "If you went down you'd probably take me with you. Then we'd both be screwed."

He chuckled and sank a bit more into the chair. He was done.

"This is an important party tonight. It'll do you well to meet the people there."

Seriously, it was like saying no to a toddler. "For all my political aspirations?"

"You never know when you'll need a favor."

And didn't that just show how corrupt our government was? "I'm more of a survivalist by avoidance kind of gal."

"You're going."

"Remington, I really think you'll do fine with Hale and Eric."

"Eric isn't going."

I scoffed. "Then why do I have to go?"

"Because I want you there. Go for Hale, if you won't go for me."

But Hale hadn't asked me to go. I didn't understand why it meant so much to Remington for me to be there, but knowing Eric wasn't attending, I worried who would look after the stubborn jackass on crutches.

"I'll go if you bring the scooter—just in case."

"Women. There's always a condition. Fine. I'll bring the damn scooter, but I won't need it. The crutches will be enough. Half the night we'll be sitting at a table anyway."

Shit. I honestly didn't expect him to agree that easily.

Arching a brow, he said, "You better go look in the closets downstairs. The party's at seven. We'll be leaving at six."

I helped him to his bed because I saw he was hurting from that little bit of exercise. When men like Remington hurt, the rest of the world hurt, not because he bitched and moaned and lashed out like a high-strung Sally, but because men like Remington Davenport didn't wear weak well. It wasn't right seeing him feeble and frail, and I couldn't wait until the day his strength returned.

Lord only knew what that was like. I couldn't imagine him more full-throttle.

Once I had him settled, I took a detour to find Hale. He was working at the table on the upper deck and speaking on the phone. However, this time, things were different. The moment he saw me, he put the caller on hold and rose to greet me. "Hey, beautiful."

"Hey. Your father's insisting on using the crutches tonight."

He rolled his eyes. "He's a stubborn ass."

"He's also insisting I go with him."

Hale's brows shot up. "Is he?" He studied me for a moment. "You don't want to go?"

I shrugged. "Do *you* want me to go?"

He smiled. "I'd love to have you there. I should have offered last night, but you distracted me."

I laughed. "Oh, *I* distracted you?"

"You're very distracting."

I gave him a shoulder bump. "So are you. I have to go find something to wear. Get back to your call."

He watched me, eyes heavy, as I walked away. It was rather nice having a man's attention when you wanted it.

Being that Seraphina owned her own clothing line, it was no surprise her closet was packed to the gills with dresses way too expensive for my wardrobe. Everything black was extremely low cut. I didn't have the right bra for anything like that and going braless was something I never did in public.

Okay, fine. Occasionally I put on a hoodie and went to the deli, but that was it, and no one knew about that but me.

I picked three dresses and took them to my

room. The first one was an absolute fail. I couldn't even discern the neck hole from the arm hole, and there was no way I was getting it back on the hanger, so once I wrestled it off my body I folded it and gave it a threatening glare.

The second one was okay, but I could see my bellybutton through the material. The last thing I wanted to do was appear in some upper-crust issue of fashion don'ts. Not that I was important enough to garner such attention, but who the hell knew how those things worked?

The third dress was my last hope, and if that didn't work, I was going to have to tell Remington he could leave the scooter home with me. It was a mulberry colored trumpet style gown with a high Grecian neckline. Sliding it over my head, I was surprised by how easily it fell into place. As I turned to the mirror, I was pleasantly pleased.

Though I wouldn't be able to wear a bra with it, or underwear for that matter, it didn't look too bad. The panel over my chest left my shoulders exposed and had delicate beading that would compensate for my lack of jewelry and undergarments.

Twisting my hair up, I clipped it on top of my head. If I pulled a few strands loose, I could probably get away with no earrings. Best of all, it was long. Thank God, because while Seraphina's feet were the same size as mine, all her fancy shoes had five-inch heels. Homey didn't play that.

I showered but didn't wash my hair, hoping the humidity would give me a bit of extra body. My face had nice color from working outside, but I needed a little something. Digging in my purse, I found tinted lip balm. That was all the makeup I owned. I applied a little to my lips and the apples of my cheeks and that made a slight difference.

Watching my time, I fussed with my hair until I was ready to shave it off. Using a hair tie and two clips, I managed a sloppy bun that looked purposely messy in a trendy sort of way—I hoped. And that was all she wrote.

Slipping on my flip-flops, I left my room and saw Hale had already gone upstairs. Thank God, because I totally busted my ass going up the steps, collapsing like a drunken debutant who had no business attending a ball.

"Stupid gown." I never would have made it a day in Victorian times.

When I reached the main floor, I spotted the boys on the back deck by the pool looking like a bunch of James Bond stunt doubles. Well, Hale did. Remington looked more appropriately fitted for a White House Correspondence dinner.

Sliding open the glass door, I kicked the skirt of the gown out from around my ankles and tried not to trip again. Once it seemed all wardrobe malfunctions were under control, I turned and—

"What?"

Something was wrong. I inspected my dress from chest to butt, turning like a dog chasing its tail. Did I leave a tag on or something?

I looked back at the men. "Is something wrong with what I'm wearing?"

Remington's face split with an approving grin and Hale walked to meet me at the door. "You look stunning," he whispered, brushing a kiss on my cheek.

"Oh. I thought I had a stain or something." Relieved, I smiled, a touch nervous he'd just kissed me in front of Remington. "You two look rather dashing as well."

Then our surroundings registered and I truly smiled. "Land!"

Hale laughed and Remington rolled his eyes. "You'd think she was castaway for years."

"Where are we?"

"Savannah," Hale answered, taking my arm.

"Georgia? I've never been before."

"It's one of my favorite places. Come on, we should be going."

I held back, making sure Remington was okay to stand. Once he did, we slowly made our way to the dock. Hale was truly wonderful with his father, so patient and helpful as he worked his way down the stairs and over the planks of the dock.

Once we were in the limo, I handed Remington a bottle of water. He nodded his appreciation and took a sip.

"Thank you, sweetheart."

I stilled but quickly recovered. Sweetheart? That was new. Usually, I just got Meyers. We seemed to have skipped right over my first name and jumped straight into terms of endearment.

"Did you hold up your end of the bargain?"

"Scooter's in the trunk," he muttered, twisting the cap back in place.

I anxiously bobbed my leg, scoping out the

limo. Hale lifted the hem of my dress and raised a brow at my flip-flops.

I shrugged. "Your sister's shoes were too tall."

He let the dress fall back in place and smirked.

After several minutes on the road, Remington's breathing settled, and I relaxed. "So how far away is this shindig? And do I need to know anything before we get there?"

"We should be there in about thirty minutes if we don't hit traffic." As far as my other question went, Remington didn't seem too concerned. "Just be polite and keep the conversation away from religion and politics."

I frowned. "But isn't this a political dinner?"

"What are your thoughts on government funded healthcare?"

"*Pft*, we're behind. Europe's had it in play for years and their people live four years longer than the average American."

Hale chuckled and Remington arched a brow. "That's why you steer clear of the political issues. Wes is a member of the Tea Party."

"Oh." I should have figured that. Remington was definitely a conservative and among the top one percent. I just wanted everyone to get along. "Well, I'll keep an open mind and your friend Wes can do his best to earn my vote."

My mom had a saying about politics and religion. Her theory was both topics were like a penis. It was okay to have one, but it was impolite to whip it out in mixed company or try to cram it down someone's throat. I agreed.

I'd been expecting some sort of hall, but we arrived at a house. Well, not a house, more like a mansion. An enormous fountain filled the circle drive as a line of sleek limos snaked their way around the property.

"Wow. Someone lives here?"

"Yes, but they've asked to remain anonymous."

My jaw dropped as I grinned at Remington. "Oh, you have to tell me who it is. Please."

He shook his head and the next ten minutes passed in a guessing game.

"Oprah?"

"No."

"Madonna?"

"No."

"Bono?"

"Give it a rest, Meyers."

I took Hale's arm and whispered, "Do you know who owns the house?"

He shook his head.

I gave up my guessing game as we entered the foyer. You could easily fit five SUVs in that room alone. Holy crap. This was some seriously posh shit.

Taking it slow for Remington's benefit, we went straight to the ballroom. Yes, a freaking ballroom —*in a house*. This was nicer than any wedding I'd ever attended.

As far as parties went, my family was the average plastic tablecloth type, with balloon accents and plastic forks. The only plastic at this party came in the form of American Express cards.

"Dad, they have us sitting over here."

Remington was already getting winded, so I kept to his side as Hale led the way. He whispered names and facts in my ear as we passed some of the finest dressed people I'd ever set eyes on. I found his clipped bios amusing and kept a pert smile on my mouth all the way to our table.

"That's Aberdeen Virden. Wealthiest woman in the room tonight. Six husbands in the coal industry. The one thing you can count on with coal, Meyers, is that if you're around it long enough, it'll kill you. She shops where the turnover rates are best."

Old Aberdeen didn't look like she had any more honeymoons left in her, but she sure hoisted those diamond rings around easy enough for a woman in her eighties.

"That's Lance Jacobi. Slimy little shit. Never trust him."

"Noted." Not that I'd be interacting with any of these people, but it was good to know when I needed to watch my six.

Once we were seated, Hale tucked his father's crutches against a nearby wall. Remington seemed relieved to have any signs of his injuries out of sight. However, when the fifth person stopped by our table to offer condolences about Remington's "spill" he grew irritated.

"How are you, Remington?" another thirty-something bombshell asked, caressing the sleeve of his tux.

My nose crinkled, as I struggled to see the sexual appeal. Remington was great, but I'd never see him in a carnal way. What did this woman have in common with him anyway?

"I'm fine. How's that column of yours? Have you arranged an interview with Wes?" Remington responded, strategically shifting the attention away from him.

The woman leaned closer, blatantly flirting. "I'd much rather have a few private minutes of your time. What do you say we steal away after the speeches and you can tell me all about that new deal you're working on?"

Oh, come on!

Thankfully, Remington blew her off with practiced finesse. "I'll have my people get in touch with yours after I read your column next week, highlighting how qualified our presumptive nominee is."

It was fascinating watching Remington manipulate others with such ease. He never gave anything without getting a promise of something in return. Yet somehow he managed this without ever having to verbally ask for a favor.

"Deal," the woman agreed, apparently satisfied.

Another woman appeared and helped herself to Hale's vacant seat. "Remington, you look well. I was worried when I heard the news."

He nodded, but that was all he apparently intended to comment on the subject. "Meyers, this is Eloise Clark, daughter of Donald Clark. Eloise, this is Rayne Meyers."

"Are you two an item?" the woman asked.

Talk about cutting to the issues. "I work for Remington."

She laughed and patted my arm as if we shared a special joke, but nothing I said was particularly funny. "Don't we all?" She preened, winking at Remington.

I laughed nervously. Did she work for him or not? I was confused.

"Remington," a male voice greeted. "I'm glad you made it."

Startled to feel Remington lifting to his feet, I shot out of my chair and casually held out my arm. What the hell was he doing, standing without his crutches?

"Wes, great to see you." Ah, so this was the man of the hour.

"Please, don't rise on my account." Thankfully, Remington returned to his seat. "And who is your lovely guest?"

I flushed and grinned because I might be meeting the future president. Remington noted my star struck eagerness for an introduction, rolled his eyes and muttered, "For God's sake."

Recalling that my behavior was a reflection of the Davenports, I pulled my act together and held out a hand. "It's a pleasure to meet you, Mr. Sterling."

"I assure you, the pleasure's mine."

Well, wasn't he fancy? I smiled and did a little curtsy. "This is quite an event."

He nodded, still holding onto my hand. "I owe it all to Remington."

Glancing over my shoulder I gave my boss a smile, but my pride plummeted when I saw Hale approaching. He didn't look happy.

He was gone for five minutes. Could something have happened that quickly? Drama, drama, drama. It didn't matter what side of the tracks the celebration was on, drama crashed every party.

"Perhaps after dinner we can share a dance, Ms...?"

Returning my attention to the future commander and chief, I quickly answered, "Meyers. Rayne Meyers."

And there would be no dancing for me. The only dance I did well was *Thriller* and this didn't seem like a *Thriller* crowd.

"Wes." Hale's hand immediately went to my back.

Wes released his hold of my fingers and opened his hand to Hale. "Davenport. Glad you could make it."

Hale nodded but didn't smile. Maybe he didn't realize he had a habit of making an enema face in public. This was something we should talk about, right? I mean, girlfriends helped boyfriends with that sort of thing, didn't they? *Was* I his girlfriend? A dirty voice in my head breathily declared we were not girlfriend boyfriend but *lovas*. That worked too.

"I've got to make my rounds. I'll be back later for that dance, Ms. Meyers."

Keeping it polite, I gave a non-committal smile. My eyes lit when I spotted enormous shrimp topiaries being wheeled out.

Turning to Hale, I said, "Do you see the size of those shrimp trees?"

He was scowling.

"Do you not like shrimp?"

Rather than answer, he took his seat and said, "The waitress is bringing over your martini, Dad."

Unsure what this sudden mood was, I gave him a shoulder bump. "I hope you didn't order me a Manhattan."

"I ordered you a White Russian." When he still didn't crack a smile, I decided to clam up.

As the shrimp came around, I was like an excited kid at a pony fair and my silence didn't last long. "I've never seen shrimp this big. How does one even find a shrimp this size? Holy crap, this one's practically the size of my palm."

"You'd think she never saw food before," Remington muttered.

"Oh, whatever, Remington. This is big shrimp and you know it." Hearing my words out loud, I snorted. "Big shrimp. That's what you call an oxymoron."

When no one seemed to care, I murmured to myself, "Check out the big brain on Rayne."

Hale was starting to piss me off with his seriousness. As they cleared away the first course, I leaned close and whispered, "Did something happen at the bar?"

He sipped his drink and glanced at me, but didn't answer.

"Did I do something?"

"No."

"You seem angry," I whispered.

He looked at me for a measured moment and said, "Now's not the time. We'll discuss it later."

"Pardon me, sir," the waiter placed a salad on the table.

When the next course came out, I decided I'd have a better conversation with the company to my right. "Thanks for making me come here tonight, Remington. This is really nice."

His eyes creased with a weathered grin. "You

look good in this setting, Meyers. You pull it off well."

I smiled. "Careful with that silver tongue. One of those women overhear you laying it on thick and they might end up tucking you in tonight."

He gave a gruff but authentic Remington chuckle. "Too soon. They're all just sniffing out my insurance policy after the fall."

"So prove them wrong. You aren't going anywhere. They're all pretty."

"Too young."

I was actually surprised to hear him say that. They *were* too young, but I didn't buy that as a deterrent for Remington.

I hid a smile as I realized this was about him still mending his broken heart. For that, he got his own shoulder bump.

Hale made small talk with the gentleman to his left and I wondered why he was speaking to strangers more than me.

"You have an admirer," Remington muttered, but he was looking at the table.

"What? Who?"

"Pay attention, Meyers. Take your eyes off your flambé for a second and look around."

But I never had a banana cooked in a fire. Taking another bite, I glanced around the room. I didn't see any—

Wes Sterling lifted his glass and grinned. I glimpsed behind me, but no one was looking at him. "Are you talking about that Sterling guy?"

"There you go," Remington mumbled, busying himself with his flambé.

I frowned. "But I don't want an admirer."

"He'll want that dance soon."

I glanced at Hale then back to Wes. In a panic, I turned to Remington. "He wasn't serious about that."

"Sure he was."

"Why are you acting like this is amusing? What do I do, Remington?"

"He's the host. You dance with him."

What was I, the political courtesan? "I don't know how to dance."

"He'll lead."

Growing frustrated, I hissed, "I don't want to dance with him."

"What's wrong?" Hale asked, and I gave Remington an S.O.S. look, but he was suddenly engrossed in his flambé. Oh, now Remington was over the whole debacle and had nothing to say.

"You're a troublemaker," I hissed in his ear then turned to Hale, pasting on a smile. "Nothing."

"Did Wes ask you to dance?"

"No."

Remington tsked.

Twisting in my seat, I snapped, "You *hush*."

He chuckled. "Here comes your dance partner now."

I looked up and saw Wes making his way through the tables. "I have to use the—" Was it rude to say restroom? "Excuse me." I left my napkin on my seat and went where no man could follow.

Thankfully, the bathroom wasn't far. Once I was safely closed in a stall, I leaned against the wall and waited. If I stayed in there for ten minutes the guy would go bug someone else, right?.

"Wait, you have lipstick on your teeth," a woman outside the stalls said to someone I couldn't see.

"Oh, thanks."

"Are you here with anyone?" the woman asked.

"Not yet. I'm hoping to change that once the music starts."

"Me too. I have my eye on Davenport."

My gaze narrowed and I tried to spy through the crack of the stall. One of the girls giggled. "Which one?"

"Junior or senior. Makes no difference to me."

"Junior would probably be more fun, but eventually, they all get old. Senior would only be a temporary inconvenience."

Gaping, I silently mouthed, *What the fuck?*

"There's a woman with them tonight, but I can't figure out whose date she is. Junior keeps watching her, but she's been talking to his dad more than anyone else."

"I'm going to work my way over there..." The conversation faded as they exited the restroom.

I had to see who they were so I could tell Remington to stay the hell away from them. Leaving the stall, I quickly washed my hands and pushed through the door—

"Hale."

"Everything all right?"

"Did you see two women come out of here?"

"It's the ladies' room. I've seen several women leave in the past few minutes."

"But these were harpies. They were talking about...your dad. We have to tell him to stay away from them." I went to do just that and he caught my arm.

"Remington can handle himself."

I frowned at him. "Are you okay?"

"I'm fine."

No, he wasn't. "You're lying to me. What's going on?"

"You don't know me well enough to know when I'm lying."

That was a dick thing to say. "Seriously?" I twisted my wrist out of his hand. "Maybe you're right. The way you've been acting tonight, I feel like I don't know you at all. But I can tell you I don't like it." With that, I walked away to go warn Remington about the gold diggers.

Remington was waiting at the table watching the younger crowd dance. As I sat beside him, I asked, "Did any women come over to you while I was gone?"

He glanced at me and frowned. "You're sweating."

"I have high a functioning thermoregulation system."

"That's not a thing."

"Yes, it is. I read it on a medical website."

"So you must be a doctor."

"Jesus, what is it with you Davenports? Parties are supposed to be fun."

He glanced over my shoulder. "Are they bringing the limo around?"

Turning, I found Hale standing with his father's crutches. "It's out front."

Wait. We were leaving? This party sucked. The food was good, but everything else was disturbing. Even the speeches were a bit much. I couldn't believe I got dressed up for this and we were leaving ten minutes after the music started. Still, the food had been good.

We walked Remington to the limo and Hale held me back as I moved to follow his dad inside. "Aren't we leaving?"

"We're going somewhere else. I want to talk to you. Eric will help him to bed."

That was my job. "But how will we get home?"

"Another limo's waiting."

Apparently, this had all been arranged some time ago because our limo pulled up directly after Remington's left. Once we were inside the car and on our way, I had enough.

"Why are you being a dick?"

His gaze shifted to mine. "I'm not a fan of Wes."

"Then why did you go to his party?"

"I told you why. It's a business strategy."

"And what was I? Another strategy?"

"You were my guest."

"But you didn't invite me. Your dad did."

"I know you like my dad, Rayne, but he never does anything without a motive."

My head shook. "You people are all ridiculous. He wanted me there to meet some of his associates."

"You're right. And he enjoyed proving that other men notice you."

"Look, if you were jealous, you could have been

a little more attentive." I pursed my lips. "You hardly spoke to me."

"It doesn't matter now. You went. You met the people he wanted you to meet. And now it's over."

"And boy, am I glad I agreed to go. How else would I know how boring these things are?"

"Let's drop it."

"Let's not. Is Wes your nemesis or something?"

"He's nothing."

"Then why are you acting like I did something to betray you. I was only being polite, which I assumed was expected, being that this was *his* party." I scoffed, irritated by the entire night. "You're being ridiculous for no reason."

He sent me a sidelong glance but didn't comment.

After three and a half minutes of uncomfortable silence, I couldn't take anymore. "Okay, look, I'm not used to men getting jealous, but I think it's totally unfair that you're mad at me—"

"I'm not mad at you, Rayne."

"Then what the hell are you? You've had your enema face on since we got there—"

"My what?"

"You know." I did my best impression of his stuffy face. "I'm Hale Davenport. I don't smile in public and I'm not impressed by big shrimp."

He frowned. "That's not what I look like and I don't talk like that."

"Really? You might want to check some of the C-SPAN footage. You may not talk like that, but you totally make that face."

"Now, you're the one being ridiculous."

"This whole night is ridiculous. Gah! Why are we even going anywhere? We should just go back to the boat and call it a night."

Folding my arms over my chest, I scowled at the privacy screen separating us from the driver. Men were stupid and if this was what I'd been missing, I wasn't sold on changing things.

Hale's hand settled on my knee. "I'm sorry."

Okay, that took me off-guard.

Now what? I didn't expect him to apologize for being grumpy, so I didn't have an acceptance speech prepared.

Apparently, when a woman gets caught off-guard, switching gears isn't as simple as it should be. "And what exactly are you sorry for?"

"I don't want to fight with you. I shouldn't have taken my mood out on you, but I... I've recently been burned as far as fidelity is concerned."

Oh. Great. Now he was disclosing personal secrets to me. Well, that was just fabulous. How the hell did I respond to that, because even I knew his apology was a step in the right direction.

"Hale, I'm sorry if someone cheated on you before, but I'm not that kind of girl. I *never* date, and you can pretty much disqualify my entire sex life before you. I know we're still in the early stages of whatever this is, but you have *all* my attention. I've never cheated on anyone and I wouldn't betray you like that."

He gave a subtle nod and his hand squeezed mine gently. "Thank you. I don't like needing that sort of assurance, but... maybe I do."

I supposed we all had insecurities. "Do you want to talk about it?"

His mouth pursed. "Eventually. But I'd rather not ruin anymore of this night than I already have. I'm sorry about how I acted. Suffice it to say, certain people have a long way to go to win back my trust, but it has nothing to do with you, and I shouldn't have made you feel like you did anything wrong."

"I understand."

Trust was a tricky thing and when trust was broken it sometimes was unfixable. If anything, I wanted him to know he could trust me, so I'd be patient. Every day Hale opened up a little more than the last and every new piece of the Hale puzzle made me like the big picture a little bit more.

"I forgive you."

He folded his fingers around mine and squeezed again. "When we talk, and we will, I want it to be right. I've had a rough few months and right now you're helping me in more ways than you realize."

"I am?"

He nodded. "I don't know what it is about you, but you're like a breath of fresh air. You're genuine and I'm not used to people being so. It makes me happy, but also makes me nervous because I don't want to ruin what we have."

I didn't want anything to ruin it either. Smiling up at him, I said, "Well, when you're ready to talk, I'll be ready to listen."

He kissed my temple. "Thank you for being patient."

He'd been patient with me plenty of times. It was the least I could do. Deciding that was enough seriousness for one evening, I put the drama behind us.

"So where are we going?"

"I wanted to show you one of my homes."

One of them? "You have a house in Georgia?"

He nodded. "A small one."

Curious to see what Hale's house might look like, I grinned. "Are we spending the night there?"

"I had hoped we would. But we'll have to be back to *The Lady Parr* early."

A sleepover. Fun. Did he remember condoms?

Despite the eventful night, I was already thinking about continuing my sex-ucation. Hale was a fabulous teacher. I nestled into his shoulder because that was my signature move.

Already used to my cues, he turned and offered an understanding smile. "You look beautiful tonight."

Heat filled my chest. "So do you. You wear a tux well." His thumb ran over my knuckles and that quickly my libido was ticking. "How far is your house?"

He glanced out the window. "We're about forty minutes away."

"Forty minutes? However will we pass the time?" People had sex in limos, right? That was a thing. Elle did, after prom.

His jacket shifted as he tipped his head, gauging my expression. "What did you have in mind?"

Well, I couldn't just say it. I shrugged. "I dunno."

He sat back and continued to hold my hand. Maybe Hale wasn't a limo sex kind of guy. Since I already used my shoulder nestle move, I sighed. That was my other move. I only had two.

When my second move didn't work, I casually rested my hand on his leg. "I like these pants."

I like these pants? What the fuck was wrong with me? Who said things like that? That wasn't sexy. Damn it.

He shifted and stretched his legs out as I lightly chafed my thumbnail over his knee. His hand squeezed mine, but he still didn't make a move. I didn't have any more ideas, so the ball was in his court. Maybe he missed the memo about the game being on. I gave another sigh.

Stretching his arm over the back of the seat, he touched my hair. I glanced at him and he smiled. At this pace, we'd be in Florida by the time anything happened.

Leaning close, I brushed my lips over his jaw. He made a sound of satisfaction but didn't bend me over the seat or stick his tongue in my mouth. I was out of ideas.

Another sigh.

Hale casually parted his jacket. I glanced at him, but his expression was unreadable. Glancing back at his lap, I watched in awe as he lowered the zipper of his pants. What was *this* move? When I looked at his face again, he gave a half-smile.

Wait... *Oh, I see what he's doing.* Or did I?

"Um..." Seriously, I needed some sort of signal. He always touched me first. Looking at him, I whispered, "Your pants are open."

"I'm aware."

Okay. Subtle. "Did you want something?"

"Yes."

My sex actually tightened at that single word. So we were on the same page. Okay. I was game. "What did you want?"

"Your mouth on my cock."

And now I was out of the game. Well, not out, per se, but definitely out of my league. I didn't know how to talk sex, but Hale seemed to have no problem just throwing it out there. "You want my..."

"Mouth."

"On your..."

"Cock."

"Right." I assessed the situation.

How were we going to do this? Did I just lean over his lap? Should I move to the floor and get on my knees? His impenetrable patience waited me out as I debated which way would be best.

Kicking off my shoes, I glanced at the front of the limo. "Can he—"

"He can't see us."

Right. Okay then. I lifted my gown and slid to the floor. "Down here?"

He nodded so I scooted between his knees and giggled. This was the most bizarre thing I'd ever done. "Are you going to take it out?"

"I want you to."

"Oh."

Taking a deep breath, I lifted off my heels and inspected his pants. Boys clothing was different, and I knew there was some sort of trap door in their underwear, but the limo was dark, and I didn't want to mess this up. "Lift your hips."

He lifted and I pulled his pants and briefs down his thighs. Oh, and he was hard. That was a plus. I stared but didn't touch. Glancing up at Hale, I was amazed by how calm he was with his dick waving around in the free world.

His arms rested on the back of the seat and he watched me with half-lidded eyes. Just waiting. *Here goes nothing.*

I wrapped my fingers around him and leaned over, putting him in my mouth. The second I made contact, his hand went to my hair, and he hissed, "Fuck, Rayne."

Once again, my body responded. The more he reacted, the more turned on I became. I hummed and his hand tightened over my hair. He applied a little pressure and I went lower. His fingers flexed and I found my rhythm. I was really getting good at this.

As I worked, he panted and muttered interesting phrases, dirty phrases, phrases that had my body throbbing and aroused. Maybe it shocked me that he could use such words, being that he was a rather serious guy. But somehow he managed to tell me to suck his cock with the same authority he had in every other situation. And strangest of all, I wanted to do it. I was addicted to Hale Davenport's big dick.

"Baby, I'm going to come," he muttered, flexing his hips off the seat.

I pulled back and looked around. "Where?"

His eyes met mine, his finger tracing my slightly swollen mouth. "I'd love to see you swallow it."

I didn't know if I could do that. I mean, I knew

women did that, the whole spit or swallow debate, but what if I gagged?

"I've never done that before. What if I can't?"

"It was just a suggestion. You don't have to—"

"No. I want to." And apparently, I did.

He shifted so he was sitting on the edge of the seat. "Lean back a little."

He cupped the back of my neck and angled my head as he placed a hand on the ceiling of the car and lifted off the seat, gliding his cock back in my mouth. "That's it, baby. Nice and deep. Fuck. You're incredible at this."

Every time he complimented my performance I preened and took him a little deeper. His strokes sped up and he kept hold of the back of my head, guiding me over him.

"Relax your throat, baby. Relax for me now."

He moaned and throbbed over my tongue. His flavor filled my mouth, warm and thick and I quickly swallowed, but traces lingered. Hale pumped a few more times then sagged into the seat and caught his breath.

That was astoundingly easy, like doing a shot of tequila with no chaser. Proud of myself, I rubbed my cheek against his thigh, and he brushed a hand over my hair.

I stroked him softly and placed a little goodbye kiss on his tip. I really was growing quite fond of Prince Ever-hard.

Hale sighed and pulled me onto his lap. He just held me, my head resting against his shoulder as we drove.

"We're almost home. Once we get there, I promise I'll take care of you."

The strange thing was I didn't need him to take care of me. I mean, I wasn't going to turn him down, but I was happy just to see to his needs. Never in a million years did I think I could feel that way about a man, but lo and behold, here I was feeling it.

I'm a Dirty, Dirty Girl

16

"This is what you call little?"

The limo pulled away as Hale unlocked the front door of his *toy mansion*. Nothing about this place was little.

"I haven't been here in a while, so I apologize if things are untidy."

He held the door and I stepped over the threshold as he flipped on a light. "Okay, my house could fit in your den. Is that a den?"

"Some call it a great room, but I never put much thought into it."

I drifted into the "great room" and did a three-sixty. "You Davenports don't do small, do you?"

"You get a lot for your dollar in the south." He flipped on a few more lights, and I was immediately drawn to the wall of windows, which showed a mirror reflection of us against the night sky.

"Watch this," he said, hitting another switch.

Trees, as far as the eye could see, lit up with gigantic lanterns. The branches were all covered in some sort of moss giving the appearance of weeping willows, but they were more than willows.

"Wow."

"I did the lighting myself. I used the buckets you saw in my trunk and utility lines. Each one has a portable hand lamp inside."

"I'm impressed." I recalled the day we met. "I wondered why you had all those buckets in your car."

He nodded. "I wanted to do the same at my home in Florida. Maybe around the pool, but I'm not sure how the palms will handle the weight."

Seeing this handy side of him did things to me. Glancing over my shoulder, I said, "I love seeing something you made. It's really beautiful."

Pride flashed in his eyes. His hands went to my hips and slithered up my front. "I owe you some attention," he whispered, making a slow transition to my breasts.

His body molded against my back as he caught my wrists and brought my palms to the window. He pressed my fingers into the glass.

"Stay like that." His slight command turned my insides into mush.

I stared at the view, checking if he had any nearby neighbors that might see, but all I saw were beautifully lit trees. The zipper of my gown loosened and his lips pressed into my spine, sending little shockwaves through my body.

His fingers gathered the gown at the side of my legs, slowly hiking up the material as he kissed my back. "You're not wearing a bra."

My nipples tightened under the silky material. "Or panties."

"Mmm," he groaned, and I felt his smile as his lips pressed into my shoulder. His warm palm glided under my skirt and cupped my bare ass. "Let's take this off."

I momentarily lifted my arms, but Hale pressed them back into the glass once I was naked. It was like being strip searched by the sex police.

"God, you're sexy." He lifted my foot and removed my flip-flops then tossed the shoes aside. His hands traveled over my skin, leaving goose bumps in their wake as his mouth kissed every curve and dimple.

Soon enough I was shaking. He dropped low and licked over the swell of my ass, and I giggled, slightly ticklish there. I was a trembling mess and he hadn't even touched my private parts yet.

Parting my cheeks, he kissed the base of my spine and I grew self-conscious. Angling my hips forward, I pulled away. "What are you doing back there?"

"Just touching."

That's not an entrance! I heard the memory clear as a bell in my head and bit my lips so not to giggle again.

His fingers feathered to my front and he stood. "Turn around."

Lowering my arms, I slowly pivoted. He was still fully dressed in his tux, maximizing the authority he had over the situation. My breasts lifted with each breath as I waited for him to say something.

Stepping close, he removed the clips from my

hair and untied my bun. I flinched as the little accessories went pinging across the floor.

His fingers tunneled up the back of my neck, through my hair, and he jerked my head back just as his mouth crashed over mine. Fuse lit, I went at him like a possessed woman. My hands ripped off his jacket and tossed it aside as I fumbled with the buttons of his shirt.

He backed me to the cool window and I gasped. His fingers sought the heat between my legs and I moaned as his mouth trailed over my skin.

He wasn't gentle this time. This was very different from our previous encounters, as he wasted no time getting his fingers inside of me. One, then two, and soon he was stretching me with three.

Giving up on his shirt, I held onto his shoulders as he dropped to his knees and put his mouth where I needed it most. Gasping, my hands dragged along the glass as he devoured me. Trumpets played, doves were released, and I swear to God, a parade marched right through his great room. I was riding the Macy's float to Disney World.

Finding myself on the floor—*no clue how I got there*—I sighed as Hale rolled me to my back and lifted my leg. My eyes opened at the press of his erection and I stilled.

"Relax, baby."

Ah, there was that *baby* again. Leaning over me, he pulled my knee up to his chest and made slow dips, working his way in. While he was on his knees, I was in some sort of pretzel twist, so when he filled me, I felt it in my sinuses. "Jesus H. Christ."

His movements slowed as he ran a finger across

my nipple and stared down at me. "I love the way your body feels when I'm deep inside."

Yes. More talk like that. Catching my breath, I relaxed and he flexed his hips, pulling back and thrusting deep. "Oh God."

"Can you take it?"

I wanted to take it. I wanted to be better than all the others, but he was so damn big and—fuck it. "Yes."

He thrust and I gave a high-pitched sigh followed by another as he drilled into me. His hands came down, catching his weight on the hardwood floor as he moved my leg over his arm and caught my nipple between his lips. Holy hell was I going to be sore tomorrow, but right now I just wanted more. More. More. *More!*

Realizing I was begging out loud, I told myself I sounded like an idiot, but that didn't stop me. He folded my legs back until my knees were at my chest. Sounds came out of my mouth that shouldn't be flattering, but Hale just kept talking back. We fell into some sort of perverted ad-lib and I had no clue where these thoughts were coming from.

"You want more, baby?"

"Yes! I want your big cock. Give it to me! Harder!" Seriously, this was a side of myself I'd never met.

"Tell me how good it feels with me buried inside of you."

"So good! I love your cock. I want it all over me." Clearly, I wasn't choosing my words carefully because he gave a few more hard thrusts and then withdrew.

Pulling off the condom, he stood and lifted me to my knees. "Show me how much you love it."

My lips parted as I caught his hips and he entered my mouth. I was new and still a little unsteady on my knees, but I fucking loved seeing him so out of control, so I looked up at him with big eyes and he cursed.

"I love fucking that mouth of yours. Open wide for me, baby."

The hidden whore in me took control. I never heard a man make so many sexual sounds. Who knew I could do this to a person?

"Take it deep, baby. Deeper."

He pulled me forward and held. His shoulders shook, as he throbbed over my tongue. Warm heat slid down my throat and I swallowed like a pro.

He eased out of my mouth and took a staggering step back, his eyes almost haunted as he stared at me, panting.

Lowering my bottom to my heels, I folded my hands in my lap and waited for him to say something. He shook his head and took a slow step forward, his thumb swiping at the corner of my mouth and pressing it between my lips. I tasted him and bit my lip, a little unsure.

Maybe people felt shame after something like that. I probably should have, but the only thing I recognized right now was adrenaline. It was tunneling through me like a drug. And though I was tired, I would have done it all over again.

"Come with me," he whispered, holding out a hand.

He helped me stand on shaky legs and we walked through the house, leaving our clothes behind. He never let go of my hand as he led me up the stairs, and once we made it to what I assumed was his bedroom, he walked me to the far side and lifted me off my feet.

Holding me in his arms like some damsel in distress, he sat on the bed and kissed me. The way he held me so gently took my breath away. His kisses were tender and gentle. When he turned and laid me on the bed, I felt like a princess in some sort of fairytale.

The drugging way he used his mouth put me at ease. Could sex make a person feel those things or was this something else? I wasn't sure and I was too drained to figure it out at the moment.

He pulled the covers over us and tucked me in at his side. There was no other place I'd rather be.

"Rest, baby," he whispered and my eyes closed.

I drifted in and out of a dreamless sleep, each time I awoke in the strange room Hale was right there holding me, reminding me where I was. And good God, was he a resilient son of a bitch. I realized this when he poked me sometime around dawn.

"Whatcya doin'?" I slurred, into the pillow.

Warm lips pressed into my shoulder as I was turned onto my belly and my legs were spread apart as his lips teased along my spine. "Let me have you."

Half my brow creased. The other half wasn't awake yet. "Have whatever you want. Just let me sleep."

Kisses rained down my back as fingers brushed over my folds, making slow dips into my sex. I seriously wasn't moving. It was too early for this nonsense. I groaned as he pressed between my legs. "Wassa password?"

"I want your pretty pussy," he rasped, still trying to work his way in.

I gave a sleepy chuckle and drew my legs further apart, but that was all I could manage before the sun rose. I required a minimum of seven hours sleep to be functional.

Spreading my folds, he wedged himself in, and I gasped. He hoisted my hips off the bed and folded my knees under my body as he gently fucked me. Oddly, this woke me up. Who knew sex could be more tempting than sleep? At this rate, I might be able to give up coffee.

Nah, that was crazy talk.

He didn't take me with the animal lust he had the night before. This was a different sort of passion. With every slow pump of his hips, his body covered mine in a way that exposed something I wasn't sure I was ready to unearth.

His lips traced over my shoulders and he caressed my hips as he gently reached his climax. There were no orgasms for me because I was fresh out this morning. I needed a shower and some electrolytes before I got my jollies.

But the fact that I could give Hale some morning lovin' was nice. And it wasn't like I didn't benefit. The experience was sweet and intimate. I just didn't come. But knowing coming was possible made the pressure of always having to orgasm disappear. I had no doubt I'd be coming again soon, in any event.

I might be obsessing, but men climaxed so easily. Seriously, a stiff breeze and a smile and they were done—except for Hale. He actually had remarkable staying power.

But most women took finesse. I could finesse myself in times of need, but it was nothing like what Hale did to me. He raised the bar on orgasms. But more than raising the bar, he proved a man could deliver one to me. And we weren't just talking about clitoral stimulation either. The first time we had sex, he got the job done right.

"You're an excellent lover," I sighed, rolling to my side.

He returned to the bed and grinned. "Thank you."

"I mean it. None of my past...people... You know."

"Let's not talk about other men you've been with." He pulled me close so I was lying with my head on his shoulder.

I thought about last night, how he said someone betrayed him. The more we slept together, the more I wanted to know about his personal life. Maybe now was the time to discuss his trust issues.

"Who was she?"

He grunted. "It's no one you need to worry about."

"You won't tell me about her?"

"She's in my past. That's where I'd like to leave her."

"Did you love her?"

"No."

Hale's past seemed so much bigger than mine, like some giant, gaping abyss my mother would warn me away from. I didn't want to pry, but I was curious. I didn't think telling him about my three encounters would make him open up any sooner, so I let the subject rest for now.

After we showered, Hale called for a limo to pick us up. It was a true walk of shame back to the yacht, both of us wearing our wrinkled clothes from the night before. Eric, of course, was waiting on the sky deck, looking down at the docks the moment we made the trek back to our rooms.

Unable to take his judgmental stare, I played it off like nothing was out of the ordinary. "Hey, Eric."

Hale stepped inside, leaving us alone, and Eric narrowed his eyes. "Typically, when a co-worker wants you to cover their shift, they have the courtesy to ask."

I stilled, my instincts to snap back at him squelched as I actually considered that it had been his night off. "I'm sorry. I didn't plan on going any-where after the party."

He rolled his eyes. "Of course you didn't."

"Hey, I'm not a jerk like that. It was an over-sight. I said I was sorry."

Shaking his head, he scoffed. "Whatever."

As he walked away, I stared after him, dumb-founded. I was *sorry*. But maybe I shouldn't be. It was clear no matter what I did, in his eyes, it would always be the wrong thing. Shaking off my frustra-tion, I went to my room and decided to avoid my co-worker the rest of the day.

The moment I changed and freshened up, my phone buzzed with a text from Remington asking me to join him. I didn't want to face him, because it seemed everyone onboard knew exactly what I'd been doing over the past twelve hours, but he was very classy about everything. He asked how my night was and I told him it was fine. He didn't ask for any more details and I was grateful. The rest of breakfast unfolded as usual.

Remington misplaced a file and sent me to his room to find it, but I wasn't having any luck. As I rummaged through drawers and checked in cabinets, I wondered if this file actually existed, but he swore he'd left it in his room.

"What are you doing?"

I turned from searching under the bed and found Eric standing in the doorway. "I'm looking for something for Remington."

"Mr. Davenport doesn't like people rummaging through his things."

I sat up from my place on the floor. "Well, he asked me to look in here for a specific file."

He stepped further into the room and glanced at the papers on the table. "What's the name of the file?"

"I've got it covered." I didn't need his help.

"You have a lot of things covered lately."

Scowling, I asked, "What's that supposed to mean?"

He lazily lifted a shoulder. "Do you think you're the first woman Remington hired to fuck his son?"

My jaw unhinged as I stared up at him. My brain was still processing his words, so it took me a minute to think of a comeback. I probably could have come up with something better if I wasn't so damn shocked by what he'd just said, but I didn't understand any of this rivalry between us.

"Are you upset because he didn't want to fuck you?"

He laughed. "Hardly. But if I were you, I wouldn't get too comfortable in Hale's bed. Chances are before long you'll wind up right there, kneeling at his father's."

I should have stood up and charged him like Bobby Boucher, but his accusation hit me like cannon fire. Not only was I stunned someone would say such a thing to me, I was disgusted to think there had been women that might have done what he'd insinuated.

Son to father? No. I couldn't wrap my brain around it. I'd never look at Remington that way, but what if he did hire me to entertain Hale? Oh God, was I some sort of rich boy's toy?

As I knelt on the floor, Eric's smug mouth smirked. He'd gotten the better of me and that was exactly what he wanted.

It hurt, knowing a stranger could dislike me to such a degree when, if he knew me at all, he'd know I wasn't the type of woman to do anything like that.

"I'm sure you've got this covered then." He turned and walked away.

I sat there for a few minutes, feeling sorry for myself until my legs started to fall asleep. My motivation crashed and I wanted to hide, because let's face it, that's what I did when things got too real. Forgetting the file, I went back to the sky deck.

Remington looked up the second I reached the top step. "Did you find it?"

"No. I'm done for the day. You can call Eric if you need anything else."

"Hold on just a minute, Meyers. You're done when I say you are. What's gotten into you?"

No fucking way was I going to let that little ball washer of an assistant make me cry, especially in front of my boss. Gritting my teeth, I turned back to Remington.

"Why did you hire me?"

He rolled his eyes. "We've been over this."

And he never gave me a feasible reason. "Answer the question."

"Watch your tone."

Pressing my lips tight, I said, "Tell me why you wanted me to go to that party last night."

Maybe I was just a temporary fix, and that was why he started pushing my buttons about other men, knowing his son had a jealous streak. Was he trying to prove something to Hale?

He scowled. "Go take a nap, Meyers. You're out of line and I—"

"Am I here as some sort of entertainment?" I interrupted.

"What the hell are you talking about?"

"Oh, come on, Remington! I have no experience. I'm a clod in any sort of sophisticated setting. I don't fit the part. And I know absolutely nothing about what it is you do. The other two were more than qualified. Did Hale tell you to hire me?"

"I think you should lower your voice and take a walk until you calm down."

Pressure built in my chest. I couldn't hold back my tears much longer. If I was some sort of a pawn to these people when I trusted them... I felt utterly stupid and out of my league. "You think you can buy anything."

His gaze shifted over my shoulder and I sensed we were no longer alone. My eyes closed when I heard Hale ask, "What's going on?"

"The hell if I know," Remington snapped. "You try to talk some sense into her. You're done for the day, Meyers—because *I* said so."

I turned and Hale looked at me with concern. "Rayne?"

As he reached for me, I jerked back and snapped, "Don't touch me."

I made a quick escape to my room where I locked the door. I wanted to call Elle, but what Eric said was so mortifying I couldn't bring myself to repeat it.

There was a knock at the door. "Rayne. Open the door."

My arms crossed protectively over my stomach as it started to cramp. "Go away."

"You're being childish. Open the door so we can talk."

Fuck you, I wanted to shout, but I was too busy silently wiping my tears so I said nothing.

Every time he challenged me to give a bit more of myself I did. All the while I patiently waited until he was ready to open up to me. Well, this time was different. I couldn't bear the thought of discussing what was said upstairs. How would I ever stand to look at Eric again, knowing he's said such things to me?

Climbing onto the bed, I crawled to the headboard and wrapped my arms around my knees, covering my ears as Hale knocked again.

"Rayne, *please* open the door. I have no idea why you're upset." I heard his phone ring through the wall and he cursed. "I'll be back in a few minutes and we'll talk."

Saved by the bell.

He was gone for more than a few minutes. I rested on my side and shut my eyes. I wasn't sure if he knocked while I was sleeping, but when I woke up several hours later no one was around. I quietly opened my door and saw his room was empty.

Shutting the door, I dug through my bag for cookies and sat on the edge of the bed, shoving one after another into my mouth as I thought about what to do now. Humiliation had a way of paralyzing a person and for the life of me, I couldn't think of a single sensible solution.

Is that what they did, hire women, sleep with them, and then pass them off once they got bored?

I couldn't even imagine such twisted relationships, if that's even what you called something that fucked up. The thought of looking at any of them turned my stomach. It wasn't like I could just pack up and walk off. We were on a boat for Christ's sake. We had at least two days left at sea.

I wondered if we'd be making another stop. Pulling out my phone, I checked Remington's schedule. Seeing the calendar reminded me how short of a time I'd been involved with the Davenports.

The amount of emotion I'd invested didn't equate with our timeframe. The Davenports seemed to fit me like an old shoe, but really, I didn't fit here at all. Even my grasp of time was fucked up.

Unfortunately, Eric was in charge of the calendar, and everything was written in abbreviations I didn't understand. He probably did that on purpose to make me feel dumb.

I couldn't grasp why he hated me, but if what he said was true and I wasn't the first woman in this position, then I could sort of see why he didn't like me from the start.

I recalled the day Hale showed me the crew barracks and how he made some comment about Eric being used to the arrangements. God, were they even trying to hide it? Truthfully, Hale was so out of my league and so set on having me, an unqualified woman hired as an assistant, it made too much sense.

I *was* here for his entertainment. He'd recently been betrayed and I was his hired rebound. If he had been the one to pass my resume along, it made perfect sense that I'd be the one his father chose for the job.

I flopped back on the bed, shoving the cookies away. I had a couple days left and then there would be some distance between all of us. I'd talk to Remington and get some answers because this seemed so farfetched I didn't have a clue what the truth was.

Hale would go to his place in Florida, and I'd focus on my purpose—personal assistant. I'd prove I could do the job I applied for. Everything else had to stop.

If I didn't drown Eric in the meantime, I'd consider it a win. Not having manslaughter on my record was always a plus.

But if I remotely suspected any truth to what Eric said, I was done. Back to Oregon I'd go. If Eric lied...well...I really should tell Remington. But how could someone just make something like that up? One would have to be a true scumbag to even think up such a twisted scenario, which made it all the more plausible.

I'd wait and see what happened. That was all I could do. So why didn't I feel better now that I had a plan?

The few relationships I had, when I sensed they were over they were over. Having a plan usually helped, but in this case it made me sick to my stomach. I didn't want us to end and I didn't want to believe people I'd come to care about had manipulated me in any way.

This was why I didn't do serious. Serious scared me. I liked loose and easy. I should be happy this was nothing personal and I was just Hale's bedroom boat buddy or whatever the fuck my title was around here.

Something pinched in my chest as I momentarily placed myself in the meaningless column. It definitely hurt, because Hale had meant something to me.

If my position was really invented for something so tawdry, I'd never be able to face any of them again. Feeling betrayed was one thing, but the fact that Remington—a man I'd come to trust—would exploit me in such a way...it just hurt.

I never had a father and I knew Remington was

the farthest thing from my dad. But I'd looked at him as someone I could count on to look out for me. I must be such a joke in their eyes.

And Hale... How could he go on about betrayal if I wasn't even hired for honest reasons?

"Rayne?" There was a soft tap at the door.

Oh God, I couldn't do this. "Please go away, Hale."

The knob jiggled. "I'm not leaving until I see you." He waited another minute then said, "You can't stay in there forever. Please, open the door."

Fed up, I slid off the bed and unlocked the door, but positioned myself in front of it so he couldn't come in. "I just want to be alone."

His gaze moved over my face and he scowled. "You've been crying."

"No." That was a lie, but I was a big believer that there should be no crying in baseball or on boat trips.

His scowl turned to worry. "I don't understand what upset you. Did my father offend you?"

My brows twitched. It was hard to assign the blame to anyone in particular without all the facts. At the moment they were all involved.

"I don't want to talk about it. You saw me, now please leave me alone."

I shut the door, but he caught it with his palm. "No." Shouldering his way inside he stared at me. "That's not how this works. You don't get to just shut me out without telling me why."

"Oh really? Whose dumb rule is that?"

His eyes narrowed. "Is it something I did?"

"Just leave, Hale. I'm not talking about this." I turned and he caught my shoulders.

"I don't want to leave. I want to know what happened and why you're so upset. How you feel matters to me, Rayne."

"Does it?"

"Of course it does. Why won't you talk to me?"

His concern didn't fit the accusations that upset me. "Fine, but first, you answer my questions." I shifted out of his hold and took a step back. "Who was the last person to sleep in this room?"

His eyes moved to the bed and back to me. "I have no fucking idea."

"Who was your dad's last PA?"

"What? I don't know. He has a lot of assistants. There's Eric, Katherine, Jill, and a few interns here and there."

Wow. I suspected there were other women, but hearing their names made me want to vomit. "Did you sleep with those women?"

He drew back. "Are you kidding me? Jill's a child, and Katherine's my mother's age."

There had to be someone else. Eric wouldn't have just made up something so outlandish. People didn't do that. "How many women on your father's payroll have you slept with?"

"This is bullshit, Rayne. Whatever was before is over. I'm not getting into—"

"How many?"

His jaw clenched. "Three."

My eyes closed. Part of me held out hope that Eric was just a sociopath making groundless accusations, but Hale just admitted I wasn't the first. "Then we have nothing to talk about."

"Why? Because I've been with other women? You knew that."

The walls were literally closing in on me. I was stuck here, but I couldn't continue to work here. I needed to go home. I wanted my room and my things and to make all of these people disappear. I couldn't do this.

"When will we dock again?"

"When we reach Florida, the day after tomorrow. Why?"

I scanned my room. "You need to find someone else to help your father. I can't work for you people anymore."

"You people?" He caught my arm and I jerked back, but he held tight. "Stop. Enough. What the hell is this about, Rayne? You don't just take a job and walk away five days later."

He obviously didn't know me. "The job expectations aren't what I thought."

His expression turned wounded and he whispered, "I don't want you to leave."

"Someone will eventually take my place." The truth of my words sickened me.

"I'm not talking about the fucking job! I'm talking about us. How the hell do you just walk away? What about us?"

"Like I said, someone will eventually take my place."

Releasing my arm, he took a staggering step back. "I'm going to find out what happened. I'm not letting you just walk away without good reason."

I said nothing. Eric survived eleven years

working with the Davenports. He wasn't going to make a peep when Hale asked around. Of that I was certain.

I just needed to get to Florida and get home, so I could lick my wounds privately. "You do what you need to do."

Old Habits Die Hard

17

I woke up the following morning to a text from Remington demanding my presence on the sky deck. I didn't rush to meet him though.

Once I had myself dressed and somewhat ready for the day, I took a roundabout way to the top floor of the yacht, so not to cross paths with anyone, but when I stepped onto the sky deck the first person I saw was Eric. My steps faltered and I quickly dropped my gaze, waiting for Remington's direction.

"Leave us, Eric." The other assistant took the front steps to the deck below. "Have a seat, Meyers."

Keeping my mouth shut, I took my usual place across from him at the table.

"Hale tells me you no longer want the job."

I shook my head.

"I can't hear you."

"I think it would be best if you found someone else," I mumbled.

"I see." He eased back in his chair and casually

tapped his fingernail on the table. "I find myself in a strange position. As far as assistants go, you're passable. I'd have no trouble finding an eager replacement, yet I don't want to see you leave."

I'd only worked for the Davenports for a week, but it seemed so much longer. Walking away meant never seeing them again, because let's be realistic. Remington was busy, and I was no one. I was absolutely replaceable.

"Nothing to say?"

I shrugged. "I'm sorry."

He sighed. "You asked why I hired you. The truth is, no one else would have, Meyers. You showed up in street clothes, you answered every question wrong during the interview, and the competition was fierce. But I'm not used to being dependent on others, and while Pendleton was a tolerable kid, that other one would've got under my skin by the second day. I needed someone to put up with me and they had to be someone I could tolerate. My logic, Meyers, was that I liked you, so I took a chance."

Tightness twisted inside my chest. I liked him too, but... "You hired me as your *personal assistant*?"

"No, I hired you as a tax consultant. Christ, Meyers, you don't make it easy."

Lifting my face, I looked into his eyes. I needed to read his response as much as I needed to hear it. "Did my position have anything to do with Hale?"

His dark brows drew together. "Hale's a constant in my business, so I had him vet the resumes, but you're *my* employee."

Yesterday, when my emotions were running

high, and Eric had gotten the better of me, it seemed so reasonable that I was a part of some ploy. But now, looking at Remington and hearing how simple the whole situation was I felt like a total jackass.

"I'm sorry for the way I acted yesterday."

"I like you, Meyers, but I won't tolerate disrespect. You want to snap at people and have womanly mood swings, you can throw your fits somewhere else. Now, if something happened yesterday and you want to talk about it like a rational individual, I'd be happy to discuss it."

I just wanted to put the whole episode behind me. "No. I think I figured it out."

"Good. Now, do I need to have Hale pull out the resumes or are we stable?"

I wasn't sure where Hale and I stood or where I *wanted* to stand with him, but I wasn't ready to give up my job as Remington's assistant just yet. I did, however, want to apply every ounce of energy to making Eric obsolete.

"I'd like to continue working for you."

"Good. How's the party coming along?"

"The party's done. I have to pick up some things once we dock, but all the plans are confirmed and ready to go. If you want me to take on more, I can. I'm not afraid of a little work, Remington."

"Well, that's what I like to hear." He lifted a stack of folders. "These are portfolios sent over from various energy companies. Reading them is like watching paint dry. I need someone to go through each one, make a list of pros and cons, and have the basic details summarized by tomorrow. I was going to give it to Eric because he has experience—"

"I'll do it."

"You're sure? This isn't exciting work."

I nodded. "I'll start now." I took the pile of portfolios and stood. "Thanks for talking to me, Remington."

He nodded. "Send Eric back up here on your way down."

"Yes, sir."

I carried the files to the upper deck where Eric waited on the sofa. His eyes followed me as I dropped the heavy pile on the table.

"He wants you."

Eric stood and took a step toward the stairs, but I stepped in front of him.

"You were out of line yesterday. I don't know you, and I don't care to, but I will tell you a little something about me. I'm not here to compete with you. You're nothing to me. *Nothing*. But what you said not only insulted me, it insulted the Davenports, and they're people I care about."

I took a step closer to him and lowered my voice. "You're not one of them. Do you know what you are? You're an insecure, lying, little shit. But I got you by the balls, now, Eric. You and I both know if I breathe a word of what you said yesterday, your ass is done here."

I stepped back and smiled. "Have a nice day."

Looking somewhat like a poached armadillo, he took the stairs. I was glad to see I, too, could fuck up his day the way he'd fucked up mine. That would be the absolute last time I let him get the better of me.

Once I was alone, I dug into the portfolios. Remington wasn't kidding. This shit was like reading Japanese stereo instructions. Who knew there were so many energy options out there? Windmills, coal, solar, natural gas, each candidate made valid points, and every time I thought I found the best option, the next pitch proved me wrong.

I drew a chart and used some boat tool as a ruler to make it legible. Once I had that done, it was just a matter of plugging in all the details.

Just before lunch, I snuck into the galley and made myself a sandwich, which I took to the upper deck and ate as I continued working. I didn't see Hale all day, which was fine because I wasn't ready to face my confusing emotions.

I closed up shop around five and took everything inside. I was overdue for a phone call to Elle, and I desperately needed her judgment, because certain things were out of my wheelhouse.

"What a piece of shit," she said after I told her what Eric had done. "You should've told Remington."

"I didn't want to get into it."

"Are you going to tell Hale?" Elle asked.

"No. The truth is, he has a reputation of sleeping with employees. He doesn't like discussing his past and I honestly don't know if I could handle it."

"I get the feeling he's not going to let it go, Ray. The way you described it, he sounded pretty upset."

"Well..." And this was the part that made my

stomach hurt. "He can't get me to tell him anything if I'm just his dad's employee."

"Oh, no." Elle tsked. "Don't do this, Rayne."

It was happening. I couldn't help it. Shutting my eyes, I confessed, "It's just too much."

"No, this is just a little hiccup. If you talk it through, everything will work out."

For how long? "He has a past and I'm not sure he's left that behind."

"We all have a past, Ray."

"I don't want to compete with his."

The mere thought of how women went after him at parties overwhelmed me. Every gold digger out there would do anything they could to have a crack at the Davenports—any one of them. The competition was too fierce and intimidating for someone as inexperienced as myself.

"This was supposed to be a fun experience."

"And it still can be. Talk to him. If he cares about you, you'll work through this. Maybe he'll even knock out Eric."

Hale wasn't that sort of guy. I couldn't imagine his control slipping like that. And what if he didn't care? If anything, this whole debacle showed me that I was investing way too much into our connection.

Elle's voice turned quiet. "Rayne, honey, not every man is your father. Some guys can handle complications and not run scared. You have to give people the benefit of the doubt if you ever want to have a real relationship."

"I know not all men are my father, but... I don't know how to do this and the thought of rejection paralyzes me. I've had enough of that in my life."

"He's trying to get you to open up. It doesn't sound like he's planning on rejecting you."

"It's just too much for me. I can't handle both. I can either work for Remington or be with Hale. At least with Remington, I have the stability of a six-month contract."

She sighed. "Fine, but don't close out the possibility completely."

The door was already shut. "I'll keep you posted."

After my phone call with Elle, I changed into one of Seraphina's swimsuits and went to the main deck. Remington was napping, and there was an hour until dinner. I shut my eyes and floated in the pool, trying to take my mind off my worries.

"Make the reservation for seven o'clock on Friday."

My ears perked up as I heard Hale's voice. Rolling to my stomach, I swam to the edge of the pool and tucked my legs under the ledge where I was less noticeable.

"Something in the back. I want privacy."

Where was he? My eyes scanned the upper deck, but I didn't see him.

"Put her up in the Bell Monte. I don't want her crossing paths with anyone."

I finally tracked his voice to the side balcony. He was speaking on the phone, making arrangements to meet up with some woman.

This was exactly why I couldn't date him. It was just too much work and I was way out of my league. Plus, jealousy hurt. I wasn't used to it and I didn't like it taking up space in my heart.

I swam for a few more minutes then grabbed my towel and sat on the edge of the pool waiting for my suit to dry. The door opened and I took a steadying breath, anticipating Hale.

Realizing I couldn't avoid him forever, I turned. "Hey."

"Hey." He slowly approached, phone still in his hand as it hung by his hip. "Are you done for the day?"

I nodded.

"Rayne." He lowered himself to the bench seat that surrounded the pool. "Whatever I did, I'm sorry. I don't want to fight with you."

"We aren't fighting." My feet made slow circles in the placid surface. He touched my shoulder and I leaned away.

"You're acting different."

"I can't do this, Hale."

"What are you talking about?"

I couldn't bring myself to look at him, so I just stared at my feet. "I can't sleep with you anymore. It's not right. I work for your dad."

He was quiet for a long moment. "I know something happened to change your mind about us. I wish you would tell me what it was."

Telling him would only humiliate all of us and I just wanted to do the job I came here to do and leave all this drama behind. "It doesn't matter."

"It does to me." His fingers closed over mine and squeezed. "I like you, Rayne."

My eyes closed again, this time to fight the start of tears. I didn't open them until I was certain my emotions were under control.

"I don't want things to be weird between us. I'm not mad at you or anything, so hopefully we can still be friends."

His hand released mine. "No," he said quietly, refusing my wishes. "I don't want to just be your friend, Rayne. I want more than that."

"Hale—"

"I don't understand you. Everything was fine and now this? It's great you're not mad at me, but I'm mad at you." He stood. "I'll see you at dinner."

Tomorrow night he'd be having dinner with someone else, proving once more that I wasn't suited for the life he led. Letting whatever we had go, was really for the best.

Not Enough Alcohol in the World...

18

The last twenty-four hours aboard *The Lady Parr* were quiet. Hale acted like I was invisible, only offering polite head nods whenever our gazes accidentally crossed, and Eric avoided eye contact at all costs.

Rather than hide away in my room, I joined the crew for a game of Five Hundred Rummy in the Captain's quarters. Once the first game was over, I convinced them we should be playing Pass the Garbage and the mood picked up.

I didn't know if it was inappropriate to hang with the crew. Eric never did, but he was a social misfit as far as I was concerned. Waking up a little hung over didn't help matters, especially when the light of a thousand suns reflected off the coast of the Keys.

"Have a little too much fun last night?" Remington commented as he reviewed my notes from the day before.

I grumbled into my mug.

"I could hear you cackling from my room last night. Quite a set of lungs you have on you."

I cupped my forehead and sipped my coffee. "Sorry."

He turned a page. "This is good work, Meyers." He sat back, pushing the report aside and studied me.

I adjusted my sunglasses and picked at my toast. "Some say it's rude to stare, Remington."

"What's going on with you and Hale?"

I tossed my toast on the plate and dusted the buttery crumbs off my fingers—appetite gone. "Nothing."

"So you wouldn't object if I asked him to stay at the house with us?"

"It's your house."

"I've given the crew the night off. You should take some time for yourself. Explore the island."

Apparently, it was customary for Remington to treat the crew to a night at a hotel after a long voyage. Marta had told me that they were all staying at the Waldorf Astoria and venturing out for supper. We were expected to dock around noon and that gave everyone time to settle in while I accompanied the Davenports back to the main house.

Remington's home was on a private section of the beach toward the tip of the peninsula. He said it was one of his favorite homes because he could golf right off the patio and the balconies were so high he could piss on the tops of palm trees. When I asked Marta about it, she said it was stunning. I hadn't realized she was also his maid at home, but I was glad she'd still be with us.

"How far is Hale's house from yours?" I asked, certain no one but Remington was in earshot.

He gave me a sidelong glance. "It's a short walk down the beach. By car it takes about ten minutes."

"How is that?"

"Traffic. No one knows where the hell they're going. Half the population's on vacation. You'll see everything's faster on foot. You should invest in a bike."

I smiled. Bikes were big in Oregon. I was better on two wheels than four, so the idea appealed to me. "I might do that."

Sound traveled from below, and I sat up, sensing someone coming. Hale stepped onto the sky deck and gave his customary nod.

Right. I stood to take my leave. "I'm going to make sure I have everything packed." Remington nodded and Hale said nothing.

At the bottom of the stairs, I stopped and caught my breath. It was really difficult seeing him with this chill between us.

"I won't be around tonight," Hale said from above.

"I told you to avoid this mess."

"I'll handle it."

"Cut her a check and put it to rest."

"I said I'll handle it," Hale groused. "I'm leaving as soon as we dock. I won't be back until morning."

"I gave Rayne the night off." There was a momentary pause. "What the hell is going on with you two?"

"The hell if I know."

"Well, fix it. I don't like seeing her upset."

"I didn't do anything," Hale snapped.

"Clowns juggle. Davenports manage their shit. You need to get this cleaned up privately before you have a mess on your hands more than you already do. I told you to stay out of it months ago."

I frowned. Was I the mess?

"I can't do anything about Rayne until—"

"You should leave her alone until you know where you stand on other fronts."

Silence.

Someone muttered something, but the yacht horn blew and scared the shit out of me. Afraid they'd see me lingering, I rushed to my room to finish packing.

There was an envelope on my bed with my name scrolled on the front.

"What is this?" I muttered, examining it like a bomb. Slicing the flap open I pulled out a thick slip of paper.

"Holy fuck." Was this my paycheck?

I flipped it over, certain there'd been some mistake. Was he paying me for the whole six months? Wait, this wasn't a check.

I read over the calculations. It was a receipt. The money had been directly deposited in my bank account so it would already be available. Sweet! And it was for one week. This was like six times what I was making waiting tables. Oh, Momma was definitely getting some new shoes.

As I stuffed my clothes in plastic bags, I saw the harbor come into view. By the time I had everything upstairs we were docked. Remington and Eric waited on the main deck as Wyatt and the crew went over some details about the marina. I didn't see Hale.

Eric rode in the front of the limo with a man named Alfonse as Remington and I sat in the back. I should have been relieved to be off the boat, but I couldn't stop worrying when I would see Hale again.

"Is Hale really staying at the house?"

"No."

"So you just wanted to make me uncomfortable this morning?"

"You didn't seem uncomfortable," Remington replied. "Hale has his own business to manage. I think the space might do you good."

I looked at him as he stared out the window. Key West was alive and bright, yet I couldn't get in the mood to take it all in.

"You don't have to worry about me and Hale, Remington."

I wasn't sure if he was working toward warning me away or what, but I figured I should let him know there was nothing going on anymore.

"I'm not worried." Whatever the hell that meant.

REMINGTON'S HOUSE WAS ABSOLUTELY stunning. The ceilings were over eighteen feet high. The back patio rolled right into a pool that went to the edge of the property, dropping off in a waterfall cliff that overlooked the cerulean blue ocean. It was the prettiest sight I'd ever seen, even better than the ad for tequila that started my quest.

Two hours passed while situating Remington and having his belongings deposited into the right rooms. The house had an office, which was where Eric orbited.

I stuck by Remington's side, learning the layout of the home and helping him set up a workstation in the room that overlooked the beach. He made several phone calls and sent me to find lunch for him.

I was so impressed with everything I couldn't stop exploring and peeking in doors. After he ate, I took his plate to the kitchen and returned to his side.

"Why are you still here, Meyers?"

"I'm sorry?"

"Go out. I told you to take the night off."

"But it's only three o'clock." He shot me a look that said he wasn't in the mood to argue. "Okay."

I'd chosen a guest room on the first floor, away from the other bedrooms. It had a private entrance to the pool and was close to the kitchen. Since I didn't have much to unpack, I checked my bank account and Googled local shops once I saw the money had cleared.

After days at sea, the noise of the vacation town abraded my nerves. I jumped at the mere sound of cars going by and found myself anxious to get back to the house, but I forced myself to endure.

I Ubered my way to a little market that sold bohemian clothing and I took out my stress there. I was a little swipe happy with my debit card, but I was sick and tired of wearing black polo shirts, and my flip-flops were on their last mile. I needed something pretty to lift my spirits, so I bought a shit load of cheap sundresses.

When I returned to the house, I saw why they called this part of The Keys Sunset Island. The view was spectacular.

Marta invited me to a late dinner with her and her husband, Raoul. I debated going, because my earlier outing had left me feeling lonelier than entertained, but I couldn't see wasting a night off.

After showering and changing into one of my new dresses, I went to check on Remington. I knew it was my night off, but I couldn't just walk out without saying goodnight.

"Well, look at you," he smiled and put down whatever he was reading. "Very nice, Meyers."

"I'm meeting Marta and Raoul for dinner and drinks."

He nodded his approval. "Where?"

"Some place called Marcos?"

He waved a hand. "No, let me make a call."

I tried to stop him, being that it wasn't my dinner, and I was merely invited along, but he blew me off. He was on the phone making reservations within seconds.

When he hung up, I pursed my lips. "You didn't have to do that."

"Don't be ridiculous. This place is much better. How are you getting there?"

"Uber."

He scowled. "I'll have Eric take you."

This time, I did intervene, because I'd rather

walk over hot coals than ask anything of that fucker. "No, Remington. It's fine."

His gray eyes studied me for a pregnant minute. "All right."

I didn't trust how easily he conceded, but I accepted it all the same.

"You enjoy yourself. You know the gate codes?"

Yes, Dad, I almost said, but instead I nodded and patted my purse. "I have them in my phone. You're sure you're okay for the night?"

"Alfonse is here if I need anything."

"Okay."

I left and called Marta, who was spending the night at the hotel with the others. I explained that Remington insisted we eat at the restaurant he recommended instead of Marco's. She was a little concerned about the cost and I felt terrible for putting them in an uncomfortable situation. I had the idea to treat them until I saw the price of the appetizers. Holy hell, this place was crazy expensive.

Just as we were ordering our drinks, my phone buzzed. Normally I would have ignored it, but it was Remington.

"Sorry," I said, opening the text.

Order the shrimp. You'll love it.

I SMIRKED AND TUCKED MY PHONE AWAY.

Dinner was outstanding. The food was fresh and the breeze coming off the ocean was invigorating. Since I could only afford the shrimp appetizer and a salad, the alcohol was gaining on me. Did I not mention alcohol was always figured into the budget first?

A little over one margarita and I was laughing and talking in my drunken voice, but we were enjoying ourselves, and that was what mattered.

The waiter seemed to have forgotten about us, so I flagged him over. "Can we have the check please?"

He frowned. "It's been taken care of, ma'am."

"What do you mean?"

"Mr. Davenport handled everything. Can I get you another margarita?"

I stared blankly at him then muttered, "Sure."

When he left our table I turned back to Marta and Raoul, who also looked startled. "I swear to God I'm not sleeping with him," I blurted.

Marta muttered something in Spanish and Raoul laughed. "It's okay, *nena*. You are good to Mr. Davenport. One does not look a gift horse in the mouth."

"But really, I'm not sleeping with him. It's not like that."

Another round of drinks got delivered and then another, followed by a second glance at the menu when we decided dessert wasn't such a bad idea after all.

"Are you sure you're all right to get home? Maybe Raoul should call and have a driver come get you," Marta fussed.

"No, I'm fine." No one saw me stumble just then. "You two go back to your hotel and enjoy your night off." I pulled out my phone. "I'm calling for a ride now." It was a beautiful night and it wouldn't hurt me to wait on a bench for a few minutes.

"Okay then, *nena*. Be safe."

We parted on the sidewalk and I watched them walk off, hand in hand, and smiled. They were adorable, with their wrinkled smiles and pudgy butts. I wanted to be them when I grew up.

The street outside of the restaurant was bustling with tourists. I searched for a bench—"Well, well, well, what do we have here?"

A man to my right looked at me in question.

"Sorry. I was talking to myself."

Tucking away my phone, I took in the impressive Bell Monte hotel across the street, recognizing the name from the phone conversation I'd overheard. Was Hale in there—with his mystery date? My feet were suddenly moving.

Hardly paying attention to what I was doing, I found myself standing in the posh lobby of a hotel a few seconds later. Interesting. Where would one eat around here?

Trotting over to the front desk, I leaned sloppily on the cool marble counter. "'S'cuse me. Is there a restaurant here?"

The man pointed over my shoulder and I gave him an exaggerated wink.

"Thank you."

Time to check out the competition. Slinking around the large fern in the lobby, I scoped out the bar. No Hale. Taking a seat at one of the upholstered stools, I craned my neck toward the restaurant.

"Can I get you something?"

Turning to the bartender, I smiled, feeling quite the spy. "I'll take a…" *Keep it in the family.* "What's good that has tequila?"

"I have something for you."

I nodded, trusting his expertise. A moment later a beautiful concoction sat in front of me on a palm leaf coaster. I tasted it and gave him a thumbs up. "Delicious. Thank you."

He grinned and folded his elbows on the bar. "You from out of town?"

"Oregon."

He raised a brow. "I hear it's beautiful there."

We got to talking and I forgot I was supposed to be spying on Hale. The bartender was really nice. He kept bringing me drinks and kept me company in between his other customers. I wished Elle were here because I would have totally fixed her up with him.

"Are you single?" I asked, thinking Elle could at least check him out on Facebook.

He smiled. "Yup."

I gave a thumbs up and slid a little off my stool. "Oops! I'm okay."

"My shift's over in an hour."

"Oh, she lives far. We'll never make it in time."

He frowned. "How about a soda?"

"Sure." Grinning, I scanned the bar, which was emptying, and my mouth suddenly went numb. "Shit." I slouched low and cupped my face, like that would make me invisible.

Hale was standing on the other side of the lobby speaking to some blonde. I couldn't see much of her on account of the gigantic fern. Digging in my purse, I grabbed some cash and put it on the bar. "I have to go. Thanks."

"You're leaving? Can I get your number?"

As if in slow motion, Hale's head lifted and our gazes met. His brow lowered then he was walking toward me. Crap. I couldn't move.

"Hey," the bartender said, waiting for an answer, but Hale was now scowling and getting closer. "I didn't get your name."

Hale didn't stop until he was right in front of me. "What are you doing here?" he asked, not even pretending to be happy to see me.

"Having a drink?" It came out like more of a question.

He glared at my bartender friend. "How many? You're wasted."

"Two-leven." Yeah. That was a number. I shrugged. "I lost count at dinner with Marta and…" The blonde looked over and I started to sweat. "You're busy. I'll just go."

He caught my arm. "How are you getting home?"

"Uber."

"I'll have Eric come get you."

"No, I'm not getting in the car with that douchebag!" Okay, that came out a little harsher than intended. I pulled out my phone and tried to find the car service app. "See, I'm already calling for a ride. I'm fine."

He took the phone out of my hand. "I'm not

letting you get in the car with a stranger in your condition. I'll drive you."

The blonde was crossing the lobby. "You can't. You have company."

Hale turned, cursed, and left me there.

"Give me back my…" My words cut off as I fully saw the woman.

There was no mistaking, by the look in her eyes, that she and Hale had been naked together. But that wasn't what I was staring at. No. Her face was hard to notice because my attention was fused to her gigantic pregnant stomach.

"Oh, fuck."

And didn't that just make my life perfect. The woman touched his arm affectionately, and Hale made the slightest hand movement, apparently oblivious to the woman's baby belly. He was talking, but I didn't have a clue what he was saying, and then the pregnant woman brushed a kiss on his cheek and walked away.

When she disappeared into the elevators, I looked down, my heart heavy with the weight of too much reality.

He returned to my side and my face slowly lifted. I couldn't hide my shock.

Blinking at him, I whispered, "You're having a baby."

Too Much Information

19

Hale's jaw twitched as I waited for him to deny the accusation. He didn't.

"Oh my God," I muttered, suddenly feeling sick.

"Come with me," he said, taking my hand and towing me through the lobby and out of the hotel. I was in no state to make decisions so I let him pull me until I was tired of being pulled.

Once on the sidewalk, I yanked my hand out of his grip. "Wait a minute." I rubbed my temples. Everything was happening too fast and why had I had so much tequila? "That woman was pregnant."

His lips flattened, but finally he said, "Yes."

"You...you were with her. That's your ex."

"Yes."

"Did you know she was pregnant when you and I...?"

"Yes."

There was no hiding how wounded that made

me feel. "Why didn't you say something? Hale, that's your child."

"It's not that simple, Rayne."

"Because she cheated on you?"

"Because it's not that simple. Let me take you home and we'll talk about this later."

Knowing him, later might never come. I felt disgusting and evil. He was having a baby with another woman and I implanted myself in their drama.

"You should stay here with her."

"It's not like that."

I looked at him, confused and trying to reconcile the man in front of me with the dignified person I assumed he was. "But...how can you just walk away?"

My father had walked away, and the true impact of his abandonment didn't hit until I was a teenager, but when it did, it knocked me to my knees. There were so many moments I'd wished he'd been present. I didn't care if he was rich or poor or if he liked the same sort of things as me or not. He was my father and the only person who could ever claim that title. But he'd made it clear, after all of my unanswered letters and failed attempts to connect with him, that he didn't want me. Even now, that sort of rejection damaged me.

I hated that Hale might be doing that to someone else. "Give me my phone."

"I'll drive you home."

"No. Go back to your...*family* or whatever. I can't be involved in this."

"I wasn't staying here anyway, Rayne. For God's sake, let me take you home."

He'd never snapped at me before. I was drunk and confused and in no state to argue. If he truly wasn't staying at the hotel, it might be safer letting him give me a ride.

"Fine."

The drive was quick because I passed out. When Hale opened my door, I was disoriented and—

"This isn't home."

"This is my house."

I drew back as he held out a hand. "I'm not going in there."

"We need to talk, Rayne."

Did we? What was there left to say? He was having a baby with that woman and I'd slept with him. We already established that was a mistake, so this was really none of my business.

"Please take me home, Hale."

"I promise I'll take you home as soon as you hear me out."

Reluctantly, I got out of the car, but I didn't take his hand each time he offered it. The house was unfamiliar and strange, so I never quite found a comfortable place to rest once inside.

Sitting on the edge of a sofa, I stared at the coffee table. Hale handed me a bottle of water, which I gratefully accepted.

"Where were you tonight?" He sat on the chair adjacent to the sofa.

"I went to dinner with Marta and Raoul."

"At the Bell Monte?"

"No. Across the street."

"What were you doing at the hotel?"

"I thought we were talking about you," I deflected.

He let the inquisition drop. "The baby's not mine, Rayne."

My gaze lifted to his. "How do you know?"

"Because I know."

If this woman cheated on him, it made sense that the paternity was up for debate. I didn't know enough about parenthood or science to know if there was a way to determine the identity of the father during pregnancy.

"So why were you meeting with her?"

"She's telling people I'm the father."

I scoffed on his behalf. "Well, tell her to stop."

"I can't. I'm going to adopt the baby and she's going to sign over custody."

My head cocked as my breath held. I must have heard that wrong. "What?"

"It's a complicated situation, but this is the best solution."

"How is this the best solution, Hale? Where's the real dad?"

"He doesn't want it."

So let her take responsibility. "I'm sure there are plenty of people out there willing to adopt—"

"The paperwork's already drawn up. She's due at the end of the month and the baby will be mine."

I laughed, because once again, this clearly didn't concern me. "Do you know what you're having?" It was the stupidest thing I could ask, but what the hell else was I going to say? None of this made any sense.

"It's a girl."

"So you're going to be a father in less than twenty days?"

"Yes."

I glanced around his house, taking it in for the first time. Sharp marble corners and glass tabletops. "Are you ready to raise a child?"

"I'll figure it out."

He seemed so detached from the entire situation, so blasé, as if he were picking out floor tile. "Hale, a baby is a big responsibility. You're talking about an eighteen-year commitment. Minimum."

"I'm aware that there will be some sacrifices in my future, but I've made up my mind. Trust me that all the emotions have run their course and the decision was made months ago. I'm not rushing into this."

I scoffed. "Do you have a nursery set up? Have you decided where you'll live?"

"Those details are small."

"Were you planning to tell me?"

I mean, really. What if we continued sleeping together? Would we be fooling around to the sound of baby squalls and I'd mysteriously find rattles kicking about his place and milk stains on the pillows?

"This was the important conversation I was hoping to have, but first I had to meet with her one last time to finalize the last of the agreement. There have been some amendments."

This was so bizarre it was no wonder he'd been putting it off.

Holy crap. "Does Remington know?"

"He knows."

"Damn, you people sure keep your secrets." He

never even hinted at the idea of becoming a grandfather.

"I don't want this to change anything between us, Rayne."

I frowned, had he missed the last few days? "There is no *us*, Hale."

His eyes narrowed. "That's up for debate."

"Hale, you are having a *baby*. I think your plate's full."

"Do you not like children? You were going to be a teacher."

If this was some sort of scheme to find the next Davenport au pair, they hired the wrong girl. I didn't work with children because other people's kids made me nervous. I blew out a long breath. *Not the point!*

"My feelings on kids are irrelevant."

"It's very relevant to me."

Man, this must be what men felt like when they claimed women came with baggage. I couldn't even keep track of my own luggage. Maybe I was a man trapped in a woman's body because I wasn't experiencing any of the expected excitement girls likely felt when babies were mentioned. This just struck me as big, heavy baggage.

A baby majorly changed things. Hale already intimidated me, but now he scared the hell out of me. Babies were serious shit. Serious, crying, hungry, shitting shit. I was not ready for this.

"Okay. You've had, like, what, eight months to adjust to this? I'm drunk and not processing this real well. So how about you take me home and I'll see you around—*tomorrow.*" Damn it. That was supposed to sound more casual.

"I understand the timing isn't ideal."

He was freakishly calm, which made me seem all the more spastic. I waved a hand. "Hey, as long as you're ready."

If there was a secret passage way out of here I'd be using it. Where was a warp zone when you needed one?

"You don't want children," he said, his expression remorseful.

"Hale," I shook my head because this was just crazy. "I have nothing to do with your situation. Maybe one day I'll have children. I don't know. I'd have to find a husband first, and that's like number seven on my to-do list. This is *your* life. So long as you want children, my thoughts on the issue shouldn't matter."

He sat back, a look of intense consideration on his face as he rubbed his jaw. "Why did you say that about Eric?"

My brain shifted gears and—due to too much alcohol consumption—sort of fell off the track. "What?"

"When I suggested having him pick you up tonight."

Oh. That. I couldn't recall my exact words, but I knew they weren't flattering. "We share a mutual dislike for each other, but it's fine."

He studied me for a moment, and I sensed him letting go of the Eric conversation, but my intuition had never been that great. "Did he upset you the other night? Is that why you wouldn't talk to me?"

"It doesn't matter now—"

"What did he say to you?"

"Nothing. Jeez."

"Remember when we talked about lying. I can tell when you're hiding something, Rayne. Tell me what he said to you."

Nothing in his tone made me think he was bluffing. In a small voice, I said, "It doesn't matter. I handled it."

His shoulders slowly rose. "Did he come onto you?"

"God, no!"

"Then what?"

Shutting my eyes, I tried to figure out why I was even protecting that little shit. Perhaps sober I'd regret giving up my secret, but I was tired, Hale was having another man's baby, and none of this mattered anymore.

"He said your dad hired me to sleep with you."

Hale remained utterly still. "I'll take you home now."

Taken aback that he didn't deny the accusation, I gathered my purse and stood. The ride back to Remington's was made in silence. Hale didn't open my door when we reached the house, and as I unlocked the front door, he stared through me, hands tight on the wheel. Gone were the days of him watching me go.

Well, that nipped that in the bud...

Getting into bed was eventful. After stubbing my toe and eating the last of my cookies, I passed out upside down on the bed. I awoke in much the same position, but I think someone rammed a hatchet between my eyes. That was the only explanation for the excruciating pain in my head.

Stumbling into the bathroom, I showered and took twice as long to dress as I usually did. When I found my phone, I balked. It was eleven o'clock. But I had no texts from Remington. "Shit."

Feeling like I had taken advantage of his generosity, I went to find him. He was sitting on the patio by the pool speaking with Hale. Great. That guy again. Even sober, my brain couldn't fathom everything he'd confessed the night before.

He was adopting another man's baby from his ex. Yup. That was the gist. Still not computing.

Sliding the glass door open, I winced as the sun pierced the back of my skull. "Good...afternoon."

"I was about to send Marta in with a mirror to check if you were still breathing," Remington greeted.

Hale stood without saying a word and disappeared inside.

"You had an eventful night," Remington observed as I massaged my temples.

"The tequila's stronger here than the stuff I'm used to."

He slid the carafe forward. "Have some coffee." My mug was waiting.

Moving at a sloth's pace, I doctored up a cup and savored a few sips before speaking again. "Thank you for treating last night."

"Good employees and all that nonsense."

I started to laugh, but it hurt, so I just breathed.

"Well, Meyers, I find myself down to one assistant, so we have a lot to cover."

What was he rambling about? "Where's Eric?"

"Gone."

I frowned. "When will he be back?"

I didn't mind the work, but right now it felt like my skull was imploding. I wouldn't be much help until I had at least two more cups of coffee and something in my stomach to sop up all the alcohol.

"He's not coming back."

My face lifted and I winced as pain reverberated down my neck. "What?"

"After Hale had at him—I'm amazed you slept through that ruckus—I was caught up to speed and I let him go."

"You...you *fired* him?"

"What do you expect, Meyers? Not only did he insult my staff, he painted my family in an undigni-fied light. Rule number one of being a PA, never make the family look bad. That applies to *all* au-diences."

I was speechless.

"Drink your coffee."

Eric worked for Remington for over a decade. The fact that he could let him go so easily was a bit frightening. It sort of put my relationship with the Davenports in perspective.

I worked hard to hide my hangover because Eric's absence was a brutal reminder that this *was* work and Remington was my employer. If I didn't get my act together, I could wind up fired too.

When I finished my coffee, he refilled my cup. "You're not finished yet."

"I'm okay. We can get to work." I wanted to keep my job.

"Not yet." He folded his hands and eyed me. "Like I said, personal assistant rule number one is making sure your employer always appears in a flattering light."

"I know I had a little too much to drink last night, but it's not like I was handing out business cards."

"I'm not talking about that." He waved a hand. "Hale told me you saw Jasmine."

"Who?"

He arched a brow.

Oh, the pregnant chick. "Yes."

"It's important we handle this situation with care, Meyers."

"I really don't have anything to do with the situation, Remington. That's Hale's business and I have no intentions of airing his laundry."

"Good." He glanced toward the ocean. "As far as anyone else is concerned, the baby is Hale's and the mother's not involved. End of story."

I supposed the press would have a field day if they suspected any sort of scandal involving the Davenports. "What if the baby looks nothing like him?"

"She will." There was that god complex again.

I rolled my eyes. "How can you be so sure?"

He leveled me with those silver eyes. "Because the baby's mine."

Where is Archie Bunker When You Need Him?

20

My footsteps echoed over the marble as I marched to the office and flung open the door. *"It's your father's?"*

"I'll call you back." Hale hung up the phone and stood, shutting the office door. "He said he was going to have a talk with you about discretion."

Contrite, I covered my mouth. "Sorry." Then I hissed, *"Your fucking dad's the father?"*

He took my hands and led me to the settee. Once we were both seated, he let out a deep breath. "Yes."

I shook my head. "How does that even happen? I mean, how are you two still working together and why the hell isn't he taking responsibility?" I had a lot of questions.

Hale sighed, and for once I saw a flash of stress in his eyes. "Jasmine and I weren't serious."

"But you were sleeping together."

"We have a past, yes."

Ew. What was wrong with this family? "I don't

think I can look at your dad for a while." If ever again.

Hale held up a hand. "Understandable, but I need you to get over this as quickly as possible. We're past it and my anger's been resolved."

"Really? How is that, Hale? Because he did something..." Words failed me. "...to *his son's girl-friend* and something really not nice to *his son*. And now you're going to be a parent. In what universe does that deflate anger?"

"First, she's not my girlfriend. You're my girlfriend."

Stalker. "No, I'm not." Single people upgraded to girlfriend-boyfriend status. This man was so not single at the moment.

"We'll get to that. Second, I don't care who the father is. That baby is my family. I know what would have happened if Remington had had his say."

Oh. Too much reality. Now, I was starting to connect the dots.

The most upsetting part of all of this was the poor impression of Remington it was leaving. Why couldn't he just be a grumpy old billionaire? Damn men and their penises!

"My dad's old, Rayne. He just had a heart attack and took a spill. He is in no shape to raise a child. He was done having children twenty years ago. He would have paid her off to make it go away."

"So he just gets a pass?" That was bullshit. "What about the kid? What about when she asks about her dad and wants to know where the hell he is and why he didn't want her—"

"She'll have a father. Me. Look, I know this isn't an ideal situation, but it's what I've decided. I'm not changing my mind."

"You might. Then what?"

"I won't. I'm not someone who enters into any situation lightly."

This was crazy. "What about the mother? You're just going to force her out of the baby's life?"

"No one is being forced anywhere. She came to Remington to tell him about her predicament, knowing he'd send her to the nicest clinic, followed by an all-expense paid vacation as she recuperated. No one wanted this baby."

My heart broke as the words left his mouth. "Why?"

I couldn't help wondering if I was once that baby, unwanted, a consequence that could simply get washed away.

"Because it was conceived when Rachel was still alive."

Something ugly settled in my stomach and I couldn't escape the nausea it brought. "But your dad loved Rachel."

"Yes, very much."

"I don't understand any of this. Why would he cheat on a wife he loved?" He should have his tally-whacker cut off. "How can no one take responsibility for an innocent child?"

"I'm taking responsibility."

I hadn't realized I was crying until I looked up and my vision blurred. There were good men, shitty men, honorable men, and dishonest men, but I had never met a man willing to do what Hale was doing.

It was a lot, changing his entire life and future for a child that wasn't his and no one else wanted. "I don't know what to say."

"Just listen. I know this isn't what you expected, but I can't control the timing. I had to pay Jasmine off just so she'd keep the pregnancy. In two weeks my free time is going to be cut down by half. My dad isn't going to be able to depend on me to help him with personal care and I just beat up his male PA. Right now, I need you to go through these applications and pick three candidates for the job. If you could help me with that, I'd really appreciate it."

"You beat up Eric?"

He cocked his head and gave me a skeptical look. "Did you think I'd just stand there after someone insulted my girl?"

My chin trembled as I looked at him, wondering how it was this incredible guy actually liked *me* enough to literally fight for me.

Wiping my eyes, I muttered, "You make it really hard, Davenport."

"What do you mean?"

"I don't want to like you, but you say all these sweet things and beat up douchebags, and adopt orphaned children, and— *Gah!* Why can't you just be a normal asshole guy?"

He laughed and gave me a shoulder bump. "I can be an asshole. I'm sure you'll see that side of me eventually, but right now I'm trying really hard to impress you."

Sniffling, I chuckled. "Give me the damn resumes."

He stood and grabbed a pile of papers off his desk. "These are the most recent."

I sank a little under the weight of the pile. "Holy crap."

"We need to make sure they understand there will be some light...personal care involved until he gets his cast off."

"Okay."

"And Rayne?"

I turned back to face him, still shaken from the emotional rollercoaster I'd been on. "Yeah."

"Don't make plans tonight. I'm taking you out to dinner."

I smiled, a thousand girlie emotions cutting loose in my belly. No matter how I tried to avoid it, I was back on team Hale. Now, what did I know about babies?

AFTER I CHOSE A FEW CANDIDATES, Remington reviewed my selection. "Pendleton's on this list."

Though I had no choice but to talk to my boss, I kept my focus on other objects around the room. "Was there really anything wrong with Miles, Remington?"

He grunted. "Seems only fair you invite the other one back, too."

"Hale said it should be a guy."

Remington scoffed. "He's trying to punish me."

"Do you really want a woman like Cadence in

the same room with you when all your assets are exposed?"

"Point taken, Meyers. This list looks fine. Call them and see who can get here by tomorrow. Anyone who can't move that fast doesn't want the job."

I made the calls and was happy that Miles could make it. I felt really bad about out-performing him in the last interview.

Hale showed me how to set up an account with the airport so that each candidate could make his own arrangements at Remington's expense. I'm not going to lie, I felt super important making those calls and thought about investing in a clipboard. Possibly a woman's power suit.

Once my workday was done, I left Remington to Alfonse's care. Alfonse was the groundskeeper, but he did other things when needed.

I had a ten-minute mental debate as I eyed my razor in the shower. It was hot in Florida, so shaving was unavoidable, but there was a distinct difference between an everyday shave and a date shave. Was this a date? And was my pubic hair treading on retro territory?

I didn't want to look like I walked off the set of a seventies porn shoot. But on the other hand, beards were in. Maybe that implied other furry throwbacks.

Not having a clue, I reached out of the shower, grabbed my phone, and texted Elle.

Bush—hairy or bald?

HER RESPONSE CAME IMMEDIATELY.

> Ew! Always shaved! No guy
> wants to make out with a
> wookie!

I THREW MY PHONE ON A PILE OF TOWELS and got to work. Dear Lord, there was a lot of hair coming off. I mean, sweet Jesus, it was like thinning out the African Congo!

Mental note, buy a new razor.

"Well, that was exhausting," I muttered, stepping out of the steamy bathroom.

My phone was full of texts from Elle, questioning why I'd shave my vagina if I wasn't having sex anymore. Maybe I just liked to be up on my labial fashion.

I didn't have an answer because I still wasn't sure if this was a date or an olive branch or something in between. The whole Hale saga just got a thousand times more complicated and I hadn't figured anything out by the time I heard his voice in the house.

Giving up on my hair, I grabbed my purse and went to find him. Once again, I was underdressed. My steps staggered as I spotted Hale looking like Don Draper's sexier twin in a three-piece suit.

"You're dressed up."

He smiled and walked over to me. "You look beautiful. Is that a new dress?"

Yes, and I paid twelve dollars for it. "I look like a hippie and you look like a Rockefeller."

"I think you look perfect."

Frowning, I mentally skimmed over my new wardrobe. "I have a different dress..." It wasn't formal, but it was darker.

Hale chuckled. "What you're wearing is fine. If you're worried—" He took off his jacket and vest and folded them over the banister. "There. Now, no one's overdressed."

I smiled. It was the simplest solution and very considerate of him. "Thanks."

He took my hand and walked me to the door. I hesitated. Remington was watching television and I felt like I should ask if he needed anything before we left, though I was still avoiding him.

"He's fine. Come on."

Hale opened my door and I fidgeted as I waited for him to get in the car. He smelled really good and I wanted to rub up against him, but I wasn't sure if that was proper.

When he started the car I blurted, "Is this a date?"

He grinned and backed out of the driveway. "This is a date."

"Oh. Okay." Now that we had that cleared up I felt better. "Where are we going?"

"Louie's."

"Who's Louie?"

"Louie's is a restaurant, not a person."

"Oh. Well, I'm sure they named it after someone."

His fingers caught mine as his thumb rubbed over my knuckles. "You seem nervous. It's just us."

Right. But I wasn't sure if this was the *us* who had wild monkey sex or the *us* who sometimes worked together or the *us* who avoided casual conversations about secret illegitimate children.

"I know. I'm just a little...you know."

He laughed. "A little what?"

"I don't know. I have the sex jitters. But maybe we aren't having sex and I just have gas. Oh, God. Never mind. Pretend I didn't just say that—where are you going?"

He turned the car around right in the middle of traffic and doubled his speed. "My place."

"What about dinner? Slow down!"

"We'll go there after." He tapped the wheel as he anxiously waited for the traffic light to turn green.

"After what?"

"Sex." The light changed and he turned, speeding in the direction of his house.

He tore into his driveway and threw the car into park. Before I even had time to unearth my death grip from the dashboard he was on me, unbuckling my seatbelt and sending my seat into a reclined position.

I laughed against his mouth as his hand went up my dress and dipped into the front of my panties.

"Hale! We're in a car!"

"I don't care. I've been dying to touch you for days."

My body rapidly responded the second he grazed my clit. I moaned and pulled him over me, but the stupid cup holder was in the way. His fingers delved between my thighs and I arched. The clank of his belt buckle rattled against the wood interior as he caught my hand and brought it to his body.

Heated, hard flesh filled my grip as he thrust into my palm and sighed into my mouth. "God, Rayne...I was so afraid I was losing you."

His lips worked over my shoulder as my dress was pushed to my waist. My bra came down and his warm mouth closed over my nipple. Dear Lord, I missed this! His fingers and mouth were relentless and soon I was coming right on his Rolls Royce leather seats.

Sending his seat back, he pulled out a condom and rolled it over his length. I giggled, because he must have literally had one up his sleeve, it appeared so fast.

Catching me by the ribs, he hauled me to his lap and the horn blew. "Shit." He pulled the seat back some more and my knees fit beside his hips.

"I've never had sex this way," I warned.

"In a car?"

"That too."

Leaning forward, he cupped the back of my head and drew me in for a kiss as he lined his body up with mine. "You have no idea how much I missed you."

As he pressed upward, I caught my breath and rasped, "I missed you too." He filled my body and I sighed with pleasure.

But it wasn't just the sex I missed. I missed our closeness. I missed making him crack a smile and the special moments I actually got him to laugh. I missed hearing his voice and the way he looked in my eyes. But most of all I missed that important way he made me feel. To Hale, I mattered, and that meant something I hadn't yet defined.

"It's not just the incredible sex," he murmured, echoing my thoughts. "It's like you're my clarity, my peace of mind. I know that's crazy because we only just met, but when you're gone I feel like part of my world is missing."

I sort of felt the same, but different. Hale was so monumental to my every thought, our relationship scared the shit out of me on a regular basis. But I was working on my issues and trying to get past my bullshit. The sex was definitely helping.

My hands caught his shoulders as I sank lower. Jesus, he was deep. If I opened my mouth wide enough, he might see the top of his penis.

"Is this okay?"

I nodded, my skin beading with sweat. "Yeah, just really, really... in there."

He chuckled. "Just the way I like it."

His hand cupped my ass as his other one held my neck, and he stared into my eyes, slowly guiding me over him. Our breath mingled as he penetrated even deeper. This was a very intimate position, one that couldn't be rushed.

He kissed me slowly, softly, and I wondered how I'd ever given up such tenderness. The more I considered all the feelings trapped inside, the more they wanted to get out. My body shook as he struck a nerve and we came together in every sense of the word.

Panting, holding each other through our damp clothes, we stared and smiled. I was falling in lo—

Wait. No. Scratch that thought. Way too soon.

I wasn't in love with him. I couldn't be. He was having a baby and we met a little over a week ago. But as I looked into his eyes, I knew this was more than a heavy *like*. There had to be a word for that. I desperately wanted to know if he felt the same.

His lips found mine as he pulled me close and held me tight. This man beat someone up for me. That was crazy. Shit like that didn't happen. I wasn't a fan of violence, but I also wasn't a fan of douchebags that made women cry. Part of me was pissed I'd missed it.

The things that Hale made me feel came without names and were so far away from my usual vocabulary I had no way of defining them. He made me happy, abundantly happy. In his eyes I was desirable. He got my humor and didn't care when I wore flip-flops with ball gowns. He'd taken off his suit jacket and vest so I wouldn't feel underdressed. That was some sexy ass, suave shit right there. And he saved a baby. He was literally reorganizing his life just so that little girl could have one, with a dad.

Yes, there was a very heavy *like* filling my heart, maybe something remarkably close to love.

Since When am I Prepared?

21

Hello, my name is Rayne Meyers, and I really like sex. Really. Dr. Seuss could have written smutty poetry about me. I did it on a boat and by a moat. I did it in a car and on a bar. I did it on the floor and by a door. I did it here and there. I did it *everywhere!*

Of course, these stories would not be for the children, but the other deviants of the world would appreciate them.

Exhausted, and running on about two hours sleep, I rummaged through Hale's fridge. "You have *nothing.*"

"We got here two days ago and I've been busy. I'll go to the store today."

I sent him a skeptical glance. "You do your own grocery shopping? And where did you get that apple?"

He smirked and took a big bite of the Granny Smith. "*Marduh dussit.*"

I snorted. "Marta does it? You're a grown man.

Get a bonus card and do your own shopping." I grabbed my left over linguini from last night's dinner and popped open the takeout box.

"It's seven in the morning. How are you eating that?" He made a disgusted face. "It's not even warm."

I popped a shrimp in my mouth. "Still good. You have to take me home. I need coffee and you don't have creamer."

As I tried to slip past him he caught my arm and pulled me into a kiss then grimaced. "Never mind. I can't do shrimp kisses this early in the morning."

I swatted his shoulder and licked his cheek. "Now it's on you. Take me home. I have interviews today."

As we drove the whole two blocks to his dad's I grinned. "Did you hurt Eric?"

Hale kept his eyes on the road. "I made my point."

I turned my cheek on the leather upholstery and continued to grin at him. "No one's ever gotten in a fight defending my honor."

Glancing to his right, he smirked. "I'll always defend your honor."

I sighed, because what girl wouldn't? "You're going to be a good dad, Hale."

His face slightly paled. "Thanks."

"But maybe pick up a parenting book and some baby paraphernalia. The end of the month is going to be here before you know it. You're a little un-prepared."

He pulled at his collar. "I'll figure it out."

I truly hoped he realized a baby wasn't a situation one could throw money at and walk away from. This was a person and people came with needs and feelings, even the little ones. Aside from his overwhelming commitment to do the right thing, he had nothing prepared.

Why did men always wait until the last possible minute to organize? Another quality I usually had in common with the opposite sex. It was a wonder we ever accomplished anything in this world. I didn't want to stress him out, so I let it go. But if I didn't see any baby stuff soon, I was bringing it up again.

The interviews went well. Remington practiced his same old tricks, asking me to remove the legs of the sofa so the candidate sat with their knees up to their chests and having me put one glass of water next to the pitcher to see who took it first.

"How is he?" Miles whispered, when he was sent to what Remington called the isolation booth —it was the back patio, where a chair sat in direct sun. The old coot sure liked to have his fun.

I was still in denial about Remington's part in Hale's situation, so I pretended those secrets didn't exist. "He's great. Ornery, short-tempered, egotistical, but really a marshmallow on the inside." Okay, fine. I wasn't ready to dislike the man so I selfishly convinced myself his misdeeds were oversights and he was genuinely sorry for putting his penis where it didn't belong.

"He sure seems to like you," Miles commented.

I smiled. We did have a special sort of bond. "I think he's partial to women. I don't put up with his crap, but I fluff his pillows so it's a give and take."

He brushed his sleeve over his brow. "Do you think I'll have to wait out here much longer? It's a hundred degrees in the sun."

"*Meyers!*" Remington yelled from the den.

I hitched a thumb over my shoulder. "That's my cue. I'll see if I can move things along for you."

Bustling into the den, I rolled my eyes. "He's melting out there, Remington."

He didn't appear concerned. "I dropped the damn remote."

Dipping to my knees, I reached under the sofa and handed it to him. "Are you done with the interviews?"

"I already sent the other two back to the airport with Alfonse. Tell your friend he has the job."

I frowned at his disinterested, clipped tone. "Are you okay?"

"I'm fine." He didn't seem fine.

"Can I get you anything? Is your foot hurting?"

"For the love of God, Meyers, I said I'm fine. Go show Pendleton around and let me rest."

Snapping my mouth shut, I just blinked at him and turned to give Miles the news. He was thrilled and a bit nervous I could tell, but once I introduced him to the staff and showed him where they kept the good snacks, he relaxed.

I found Remington in his room a while later, struggling to get into his bed. Rushing to his side, I snapped, "What are you doing? You should have called someone to help."

"Everyone's busy."

I lowered him to the bed and adjusted his pillows. "You're cranky today."

He grumbled something under his breath.

"Is there anything you want me to work on while you rest?"

"No, but don't go far. Wake me up before five."

"Yes, sir."

He sighed and shut his eyes, his face tight with a grimace.

"You sure you don't want a pain pill—"

"Meyers."

"Okay. Just checking." I let myself out and shut the door. Then I went to find Hale.

Finding him in the office, I smiled and slipped inside. Hale was on the phone, but he waved me over. Hopping onto the desk, I swung my legs and waited for him to finish his call.

"Right," he said, face serious. "No, you'll want to go with the first option." His palm caught my knee, stilling my legs. "Read it to me."

His hand slid up my thigh, parting my legs and disappearing under my dress. Angling the phone between his shoulder and his ear, he held a finger to his mouth telling me to be quiet as the hand under my dress slid my panties aside.

Oh, this was naughty. His fingers brushed over my folds, teasing and softly petting. Last night, when he saw how I'd shaved myself bare, he went nuts. It looked like I was going to have to join one of those razor of the month clubs.

"Stop there. Write back and tell him we'll cut it down to a three percent annual increase, but that's as low as we go. He won't find anything lower on the market."

I smirked. Hale the negotiator was sexy.

He lifted his chin toward my chest and I lifted a hand to the buttons in question. He nodded so I slipped one through the little hole. He angled his chin again and I did another, teasing him.

His finger slipped inside of me and I gasped, arching back on the desk. That earned him another button. He slowly fingered me as he used fancy terms like escrow and yield and power of attorney. It was all very Ally McBeal.

When my lips parted and my breathing accelerated, his gaze turned heavy and he silently mouthed, *fucking hot.*

Rising over me, he slowly licked the tip of my nipple, making comments on the phone whenever required. He was quite the multitasker. When he pinched the tip of my nipple I gasped and he smirked.

"Sounds good. I'll be in touch." He practically threw the phone as he grabbed for me, yanking my bottom to the edge of the desk. His mouth crashed over mine and he growled, "Do you have any idea how fucking sexy you are?"

I giggled. "No, but you should keep telling me."

He growled again and worked his hand back under my dress. My knees slid apart as he pressed his fingers deep inside of me. "I want you to come all over my fingers so I can smell you on my skin for the rest of the day."

"Okay," I gasped, as he pressed deeper. I shut my eyes and moaned as his fingers hooked inside of me and tapped on a sensitive spot.

"Shh, not too loud."

His hand moved quickly as his other palm applied pressure to the lowest part of my abdomen and suddenly I was soaking wet and gasping. He teased my folds and I jerked with a shiver, everything was so sensitive.

Leaning over he kissed me softly. "Beautiful. You turn me on to no end."

"It's fun being able to fool around at work."

He glanced at me from under his lashes and smirked. "I love having you close enough to fuck at a moment's notice."

I drew in a deep breath, as his little comment doubled my arousal. "Did you want to?" The idea of him bending me over that desk was incredibly erotic.

He brushed his mouth over mine and bit my lower lip. "You have no idea how badly I want to, but my schedule's nuts today."

He slid my panties back into place and lowered my dress to my knees. Helping me sit up, he laughed.

If I looked as drunk as I felt it was probably quite the sight. I never knew sex could have the same effect as vodka, but I was becoming a raging sexaholic.

"How did the interviews go?"

I buttoned my dress. "Good. We hired Miles."

"Miles?"

"The guy who interviewed with me before. He was nice and I felt bad beating him out of the job."

Brushing my hands away, he closed the last button. "You're fond of him."

Using my caveman voice I said, "Hale no like

when Rayne has male friends. Hale needs to get with times."

He caught my chin and bit my lip again. "Rayne is smart ass."

I grinned and gave his mouth a lick. "Miles is cool, but I don't really know him."

"Well, I'm glad you found someone you can work with."

"I can work with anyone."

He held up his hands impassively. "I wasn't saying you couldn't."

"Okay. Just so we're clear. I'm not the one that made the last assistant leave."

He rolled his eyes. "We could have left him in Georgia if you'd confided in me sooner."

Snapping my fingers, I tsked. "You're right. How foolish. I don't know why I avoid situations I'm not emotionally equipped to handle. Avoidance is so passé. By the way, did you buy that bassinet yet?"

He laughed. "What's a bassinet?"

I just gaped at him. "Seriously, get a baby book. It doesn't even have to be new. Take one out from the library for the day. Please."

He glanced at his watch and grimaced. "I have a conference call in a few minutes."

"Yeah, I have to update my Linkedin account. So many new job skills to report this week. Office orgasms. Car sex. My qualifications are mounting up." When he didn't laugh, I saw he wasn't listening. "Hale?"

"Hmm?"

"You okay?"

"Yeah. I gotta make that call."

And that was my cue to leave. Maybe tonight I could have a serious conversation with him about the baby. He'd made up his mind, but every time I talked about normal things babies required, he deflected the conversation to something else.

It wasn't my place, but it wasn't like Remington was offering much advice. I wasn't even sure if Hale's brother and sister knew what was going on or how much they knew of the true situation. All things I should probably find out.

With thirty minutes to spare, I snuck away to call Elle. She'd been blowing up my phone since the big shave inquiry. I caught her up to speed on my latest sex-a-thon and then dropped the bomb about Hale's life, leaving out the scandalous secrets involving Remington's paternity.

"Uh-uh. No way. Baby drama comes with momma drama. Get out of there, Rayne."

"I don't think the mom's going to be an issue. She's literally uninvolved. She's only in town because Hale wants to be there when the baby's born and it could be any day now."

"And what exactly are you going to do when he's tied down with a kid?" Elle asked. "There goes the sex."

"That's not true. Babies sleep."

"Have you looked at mothers lately? I'm not talking about the ones on tampon commercials. I mean real women with kids. You see it in their eyes. There's an anger banked there that hisses and lets the world know if a penis comes within grabbing distance they're ripping it *right off!*"

"Well, maybe they look like that because they recently gave birth. I mean, no woman would enjoy that." Hale's situation was different.

Elle sighed. "I think that look in their eyes is sheer exhaustion. Remember my friend Val, the one who got married and had all those kids?"

"Yeah."

"Look her up on Facebook. You'll see what I'm talking about."

I rolled my eyes. "We're way off topic, and you're supposed to be reassuring me, not terrifying the crap out of me."

I mean really, if I wanted this sort of feedback I would have called Tyler, which I needed to do soon.

"I don't understand how you're even remotely entertaining this idea. Babies equal commitment. You don't commit."

"I commit."

Elle scoffed. "You can't even commit to one flavor of ice cream. You always buy at least two pints at a time."

"That's just good sense. If I drove to the store every time I wanted Ben and Jerry's do you know the damage I'd be doing to the environment?" But she had a point. "Look, I know what babies mean, but it's not my baby. I just want to do stuff with daddy. Wait, that sounded dirty and not in a good way. My relationship is with Hale. Period. The baby's just a relative."

"I don't know, Ray. First you'll be all, *Oh, can I hold it.* Then he'll be like, *Could you take the baby for a minute?* Next thing you know, he's running out for a pack of smokes, and you're barefoot with another woman's baby in your arms."

"You have way too many clichés in that scenario and none of that is going to happen. First, babies are loud and sticky. Pass. Second, they cost money. Pass. Third, this is not my kid. I'm absolved of all parental responsibility."

Of course, if he wanted someone to help him ready the nursery that might be fun, but that was it. I drew the line there. Maybe an outfit or two. No. No clothes. Not my kid. Not my circus.

I glanced at the clock. "Shit. I have to go. I was supposed to wake up my boss ten minutes ago."

"Don't look at the baby. Its cuteness will suck you in!" she shouted, and I hung up the phone.

22

Guilt was an utterly useless emotion, but man could it bind a girl up. Remington had been in a shitty mood for days. He claimed it wasn't his foot, and I believed that was half true, but something crawled up his ass.

Miles was likely rethinking his enthusiasm about the job because Remington snapped at him more than anyone. But no one was immune. Even Hale took his licks here and there.

Joining my boss on the veranda—he'd been purposely moved out there so the staff didn't have to hear him—I shuffled a deck of cards and straddled the lounge chair next to his.

"So…" I dealt out a hand of Solitaire. "You want to tell me why you've been in a mood?"

"Do I look like someone who enjoys daytime television, Meyers?"

I shrugged. "You might DVR *The View* and watch it in secret."

He grumbled, "Men don't discuss feelings."

Rolling my eyes, I moved the five of hearts and said, "They can get away with that if they hide them. You're waving yours around like you just don't care."

"Jesus, Meyers, move the damn nine of clubs. It's right in front of you."

I moved the nine. "Seraphina's coming tomorrow. That should make you happy."

He nodded. "The Jack of clubs."

I was basically playing for him at this point. "We picked up everything for the party and *The Lady Parr's* been cleaned from top to bottom."

"Good." He pointed. "Stack your piles."

"Are you happy with Miles?"

"He's fine. I'll be happy when I get this damn cast off. You're terrible at Solitaire. The four, Meyers."

I moved the four. "A few more weeks and you'll be a free man. We'll have to pin a bell to your clothes so we don't lose you. I'm not used to you getting around quickly."

"I can't stand being limited. It's against my nature."

If Remington were a wild animal, he'd be the sort that chewed off its own leg when in jeopardy. "I made dinner arrangements for you and your kids at Le Blue tomorrow night."

"Is Barrett bringing anyone?"

"No. Hale said Barrett's coming alone because there's a party with Seraphina's friends." The way Hale spoke of his brother, I got the impression he was a bit of a womanizer.

"Make sure the reservation's for five."

I cleaned up the cards and stacked them in my palm. "That early?"

"Five people, not five o'clock."

I arched a brow. "Are you bringing a date?"

"No. I want you there."

My shoulders tensed. "Remington, I don't think—"

"I didn't ask your opinion, I asked you to make the reservation."

"But this is the first time your family's been together in months. I don't want to intrude on your time with your kids."

He eyed me for a long moment then grumbled, "Make the reservation, Meyers."

After I finished up my tasks for the day, I took a walk down the beach to Hale's. It had been days and he'd done nothing as far as baby preparations. This wasn't my problem, but some deep-seated responsible side of my personality insisted I light a fuse under his ass.

As I climbed the steps to his back deck, my phone buzzed with a text from him asking what I was doing. I texted back.

I'm stalking you.

STANDING AT THE BACK WINDOW, I watched him check his phone, and I tapped on the glass. He looked up and laughed.

Opening the door, he greeted me with a kiss. "Stalker."

"It's what I do." I glanced around to make sure he was alone. "Are you doing anything?"

"I'm done for the day. Did you want to grab dinner?"

"I actually did want to go out. I need to go to the store. Will you take me?"

"Sure. Let me grab my keys."

I'd Googled a small baby boutique about ten miles away and gave Hale directions as he drove. When we arrived at our destination, he gripped the wheel and stared at the sign.

"What is this place?"

"This is a baby store. You need to start preparing, Hale."

He glanced at me, as if I were suggesting he drive off a cliff. "You're okay with this?"

"Shopping? Sure. Come on." It wasn't my baby. For some reason, I kept repeating that in my head.

When we approached the store, I could swear Hale's pace slowed by half. I had to literally take his hand and pull him inside.

Everything was soft shades of pastel and smelled like love. My uterus might have sighed.

"Oh my God." I moved to the display of plush stuffed animals. "Look at this sheep. You need this sheep."

Hale approached slowly as if I held a live tarantula. He frowned at the little plush toy. "It's a sheep."

"The baby needs this sheep, Hale."

He nodded and took the stuffed animal from me, holding it like a hot casserole. I moved toward the showroom where multiple cribs were dressed in ruffled sets with lavish mobiles suspended overhead.

"Do you have a nursery theme in mind?"

He trailed along, sheep in hand, a pallid expression on his face. "A theme?"

"Like an idea how you want to decorate the baby's room."

"It's a girl," he said as if this were all the necessary information needed.

I laughed. "I know it's a girl, but what sort of girl do you think she'll be? Will she be a princess?" I moved to the canopy crib that looked like Cinderella's carriage. "Or maybe she'll be adventurous like her dad." I pointed to a Swiss Family Robinson sort of set.

Hale hooked a finger in his collar and gave it a tug. "Maybe something neutral."

"Okay." There was a simple white crib in the corner. "How about this?"

"That won't fit in my car."

"They have delivery." I frowned at him. "Do you need to sit down?"

He glanced at the row of upholstered rocking chairs and shuffled toward them, dropping into the first of the line.

I crouched in front of him and whispered, "Hey. I'm sorry for springing this on you. I was just trying to help."

He caught my hand and squeezed so tight, it startled me. His silver eyes were stark against his pale coloring and he hadn't blinked in a while.

I cupped his cheek with my free hand. "We can go if this is too much."

He swallowed, his Adams apple shifting under the shadow of his throat. "No. You're right. I need this stuff. I just..." He exhaled and shook his head slowly. "I don't like being unprepared."

That was a step in the right direction—not that I was an expert on preparedness. My methods would get me killed in the wilderness because I never had a plan, but Hale was different. He was capable of anything. It was just his personality. I didn't see why this should be an exception.

This whole baby thing was likely his first experience with procrastination, going by his usual behavior. Everyone had a right to stage fright once in a while, but if he prepped a little, he might feel more in control. It was my guess that his lack of control was the true stressor here.

I smiled. This could actually be fun. "Do you want me to help you do this?"

His hand tightened around mine. "Yes."

"Okay. You wait here. I'll be right back."

Reluctantly, he let go of my fingers, and I went to the front of the store where a young woman stood. She wore an apron with a giraffe on the front.

"Do you work here?" I didn't think anyone else would rock a giraffe apron in public, but you never knew.

"Yes. Can I help you?"

"Is there some sort of baby checklist to help new parents?"

The woman nodded and produced a slip of paper from her apron pocket. "The list is organized by department and there's a map of the store on the back to help you find everything."

"Perfect. Thanks."

"Do you need a cart?"

I eyed the carts and wondered if two would be enough. This was a long ass list for a person the size of a pineapple. "Thanks."

I found Hale exactly where I left him, sitting on the rocking chair holding his sheep. "I got a list."

He stared at me like I was a stranger, then asked the question of all questions, "Am I making a mistake?"

My smile faltered. Abandoning the cart, I sat on the chair next to his. This was a serious question and it deserved all of my attention. "I can't answer that, Hale."

His brow creased as he looked down at the sheep in his hands. "Usually, I have a sense when I'm making the right decision. I don't feel that now and it's scaring the shit out of me, Rayne."

"Maybe that's just parenting."

His eyes turned pleading as he glanced at me. "She's going to change everything."

"Yes." There was no point in lying to him.

He swallowed again and brushed a hand over the sheep. "I've never even changed a diaper."

"You'll learn."

He sighed. "Thank you for taking this so well."

And now came the FBI warning that flashed before every good story. "It's not happening to me. This is your decision, your responsibility, Hale. I'm just lost somewhere in the background watching it happen. But it's happening to you, not me."

"But you won't leave?"

I frowned. "I don't plan to walk away just because your life gets a little complicated, but…" Why was this so hard to say? "She *is* going to complicate your life. You might not have time for me. You're going to be in love with someone else."

His head lifted. "What do you mean?"

I laughed softly and smiled. "Hale, she's going to be the most important girl in your world."

He seemed to truly concentrate on every word I said as if I were speaking a new language to him. "How do you know that?"

My heart pinched. "Because that's what daughters are to their dads."

At least that was the way it was supposed to be.

"You're going to be everything to her, and when she cries, it'll rip out your heart. When she laughs, it'll be the best sound in the world. And when she sets her mind to something, I have no doubt you'll do everything in your power to make her dreams come true, because you're Hale Davenport, and you don't do anything half ass."

His chest moved as he breathed a little faster and studied me. "Do you really believe that?"

"Yes." My smile turned sad, but I was still happy for him. "So when the time comes that I want to be with you, but she has a dance recital or wants you to take her to the park, I wouldn't want you to put *anyone* in front of her. Not even me. Your life is about to get very busy for the next twenty years, but that's okay because it's going to be great. *You're* going to be great."

Dear God, was I about to cry? Where the ever-loving hell was this gushy feeling coming from?

I scowled at the pink and blue ruffles surrounding me. Were they pumping tear gas through the air ducts? We needed to get the shopping done and go do something normal. This place was infectious and I was coming down with baby fever.

I stood and held out a hand. "What do you say we shop for your daughter?"

He smiled, something alive in his gaze for the first time since we entered this fertile petri dish of a store. I seriously wanted a lead bib to protect my ovaries from implantation, because this stuff was enchanting enough to make me impulse buy a human. I couldn't keep fish alive, so I should never own a human.

Once Hale accepted the task, he took over. By the time we filled the second cart, he seemed like a true authority on all things baby.

He wanted only the best for his daughter. The crib was ordered along with a luxurious dresser and daybed. Everything he chose was in shades of ivory, cream, and delicate pink. He even shopped from the store's catalogue and ordered chandeliers, sconces, and accent rugs. With unlimited funds, nothing was out of the question.

The clothing section of the store did me in. While Hale read diaper packages, comparing one brand to the other, I held a teeny-tiny set of baby work boots and started to cry.

"Hey," he said, glancing up from the diapers. "Are you okay?"

I presented the baby work boots like two fragile eggs resting in my palms and whimpered, "I don't know why."

He laughed as my face crumpled and a tear slipped from my eye.

"Aw. They're cute, but I think they're for boys."

I sniffled and gave him a stern look. "You are buying these booties, Hale. She might have to build something."

"What's she going to build?"

"She needs them, Hale. She might have to hammer something. The other babies won't take her seriously if she doesn't dress like a hard ass."

He kissed me and chuckled. "Okay. Put them in the cart."

I seriously had to get out of this place. I wasn't sure what these feelings were, but at one point I found a miniature bug catching set, and I insisted he buy that too. The kid might not even like bugs. I did, but I was weird.

The total bill hurt my brain, but Hale didn't flinch. He decided to have everything delivered together, but he held onto the stuffed sheep, wedging it in the corner of the dashboard of his Rolls Royce.

As we drove home, he held my hand the entire way and smiled. "I can't thank you enough for making me do that."

"It's no problem."

Hale was happy. I should have been happy too. But all I felt was sad like I left something behind in that store. My ovaries were depressed.

Wanting to take my mind off babies for a while, I threw out a sigh. I needed some adult time.

Hale, in tune with my signals, glanced at me. He gave my hand another squeeze. Oh yeah, he knew. Someone cover the sheep's eyes because the next hour was going to be rated R.

Well, Fuck

23

The Davenports—the other ones—arrived the following afternoon. Hale was busy painting the room he deemed would be the nursery and Miles was taking the brunt of Remington's moods, having to help him in the bathroom and do all the personal things I was exempt from. I took pity on him, so I brought him a cookie.

Seraphina was difficult to look at because she was utterly perfect. Her dark hair was thick and shiny, her teeth were white as paper, her eyes were the same exotic gray as her brothers' and father's, and she had a body that should have been air-brushed, but it wasn't. It was totally real.

The Hot One—who I really didn't think deserved that title anymore because Hale was so much more than *The Other One*—made me nervous. Barrett was easy going and laidback and had a way about him that made me turn into a puddle of pre-teen hormones whenever he addressed me directly.

Barrett didn't have the Davenport edge, that air

of sophistication that smelled of wealth and authority. He had something else—utter confidence—but I wasn't sure which was more potent.

Every time he looked at me I giggled, because men like that shouldn't look at me. It filled me with butterflies and made me feel special, but in a totally ridiculous way. He was woman kryptonite, and I needed to stay away from him, because he was aware of his powers and unapologetically abused them.

I was totally unprepared to see Hale's brother in his underwear, but I didn't have much choice or warning. Apparently, at his sister's insistence, he'd volunteered to help get her men's clothing line off the ground by posing for a few pictures. I had no idea he was a model, but it made perfect sense.

"What do you think, Rayne?" Seraphina asked, shoving the proofs across the table.

Penis! I immediately looked away. Everything was covered, but there was a definite bulge under those briefs. "Um..."

"Come on. I need an outsider's opinion. He's my brother so I can only go by what other women see. Do they look okay?"

Not since Marky Mark left the Funky Bunch had a man worn underwear so well. Sweet Hades, Barrett looked good in color, but in black and white he looked even better.

I swallowed thickly, my voice off its usual pitch. "Oh, I'd say these are good."

Barrett's deep voice whispered over my shoulder, "Like what you see, Meyers?"

"Jesus!" Face burning, I edged away from the pictures and scowled at Hale's brother.

He laughed and bit into a pear. "I like the one where my butt cheek's exposed. Show her that one, Phina."

"I'll pass." Needing air, I escaped to my room to change for dinner.

Remington was happy to see his children in his own Remington way. He was hard on Seraphina, but in a manner I admired. Sometimes he bullied her into conversations about investments and critiqued the way she ran her clothing company, but Seraphina was no joke. She had young values and stuck to them with a spirit I could almost remember possessing myself.

When I looked at her, I saw youth, promise, and beauty. With Barrett, I saw trouble, sex appeal, and cockiness. It seemed interesting they were all alike, but so different and unique in their own way. But Hale was my favorite, all quiet sophistication, authority, and honor. What amazed me most, was that each one of these characteristics stemmed from the one common denominator—Remington.

Remington, though older and cynical, once possessed all the ambition of his daughter. There was no debate where his second son inherited his boyish charms. And that intimidating control that defined Hale, that came from Remington too. I wondered what his wives could claim because he was definitely the dominant gene carrier.

There was a knock on my bedroom door and I turned to find Hale standing in a suit. I sighed because he just had that effect on me. "You look nice."

"So do you." He approached and brushed a kiss on my cheek.

"Did you get the nursery done?"

He nodded. "Will you come see it after dinner?"

"Of course." I actually couldn't wait to see all the things we bought, out of their packages and put together.

"Ready to go? I figured we'd drive separate, let them have the limo."

"Okay, but stay close. Your father will need help getting in and out."

"Barrett's with him."

The restaurant was perhaps the fanciest place I'd ever eaten. They had little dishes with warm wet cloths for people to wash their fingers mid-meal, and about seventy-two pieces of silverware on the table.

"So, Rayne, how do you like working for my dad?" Barrett asked, and I giggled once again picturing him in his underwear.

Bad Rayne.

My cheeks got hot whenever he asked me a direct question. It was sort of annoying, because, despite his indisputable good looks, I wasn't interested in him that way and I was definitely sleeping with his brother. So not a good thing.

"It's not my least favorite job. I've had worse."

Barrett smirked. "Well, that's honest."

"I think you have the magic touch, Rayne. I've never seen Daddy so laid back around his employees," Seraphina commented.

"It's probably the drugs," I remarked, then wondered if that was wrong to say.

Barrett laughed. "How long until you get the cast off, Dad?"

The conversation flowed in an intimate volley of

current events, but no one brought up the biggest news of the soon to arrive baby Davenport. By the dessert course, I wondered if Phina and Barrett even knew they were getting a niece in a few weeks. Hale didn't mention a single thing relating to his renovations. It was weird.

This wasn't some rich person thing. This was a weird person thing. Was a baby just going to show up and everyone would wonder where it came from?

Every once in a while on the news, there was a story about a girl suddenly giving birth in a bathroom because she didn't realize she was pregnant. Was this going to be like that? I mean, come on. How does someone overlook missing nine periods?

I wiped my mouth and stilled. Oh God. It was July eleventh.

I started working for Remington last month. I bought tampons, but... I hadn't used them. No, wait...we used condoms. Everything was fine. *Everything was fine!*

I couldn't breathe. Everything was *not* fine.

I had no idea what anyone said during the last portion of the meal because every minion in my head was running around on high alert. All systems were go, sirens were blaring, arms were waving, parachutes were getting strapped on, and my mind minions were crashing into walls like crazy kamikaze underlings terrified of implantation.

I could *not* be pregnant.

Hardly feeling my feet move, we walked to the car, and Hale opened my door. I was sweating. I was definitely sweating.

The second his door closed I blurted, *"We need to go to a pharmacy!"*

Brow pinched with concern, he looked at me. "Are you sick?"

"No, but I might be pregnant."

"What?"

"Just drive!"

He put the car in drive and two minutes later we were pulling up to CVS. "I'll be right out."

"Do you want me to come in with—"

I slammed the door in his face. I couldn't be expected to sit around discussing the weather when a person might be getting drunk off a vodka-fermented umbilical cord in my uterus. Come on people!

I went down the aisles until I found the one with tampons, condoms, and—ooh, heated massage oil. *Focus!* Right.

Oh, God, there were twenty different kinds. Holding up my basket, I knocked one of each brand off the shelf and into my basket. Detouring down aisle two, I covered the pregnancy tests with a box of cookies, because shit like this called for cookies.

At the register, I feared the clerk might call out a price check, but it was nothing quite so dramatic. But damn, pregnancy tests were expensive. What a racket! People knew these were essentially sticks you peed on, right?

Flopping into the car I caught my breath. Hale scrutinized the two bags.

"How many did you buy?"

I waved a hand for him to go. "It's good to be sure."

When we got to his house, I went straight to the bathroom. Hale waited outside the door. He didn't seem to be pacing, which I would have been, but currently, I was trying to aim a stream of urine onto a narrow stick—basically pissing all over my hand. "Damn it."

I buckled my knees together. "Can you get me a cup?"

I wasn't coordinated enough for this crap, but I'd done my fair share of tailgating so I could pee into a cup like nobody's business.

Hale opened the door and held out a crystal glass.

"What are we having, a wedding? A plastic cup!" I couldn't hold it much longer.

Hale returned with a glass mug. "This is the best I can do."

I grabbed the mug and sent him a withering look. "Privacy?"

He closed the door and I unleashed the floodgates. When I was finished, I washed my hands and opened three tests, saving some for morning—something about the pregnancy chemical being strongest then.

Biting my lip, I frowned at the three little sticks. *Please don't be positive. Please.*

Hale knocked. "Anything?"

"You can come in."

He stood behind me, staring at the sink as we waited. Pictures of neglected houseplants played through my mind.

I had an image of myself in my grandmother's apron, with my hair in a sloppy brothel bun. I was smoking cigarettes, holding a kid on each hip and had one in my belly. There were houseflies and screaming children and I think we were in some sort of shed house with a dirt floor.

Then I pictured myself being handed a huge wad of sweaty cash and my baby being taken away by Remington and put into some lame sailor suit as they cruised him off to prep school. The image was so clear and terrifying.

"I'm not selling you my baby!" I blurted.

"What?"

Oh God, I couldn't breathe.

"They're negative," Hale muttered and walked out of the bathroom.

I hung back, checking each package booklet to be sure the signs all matched. Relief didn't immediately kick in. I threw the tests in the trashcan and sat on the toilet seat. I needed to go on the pill.

When I finally emerged from the bathroom, Hale was sitting on the couch having a drink. Feeling like I might have overreacted a tad, I approached slowly.

"Sorry. I'm just not ready for anything like that. I freaked out."

He glanced at me but said nothing. Okay, maybe the selling my baby thing was crossing a line, but look at the situation he was in now.

"I kill a lot of goldfish and houseplants," I lamely explained.

He frowned, those silver eyes observing too much.

Great, now he was probably thinking he should keep me away from his daughter. Not a bad call, but

I at least wanted a chance to play with her a little. I didn't dislike babies for malicious reasons. It was more about my tendency for calamity and habit of dropping expensive things and my forgetfulness when I was supposed to be taking care of something.

He still wasn't talking.

"Are you mad at me?" I asked, wishing I'd kept my panic to myself.

"If you were to get pregnant, Rayne, we'd figure it out together."

I knew that, but these were Davenports. They had more power than me. I was just a Meyers. The only cool things Meyers did were write vampire books. And those people weren't my relatives anyway.

I sat stiffly beside him. "Okay."

"If this is too much for you, I need to know now."

"You can't say things like that, Hale. How am I supposed to know where we'll be in a few weeks?"

He put his glass on the table and faced me. "If it were my choice, we'd be together. I know my life's going to change, but I don't want us to change."

But we were going to change. *He* was going to change. "I think we just have to see how everything plays out." It wasn't my baby.

His eyes showed intense concentration as he stared at me. "I'm in love with you, Rayne."

My face went numb, my voice suddenly seeming very far away. "What?"

"I love you."

I slowly recoiled and wrung my hands. "Okay."

"Okay?"

I shrugged. "I don't know what to say."

He scoffed. "Do you love me?"

Crap. Panic. "I...I don't know." Maybe. Probably. My palms were clammy. Fuck.

He picked up his drink and finished it. "Well, this night didn't go as planned." He stood and walked to the bar.

"That's not fair. How was I supposed to know my period would be late for no reason?"

"I'm not talking about that."

"Then what are you talking about?" God, I sucked—absolutely sucked—at relationship communication.

"I'm talking about us, Rayne. You and me."

"I understand that, but why are you angry?"

"I don't know!" He paced and gripped the back of his neck. "I'm upset the test was negative—and I hear how crazy that sounds."

Whoa. "Um..." I looked for reinforcements, but we were still alone in his house. "Hale, I'm not ready to have a baby. I don't even know if I'll ever have children."

"Do you want them?"

I leaned back and blew out a breath. "That's a big decision."

"You're thirty. You had to have considered the possibility at some point."

Shutting my eyes, I silently counted to ten. "Look, I don't really get why we're fighting—"

"We're not fighting."

"*But* I'm just going to be honest with you. I admire what you're doing. I don't know anyone else that would make such a sacrifice just because it was the right thing to do. But it scares me. Your life's going to be unrecognizable from what it was and this baby will be yours, not mine. We've known each other for weeks, not months, not years, *weeks*. You can't expect me to make some life-altering commitment just because it fits into your timetable."

Just the mention of commitment had me searching for an exit. I wasn't even sure he really loved me. Maybe he was rushing things out of desperation, hoping to find a maternal figure in this mess.

"Parenting's a *huge* deal, which is why it terrifies me. I'm willing to see if our relationship will still work once you're a father, but I'm far from ready to be a mother."

He made a sound confirming he'd heard me, his expression unreadable.

"Please say something."

"I just assumed you'd be involved."

"You didn't even know me a month ago. You agreed to adopt this baby way before then."

"I know. I'm completely aware that this is *my* responsibility, and I signed up for it, but I...I want her to know you."

My lips twitched. For some reason that made me smile, but I was still unsure. "And I'll meet her when she gets here."

He returned to the couch and sighed like a teapot holding in too much steam. "I can't remember a time I've ever been this stressed out."

My fear and ego took a backseat for a moment as

I tried, once again, to fathom how big this was. I gave him a shoulder nudge. "I have faith in you."

"Thanks."

He kissed my forehead and rested his arm over my shoulders, both of us staring straight ahead, thoughts distracted.

"Are you close with your dad?" His question startled me.

I wasn't used to those close to me discussing something that was hardly on the table as a conversation piece.

Everything inside of me locked up. This was exactly why it was too soon to say *I love you*. There was still so much we didn't know about each other.

"I never met my dad."

He turned, his surprise clear in the crease of his brow. "Really?"

"Really." I nodded, pushing away the painful sense of inadequacy. "He didn't want to be tied down. Through the years I tried to contact him. A few times he sent a Christmas card, but only signed his name. He never sent birthday cards or called."

Part of me believed that was because my birth was so unremarkable in his world, he'd forgotten the date I was born.

"I'm sorry. I didn't know."

I gave a sad smile. "It's okay." It wasn't, but what could I say? "So you see, what you're doing, raising this baby that needs a father, it's probably the most selfless thing I've ever seen. You want the daughter that no one else wanted. She needs a dad and the first thing you'll ever do for her is be one—a good one, who's there when no one else is. That's pretty incredible."

It also made me want to punch Remington right in the dick, but he was old.

His gaze found mine, and a gentle smile curved his lips. "And that's why I love you."

There was that sticky word again. "Will you show me the nursery?"

He nodded and took my hand as we stood.

The baby's room was amazaballs. It had everything. Seriously, if Hale could use a breast pump he would have bought one.

"This is beautiful."

"Thanks. Do you think she'll like it?"

He still needed to brush up on his reading, because I didn't think he had a grasp of developmental stages just yet. But I humored him. "I think she'll love it."

We walked over to the crib and stared inside at the delicate bunting. There was going to be a baby in there soon. It would make noise and spit up and shit all over that pale pink quilt. I told myself this because I didn't like children. And I told myself I didn't like children because I didn't understand why part of me wanted his baby to be mine.

Dangerous, dangerous, crazy territory. Once again, my ovaries were depressed.

24

Of course, I got my period the next morning and why wouldn't I? It was only the busiest day I'd had since working for Remington.

First, I had to run home and get tampons. Then I was off to the marina making sure all the deliveries had arrived for the party and the casino games were in their proper places. Next, it was back to the house because Remington thought this was the perfect day to go over the energy notes I'd made from the proposals. That was an hour I really couldn't spare. Then it was back to the marina.

The Lady Parr was shaping up to look like a casino cruise designed for the elite and everything was going smooth until I heard thunder.

"What the hell was that?"

Marta pointed at a patch of storm clouds approaching from the east. "There's supposed to be showers over the next hour."

"What the ever-loving fuck?" I growled. "Move

381

the linens off the deck and get them inside. Someone grab the raffle baskets!"

I hustled from the main deck up to the sky deck and gathered the favors I'd been piecing together. I was sweating like a heifer on her way to slaughter by the time I had everything back in a box.

My phone rang and I snapped, "Meyers."

"Hey, Rayne."

It was Phina. I clamped my lips shut as I gathered all the crap off the table. Didn't she know we were in a red alert, all hands on deck, batten down the hatches situation?

Apparently, she didn't. "We were going to take a ride over to see the yacht. Is that cool?"

Goddamn it. Nothing's ready yet.

Keeping my voice as pleasant as possible, I said, "It's going to rain. I'd wait another hour until the storm passes." Another roll of thunder.

"We're just going to peek."

Motherfucking, cock licking, ball sniffing damn it. I kept my voice calm and sweet. "I think your dad wanted you to see it when it was all done."

Please just give me more time...

"Oh, all right." She sighed. "I guess I can wait. I'm so excited! We'll be there about an hour before the guests arrive. Just me and a few close friends. We want to have a bottle on the sky deck to kick things off."

"Okay. I'll make sure it's ready for you."

"Thanks, Rayne. I can't wait!"

"See you then." I ended the call and raced inside just as the first raindrops pelted my shoulders.

Seraphina called three more times over the next

two hours. I prided myself on not freaking out, but inside my head, I was stabbing voodoo dolls. This party planning shit was for the birds.

By ten of six, everything was once again dry. The auction baskets were set up along the main deck where guests would see them upon arrival. The furniture in the main living room had been rearranged to make it look like a lounge and all the lighting had been switched out with dim bulbs to complement the burgundy and gold fabric I used to swath the room.

An enormous roulette wheel was situated on the upper deck and the hired staff was dressed to the nines in bow ties and white gloves. Laurent had hors d'oeuvres ready to roll and the butler crew was briefed on their stations. There was a bar on every floor and two on the upper deck, one inside and one out.

I ran the bottle that had been chilling on ice up to the sky deck and put it down just as I heard Seraphina's voice below. Her small group of friends added up to fifteen people. As I went down to greet them, I saw Miles helping Remington out of the limo.

"Here we go," I whispered, pasting on a smile and taking the stairs to greet the guest of honor. "Welcome to Seraphina's Casino Royale."

She beamed and rushed to give me a loving hug. "Everything looks fabulous, Rayne!"

"It was all your father's doing." Passing the praise wasn't too painful. At least this way, if anything went wrong, I'd only be partially accountable.

"You're all set up on the sky deck. The DJ will start in about ten minutes."

As the group of friends disappeared above, I overheard comments of praise dappling their conversation and felt a pinch of satisfaction.

"Meyers, you're not dressed," Remington said in greeting.

Glancing down at my usual yacht uniform, I sighed. I'd considered wearing something nicer, but after being on my feet all day and running from one end of the boat to the other, it just seemed more sensible to wear something easy.

"I'll stay in the background."

"Hell no." He frowned. "Go change."

"I still have to—"

"Meyers," he warned.

Gritting my teeth, I nodded and slipped down to the stateroom where I'd hung my dress. Of course, ten people stopped me along the way to ask where I wanted something. I was swiftly reaching the point of screaming, *I don't fucking care!*

My dress was nothing special, just a plain black wrap, but the shoes were fancy. I debated if I could get away with wearing my sneakers, but I knew that wouldn't fly.

Slipping off my shoes, I hissed. There was a lovely blister on my heel.

Well, that's gonna feel great with pumps.

Hale had texted me several times that day, but I only had the time to send him one word replies. Just as guests started to arrive, I got another text from him asking where I was, but the marble to the roulette wheel was missing, and I needed to find where we stashed the box of backup marbles. Finally, I found it and ran it up to the guy manning the wheel.

Music was pumping, people were mingling, drinks were flowing, and I was suffocating. I crept through the back stairwell, planning to catch my breath in my room, but Barrett was showing some woman where he slept. Backing up the stairs, I slipped into Remington's room and shut the door.

Closing my eyes, I pressed my weight into the door and simply breathed. My fragile hold on my sanity slipped as my phone rang. "Hello?"

"Where are you?"

Hale. His name came on a mental exhale that eased a great deal of my tension. Him I could handle. It was all those other people depending on me to wipe their asses who were making me crazy.

My head tipped against the door. "Hiding."

He chuckled softly and the sound was so full of intimate understand, it teased my senses into a calmer place.

"Location?"

"Your father's room."

There was a tap on the other side of the door and he whispered, "Little pig, little pig."

Grinning, I opened the door and bashfully smirked. "It's crazy out there."

He pocketed his phone and smiled. "You did great."

I cracked the door only enough so he could slip in. "I need ten minutes before I can go back out there." My phone pinged and I growled, but Hale took it out of my hand.

"Ignore it."

"I—"

"They'll be fine, Rayne. Take a breath."

Nodding, I sat on the edge of the bed and pulled off my shoe, wincing at my blister.

Hale held out a gift bag. "I thought you might need this."

"You got me a present?" *Sweet man.*

"I know my girl."

For the first time that day, all the little obligations fell away. "That's really sweet."

He glanced around the room, his attention on other objects, as we shared a silent moment that said so much. He did know me. He was this buttoned up, sophisticated guy, and I was a walking disaster, but somehow we fit together and we fit better than I ever thought two people could.

I think we both drew some sort of comfort in identifying the rightness that came from finding each other. We really were an odd suited couple, but his rigidness was the perfect match for my scribble scrabble chaotic squish of a personality. His sharp edges didn't bother me. And my lunacy didn't seem to bother him.

"Open it." He pressed the gift into my hands.

Accepting the bag, I parted the tissue paper and laughed. "Yes, you definitely know me." I lifted out a pair of flip-flops and rose to kiss him.

His lips were soft and his body warm and comforting. I wished I could fall into his hold and hide for the rest of the night.

"There's more."

Feeling the bag was still weighted, I dug deeper and this time, I really laughed. "You got me tequila!"

It was one of those little airport bottles, but it would definitely come in handy. I stuffed the bottle in my bra and gave him a shoulder bump. "Thank you."

"You did a really nice job with the party, baby. Phina loves everything, especially the silent auction."

"I'm glad."

Once again I recognized the strong affection he held for his siblings. It was no wonder he couldn't bare the thought of losing one. They were, after all, half siblings at best, Remington being the one link in their relationship. This baby was no different and Hale would always protect his siblings.

"It's okay to take credit, Rayne."

Flushing, I smiled. "This is your father's thing."

"No. This is all you. You did great."

My nerves settled and I blew out a breath, finally feeling some of my confidence slip back into place. "I think I'm ready to go back out there now." Slipping on my flip-flops, I stuck my pumps in the bag and tucked it away on Remington's shelf.

Once I had something in my stomach, everything started to flow. The guests were happy. Seraphina was happy. Remington was happy. And all of that made me happy.

The seas were calm and the sunset was one for postcards. I couldn't have asked for a better night. As each hour passed and my plans played out, my pride warmed a bit more. Just as I started to relax and truly enjoy all that I'd created, Hale was pulled away.

"Excuse me," he muttered, plugging his finger in his ear and holding his phone to the other one.

Cake was being served and all the guests gathered around the railings to sing as Phina blew out her candles on the main deck. Seeing how cheerful she was made all the stress worth it. One hour to go and it would all be over.

Hale returned and I could see he was irritated. "What's the matter?"

"Jasmine's having something called Braxton-Hicks. She saw the obstetrician this afternoon and they said it's normal, but she's in a lot of pain."

"What's Braxton-Hicks?"

"False contractions."

I frowned. What the fuck was a false contraction? The only thing I knew about childbirth was that it hurt. How could a contraction be false? That was like calling a cramp fake. They all hurt. A contraction was a contraction. This had to be a phrase a man lacking a uterus coined.

"Is she okay?"

"Yeah. I told her to call me if they get worse."

But we were on a boat. We were forty-five minutes away from port and I was one cocktail away from feeling good and there were two whole weeks until the due date.

Okay, calling the contractions false sort of helped. Kind of like a false alarm situation. That was why the contractions didn't count.

Appearing out of nowhere, Barrett slung an arm over my shoulder. "You did good, Rayne. Great party."

Jesus, I couldn't breathe when he touched me.

It was like being dunked in a tank full of testosterone—too many pheromones and what not.

I shouldered out of his hold and answered with little inflection, my mind still worrying over the phony labor pains. "Thanks."

Barrett looked at his brother and back to me. "You guys okay?"

Apparently Hale wasn't buying the whole false contraction thing either. "Yeah." He rubbed the back of his neck. "I'm going to go check in with Wyatt and see what our schedule looks like."

Reading his concern, I nodded, wishing I could say more, but still unsure how much his brother knew. "Okay."

He left me with Barrett. *Great.*

His brother smiled. "Dance?"

I shook my head, staring at the door Hale disappeared through, my mind a bit preoccupied. "I only dance to *Thriller.*"

His grin doubled. "We can arrange that."

Distracted, I looked at him and frowned. "What? No."

"Oh, have a little fun, Meyers." He grabbed my arm and dragged me to the main deck where the speakers were pumping. He left me in a herd of young, gyrating people and went to say something to the DJ. The DJ typed on his computer and handed Barrett a microphone and then the recognizable intro echoed.

I was going to kill him.

"You all having a good time?" Barrett's voice rumbled through the speakers. Everyone cheered.

Dead. He was fucking dead.

"I wanted to wish my beautiful sister a happy birthday and thank my dad for hosting such a fun night." More cheers. "But I also want to thank the woman behind the scenes who organized this bash."

World, swallow me now.

I dug the tequila out of my bra, cracked the seal, and guzzled it down.

"That's Rayne." He pointed.

I hid the empty bottle in my palm and gasped as the liquor burned the hell out of my esophagus.

"I think she's worked hard enough and it's time for her to join the party. What do you say we start her off with a toast and a dance?" He lifted his glass. "To Rayne, party planner extraordinaire."

Everyone raised his or her drinks and cheered. I shyly waved my empty bottle and wondered how long it would take me to find bullets and a gun. I'd need a shovel too.

"Come on," he yelled, tugging me onto the dance floor.

Seraphina ran over and gave me another bear hug as one of her friends handed me a cocktail. Everyone spoke at once, and I stared, unblinking, as they crowded around me. Where was Hale?

"Drink up!" someone called and I tipped back the glass, taking a fast train to Drunksville.

"Party's awesome!"

"Love how you transformed the yacht!"

"I can't believe Lola Judd is here!"

"Do you do other parties?"

"I'd love to hire you for my wedding!"

"Do you have a card?"

The enthusiastic comments and questions came

too fast to answer as the music got louder and the alcohol hit my system like a heat seeking missile. Suddenly, all I heard was Michael Jackson screaming, '*Cause this is Thriller!*

Okay—side bar—when we were in high school we thought it would be fun to learn the *Thriller* dance. But no one tells you the song will then be like an incurable disease, something you can't ignore whenever it plays. It's a song that just has to be danced to. These are the laws of pop culture. If you know *Thriller,* you dance. There is no choice. It's just a freak impulse, a reflex, like a seizure on a dance floor to a badass song that makes it okay to pretend you're a zombie.

So I handed off my cup, threw up my arms and got my crypt walk on. Thankfully, other guests had also been infected, because they jumped right in, lurching and sliding, and clapping and laughing.

I sort of led the show and dominated the lineup, because no one loved *Thriller* as much as me. And once we were all synchronized and waving our hands to the beat, I forgot why I didn't want to dance in the first place. I was a rhythmic motherfucker.

Owning the dance floor like Jennifer Beils in *Flashdance,* I gave them the best show since Johnny and Baby lit it up at Kellermen's.

I. Was. On. Fire. But I was also rapidly approaching drunk, so there was a teeny tiny chance I looked like I was having an epileptic seizure. The beauty of alcohol was I no longer cared.

The song closed and everyone cheered. Stage fright compensated by booze, I howled and bounced as another drink miraculously landed in my hands. "Play *Footloose!*"

The crowd parted and my excitement faltered as my gaze fell on Hale. Realizing something was wrong I took a hearty sip—so not to spill—and stumbled over to him.

"Y'all right?" Fuck. There went that fine line between okay and plastered. I was way past that line. Again.

"We'll be back to the marina in about thirty minutes. I have to take Jasmine to the ER."

My brow creased. "Did something else happen?"

"The contractions are getting worse and I want a second opinion. She's alone at the hotel, so as soon as we get back I have to go."

Fuck. Why did I drink so much? "Is she having the baby?"

I saw the panic in his eyes, the possibility not an improbable one if her contractions were getting closer. Holy crap, Hale might have a child by morning. A person. A little human who needed him to be responsible all the time no matter what.

Holy fuck, he was having a *person*!

Yet he kept his remarkable calm—sort of. "I won't know anything until we see a doctor."

Okay, that was enough bullshit. I leaned close and whispered, "How are you so calm?"

He pursed his lips. "I have to talk to Barrett and Phina."

My jaw unhinged. I knew it. I fucking knew it. "They don't know, do they?"

At least he looked a little guilty. "I didn't know how to tell them."

I pulled him aside where less people were standing. "Will you tell them...everything?"

He met my gaze and let out a slow breath. "No. This is my baby." Worry lines formed beneath his hairline, as his eyes were a tad unsure. He met my stare, face blank, and rasped, "I'm having a baby."

Well, duh. Did he think he was decorating rooms for the fun of it? His skin actually wore a sheen of sweat I knew had nothing to do with the heat. He suddenly looked so...human.

"Are you okay?" I shouted, as the music got louder.

"I'm having a baby," he repeated, face trapped in some sort of shock paralysis.

I touched his shoulder. "Hale?" I never saw him look so uncertain, not even when we were at the baby store. It was a little scary.

"Fuck," he snapped, running his fingers through his hair and leaving it standing on end. "I'm having a *baby!*"

Thank God this wasn't like the movies when statements like that send the record skidding and plunge the world into silence. No one appeared to hear his outburst but me. Still, that was not the sort of shit to go shouting in mixed company before the proper authorities had been notified.

I took his hand and pulled him inside, but people were lingering there too. I walked him down the hall and up the steps until we were in the little server. Shutting the door, I grabbed his shoulders and shook him. "Breathe."

He let out a gusty breath. "I'm having a baby."

"You can handle this, Hale." Was I the grown up here? That didn't seem right.

"What if she's early? What if the baby comes tonight?"

Yeah, he was *not* ready. All that decorating hadn't made a dent in his avoidance. But I was a pro at being stuck in situations I hadn't prepared for, so I gave him the best advice I could—much like Elle usually did for me.

"Look, if the baby comes tonight, then she gets to share a birthday with her aunt. That's cool. They'll be birthday buddies. But this might be nothing. Maybe that Braxton Hicks guy just has Jasmine in a bit of a headlock right now and tomorrow everything will be back to normal." Right? False alarms and whatnot. "But you might want to start thinking about a name."

"Jesus Christ! I don't have a name!"

My eyes went wide. I was not used to seeing him frazzled. "Do you want a drink?"

"No, I have to drive."

"Do you want me to get your dad?"

He scowled. "Fuck, no."

"Okay. Relax." I held up my hands. I needed to relax too. *Think, Rayne. Think!* "How about Barrett?"

Hale nodded. I was amused to see that he also sweated when he was nervous.

"I'll be right back. Stay here."

Speed walking out to the deck I was relieved to find Barrett still on the dance floor. Shouldering my way through all the women orbiting around him, I yelled, "Barrett, I need you for a minute."

His lashes lowered as he gave a gratified smirk

and arched a brow. "It'll take longer than a minute, Meyers. We Davenports don't believe in doing anything half ass."

Good God, the man never stopped. "For the love of fuck," I muttered, grabbing his arm and yanking him away from the dance floor. "Just come with me and calm your balls."

"Where are we going?"

I led him toward the server and he chuckled when I gestured for him to enter.

He eyed me from head to toe, way too much implication in his expression. "I can work my way around a tight space."

As much as I was trying to regroup and locate my big girl panties, I needed to call a time out and address this game he was playing. "You do realize I'm with your brother."

"Davenport men are like potato chips, you can't just have—"

"Stop." I held up a hand because I simply couldn't take anymore. "I'm going to pretend you didn't just say that because I know you've had a lot to drink and all these women have you raring to go, but I want to make this clear. Your brother and I..." How to put it? "We..." Great. Now *I* was sweating. "Hale's very important to me and I'd never—*ever* —do anything to hurt him."

Barrett dropped the smolder and tipped his head, a genuine smile curving his lips. "You're in love with him."

Wait, what? I frowned. "Am not."

He chuckled, and though I never had a brother,

something told me that look I was getting was full of brotherly affection.

"For the record, I'd never poach from Hale. I was just testing you." He patted my shoulder, not like the manwhore he'd been acting like since we met, but like a friend. "You passed with flying colors."

Letting out a breath I sighed in relief. Then I shoved him. "Jerk." Thank God he hadn't been seriously flirting with me. "I should punch you in the throat for messing with me, but there isn't time. Hale's having a bit of a conniption."

Barrett flipped a switch fast, showing a serious side of him I didn't know he possessed. All signs of jovial flirt disappeared as that Davenport authority kicked into overdrive.

"Where is he?"

"In the server." I barely had the sentence out before he was opening the pocket door.

I followed him quickly inside. Barrett was asking what was wrong before I even closed the door to the cramped room. Hale paced and—Wow, there was a lot of testosterone in here.

Rather than answering his brother, Hale looked at me and asked, "What do you think of the name Julia? Or how about Grace? Do girls still go by traditional names? Or do you like something more original?"

"What's going on?" Barrett asked, totally confused.

Hale stilled and caught his breath but said nothing. Not a word. He looked at his brother and...nada.

I cleared my throat. "Okay." Damn my palms were clammy. "Barrett…Hale is having a baby. Possibly tonight." There. That was easy and could have been done months ago.

Barrett chuckled, but when Hale looked at him, eyes alarmingly wide, his laughter faded. Barrett's gaze snapped to me, dropped to my stomach, and then shot back to Hale.

"What's that now?"

"A girl. I'm having a girl and I don't have a fucking name."

Barrett laughed again, this time slow and slightly nervous. "Okay, what the hell are you talking about?"

I looked back at Hale because this part was all him. If he honestly planned on keeping Remington's involvement from his siblings he was going to have to start practicing his speech now.

The panic in his eyes slowly banked and something shifted in him as he regained his composure. It was truly amazing to see him transform back into a mature, capable man, so beyond any talent I personally possessed. Adulting would never cease impressing me.

Swallowing, he straightened his shoulders and looked his brother in the eye. Voice steady, he said, "I'm going to be a father."

I smiled, knowing this was difficult but proud of how he owned it. The world needed more Hales.

"Seriously?" Barrett practically shrieked.

Hale simply nodded. "As soon as we dock I have to take the mother to the hospital, but she's been having contractions all day, and she thinks it might be time."

Barrett looked at me, eyes wide. "How do you play into all this?"

Holding up my hands, I quickly stepped back. "I don't." Then I looked at Hale and whispered, "But I think I'm in love with the baby's father."

Hale's attention jerked to me as he stepped to my front, shoving his brother aside and cupping my face, he pressed his lips to mine and breathed as if every worry in the world just got a little lighter.

"Is that true?" he rasped.

Was it? The words just sort of fell out, but I nodded anyway.

His lips brushed mine again and he whispered, "I love you too."

I flinched as the horn blared, signaling we were approaching the marina. I placed my hand over his and whispered, "You got this."

He nodded and slowly released me. Barrett looked like he'd seen a ghost, but Hale was back in control.

"Let's wait until we know anything, before we mention this to Phina. I don't want to interrupt her night. I'll text you when I get to the hospital, and hopefully everything will be fine, and I can tell her tomorrow when she's sober."

That was the Hale I knew! And yes, sober would be good. It was remarkable how lucid I felt after watching Hale lose it. Not an easy thing to picture when he's always in such control of his emotions. But good to know he was human.

As soon as we were in the marina, Hale was the

first to leave. The party went on and no one was the wiser. Barrett had switched to water, as did I, both of us checking our phones every thirty seconds as we waited on a bench away from the remaining crowd.

"Is it Jasmine's?" Barrett asked, not looking at me.

I glanced at him until he faced me and then I simply said, "It's Hale's."

He nodded and I wondered how much he could figure out on his own based on his father's reputation, but I didn't say a word. The guests trickled off the boat in increments and the DJ closed up shop. Only Seraphina and her fifteen friends remained as we waited for any word from Hale.

Miles took Remington back to the house and Barrett and I decided to join him. The crew would break down the party and I'd be back in the morning to check on everything.

As we drove home, Remington and Barrett were silent. No one mentioned Hale and I wondered if Remington realized what was happening.

When we got to the house, I texted Hale to ask if everything was okay. It had been two hours since he left and I hadn't heard a peep. I helped Remington to bed and my phone rang just as I was closing his door.

"Hello?" I whispered, standing in the hall outside of his father's bedroom.

I could hear him breathing, but he didn't speak.

"Hale?"

He sighed, a low chuckle lost in his voice. "I have a daughter." And I knew then nothing would ever be the same.

Nope. Definitely Not In Kansas

25

Once I got the call, I woke Barrett, and we took a cab to the hospital to meet the newest Davenport. I was a bundle of nerves the whole way there. Barrett was stoic and silent until we got to the hospital lobby where he hesitated at the elevator.

I looked at him as the doors prepared to close. "What are you doing? Come on."

He shook his head. "I think you should go up first. You and Hale should have a minute alone."

I frowned. "Don't be ridiculous. You're his brother."

He looked at me for a long moment as I held the door. "Trust me on this." He slid my hand off the door and I stared at him as the metal doors closed.

The ride to the maternity ward was quick and unnerving. I should go back down and get Barrett. This was crazy. It was *his* niece. I was just the uninvolved girlfriend slash employee. Why wasn't he here with me to see his brother? And did I tell Hale I loved him? Sobriety was coming too fast with all of these emergencies.

The doors opened and I reached to hit the button to send me back down but stilled as I saw Hale's back. He stared at a long glass window, perfectly still, suit jacket gone, sleeves rolled up to his elbows.

I stepped off the lift. "Hale?"

He turned as if in a daze and smiled.

I walked to his side and stared down at the row of bassinets. Something inside of me cooed sweetly as I looked at the row of precious faces and then I spotted the one that said *Davenport.*

"She's beautiful," I heard myself say.

"I know," he whispered, not taking his eyes off the glass.

I took my hand and folded it around his, squeezing lightly. He entwined our fingers and securely held my palm.

"It was amazing," he rasped, voice gravelly. "The whole thing. I never saw anything like it." He quietly laughed, the small sort of titter reserved for miracles alone. "I cut the cord."

An unexpected sadness swept over me and I wasn't sure where it came from. This woman who did this amazing thing and brought this person into the world, she and Hale had a past.

Was this why Barrett wanted me to go up alone, so he didn't have to see this part? Was this... My chest suddenly ached. Was this the breakup?

What if, despite the child not being his, they could work this out and be a family? I didn't know Jasmine's reasons for giving up the baby. I never put much thought into it, being that sometimes parents weren't able to make commitments. But thinking about all the pain I suffered over the years, wondering where my dad was and if he was thinking about me, I worried for this little angel and didn't want her to have those thoughts. I didn't want to be the obstacle that separated a family.

Swallowing the lump in my throat, I whispered, "How's Jasmine doing?"

"She's resting."

A nurse smiled and lifted Hale's daughter, carrying her to the window, and I sucked in a breath as I recognized the unmistakable Davenport features in her face.

I wiped my eyes, taken off guard by my tears. "She's a little peanut."

"She's perfect," he rasped, eyes focused on the bundle of little person. "Ten fingers. Ten toes."

"Have you held her yet?" Why was I here? This had nothing to do with me. And why couldn't I stop crying?

"When she was first born, but then they had to run some tests. They're going to bring her to me in a few minutes. I have a room."

Of course they did. "Well, I should—"

The nursery door opened and a woman in scrubs peeked out. "We're going to bring her down now. I think she's ready for a little formula, Dad."

Hale nodded, a proud but unsure smile on his face.

I couldn't do this. This wasn't right. "Barrett's downstairs. I'll tell him your room number." Then I'd check myself in to the psych ward because I was pretty sure I needed to scream into a pillow and sob inconsolably.

His brow creased. "Don't you want to meet her?"

Yes, but I didn't want to meet Jasmine, and I certainly didn't want any part in breaking up a family. I wiped my eyes. "I should go."

His smile disappeared. "I don't want you to go."

I rubbed my nose on the back of my hand. "You should be with your daughter, Hale. This is a family thing."

His hand tightened around mine, his grip pleading. "Please stay."

It hurt, not his hold, but my heart. Still, I nodded. "For a few minutes."

We walked through the halls in silence. Nurses worked quietly at random desks. It was late, so the hospital was peaceful.

Hale pushed open a door to a private room and I stopped in my tracks as I spotted the empty bed. "Where's Jasmine?"

"Her room's in the other wing. This is where I'm staying."

"You aren't sharing a room?"

He tilted his head and frowned as if my assumption wasn't something he'd even considered. "She thought it would be easier if she didn't spend time with the baby."

My lips parted. This was so strange. "Has she seen her?"

"Of course, but she didn't want to hold her."

Was this how my birth was? Did my dad lack the courage to hold me? I shoved those thoughts away. I had no idea it could be like that. I didn't know what to say. "She really is okay with this?"

"She did me a huge favor, Rayne."

I wondered how much he actually paid her to carry the baby to term. He'd said she didn't want a baby, but...I might have said that too in a similar situation, but eventually, I would have crumbled.

I simply couldn't fathom that level of commitment, not the amount required to be a parent *or* the level of commitment to never get involved—ever. I never expected her to actually stick to her guns.

"Mr. Davenport?"

Hale turned and smiled as the nurse rolled his daughter's bassinet into the room.

"She's ready for a bottle. I just changed her, so she'll probably go right to sleep for you."

Whoa, this was serious territory. I shuffled over to the side of the room and watched as the nurse gently placed the baby in Hale's arms. My mouth twitched as he shifted and cautiously figured out the best way to hold something so breakable. They spoke quietly as she handed him a tiny bottle.

Hale touched the rubber tip to his daughter's mouth and laughed softly. "She's a fast learner."

"I'll leave you two alone."

He took a few minutes to simply stare at her, but then he looked up at me and whispered, "She's perfect, isn't she?"

Perfect and beautiful, that seemed to be his final verdict. I couldn't disagree.

My heart stuttered as I watched him, so caring and gentle, so in love with this new little person.

That's how dads were supposed to be, immediately in love with their children.

Great. Here come the tears again...

Wiping my eyes, I smiled at him and nodded because speaking was impossible at the moment. If I was in love with him before, I didn't know what to call the emotions I felt now. He was the best guy I'd ever met.

"Her eyes are open," he whispered. "Come see."

I drifted closer one baby step at a time. There were those silver-gray Davenport eyes, only hers were slightly bluer than Hale's.

"She really is beautiful."

He glanced up at me, face serene, and we both looked back at her, in awe of this indefinable moment. "I was thinking of calling her Elara."

"That's a lovely name." I wanted to hold her so badly I folded my hands behind my back.

"Knock-knock." Barrett stepped inside and grinned at his brother. "I heard I have a niece."

Hale's expression was dominated by immeasurable pride. "Come meet Elara."

I took the opportunity to slip out of the room and catch my breath. Once in the hall, I leaned into the wall and sucked in a deep gulp of air. I didn't expect this to be so intense.

Wandering off, I found a machine that dispensed ice chips and filled a cup. Sitting on a chair at the end of the wing, I stared at the floor and nibbled the ice. Every now and then a baby would cry, but the hospital was mostly quiet. Even my brain was quiet, because there was no precedence for a situation like this and I didn't know how to process it.

Sometime later, Barrett found me and grinned as he approached. "Well, this was unexpected."

I laughed, sort of outside of myself. "No kidding."

"I'm going to take off. I think he wants you to stay."

I wasn't sure that was such a good idea. I considered Barrett. He had to know something was up with this situation.

"Will you tell your father and sister?" They should be here.

Barrett nodded. "I'll make sure they know."

"Do you think Hale realizes what he's doing?"

I wanted to believe he did, but everything was happening so fast. What if he changed his mind and the poor peanut was abandoned? I couldn't dwell on thoughts like that. Despite doubting men—mostly my father—I had strong faith in Hale.

"I think he knows he's doing the right thing and that's all Hale ever wanted to do. You probably realize he isn't one to stray outside of the lines."

He made it sound like Hale was perfect, but I knew he wasn't. He drove too fast and got jealous and crossed many lines when it came to intimacy, but somehow he managed to convince the outside world he was always in control.

Maybe I was an outlet for him, someone who let him know it was okay to swear and speed and be less than perfect at times. I liked thinking I might be that outlet for him, because Hale was so complete, I often wondered why I was necessary to him at all. More things to consider at a later date.

I nodded at Barrett, unsure if I'd make it

through the night at his brother's side. "I'll see you tomorrow."

A while later I found my way back to Hale's room. When I entered he still held Elara, only now he was whispering something to her. It was possibly the cutest thing I ever saw.

I sat on the bed and he looked up, abashed. "I didn't hear you come in."

"Don't stop on my account."

His cheeks flushed. "It's something my mom used to sing to me."

It was sweet.

Though he appeared to be exactly where he wanted to be, it was almost dawn, and I was fading. "Aren't you tired?"

"I was, but I got a second wind. You can lie down if you want."

I rolled to my side on the bed, watching him in between long blinks. When my eyes couldn't open anymore, I heard him sing again.

Just close your eyes and I'll be there...

I STIRRED AFTER THE SUN WAS UP. HALE was already awake and having quite the conversation over the bassinet.

"Well, this isn't very ladylike, but I won't tell anyone."

He lifted a soiled diaper and tossed it into the trash with a splat.

"I'll have them burn that."

The baby made the softest sound and, I swear, my ovaries quivered in delight.

"There. Good as new."

"You sound like a pro."

He turned and grinned. "There's my other beautiful girl. I think I'm finally getting the hang of diapers."

I sat up and ran a hand over my hair. "I need to go home and change." I also needed to check on the cleanup at the yacht. "Can I bring you back anything?"

"I have a bag with me, but I'd like to see my sister."

Let's just hope Barrett delivered the news, because I'd had enough awkward for one week. "Okay." I hesitated, unsure if I should kiss him or what. "I guess I'll see you."

Leaving the baby in the bassinet, he turned and hugged me—hard. "Thank you for being here."

"You're...welcome." Tongue-tied as usual, I patted his back.

He kissed my head. "Be careful getting home. I love you."

So I supposed we were saying that now. "I..." *Just say it!* "...love you too." There. That wasn't so hard.

His gaze held me immobile for a split second, those gray eyes of his holding an understanding of things too complex for me to decipher. This was not my life. These were not my people. Yet here I was, proclaiming my love for a man I hardly knew.

But those feelings, they were all true. I did love him and I wasn't sure how that happened or what it meant for my fragile heart. I only knew speaking such sentiments made things real and scared the ever-loving shit out of me.

When I got home from the marina, Remington was sitting on the couch. It was no mystery I was gone all night, as I still wore my dress from the party.

"I was at the hospital," I announced.

"I know where you were," he mumbled, keeping his attention on the paperwork in front of him. "Are you working today?"

"I was going to go back." Taking a step closer to him, I hedged, "I figured all of us would go."

"You enjoy yourself. I have work to do."

Treading lightly, I hesitated to leave. "Remington—"

"I'll catch up with you tomorrow, Meyers. You've earned a day off."

My molars locked as I just stared at him. He knew I was still there, but he had yet to look at me. Maybe I was being irrational. I was definitely out of line, but I didn't care.

I walked up to him and snatched the paperwork out of his hand. "Your son had a child last night."

He glared at me. "I'm perfectly informed of my son's whereabouts."

"Don't you want to meet your granddaughter?" I snapped.

His eyes narrowed. "Perhaps you misunderstood the situation, Ms. Meyers, but I assure you, this is a Davenport affair, and I'll handle it as I see fit."

His words hurt because he'd led me to believe I was more than an employee and he was more than a cold asshole. "Is that how it is?"

The disappointment I bore in that moment literally crushed me. He was better than this.

When he didn't answer, I said, "Count me out of the next family dinner, Remington. Maybe we all need to remember I'm just part of the staff." I tossed the paperwork to the sofa and stormed off to my room.

SERAPHINA FOUND THE ENTIRE PROCESS OF meeting her unexpected niece exhilarating. She demanded we stop by a store and pick up something little for her niece. I figured she'd get a few balloons, maybe a rattle, but what did I know? An entire baby wardrobe later, we were finally on our way back to the hospital.

Hale looked exhausted but happy. I couldn't get over how natural he seemed to handle Elara after only half a day alone with her. His sister took to the baby like a boat takes to the sea, natural, and I envied her maternal instincts.

Hale had a long list of items he needed and Seraphina volunteered to help him. Once we were alone—well, Elara was there, which I guessed was the *new* alone—he asked the question I was dreading.

"Is my dad coming?"

Inwardly I cringed, but outwardly I tried to play it cool. "He had a lot of work to do, but he said he'd try to make it over."

Hale laughed coldly and rolled his eyes. "No, he didn't."

"I'm sorry, Hale." And I truly was, because if anyone knew what it meant to be disappointed by a parent, I did. "Maybe he just needs time."

"We'll see." He glanced at the sleeping baby. "Did you have lunch?"

Grateful for the distraction, I shook my head. "Did you want me to go get you something from the cafeteria?"

"I had Laurent make a few catering trays and deliver them to the nurses' station."

And that was how the Davenports did things. "Of course you did. Did you want me to make you up a plate?"

"I want *you* to eat. I know yesterday was crazy for you and you're probably running on empty. I thought of you when I told him to make a dessert tray."

Be still my heart. I smiled and gave him a shoulder bump. "Where did you come from?"

Catching my hands in his, he kissed my knuckles. "Go eat."

And eat I did. Trust the Davenports to put out a spread suitable for a celebrity wedding. Suffice it to say this made Hale very popular with the hospital staff.

I was filling my second plate when I heard a passing nurse whisper, "Apparently, she's on her way to Paris. They pulled out all the stops."

The woman with her murmured back, "I don't know why she wouldn't want to be involved. Did you see the ass on him?"

"Hey..." I mumbled to myself, biting into a cannoli as they walked away. Chewing, I frowned. That was my guy's ass they were talking about.

Taking my plate, I went back to the room where I could keep a close eye on said ass and make sure no one else was trying to get a peek at the new sexy father of the year. Hale was finally sleeping.

I sat on the chair and finished my cannoli and brownies. Since no one was awake, I used my finger to dab up all the sugary crumbs. Waste not, want not.

I stilled when there was a strange little sound. Looking left then right, I put my plate down and slowly rose. Yup, that was one wide awake baby. Her little head turned and she made another sound and I took a step back.

I looked at Hale, but he was still asleep.

Silently, I went to the door and looked into the hall. "Hello? Nurse people?"

No one was around. They were all down the hall with the food. I poked a thumb over my shoulder. "The little person is making noise."

I waited, but no one appeared. "Shit."

Going back to the bassinette, I stared at Elara. "Shh. Your daddy's sleeping." She didn't seem to care.

Glancing to the door and back at Hale, I tried some negotiation tactics I'd picked up over the last few weeks. "If you stop crying I'll get your daddy to buy you a pony. Every girl wants a pony."

Her little chirps got louder.

"Okay, no pony. How about a Lamborghini? Do you want a Lamborghini?"

Her face flushed and she made a little hiccup

sound, her mouth opened wide flashing a good set of gums.

"Delinquent," I hissed, reaching into the little baby bed. My hands sifted under her little glowworm wrap and gently lifted. "Shh. Shh. Shh..." I cradled her to my chest and slowly bobbed in place. "I don't know what you want."

One of those little bottles sat in the corner of the bassinet. "Are you hungry? Sometimes I cry when I'm hungry."

I took the bottle and gently lowered myself in the chair, angling her in my arms in a comfortable position. A sense of warmth stole through me like a fast summer rain, warm and full of rainbows. Was this what a biological tick felt like? I'd always assumed it would hit like a gong, but this feeling was subtly potent and nice, sort of like laughing gas.

I tipped the bottle to her pert mouth and she opened. "You're a little thing. Someday you'll appreciate compliments like that."

I watched her suckle and had flashbacks to the time my mother rescued a litter of kittens. They were blind, little fuzz balls and we had to nurse them from bottles. This was sort of like that.

Once she latched on, she really started to tug. "Wow. A girl after my own heart."

As her little mouth pulled at the bottle, my tension eased a bit. This wasn't too bad. I watched her drink and wondered about things like breast-feeding. Though I never gave it much thought, I bet it was pretty cool to provide for your young in such a way.

"You're like a little kangaroo in your little

pouch," I whispered, admiring her burrito wrap blanket. "I have a snuggie."

The longer she ate, the heavier her eyes grew. She had so many miniature features, pencil thin eyebrows, soft little lashes. I didn't expect her to come out missing parts but seeing these little characteristics mesmerized me.

"You look like a natural."

My head turned toward the bed where Hale still laid on his side, his half lidded gaze focused on me.

"She made noise."

"She does that."

"I gave her the bottle that was in the crib thing."

He smiled. "Do you want me to take her?"

My hold turned protective by the slightest degree. "That's okay." It wouldn't hurt to hold her a little while longer.

My pinky finger gently brushed over her tiny digits and I sucked in a breath as she gripped me. "We're holding hands." Her fingernails were so petite. "Do you see her holding my—"

As I glanced back at him, I saw he'd fallen back to sleep. Lowering my voice, I whispered, "We'll call this our secret handshake."

Hale slept for over an hour and Elara was ready to party. I told her about *The Lady Parr* and warned her about her crotchety old grandfather. I might have embellished a tad when I explained he was fighting a scary demon that broke the heart of his princess, but I promised her as soon as he found his way out of the woods he'd come and see her because she was the new princess in town.

I never knew babies could have so much personality when they were only a day old. Elara made faces and watched me closely as I made them back. She moved her arms and cooed sweetly. She also made a hell of a stink when she poodled. I could have woken Hale, but he needed sleep, so I laid her on her little baby bed and nearly fell to pieces when I discovered her itty-bitty diapers.

"Well, this is just absolutely ridiculous," I said, examining the tiny diaper. My Cabbage Patch dolls had bigger bottoms.

My voice took on a new tenor as I spoke to her, a sort of singsong quality that was similar to the one I used at the zoo when speaking for the animals. Not for the lions, of course, because everyone knew lions sounded like New Yorkers, but all the little fuzzy critters got the singsong voice.

"Look at these little chicken legs! I'm gonna bite them." She started to cry, and I cursed. "Sorry. I won't eat you. I mean, come on, there's a tray of brownies out there, and we aren't stranded in the Andes."

Her cries got louder and I rushed to wrap her back up in her blanket, but I had no idea how they got it so tight before.

"Is she okay?" Hale rasped in a waking voice.

Panicked, I turned to him. "I swear she was happy the whole time you slept."

He laughed and slowly sat up. "I believe you."

I stepped back and let him handle the blanket, studying his technique. "It's like wrapping a hoagie," I observed.

As I watched him, I realized a few things. One, we only spoke in whispers since the baby was born.

Two, Hale was a natural. Three, babies weren't so scary. And four, Remington was missing so much.

Hale was scheduled to leave the following morning and it broke my heart that his dad would never be able to say he was at the hospital the day his first grandchild was born.

I was over the whole scandal. This was absolutely Hale's baby. If he could make this amazing compromise and adapt his entire life accordingly, why the hell couldn't Remington?

He wouldn't have to do anything but be a grandfather. That required slipping kids candy and making pull my finger jokes. Elara could pull a finger, but she was years away from candy. So why couldn't he be here for that?

When it got late, I went home. The room only had one bed and Hale needed to get all the sleep he could while he had the hospital nurses there to help. I also wanted to take another crack at Remington.

When I walked in the house, Miles was standing in the kitchen. "Hey," I greeted, putting my purse on the counter.

"I'm glad you're back. He's been in a mood all day. Do you think you can finish the night for me?"

Taking pity on the man I nodded. "Sure. I wanted to talk to him anyway."

I found Remington already in bed, but still surrounded by work. "Hi."

He glanced at me over the rim of his reading glasses, but then looked back at his paperwork. "Where's Miles?"

"I told him I'd finish up for him."

He grumbled something under his breath and I sat on the edge of the bed.

"Her name's Elara." I waited for him to comment, but he didn't. "She looks like a Davenport." When he still didn't respond my chest got that tight pinch again. I sighed. "You'll eventually have to meet her, Remington. Hale's in love with her."

"Maybe Hale falls in love a little too easily."

My expression faltered as I slowly drew back. My eyes tingled and, if I allowed it, I could have cried in that instant, but I absolutely forbade it.

Rising to my feet, I asked, "Do you need anything else?"

He sighed and removed his glasses. "That was cruel of me."

And that was no apology. Keeping my jaw locked, I waited, but that was all he apparently had to say.

"I'll see you in the morning," I mumbled, and left.

I don't think my jaw unlocked the entire time I showered and prepared for bed. At one point I was so irritated, I considered storming back into his room and asking what game he was playing.

Though I'd been talking about the baby, I had no doubt his comment was a barb toward me. And it hurt.

He'd been the one to hire me and he'd orchestrated a great deal of the interactions Hale and I shared. The benefits and family dinners, why do all of that if he didn't want his son to fall in love with someone like me?

He had a lot of nerve. The man had four wives and chances were this wasn't the first of his illegitimate offspring. Why could he love whoever he wanted, but Hale couldn't?

I didn't find calm as I lay in bed and I wasn't sure I would in the days that followed. Remington was my boss and from now on he'd get an employee out of me and that was it. I refused to let him hurt me because he couldn't come to terms with his own issues.

Also, now that I admitted I loved Hale, I wasn't taking it back. Screw anyone who had a problem with my feelings. They were mine. So was Hale.

Too Close to Home

26

Apparently, I wasn't the only person who planned on evoking some distance. The following morning I found Remington on the veranda already enjoying his breakfast with his daughter. Sliding open the door, I paused as she finished telling him something about the baby. Though I wasn't sure what Barrett knew, it was clear Seraphina believed Elara was Hale's biological child.

"Rayne, come join us," she called as she finished her story.

Prepared to make an excuse, I opened my mouth, but Remington spoke first. "I'll need you to confirm with all the rentals that the balances from the party have been paid and I want you to take a ride into town today and meet with the interior designer working on the Riverton Estate."

The Riverton Estate was one of Remington's many homes, this one located in New England. "Yes, sir."

"Barrett went to get Hale," Seraphina said, face

alight with joy. "I wish I'd known this was happening. I would have made arrangements to stay longer." She twisted her lips. "Maybe I could manage a few more days."

"You have people depending on you, Phina," Remington commented, and my eyes narrowed. I really disliked him lately.

Phina sighed. "I know. Maybe I'll plan a trip back in a few weeks."

When Remington ignored his daughter's enthusiasm for the baby, I said, "If there's nothing else, I'll contact the vendors and be back in a bit to get the address for the meeting."

He waved a hand, dismissing me.

I didn't understand why his indifference crushed me. My anger faded into upset and as I worked through the list of the contracts I found myself distracted to the verge of tears.

By the time I finished calling everyone Seraphina was gone. I knew she was likely at Hale's welcoming home the baby and part of me envied the freedom they had to take part in that moment. Another part of me thought it was best I leave such events to the family and stay out of it.

"I'm finished. All the balances have been paid and the contracts are all in your office in a file labeled *Casino Royale Party*."

Remington nodded. "I'll text you the address. You can take the SUV in the garage."

"I'll just call a cab."

"Or you could argue with me, the one thing you seem to excel at above all else."

There was that crushing feeling again. "Where are the keys?"

As I sat behind the wheel of the very sophisticated Mercedes GLE, I tried to wipe the sweat off my palms. This car was easily over a hundred thousand dollars. I wasn't on the insurance policy and I hadn't driven anywhere in weeks. There was a seventy-five percent chance I would be returning the car bruised.

Once I figured out how to use the GPS I plugged in the address and a polite British voice directed me. The drive was about twenty minutes and when I reached the posh office complex, I wondered what I was supposed to do there. Remington hadn't been very specific.

I followed the lobby kiosk map to the office of Lynette Jones, Remington's designer on the project. Lynette was a young woman, about my age, only she'd nailed the responsible and thirty look. Her pencil skirt and silk blouse were at total odds with my boho sundress.

"You must be Ms. Meyers," she greeted, shaking my hand.

"It's nice to meet you."

She led me into a small conference room with a polished table and several stacks of sample flooring off to the side. "I suppose Remington sent a woman since the house is for a female client."

I frowned as she took a seat and opened a portfolio. "Aren't we doing something with the Riverton Estate?"

She nodded. "The far end of the estate, his son's portion of the land." She made an apologetic face. "I always get their names confused. Which one's the older one?"

"Hale," I supplied, still puzzled.

"Yes. I need to remember that. So this is Hale's portion of the land. He's selling it to a client. The major renovations were completed last week and now it's just a matter of the final details."

I shook my head, totally lost. This was a family property. "He's selling his entire portion?"

"I believe so. The new tenant's deed is for twenty-six acres."

Why would he do that? His siblings each had a stake in that estate and... An unwelcome sense of nausea stole over me. "Who's the buyer?"

"Well, Hale is, but the client's name is Jasmine Wacom."

I blinked at the table, wondering how I could have misread a person so severely. Remington sent me here on purpose. This wasn't his project. It was Hale's, and Hale was preoccupied at the moment.

Swallowing, I rasped, "Will you excuse me for a minute? I need to make a phone call."

"Of course." She stood and left the conference room.

Sliding out my phone, I stared at the screen, debating if I should bother Hale with this matter or go right to Remington. I had so many questions.

What message was Remington trying to send? Why hadn't Hale bought her a different house, somewhere away from his family? It was completely inappropriate for me to pick out this woman's drapes and flooring. I had no personal issues with her, but I didn't want to know what her kitchen counters looked like.

Swallowing again, I dialed Hale. Maybe I'd just feel him out. He might not even answer.

"Hey, baby."

Crap. "Hey. What are you doing?"

"We just got home. Phina's giving Elara a bottle and Barrett's helping me put together the baby swing." It sounded like such a lovely family moment.

"Oh. Good. I just wanted to say hi and make sure everything went okay at the hospital."

"Everything's great. How's your day going?"

"Fine." I kept it simple because I was a terrible liar and I absolutely hated lying to Hale, but I didn't want to interfere with his happy day. "Do you want me to come over tonight?"

"I was planning on it. It's Phina's last night here, so I thought we could order in and just hang out."

"Are you sure you want me there?"

He laughed. "Of course I do. I'll see you around five."

When I hung up the phone a steady rage washed over me. The Davenports were happy—all but one. Remington sent me here to tamper with his son's happiness and that infuriated me. Anger had never been my source of motivation in life, but I was fucking angry now and I'd had enough.

Rising, I found Lynette and told her I was ready. I decorated the fuck out of that house. The blueprints were incredible and this woman was walking away with everything due her.

Part of me wanted to villainize Jasmine, but that

was wrong. She'd done nothing to hurt the people I cared about. She'd only found herself in a position plenty of women had been in before. She had every right to be a parent, give the child up for adoption, or even terminate the pregnancy. Hale said she would have gone through with the latter had he not intercepted. In all truth, it was big of her to consent to the adoption when it wasn't her first choice. And in turn, her cooperation made Hale incredibly happy. So I did my best to make her home nice.

I chose the best of the best, pretending I was picking for myself and the sky was the limit. Lynette was great. She made wonderful points about color schemes and had swatches and samples for everything from bathroom fixtures to wood flooring. We wrapped up around five o'clock and that was when the punch line hit me right in the face.

"So I'll just need Hale's signature on all of this and then we'll get started on the installation."

I wasn't sure if Remington's intention was to hurt his son or me. The only thing I was clear on was the fact that my boss was a callous asshole.

"I'll make sure he signs them. I can run them back in a few days. Will that be soon enough?"

"Oh, we have plenty of time. The client's in France until November." She leaned in and smiled. "Could you imagine living in Europe for half a year? I'm telling you, I must be doing something wrong because that's doing it right."

My grin was forced. "It must be nice."

I left the paperwork on the front seat of the Benz where it taunted me the entire ride home. When I reached the house, I went in search for

Remington, who was in the process of explaining something to Miles.

Stepping into the room, I interrupted, "Will you excuse us for a minute, Miles?"

Remington scowled. "We're in the middle of something, Meyers."

"This will only take a second."

Miles looked from me to Remington, who nodded so the other assistant could be momentarily excused. Once we were alone, Remington folded his arms over his chest and continued to scowl. "You misjudge your position in this household, Meyers."

"Probably. I wanted to let you know Jasmine's plans are complete. It was nice of you to handle that for Hale since he's preoccupied with family." I had the pleasure of watching a bit of his smugness fade.

"If you object to the assignments I give you—"

"I don't. I just wanted to let you know it's done." I'd be damned if I'd give him the satisfaction of letting him know this bothered me. "Is there anything else?"

"Does Hale know where you were?"

I shrugged. "You'd have to ask him."

"I'm asking you."

"The last thing I'd assume to do is speak for a Davenport. I suggest you take that up with your son."

He glared at me and my stomach started to cramp. I needed to get away from him. First he'd hurt me, but now I was just pissed. "If that's all for the day—"

"Alfonse is going to take you driving."

I frowned. "What?"

"I'm short a limo driver now that Eric's gone."

"Miles is learning. Wouldn't he be better suited?"

"No. He has a background in business. He's better suited for working by my side."

"I see." The waitress gets the demotion.

"Be back by eight to help me to bed."

My lips compressed. So Miles was also overqualified for tucking him in. Without another word, I turned on my heel and went to find Alfonse.

Several hours later I was in need of a big glass of wine. Alfonse needed something a bit stronger.

So I wasn't the best limo driver. I was lucky I managed not to kill myself in my own little two-door car over the past decade. The limousine was three times the length of what I was used to.

Hale had texted me several times asking where I was, but Alfonse freaked out and took my phone the second I attempted to reply while driving. When we got back to the house I called Hale, but there was no answer.

Seeing that Remington was showered and ready for bed, I went about situating his medicine and pillows. The chill between us had not thawed and I was anxious to get to Hale's.

"You'll need to have Hale sign the plans for the estate," he said, shifting into bed.

"I will."

"I'll also need to see them."

I paused, knowing full well this had nothing to do with him, but I was *his* employee, and my loyalties were divided. Having had enough, I faced him.

"What is it you're trying to prove here, Remington?"

"I don't know what you're talking about."

"Oh, cut the crap. Is this about you not wanting me to date your son or is this about the baby or is it something I did that I'm not even aware of?"

He stared at me for a long moment, then admitted, "I don't want you to date my son."

That hurt a little more than I expected. My voice turned small as I worked it past the lump in my throat and the crushing insecurity resting on my heart. "Why?"

"I don't think it needs to be spelled out."

"Then you should have hired someone a little brighter than me because I'm a touch dense. You were fine with everything a week ago."

"I misjudged you."

I frowned, perfectly aware I had faults, but confident I was still a decent person. "How so?"

"How is it, Meyers, that he won't let you look at another man, yet you can accept all his baggage left by another woman?"

That *baggage* was Hale's daughter and partially his, too. I shook my head, truly feeling sorry for him. "Hale did you a favor, Remington."

"He did me no favor. It's a goddamn complication."

"That complication is your granddaughter," I snapped.

He shook his head and looked away. "I'll have nothing to do with that child."

No matter how many breaths I took, I couldn't get enough air. "How can you say that? You and I both know that child is something to you. How can you punish her? She's innocent."

"That child will have every bit of my legacy that my future grandchildren will, but I refuse to celebrate this perverse version of...I don't even have a word for it."

I wanted to hit him. But for all the rage I felt, it was nothing compared to my disappointment and pity.

"I thought you were a nice guy."

He laughed, coldly. "Your mistake."

Speechless, I stared at him for a solid minute. "Yes. My mistake." Lowering my head my vision swam behind a sheen of unshed tears as I finally figured it all out. "You used me. Eric was right."

When he said nothing, I accepted the truth.

"You hired me because you thought I'd distract Hale. Maybe he'd realize he wasn't ready to be tied down with a child. How long was I supposed to hold his interest, Remington? A few weeks? Months?"

"You could have married him, so long as it kept him from going through with this nonsense."

A tear escaped and I quickly dashed it away. "I'll start looking for my replacement tomorrow."

He sat up. "Now, just a minute, Meyers. We have an arrangement."

"Which one is that?" I snapped. "There have been so many I can't keep track." My body shook with indignant pressure as I tried to hold it together.

"The one where you work for me and we cut the bullshit."

"Then cut it!" I shouted. "Don't use me to manipulate your kids! If you want me to drive your limo, fine. I don't care if you want me to spoon-feed you, but I'm not going to be a part of your games, especially where Hale's concerned. The only perverse thing about this whole situation is *you*. I'm sorry you lost your wife. But you did this. *You*. This isn't Hale's fault, and you should be thanking him for fixing your screw up, but all you can think of is yourself. That baby needs a father and he's going to be one for her.

"Do you know how incredible that is? How can you sit here and act like nothing remarkable is happening? Why do you have to be so hard on them? Don't you ever just look at your kids and feel proud of them? Because that's all they want."

I choked, my words getting ahead of me. Somewhere in the midst of all that I'd lost control of my emotions and begun shouting through my tears. Even I, in the short span of time I'd known Remington, had become desperate for his approval.

I quickly blotted my eyes and whispered, "They just want your approval."

The look on Remington's face was the closest thing to fear I'd ever saw him express. Neither of us said anything for some time. I frowned as he twisted his legs off the bed and made to stand.

Out of habit, I took a step forward, but he held out a staying hand. Struggling, he held the bedpost and wobbled to his feet.

I was too hurt to detect his motive as he staggered to the end of the bed and gripped the other post. Face red, he looked in my eyes and frowned.

Reaching into the silk pocket of his blue pajama

set, he withdrew a linen square and pressed it into my hand. "The one thing I can't take is a woman's tears, Meyers."

I looked down at the handkerchief with the initials RD sewn into the corner. "I don't understand you, Remington."

All of this discord was killing me. I didn't like the level of consequence connected to his every action, and it wasn't fair that his indifference could cause so much heartache.

He lowered himself to the edge of the bed and caught his breath, hand still gripping the bedpost. Head low, he muttered, "I'm proud of my children."

I wiped my eyes unable to continue this argument. My hands were tied and I hated it, hated that he had so much authority over those that loved him and he continuously abused it. Dads weren't supposed to be like that.

He frowned as he stared at the wall ahead of him. "I'm old, damn it. I'm supposed to die with dignity. That night...it meant nothing. But to Rachel it meant everything. She never looked at me the same after she caught us together. I swore I'd make it right by her, but...I never had the chance."

I sat beside him on the bed, also staring at the wall. Rachel was dead. Those were his demons and he had to deal with them privately.

"Punishing Hale won't make your regret any easier."

He glanced at me and I couldn't tell if he thought I was just a naïve girl or if he thought I had a point. "A few weeks ago you told me you didn't date."

I shrugged. "I told you the truth." As much as this family rift was upsetting me, it had very little to do with me.

"You're in love with him."

I shrugged again. "I haven't had a lot of men in my life, so it's a little hard for me to define what I feel, but it's a lot."

It was love. There was no denying it. But that shouldn't influence the family situation one way or another. Our love was private, mine and Hale's.

I really missed the nice side of Remington when it came to defining things I had little experience with, because he had an astounding way of clarifying the things that confused me in this world. Had the baby not come when she did, I would have told him about my drunken confession the other night and asked him to make sense of all the confusion in my head, but he'd been unreachable for the past week, and I had no one to simplify these emotions.

Elle was just a phone call away, but since the news of the baby, she'd been advising me against further involvement with Hale. The fact that I shelved her advice was the first indication that I was more than a little emotionally involved. Hale was the first thing in my life I wanted regardless of other people's opinions on the subject.

Remington sighed. "He's a lot like me, Meyers."

In some ways, yes, but not all. "No matter how upset I am with you, Remington, I do believe there's some good in your soul."

"You're good for him."

I laughed without humor. Now he was contradicting himself. "But you want better for him."

He waved a tired hand. "Of all the women I've known, I've never had trouble figuring them out. You're different."

"Why?"

He frowned, shaking his head as if *up* was suddenly *down* and purple was now yellow. "You're a mess."

I laughed again. No arguing with that.

"Hale doesn't do messy. He's always had an aversion to it. He used to keep his blocks stacked neatly in a pile when he was a boy and I'd ask him why he never played with them. I suppose he wanted to please me, so he built a castle. I watched as he walked to the wall, carefully selecting each one and carrying it back only when he was sure it would fit seamlessly into his plans. He worked on that castle for a week. Barrett had built several things in that time, but nothing was as impressive as the one Hale constructed."

"He is meticulous."

"Babies are messy," he commented. "I'm not talking about sticky fingers and spilt milk. I'm talking about the stuff inside. You worry if they're going to get bullied, if they're going to *be* a bully, and you try to steer them somewhere in between soft and hard so you're confident they'll someday be able to take care of themselves. I had three incredible women help raise my children. How is Hale going to do this alone?"

A bit of my anger faded as I understood his distance was partially made up of concern. "You're worried about him."

"Of course I am. He doesn't have a clue what he's committing to. It's hard enough raising your own children. I couldn't imagine taking on someone else's."

Taking a deep breath, I gave him the truth. "The baby's his, Remington. If you'd meet her, you'd see. He loves her already." Even I was a bit taken aback by how fast he'd fallen, how absolute Hale's love was once he gave it.

"And then there's you."

My defenses went back up. "What about me?"

"You don't date, yet you're in love with my son. How strong is that love, Meyers? Is it strong enough to share? As much as I loved each of my wives, I never loved any woman to the degree I loved my daughter. Hale needs a woman who will help him if he's really going to do this."

"Who says?"

"Time. Time says."

"Remington, my mom raised me alone and she did fine."

For the most part. I knew I was a bit odd and irresponsible, but I was working on it.

He studied me for a long moment. "Where was your father?"

I shrugged. "Away doing something else."

"That explains a lot."

"Gee, thanks."

"You know what I mean."

After the last few days, I was completely drained. Sighing, I said, "I can't tell you how many times I tried to contact him and came back empty-handed. I couldn't even tell you the last time was the end of my hope because I still haven't given up. I know I'll eventually try again, and he'll most likely let me down again. It's something I'll probably be bothered by for my entire life."

Reaching over, he patted my knee. "He's the one missing out. You're a good kid, Meyers. You have a lot of potential and one day he'll realize exactly who you are and that it's too late."

I laughed, despite myself. "It's a little hard to believe that when a minute ago you told me I wasn't good enough for your son."

"I never said that."

"But you don't want him to date me."

He sighed, the events of the past few days catching up to him. "You're a lot more sensitive then you appear. I don't want you to date my son, but not because I think you're not good enough. Davenport men don't make the best partners."

That might be true by Remington's record, but Hale wasn't his father. "Are you worried about *me*?"

"You make it too easy for him. A woman should challenge a man, make him strive to evolve."

"Maybe everything isn't a merger or a competition, Remington. Maybe people can just love each other."

"That's exactly the sort of liberal bullshit I'd expect from you."

I shrugged. "I am who I am."

"You're young. You should want to be more. I'd understand settling down if you had your life in order, but you don't."

No one said this was where it would end. I'd come here because I needed to shake up my life. But this whole strategized approach to dealing with people wasn't me.

"I told Hale I wouldn't walk away just because of the baby."

"And that's exactly what I meant when I said you have potential. You might not like being challenged, Meyers, but you'll be damned before you balk at one. Perhaps part of me doesn't want you to date Hale because I'm worried his choices will hold you back."

Startled by his words, I faced him. "Hold me back from what?"

"I gave you an opportunity, an open door with a private invitation to a world you never could've entered as a waitress. You should think about that before you commit to playing nursemaid."

My brow tightened. "That's not what I'm doing."

"You and I both know there's a good possibility that's how this will end. You're capable of more."

I didn't want more and I definitely didn't want to play nanny. I wanted easy. Babies equaled difficult and I'd been telling myself that since one was thrown into the picture. None of that thinking led to nursemaid.

"So what is it you want, Remington?"

"I want to see you try."

"I am trying." I was trying to make a change, trying not to strangle my new boss, trying to finally maintain an adult relationship. All of these things were new in the trying department.

He shook his head. "You need direction, Meyers. At first, I thought it would be entertaining, passing my days with someone who challenged me—sort of like a bad reality show you can't look away from—but then you surprised me. The few assignments I gave you, you tackled with aptitude. I'm never quite sure when you'll pull back and when you'll barrel in like a bull in a china shop, but you rarely disappoint me. You're a smart girl, but you let your fear get the better of you."

"I just want to be your assistant. Conquering the world is your shtick."

"Don't be an idiot, Meyers. You're more than a gofer."

No, I'm not.

"Well, that's all I want to be right now, so you can stop worrying I might return to childcare."

"So you intend to stay on as my assistant."

Tricky bastard. He wasn't even asking, more so surmising whatever kind of round about negotiation this was. I wasn't sure if continuing my job for him was right. This all started because I wanted him to see his granddaughter. "Will you think about what I said?"

"Ah, avoidance. Another area in which you excel."

"Your son needs you to be a part of this, Remington."

"Because every child wants the approval of a father," he said, almost to himself. "You're not as transparent as you once were, Meyers. You got a thick skin, but you wear that bleeding heart of yours right on your sleeve. Maybe tuck it away for a bit."

Despite his gruff, sometimes jarring approach, it seemed like he was trying to protect me in some way. From Hale? I couldn't understand why. I'd never been cynical enough to hide who I was.

Shelving his advice, I turned the conversation back to him. "Please visit them."

"I'll consider it if you consider what I've said tonight. Do something with yourself, Meyers. Don't just exist in Hale's shadow. He's not going to have an abundance of free time in the coming months. I need someone to step up to the plate and take care of the things I usually depend on him for. I want that person to be you."

Hale's shoes were definitely too big for me to fill. "You have Miles."

He waved a hand. "Miles will do fine on his own. I'm a notch on his resume at this point."

"But I'm not qualified."

He huffed. "Christ, don't make me spell it out. I need someone I can trust."

"I'll help out where I can, but I'm not your kicking post, Remington. I may look at you as more than a boss, but I'm not desperate for any man's approval. Not my dad's and certainly not yours."

I left Hale out of the equation because I lacked the foresight to imagine anything as painful as him being disappointed in me.

"There's that backbone I admire."

I wasn't letting him distract me. "You play games with people's feelings and it hurts."

"I was wrong to put you in the position I put you in today."

My brows lifted. "Was that an apology?"

"It's as close to one as you're gonna get."

I shook my head. "You're such a narcissist."

"And I have every right to be. But I hurt you today and there was no satisfaction in that."

And that was his way of saying sorry. I glared at him, hiding the affection that still remained.

Part of me believed once you loved a man like Remington you never stopped, no matter how much of a dick he could be. "Don't do it again."

His mouth pursed, but he nodded. "I can help you, Meyers."

"I don't need help."

"What about returning to school? Take a few business courses and see how you like it."

My nose scrunched as I compiled a list of qualities I worked hard to avoid. Greasy palms and tough decisions weren't my thing. "School's expensive and I'm still paying off my loans."

"I'll take care of that for you. Take a few classes and see how it fits."

His offer was tempting, but the idea of owing Remington Davenport any sort of debt was terrifying. My mind saw school as an acceptable delay to reality. I'd always been a great student. It was the post-college stuff that crippled my ambition. I couldn't waste more time on another career I didn't want.

I wasn't a businessperson. "I can't let you do that."

"You really are a pain in my ass. Think about it. It's bad form to settle negotiations in one sitting."

I chuckled. "Are we negotiating?"

"Yes."

Negotiating meant each side had a form of leverage. Realizing mine, I used it. "Fine. If you accept Hale's decision and meet your granddaughter, I'll take *one* online course."

"Deal."

"Deal? Just like that?" That was too easy. Somehow, I felt played.

He shrugged. "You were right. Children need a father. That baby has Hale and..." He waved a hand. "You get what I'm saying."

And Hale needed his father as well.

The tightness that had resonated in my shoulders over the past few days abated and I nudged him. "You're not as rotten as everyone thinks."

"I can be a bear."

"I have a better word for it, but we'll use yours."

He chuckled. "Tomorrow, we'll take a ride over and see the baby."

I smiled at him, on the verge of hugging him, but I held back. "Hale will love that. And I can show you my skills behind the wheel of the limo."

He grimaced. "There's no way in hell I'm letting you drive. I'm trying to save my life, not end it."

I gaped at him. "Then why did you have me practice?"

As soon as I asked, I had my answer. He didn't want me to go to Hale's and have an experience he couldn't abide himself.

"Never mind." I shook my head. "Sometimes you're worse than a four-year-old."

He arched a dark brow. "This conversation stays between us, Meyers."

I gave him a cheeky smile. "God forbid the world find out you have feelings."

"God forbid," he agreed. "Help me lie down. I've had enough talking for one day."

As I assisted him back to bed, my tension eased. I wasn't sure why I cared so much about this man, but I did. I cared about him, his children, and even his grandchild.

It was strange to hold so much affection for people I only recently met, but something told me they were put in my life for a reason. I was still trying to figure out what that reason might be.

27

O nce I had Remington settled, I planned to call Hale again, but Barrett came home, and I wanted to talk to him first. It was late and we were all short on sleep.

"I was just going to head over," I told him, putting down my phone.

"Don't bother. Daddy Dearest is fast asleep."

"Oh. That's probably good."

Barrett came over to the counter and gave my shoulder a squeeze. "You okay?"

"Yeah, just tired, I guess."

"Well, get some sleep. He's not going anywhere."

Impressed by what a good brother Barrett was, I smiled. "Did Phina leave for her flight?"

"About an hour ago."

"How long will you stay?"

Barrett wasn't tied to any business. He made money modeling here and there but wasn't as entrepreneurial as the rest of his family.

He shrugged. "Until I get stir crazy or my dad pisses me off. I'm in no rush to be anywhere else."

"Hale will be happy to have you around."

He laughed. "Not so sure about my father."

"He might surprise you." I didn't say any more on the subject of Remington because I didn't want to speak too soon, but my optimism was pulling for him.

After saying goodnight, I went to my room and crashed before I even changed into pajamas. The following morning, Remington and I shared a peaceful breakfast and Hale called shortly after that.

I didn't mention that his father planned to stop by because I was still unsure if he would. But I was pleasantly surprised when I saw Miles help Remington to the limo.

"Are you coming, Meyers?" he called as I showed Miles how to collapse the scooter into the trunk.

I hesitated. "I thought it would be nice for you and Hale to have some time alone."

I read the uncertainty in Remington's eyes, but he nodded, and Miles shut the door, then he joined Alfonse in the front seat.

While the house was empty, I did my laundry and called my mom. I told her about the party for Seraphina and the celebrities I brushed elbows with on the yacht. She said my new life reminded her of the old show *Dynasty*.

When I ended the call, I went to the kitchen. Marta had just what I needed, a fresh batch of homemade cinnamon buns.

"I made them for Hale. We're taking them over to him tonight. You test."

I tested three because you can never be too sure. Rich people had the best desserts. I seriously needed to get on some sort of exercise regimen.

Remington returned just before supper, and I watched him carefully, waiting for him to express any signs that his visit had been a success. I'd hoped he'd come home and tell me how beautiful Elara was or how great Hale was with her, but he said nothing. He just looked sad.

I thought about Jasmine and her refusal to hold the baby. Perhaps she was smart to stay detached. Maybe I was wrong to pressure Remington. I hadn't done it to hurt him. I only wanted to help bridge the gap between him and his son.

When Miles stepped away and we were alone, I whispered, "Did you have a nice visit?"

He appeared taken off guard by my question, almost like he missed what I'd asked. Marta appeared before he answered.

"Pardon me, sir, but I forgot to tell you Ms. Naomi called while you were out."

My ears went on high alert. Naomi, as in Hale's mom?

Remington nodded. "I'll call her back after dinner." When we were alone again, he looked at me and chuckled. "No doubt you'll be in a trifecta by the end of the week."

"What do you mean?" I was instantly nervous.

"It's one thing to compete with a man's daughter. It's a whole other thing to compete with his mother. You'll see."

My eyes went wide. "Is she coming here?"

He laughed. "Her son just had a child. What do you think?"

It was the first time he made any reference to Elara. Somehow that took precedence over my own worry. "What did you think about the baby?"

"I think...I think there might be something to be said for grandchildren. It's different in a way I didn't expect."

That was lovely and I wanted to take a minute to bask in my satisfaction, but there were other issues that needed addressing. "Where does Naomi stay when she visits?"

He frowned. "Hale's. I've had three wives since Naomi. It's been decades since we've slept under the same roof."

"How long does she usually stay?"

"Usually a week. Hale has an in-law suite and he has to get back to work, so I imagine she might stick around."

I was never having sex again. Hale was her only son, and going by his reputation and instilled manners, he wasn't the sort of son to blow off his mother.

"Do you think Miles can help you the rest of the night?"

He waved a hand. "Go."

Not wasting a single second, I shoveled the last bite of food into my mouth and left. Remington had told me I could use the Mercedes SUV whenever I needed, so I drove, not sure when I'd be coming home.

On the short trip I came up with a game plan. I'd walk in, take off my clothes, and attack.

But what about the baby? Babies slept something like eighteen hours a day in the beginning, so maybe she was sleeping. I really needed her to be asleep. This was going to suck when I not only had to consider the baby's schedule, but his mother's presence as well.

Pulling into Hale's driveway, I grabbed the keys and speed walked to the door. I didn't ring the bell, because if Elara was asleep I didn't want to wake her.

I was totally unprepared for the mayhem that greeted me.

The baby squalled from somewhere on the second floor. The sink was full of dishes and a pot of soup had boiled over on the stove. "Hale?"

Following the trail of rattles and blankets, I collected infant paraphernalia as I neared the cries.

"Hale?" He still didn't answer me.

It was amazing how powerful a few dirty diapers could smell. The stench smacked me in the face the second I stepped into that lovely white nursery, which was in shambles.

Hale worked to calm the baby as he fastened her jumper. He had an old t-shirt on and a pair of briefs.

"Where are your pants?" I frowned as I heard water running.

"Hey. Can you take her for a second? I have something on the stove."

Eyes wide, I tightened my grip on the items filling my arms. Screaming babies didn't bear the temptation sweetly cooing ones did.

"I shut off the stove. It was boiling over."

He sighed in relief, his hair in complete disarray. "Thanks."

The hamper was overflowing, but the first issue that needed attention was the trash. How the hell did something that small poop that much? I emptied my arms and tied off the bag.

"I'm going to take this outside."

He nodded and plugged a bottle in Elara's mouth, which immediately silenced her screams. On my way back to the nursery I wiped up the stove and loaded the dishwasher, frowning at the little baby items in the sink.

When I returned, Hale still looked frazzled but Elara drank heavily from the bottle, her eyes closed. "Is water running somewhere?"

"I was going to shower, but she woke up."

I went to shut off the water and realized this was not at all what I had planned. Maybe he did need Naomi here.

As I came back into the ransacked nursery, Hale was carefully placing her in the crib. I silently stacked diapers into a flipped over basket and put a new bag in the trashcan.

He backed away from the crib like a bomb might detonate at any second. I quietly watched him and joined him in the hall. "Having a rough—"

"*Shh.*"

He carefully closed the door and his pleading eyes turned on me. "This is way harder than I expected. I'm fucking exhausted."

I had no consolatory words. Selfishly, I wondered where my boyfriend went, the one who always smelled great and had perfect hair and wore pants.

"Why don't you take a shower and I'll keep an ear out in case she wakes up?"

He sighed as if I'd pardoned him from a life sentence. "Thank you."

While Hale showered, I tidied up. I didn't know where he kept stuff, so I just stuck things anywhere. Then there were things of his that were put away, but clearly in the wrong place, so I organized those shelves as well. I peeked in drawers and behind doors until I heard the shower shut off.

A few minutes later my boyfriend returned—the real one with the clean-shaven jaw and pants.

"You didn't have to clean up." He wrapped his arms around me and squeezed.

Sinking into his strength I sighed. "I missed you."

His mouth found my neck and I drew in a breath. Taking his hand, I guided it to my boob, because, let's face it, we had limited time. He chuckled and softly massaged. That's what I was talking about. I gave him another signal all systems were go and pressed my behind into his hips.

"I've been a little preoccupied lately," he whispered.

"That's okay." God, just the weight of his hand on me was extraordinary. I wanted to be sympathetic, maybe let him catch a nap, but there was time for that later. At the moment I was a single-minded sex fiend, needing to prove we still had this connection post baby.

I reached behind my back and cupped him and he groaned. His hand lowered, lifting my skirt, as his finger slid aside the silk of my panties and skirted my sex. "Fuck, baby, I missed this."

Already breathing fast, I turned and pulled him

down for a kiss. There was such haste to my motions. I hadn't realized how much I feared this part of our relationship might change or vanish.

He cupped my ass and we plummeted to the couch, his body grinding over mine as my ankle hooked over his hip and pulled him closer. My dress was shoved to the top of my chest as my bra came down. His mouth fastened to my flesh as his finger sank deep and I moaned, arching into his touch.

My hands rode over his hips and found his zipper. Undoing his pants, I stroked him, pressing my hips closer to his erection until it glided against my sex. This needed to happen *now*, before the little pooper woke up.

We both shuddered at the hot contact and he pulled back. "Condom."

I inwardly growled. He felt so good gliding against my skin. I teased and stroked him along my flesh again. It was just a tease so we were both taken a bit off guard when he slid in by the slightest degree.

Pausing, our breath mingled as he looked into my eyes. I wasn't an idiot. People that weren't ready for children used birth control. I got an A in health class, so there was really no explicable reason why my hips suddenly lifted and took him in another inch.

There was a split second where we studied each other, likely having the same list of consequences run through our minds, but neither of us objected to what was clearly happening. My period just ended so I wasn't fertile.

I gave a slight nod, my mind refusing to entertain any serious thoughts at the moment. It registered that I wasn't going to stop him, as stupid as that made me, and he thrust forward. We both moaned.

"Fuck. You feel incredible," he groaned.

My fingers pressed into his shoulders as my heel dug into his butt, edging him on. We wasted no time on regret. There was too much pleasure. My legs parted as he thrust hard and I cried out a litany of dirty words begging him never to stop. We were panting and moaning and clawing at each other's flesh, greedy for more.

Gasping, the thrills of ecstasy took hold and he pounded harder, his words demanding I give him everything. My arms fell back as I gripped the arm of the sofa, calling out his name as I arched into him and came. He thrust one last time and then he was suddenly gone, his own release coating my stomach.

Knowing we'd both done something very irresponsible, it seemed crucial to destroy all evidence before any witnesses showed up. I reached for a box of baby wipes sitting on the coffee table and Hale made quick work of cleaning up the mess.

I righted my dress and he fixed his pants. Then we both sat up and stared at the television, which was off. After several minutes he said, "We should talk about the pill."

"Yup." I nodded, because that could *not* happen again.

But it did. Once we knew what it was like to go without a condom and realized how unpredictable his daughter's schedule was, we took whatever we could get whenever we could get it.

That night we had sex in the kitchen, in the bedroom, on the steps, and in the hall. We gorged ourselves until we had nothing left and poor Hale hadn't slept a wink.

When I returned to Remington's there was no mention of our previous conversation, but there was an email in my inbox from an advisor of a local college. I deleted it.

Naomi's flight was coming in around midnight and my worry about how her presence might change our ever-shifting dynamic terrified me. I joined Hale at his house for dinner and Elara was in a pleasant mood, so I sat with her on the floor, shaking plush rattles over her, which she seemed to appreciate.

"So I think we should talk," I said, keeping my voice casual.

Hale's expression blanked. "Okay."

"I made an appointment with a doctor so I can go on the pill."

He nodded. "I was going to bring that up again."

"And...I have some paperwork for you to sign."

He frowned. "Paperwork?"

Things were about to get icky. "I met with Lynette."

His frown turned to a scowl. "When?"

"The day you came home from the hospital. It's no big deal." It totally was. "You just need to sign the plans."

He stood, clearly agitated, and busied himself by picking up items around the room that needed to be put away.

"Are you mad?"

He scoffed, but said nothing.

"Hale?"

Shaking his head, he snapped, "He had no right to send you to that meeting. I would have handled it."

Yes, Remington was high-handed. This wasn't news. "Maybe you could tell me why you're giving her part of your estate."

His eyes closed as he pinched the bridge of his nose. "I rarely stay there."

"But your family does. Isn't that going to cause some conflict down the line?"

Dropping back to the sofa, he braced his arms on the edge of his knees. "I made the offer when everything was new. I was angry with my father and I wanted to hurt him. He tampered with something I considered...mine. The estate has always been one of his favorite homes. It's his, but we inherited our portions years ago."

I couldn't deny the disappointment I felt, finding such vindictiveness beneath him. "Can you change it? Is there a way you can offer her a different property?"

"No." He eased back on the sofa and I recognized the stress in his eyes. "I've tried. Once I cooled down and realized having her there wouldn't benefit anyone, I made a counteroffer, but her lawyer turned it down."

That quickly my opinion of this woman shifted, returning to a point of distrust. I'd given her credit, witnessing how stoically she walked away in order to grant Hale's wishes, but nothing was ever black and white.

"Is she holding on to it as some sort of leverage?"

His mouth flattened. "Whether she realizes it or not, that's exactly what it is." He picked up the stuffed sheep sitting beside him and stared at it, his voice somewhat distant. "Elara's guardianship is solid. It's my name on her birth certificate, but there are always loopholes. I'll never be able to take her there."

"But Jasmine doesn't want her." That might change, however, if she saw Elara.

"No, she doesn't. She does want a life of luxury, however, which is why I've made things as easy as possible for her."

"What about your dad? Can he do something?"

"I'd rather not involve him."

But he was involved. Biologically, this woman would always be Elara's mother. Hale was not her true father and, should Jasmine contest, his shaky position might hinder his good intentions. I couldn't see Remington voluntarily disclosing his true position to protect this child, but what if his silence cost his son?

"I'm sure it will all work out." That was total bullshit, but I didn't like seeing Hale worried.

I stood, scooping Elara off the floor and rocking her in my arms as she drifted off. Once she was asleep I carried her to the nursery and gently placed her in the crib. As I shut the door, I found Hale waiting in the hall.

The intense look in his eyes gave me pause. Slowly, he approached and took my hand, drawing my fingers to his lips for a kiss. His other hand lifted and traced my jaw, that penetrating silver gaze never leaving my face.

The air thickened. A heavy pull tugged between us as I stood before him, enduring his inspection, my body slowly heating under his reverent scrutiny. I'd expected him to have very little time for intimacy, but every time his daughter went to sleep he seemed ravenous, like he couldn't get enough of me, each encounter more demanding than the last.

I wasn't sure where all this sudden intensity came from, if he was trying to prove something to himself, or me, or perhaps he just needed something outside of his role as parent for a moment.

"You need sleep, Hale."

"I need you." His lips brushed mine and I waited, unsure why this time felt different from all the other times he kissed me.

He teased me with his mouth, taunted. His eyes watched me as he silently asserted his virility with each nip and lick. He crowded closer, boxing me in, demonstrating a level of unspoken ownership as he helped himself to my body. It was enthralling and a bit unnerving at the same time. I waited to see what he'd do next, what exactly he wanted from me.

Something desperate passed between us, needy and hungry. His gaze followed his touch as it gradually traced my shoulder to the strap of my dress.

Without speaking, he lowered the zipper of my dress. Fabric whispered down my frame as the dress fell to the floor, leaving me shivering before him in nothing but my bra and underwear.

"Sometimes," he whispered, his lips brushing over my shoulder and sending chills down my back.

"You have a way of sweeping away all the bullshit, Rayne. Let me have you."

My nipples pebbled as the clasp of my bra came undone and my breasts hung heavily as he peeled the lace away. His fingers caught the silk covering my hips, stripping it to my ankles, and I stood before him completely bare and shivered.

His eyes took me in, unapologetically looking his fill. There was such need hidden in the depths of his stare, such command of everything I was and felt in those passing seconds. Perhaps he needed to feel in control after confronting the things outside of his power, in order to cope with his fears.

I could be that for him. I could give him the authority he seemed to desperately need at that moment.

I waited, showing no objection to his boldness. My surrender seemed to register as his breathing escalated. Somehow, for as unobservant as I tended to be, I always recognized this shift in him, the subtle plea in his eyes to possess my body, own me in a way no one else ever managed.

I glanced below his waist where he was noticeably hard and lifted my gaze, telling him without words, he was free to do as he pleased.

In tune with my subtle permission, he took a swift step forward, backing me to the wall with his towering body as he pinned my hands against the flat surface.

His mouth crashed over my throat. His breathing labored as he cupped my chest, mashing my delicate flesh in his palm.

The jangle of his belt coming undone was a

slight warning before my thighs were wedged apart and his fingers penetrated. I gasped, rocking into his hold as the heat of his body burned against mine.

"I love you," he hissed, pressing my back to the wall. His eyes were wild as he cupped my face and kissed me hard. "I fucking love you."

My feet lifted off the ground as he balanced my body with his strength, leaving only enough space for a gasp of surprise as he drove into me, hard. His possession was rough, needy, and almost bruising as he pulled me down to meet each blunted thrust. I caught his strong shoulders and held onto him.

Our bodies slicked with sweat. My breasts slid against his chest as he pinned me there, his breath beating starkly against my shoulder.

He stilled, deep inside of me and I waited, immobile, trapped in his hold.

"Sorry," he whispered, seeming to reclaim his senses. "I'm being too rough with you."

On the precipice of ecstasy, my hand gently cupped his head. "It's okay. You aren't hurting me."

He groaned as his hips slowly pumped. "I needed you. I couldn't wait." Somehow his words spoke of more than this moment.

"I'm here," I assured him.

He was exhausted, overwhelmed, and I was his escape. That, for some reason, gave me more purpose than so many other things in my life and I drew comfort where he took his.

"You have me, Hale. I'm not going anywhere."

Drawing his head back, he studied me, eyes unguarded, and there was so much vulnerability flashing in their depths. Withdrawing, he let my legs trail down his until my toes met the floor. Then he scooped me into his arms and carried me to his bed.

He laid my body on the duvet with utter tenderness, never taking his gaze off me as he removed the remainder of his clothes. A hollow ache formed at my core where his body had been. I wanted him back inside of me, but Hale had other ideas.

His mouth worked up my inner thigh, kissing and licking over the most sensitive places. My body stretched beneath him, opening without encouragement, begging for anything he might offer. His motions were restrained as he visibly battled to retain his control and I took pity on how much it cost him.

"I won't break," I whispered, knowing he'd never intentionally hurt me. Hale was an intense man and I wanted all of him, not just the well-rounded edges. "You don't have to be gentle."

Though I was the farthest thing from an expert on men, something told me he was holding back and needed to unleash. Others looked at him and saw a refined gentleman. I saw that too, but I also saw the animalistic side of him. The part that hungered greedily to let go of the propriety that bound him, and ached to be set free.

Catching his fingers, I gently smiled. "Take me the way you want, Hale. I won't run scared."

His brow tightened as the inner debate played over his features and then the decision was made. He caught my hips and flipped me to my stomach, dragging my body to the edge of the bed until my toes grazed the floor.

He wedged my thighs apart, his labored breath

audible in the silence, as he stilled. "I need this," his whispered.

"I know. It's okay. I'm yours."

He let out a slow exhalation that sent a chill across my shoulder. The blunt tip of his cock nudged my folds as his thighs pressed to mine. I could sense all he held inside, the rage of so much emotion dying to get out, but he seemed terrified to let himself go.

"Please, Hale. I want it...hard."

My cry echoed off the walls as he filled me to the hilt. As my body lifted, he caught my shoulder, dragging his wide palm across my chest and to my jaw, angling my head back as he thrust again. I'd never been in such a vulnerable position, his fingers curling around my throat in a way that contrasted his absolute strength with my slight size. He held me there, not cruelly, but worshipfully, and I melted into his touch, giving him total control.

His fingers dug into my hips as he roughly filled me and I gasped with each penetrating advance. Releasing my jaw, he gathered my hair in his fist and held me at a sharp angle. My body took every pounding thrust and he never slowed. Eventually, my strength waned, and his hold gentled, but he didn't stop.

Resting on my tired arms, I gasped with each plunging thrust. This was more than I anticipated, a darker side to him than I'd expected, but it was raw and honest and I wanted him to share it with me, because the idea of him showing this side to anyone else gutted me.

The slap of our slicked bodies filled the room as

I gasped under each hard advance. He cursed and grunted, his hands pulling at my limbs, cupping my curves, and his teeth scraping over my skin. I had no idea where he found the energy, but he seemed far from finished.

His fingers gripped my ass, parting my cheeks as he slowed and stared at our bodies sliding together. "You're so pretty, Rayne. Every part of you."

I should care that he was staring at my back door, but I couldn't muster the concern. My folds were wet and swollen, making it easy for him to slide in and out of my sex as it pulsed with what seemed like endless need.

He withdrew and my weak limbs sagged over the edge of the mattress. He carefully lifted me, placing me back in the center of his bed. The heat of his body blanketed mine. I was warm, but he was scorching. My body shivered as his heated flesh burned against mine.

My eyes opened as his lips gently traced mine. He looked at me questioningly and I smiled, more sexually depleted than I'd ever been.

"You okay?" he whispered, gently cupping my face.

"Mm-hm."

I was more than okay. I was thoroughly loved, needed, and wanted in ways I never assumed I'd be. My palm curved along his strong jaw as I stared into his beautiful eyes. I stopped trying to rationalize my feelings or justify how fast my emotions had evolved, and recognized them for what they were.

"I love you, Hale."

His lashes lowered as if those four words were

everything he waited for in this life. Countering his earlier urgency, his touch slowed. His caress traveled up my leg as he parted my tender skin. "A little more, okay?"

He gently slid back inside of me, filling me. I never imagined a moment like this, so unguarded and passionate. We stared into each other's eyes, breathed each other's air, as our bodies rocked as one.

Hale was the first man to bring me any level of pleasure worth mentioning, but he was also the first man to make love to me. That's what this was. There was no denying it. Wild, unrefined, tender, or slow, it was exactly what he was doing. And I was making love to him, too. It passed between us like secrets in the night as my chest ached in a pleasantly reassuring way that told me I was alive.

These feelings, all of these sharp, intense feelings, cut into my soul. They showed me just how deeply this man connected with me. For the first time in my life I felt anchored and secure, and for once, I wasn't scared.

I didn't know where the tears came from. Hale's face nuzzled mine, catching each salty truth that fell between us in those quiet moments of completion. He whispered, pressing kisses to my eyes and temples. "So beautiful, Rayne."

His lips pressed with each uttered truth. "So sweet." But my favorite, of all his words, was when he whispered, "You're mine."

I Avoid. That's What I Do

28

"Aren't you going to Hale's?"

Folding my feet beneath my legs on the couch I shrugged and reached for the remote. "Are you watching this?"

Remington eyed me suspiciously. "That depends on what you want to watch."

"*Impractical Jokers* is on."

"Then yes, I'm watching this."

I rolled my eyes and relinquished the remote. My gaze followed the crawl on the bottom of the screen reporting the same news that had been reported for the last three hours.

"Why aren't you going out, Meyers?"

I shrugged again. I was avoiding Hale's mother, but that didn't need stating. "I'm tired."

I felt Remington's scrutiny without having to see it. "You don't wear intimidation well. Naomi's nothing to be afraid of."

That was likely true, but she was Hale's mother

and I didn't have the energy to be examined. "I'm not intimidated by her."

He chuckled. "Bullshit."

Poking back, I asked, "Why did you two get divorced?"

"She took issue with the company I kept."

I pursed my lips, certain I knew exactly the sort of company he was referring to. Men like Remington were shamelessly anti-monogamous. "Why even get married?"

His head tilted. "Stability."

"Forget I asked. I don't want to know how you justify things in that head of yours."

He slid me the remote and I changed the channel. I'd already seen this episode, but it was a good one. Murray and Joe were my favorite impractical jokers.

"You'll marry some day and understand," he commented, frowning at the screen. "These men are idiots."

"I might marry, but I doubt I'll ever view the laws of fidelity the way you do." I laughed as one of the jokers got busted mid-challenge.

"Would you forgive a man for straying?"

"No."

"How can you be so sure?"

As a commercial came on I looked at Remington. "Why get married if the rules of monogamy don't apply?"

"There's more than one vow. Just because I strayed doesn't mean I didn't love my wives."

He said wives as if he were a natural polygamist. "Let's talk about something else."

He was silent for a long moment. "I expect Hale will eventually propose."

I choked, because he spoke as though he were wondering if it might rain. *"Excuse me?"*

His brows briefly lifted. "He loves you. I know my son."

"Well, let's hold off a bit on the registry." Things were moving way too fast.

He chuckled. "Any wise woman would say *yes* to a Davenport."

"And what gave you the impression I was wise? I don't care about your wealth."

"And so you shouldn't. What's mine is mine. But Hale's success is nothing to sneeze at."

So far we'd avoided any frank discussions of Hale's unarguable capital. It hung there, like an affluent smog over every detail of his life, but it wasn't what attracted me to him. "Did you get my notes on the Wes Sterling donations?"

"Now there's another kind of success. I spoke to him today. He asked how you were."

My eyes narrowed. "What are you doing, Remington?"

Feigning innocence, he blanked his expression. "The man's interested in you."

"I'm dating your son."

"Well, it isn't as though you two exchanged vows," he grumbled.

"Don't be a jerk."

"He'll be in Florida this week."

"Who?"

"Wes."

I rolled my eyes. "I said, knock it off."

"I'm joining him for dinner on Monday. I'll expect you to make the arrangements."

Pursing my lips, I kept quiet. I'd make the arrangements, because that was my job. But I wasn't attending that dinner.

"You'll attend the dinner."

I scoffed. "I'm not going to that dinner."

"I need you there. I want Wes to get onboard with a future venture of mine and I'll need all the leverage I can get."

"Then buy him jewelry or something. I'm not flirting with some guy for your financial benefit."

"You flirting would be disastrous," he mumbled. "I just need you present."

What was I, some sort of performing chimp? "The answer's no."

"You'll go."

He was wrong. I wasn't going. Irritated, I stood.

"You going to Hale's?"

Was this some way of driving me up the wall so I'd have no choice but to meet Hale's mother? I didn't like feeling maneuvered, which Remington excelled at.

"No. I'm going for a walk."

He laughed. "Chicken."

"*Buck-buck* off."

As I left him on the couch, he yelled, "That's not the sound a chicken makes."

I walked along the beach until Hale's home stood before me. What was he doing at this very moment? If he'd told his mother about me, what had he said?

The last time I saw him, things had been overwhelmingly intense between us. At the time it seemed pivotal, shoving us in the direction of something monumental, but after of day digesting all those intense emotions, I was now fearful.

I was a breaker. I broke things and I didn't want to break us. Thus me sneaking out of his house as soon as his mom notified him her flight landed. Well, not sneaking. It was more of a scurry.

His dad was right. I was a chicken. Turning back to Remington's, I intended to enter through the pool area to avoid any commentary from the peanut gallery. But when I spotted Miles sitting at the pool drinking a beer, my intentions were sidetracked.

"Hey." I grinned, desperate for a distraction.

He looked well adjusted now that Remington was no longer on a warpath. I pulled up a chair beside him and faced the ocean.

"Hey." He reached to his side. "Want a beer?"

"Sure." In companionable silence, we watched the sun set and sipped our bottles.

I casually flicked my cap across the table, landing it between two candlesticks. Miles did the same, knocking my cap out of what I already considered the goal posts.

Leaning forward, I retrieved the two caps and shot again. My cap pinged off the candle and skittered across the cobblestones and we both laughed.

An hour later, several caps were on the table and the candles had been relocated to a more sensible location. Other household items, such as a bottle of port and set of wine glasses, had also worked their way into the mix. As we hunched over opposite ends of the table, we laughed and took countering shots, working under a combination of rules that resembled table hockey, mini golf, and paper football.

Miles nailed a shot in my goal and I shouted, "No fair! I wasn't ready. I wanted to move my shoe."

"Bullshit. You already set up your pieces."

I sipped my beer and hunkered down, squaring my shoulders and lining up my shot. He angled his shoe in front of his goal. I needed this point.

Aligning my fingers, I squinted at the little cap and flicked hard. It pinged across the table and missed the goal by an inch. "Son of a bitch!"

Miles laughed and shot up a finger. "Point!"

"How is that a point?"

"You missed."

"So did you."

"No. I made the shot fair and square."

"My shoe was wrong!"

"Your ass. Don't be sour."

We continued to bicker, but it was all in good fun. I hadn't realized how much time we'd wasted playing the stupid game until the sliding doors opened and Hale appeared, expression blank.

Distracted from my next shot, I stood up. "Hale."

He glanced at Miles and back to me. "I could hear you all the way out front."

I bit my lips, trying not to laugh, only slightly sorry. Miles returned his shoe to his foot and gathered up the beer bottles. "It's getting late."

Hale stepped aside as Miles passed, returning to the house. I put the candles back and slid my flip-flops on my feet. A sense of breaking curfew stole over me, but that was silly. We were only having fun and it felt like ages since I did something as mindless as play a drinking game. "How was your day?"

He brushed a kiss over my cheek. "It was good. I thought I'd see you at some point."

"I was...busy."

He raised a brow.

"Did your mom get settled?"

"Yeah. She's great with Elara."

I supposed that was how he'd been able to show up sans child. This mother thing might just work out. "That's good."

He glanced back at the house, which was now dark. "You and Miles seem to be getting along."

"We're just having fun." Miles was a distraction, nothing more.

"I see that." He picked up a bottle, read the label and returned it to the table. "How do you feel about dinner tomorrow night?"

"With just us?" The moment I asked I saw that wasn't what he'd been suggesting. "Or all of us. Whatever."

His brow creased. "Are you avoiding my mother?"

"Maybe."

"Why?"

I shrugged, finding my reasoning pretty solid after six beers. "Because it's your mom and I've never met a boyfriend's mom before."

"You already spoke to her once. If not for her, we might not have met. She wants to meet you in person, Rayne."

And there lay the issue. She likely had all sorts of expectations about the woman in her son's life. None of which I'd meet.

"I'm sure we'll cross paths eventually."

"You'll meet her tomorrow."

Taking a step back, because that wasn't a request, my guard went up. "Hale."

"Let's not make a big deal of it. We'll have dinner and—"

"Hold on a minute." I shook my head. "You're being a bit high-handed."

His jaw twitched and I could tell he was irritated with my reluctance. "This is something I want, Rayne."

"Well, I want a unicorn. Life's full of disappointments."

He scowled. "You're being childish."

"You're being bossy."

His tone dropped as he gave me a penetrating stare. "You like when I'm bossy."

In a different context. "Not at the moment."

He took a step closer and caught my hip, yanking me to his front. His hand slid to my ass and cupped me possessively. "How about now?"

My breath hitched as I blinked at him. "That's okay," I whispered, liking where this was going. My body arched against his front as he looked into my eyes and his hand slid lower.

"I want you."

Yes, I liked *this* bossy side of him very much. Thinking this was better than bickering about his mother, I gave the slightest nod and he pulled me into the shadows where a lounge chair sat. His lips crushed mine in an almost punishing kiss and I met him lick for lick.

"Do you want me, Rayne?"

"Yes," I breathed, as he stepped closer, sliding his fingers under my dress. I rose on my toes as he bunched my skirt. "Hale..."

His thumb latched onto my panties, exposing a bit of my ass cheek. His touch moved between my legs as his other hand pulled down the top of my dress, exposing my breasts.

"Let him hear you call my name."

What?

Awareness slammed into me and I stepped back, covering myself with my dress. "What are you doing?"

He crowded me, prying my hands away from my chest. "I think my intensions are clear."

"Wait a minute." I caught his wrist. I wasn't into exhibitionism. "What is this?"

He scowled at me and pulled his touch away. "I heard you two carrying on."

"Who? Me and Miles? So what? We were playing a game."

"You didn't even call me today," he snapped, taking me off guard.

And that gave him a green light to act like a jerk? "So fucking what? I was busy."

"Drinking with Miles. I know how you get when you drink."

Speechless, I gaped at him. Possessiveness was fine when it was just the two of us, but I wasn't about putting on a show to make another man jealous and inflate my boyfriend's ego. Not to mention I was pretty sure Miles was gay.

Offended and disappointed, I fixed my dress. "I don't have to stand here and listen to this shit."

"You're just going to walk away?"

I paused and eyed him from head to toe. "From this? Yes. Call me when you grow up."

"Oh, you're one to talk."

My steps faltered. I knew in that moment Hale hadn't been lying when he said he could be an asshole. "What's wrong with you?"

"Nothing. I'd rather address whatever this problem is between us than avoid it, which I know you're doing."

I scoffed. "And that's what you were doing, addressing a problem? Don't act like you have everything under control when you don't. You're pissed I'm not ready to meet your mom and jealous I was hanging out with another man. Fucking me doesn't change that. I'm going to bed."

I went inside, shaking my head, leaving him and his insecurities out to dry. I'd definitely been avoiding his mother, but so what? There was no rule that said I had to meet his mom *now*.

Too many formalities were suddenly coming into play. Why couldn't we just be us? And what the hell was that bullshit about letting others hear us fooling around? He wanted to invite too many people into something private.

Jerk. Stupid jealous jerk.

Being territorial was one thing, but his trust issues were not my fault. I refused to pay a price every time he saw me in the vicinity of another man.

Was there some deformed Davenport gene that made the temptation of manipulating others irresistible? For such big men they sure had the frailest egos. This was the first time I saw something so incredibly Remington in Hale and I didn't like it.

Hale had trust issues, for sure, but I wouldn't enable them. If he wanted to act like such a grown up, he needed to trust people, especially where I was concerned.

Love did not entitle one person to control another. I'd never try to dictate to him the way he'd just tried dictating to me. Why did he have to say that? Why couldn't things just be uncomplicated and fun? But more than anything, why did he have to remind me so much of his father in that moment, a man I adored and disliked with equal measure?

Some Acorns Fall Far and Some Don't

29

The following day when Hale overlooked apologizing once again, I was still angry. Remington gave me a list of tasks and I attacked them one by one until they were all completed and then I demanded he give me more.

I didn't join Hale for dinner, nor did I call him. Miles was oblivious to my personal drama, as he should be, but Remington wasn't so easily fooled.

"You two have a fight?"

"Mind your own business," I'd snapped, and he must have sensed I was in no mood to discuss my issues with him.

When the weekend rolled around, Barrett returned. He'd caught up with an old flame and disappeared for a few days, but according to his father, that was normal behavior from Barrett.

With every passing day I thought about Elara. I wondered if she was growing, and worried that she'd already forgotten who I was. I couldn't hide my curiosity whenever Barrett returned from his brother's.

"Did you have a nice visit?"

"I'm out of it, Rayne. You want to talk about Hale, call him. I know he's waiting for you to pick up the phone."

"Oh is he?" I honestly didn't know if I could outlast Hale in some sort of pissing match. So I bluffed. "Well, he can go on waiting."

This was about more than Hale's mother. It was about him making me feel like a pawn in some dick-measuring contest and taking his insecurities out on me. But it was getting worse the longer he didn't call. Now it was about feeling ignored. By Monday, my anger tripled.

"Did you make the dinner reservations, Meyers?" Remington asked.

"Yes."

"Did you make them for three people?"

I scowled at him. "I told you I wasn't going."

"Your loss. Tell Miles to be ready by six."

My scowl dissolved into a pout. "Miles is going?"

"Unlike others in my employment, he appreciates the opportunity to network and make connections."

Well that was just great. At first I thought this was some ploy to get me to persuade the future president, but maybe Remington just felt the meeting would be more casual if he had an assistant present. And why was I considering how Hale played into any of this if attending such dinner meetings was just a part of my job, the same job expected of Miles?

Remington made no objection when I showed up wearing my black wrap dress for dinner and announced I'd be joining him and Wes. This was work. Period.

On the way to the restaurant, he complimented my outfit and I merely rolled my eyes. I wasn't a fan of Remington at the moment either, because while rationalizing my anger toward Hale, I'd pinned a clump of his trust issues on his father. Maybe if Remington hadn't gone sticking his dick where it didn't belong, his son wouldn't be so insecure when it came to other men hanging around his territory.

As we waited for Wes to arrive I read over the menu.

"When do you plan on getting out of this mood, Meyers?"

"You're one to talk." We all suffered plenty under the wrath of one of Remington's many temper tantrums.

"There's Wes."

I glanced up as the man of the hour entered the restaurant. His smile grew as his gaze crossed with mine. I truly hoped I wasn't playing into another Davenport scheme.

"Rayne. It's lovely to see you again."

I smiled without showing teeth. Remington went into a lengthy description of his upcoming venture and Wes appeared to only partially listen.

"Do you like the wine, Rayne?"

Taking a sip, I swallowed. "It's fine."

Remington stopped talking long enough to

watch Wes who apparently couldn't stop watching me. I supposed this was the time to practice some of those nifty networking skills I was always hearing about.

"So...president. Did you always plan to run?"

Wes's eyes—brown, not silver—softened. "I think every boy dreams of holding a position of power."

"Some just want to be veterinarians and zoo keepers." I didn't need to look at Remington to know he wasn't amused.

Wes chuckled. "Did you always want to be a personal assistant?"

"No. At one point I wanted to be Indiana Jones."

"Charming." He laughed again.

The waiter took our order and Wes humored Remington with some mild shoptalk. I switched from wine to water, because I didn't like the way Wes kept watching me. I also didn't like the way Remington made no attempt to intervene.

The conversation shifted back to lighter topics as dinner was served. I remained polite, but made no attempt to impress Wes. I wasn't interested in anything more than the pasta on my plate and honestly should have let Miles come in my place. What the hell did I have to network for?

It was a win-lose when I realized no one was ordering dessert. I never turned down dessert, but I was glad the evening was coming to an end, so I didn't make a fuss.

Wes and Remington talked as we made our way

to the valet. Once Remington was inside the limo, Wes made the move I'd been dreading.

"I'll be in town for the next few days. Perhaps I could take you out again, Rayne. No politics this time. Just the two of us."

I finally allowed myself to actually take his measure. He was a decent looking guy, older than me by at least ten years, if not more. But he was fit and fairly attractive on a politician's scale. No matter what, I couldn't see past his career. But most unappealing of all, he wasn't Hale.

I suddenly had an image of me sitting as First Lady and I laughed, because it was such a ludicrous thought.

"What's funny?"

My laughter ceased. Time to get serious. "I have a boyfriend."

"Hale?"

"Yes."

If he had any inclination I was involved with Remington's son, he shouldn't be asking me out. It seemed all so two-faced and... politician like.

He reached in his pocket and produced a card. "Well, you have my number if things change."

Appalled by his persistence, I took the card and slid into the limo. Wes leaned in and offered a polite goodbye to Remington.

Once we were on our way, Hale's father said, "Hold onto that card."

If I wasn't so opposed to littering I would have chucked it out the window just to spite him, but I made do with crumpling it in my hand. "Don't you care what your son thinks?"

"Of course I care."

"Then why encourage me to have dinner with someone else?"

"It's not for my benefit."

My brows lifted. "Oh, really. Then whose?"

"Yours. He could open doors for you."

"I can open my own damn doors," I grumbled, sick of the games. "Besides, you and I both know I'm not his type."

"There are all kinds of types, Meyers. No one's moving you into the White House, but you'd be in a comfortable position."

I gaped. "Jesus, you are such an asshole."

"But I'm honest. Marilynn wore as many smiles as Jackie Onassis, if not more. "

"My God, Remington. Shut up."

I was quickly shifting back to my stance of sex complicates life and should mostly be avoided. Seeing sex as any sort of manipulation device disgusted me.

Irritated, I asked, "How is it men can sleep with whoever they want for the simple pleasure of it, but with women it always comes down to being some sort of tool or weapon?"

"Don't turn your nose up at a good opportunity when your other options are suddenly MIA. Things change, Meyers."

My eyes closed, showing him I was finished with the conversation, but he didn't seem concerned with my limits.

"Hale won't beg. I don't know what you two are squabbling about, but you've reached an impasse. Either you bend or the game's over."

Was that true? Deep down the thought terrified me, but I hid my fear. "It's always a game with you, isn't it?"

"There's always a motive."

I narrowed my eyes. "And what's yours?"

"Which one do you want to know?"

Shifting in my seat, I looked him square in the eye. "Jasmine. Why did you sleep with her?"

His brow twitched. "She offered."

"Bullshit. You're always three moves ahead, Remington. You loved your wife and you love your son. There was a reason you crossed that line."

"When it comes to sex, men aren't that complicated, Meyers. We like to feel powerful, desired and, above all, necessary."

"Yes, I'm getting quite a lesson on man's fragile little ego lately."

"It's your own ego that makes it impossible to understand what I'm talking about. Look at you now, waspish and miserable. That's the first sign of a bruised ego."

I rolled my eyes.

"Go ahead and roll your eyes. I'm right."

"No, you're not."

"Really? Let's see if I can't piece together the puzzle. You felt threatened by another woman, not the baby or the baby's mother, but Hale's mother. That was the first prick. Rather than face your fears, you turned the tables, using poor Miles as a pawn to even the score and poke back, showing your life could be just as busy as Hale's."

"You sound crazy. Miles and I were just hanging

out and all of you Davenports are out of your minds."

"Hale saw you two together, predictably got jealous, and suddenly you aren't speaking, and you somehow changed your mind about having dinner with a man who is openly interested in you. Even if you weren't intentionally provoking him with Miles, you knew exactly what you were getting into having dinner with Wes tonight. My son won't apologize now."

Seething, I snapped, "I had dinner because it's my job to attend these functions with you."

"I gave you the option not to go."

He was turning everything around! "This has absolutely nothing to do with my question about Jasmine."

"It has everything to do with it. If not for women like her and men like Wes, you wouldn't be in this predicament."

"And you take no accountability for *this predicament*?"

"Oh, I hold the lion's share."

He glanced at his watch and sighed, his attention turning to the traffic passing by. "Rachel was gentle. She never expected anything from me but my loyalty. She was devoted, kind, everything women like Jasmine will never be. Hale knew the kind of woman Jasmine was, which was why he got involved with her—no messy emotions. In the end, she got her pay off and now she's satisfied."

"But why jeopardize what you had with Rachel for a woman like that?"

"Because I'm a man. We want it all."

I couldn't wait to get out of this car. "That's you, not every man."

"Are you sure about that?"

No, I wasn't sure about anything. Sometimes Hale was vulnerable, other times he was strong. Gentle, demanding, forgiving or rigid, there were many sides to the same man.

The other night he'd upset me, coming in like a dog ready to mark his territory. It bothered me, but also made me feel like a hypocrite, when the night before I'd let him use every part of me and encouraged every second of his intense possession. I didn't understand what made both situations so different, but they were.

By the time we returned to the house I was more confused than ever. I helped Remington to bed, but didn't linger.

"Meyers?"

I gritted my teeth and paused at the door. *So close.* "I'm tired Remington."

"There's something incredibly alluring about a woman strong enough to surrender. Don't mistake it for weakness."

I was so sick of strategizing. "And there's something to be said for a man big enough to apologize when he hurts someone he loves."

"Also true, but not a trait you'll find in any Davenport. When things are too rigid, they break. Don't be ashamed of bending where he can't."

Making no comment, I shut the door, but Remington's words stuck with me. I didn't want us to break. I just wanted Hale, uncomplicated and at my side.

After pacing for over an hour, wondering which one of us was the bigger stubborn ass, I decided nothing was worth missing him this much and someone had to make the first move. I found my phone and texted him.

> Are you awake?

MY PHONE RANG AS HIS NUMBER FLASHED on the screen. "Hey." His voice was monotone, giving me no indication of his feelings at the moment.

"Can we be done with our fight now? I don't want to be mad anymore."

He was silent for a moment. "I'm not mad at you, Rayne. I was giving you time."

"Time for what?"

He sighed. "I don't know if I can change certain things about me, Rayne. I'm fucked up for good reason. If you can't handle this..." He paused. "You're not the only one afraid of being hurt."

I understood his *reasoning*, but he also had to understand my background. He hurt me. "One of my closest friends is a guy, Hale. You can't expect me to only have female friends and you can't turn into a jerk every time I'm around other men."

"I don't expect you to only have female friends."

"Then what is it you want?"

"I want to know you're mine and that nothing will threaten what we have."

Oh, was that all? Because I'd misplaced my crystal ball and the future remained a mystery, I gave the little assurance I had. "I've never cheated on anyone, Hale."

"That's not what I'm worried about."

"Then what? It's been days and you haven't called."

"I know what I want, Rayne, but you have to figure out what *you* want. Don't think this week wasn't torture for me, but I endured it so you could have some time to decide what it is you want. I have no interest in moving backwards, but the biggest threat to us right now seems to be this impulse you have to bolt whenever things get too real."

"I wasn't bolting."

"But you were avoiding, not just my mom, but me. I know my life's complicated, but I can't filter it for you. I don't want to. Nor do I want some censored version of you. It's like I said, I want *all* of you."

Was that some sort of code for anal sex? Because I definitely wasn't ready for that. "I'm not sure I follow."

"I don't know how else to explain it other than I want all of you."

"Um..." He was going to have to give me more information than that.

"Look, Rayne, I know this is moving fast, but I've never felt so strongly about another person. When you're not around, I can't breathe. You're always on my mind and when I'm with you I don't want to let go. The thought of anything threatening that..."

I frowned, not used to anyone taking my actions so personally. "I'm not going anywhere."

"If I need you, I want you here. I want you to be there for me and, damn it, I want you to let me be there for you. This thing you do, closing yourself off from me every time things get a little intense, I won't have it. I love you. I *trust* you, but you have to be honest with me about how you're feeling."

I understood what he was saying. No masks. No more façades. "I try to always be honest with you."

"Do you?"

Okay, maybe that wasn't one hundred percent true. "I wasn't trying to upset you the other night. I just... needed space."

"Why?"

Holding the phone close to my ear, I lowered my gaze. "I don't know. I get scared. The other night was...a lot."

He paused. "I didn't mean to overwhelm you."

"You didn't—I mean, maybe you did, but I loved it. But then your mom arrived and...I don't know how to meet people's expectations. I always screw up."

"Nobody expects you to be anyone other than you, baby. She just wants to meet you, because I love you."

Love was such a big word and it didn't extend through degrees of separation. Just because Hale loved me didn't mean his mother would. Parental rejection was painful and I was terrified possibly being rejected by Naomi Davenport would tear open old wounds.

He signed and I wished I could see him. "Some

scars take lifetimes to heal, Rayne, and I think we both have some pretty deep ones. It was never my intention to scare you. I just...need you. And when I fear you pulling away I tend to hold on tighter than I probably should."

Closing my eyes, I let myself believe him for a moment. Warmth bloomed in my chest, pronouncing the empty ache that had always been there before meeting Hale.

Not being the most flexible person, the first bend hurt. "No one's ever needed me."

Five simple words, but they gutted me. I hated depending on others, because that dependency eventually became a crutch and when it disappeared I fell hard.

"I need you," he repeated. "All of you."

"Tell me how to do this, Hale. I have limited experience with relationships, and zero experience with guys like you."

"Come to the house."

"Now?"

"Yes. It's dark, so take a car. I'd come pick you up, but Elara's sleeping."

"What about your mom?"

"She's sleeping in the guesthouse."

"Okay, but I want to keep talking about this—"

"The conversation's far from over, Rayne."

"Good." Holy shit, I actually wanted to communicate. And now I was sweating. But I could do this. Hale was worth it. "I'll be there in a few minutes."

"I'll be waiting."

As I drove, I considered everything Remington

said over the past few weeks. I wanted to be what Hale needed and I wanted to prove that honest men didn't need to stray to have it all. He asked for all of me and I wanted to try to give him just that, over-looking my fears that I might somehow come up short.

When I pulled into his driveway I drew in a slow breath, unsure what I was walking into. I pulled the keys from the ignition and let myself into his house. The hall lights were on, but all the rooms were dark.

Dropping my purse on the side table, I quietly called for him. "Hale?"

"I'm in the den."

I stepped around the corner and paused as my eyes took him in. He sat on the chair next to the couch, shirt off, a weathered pair of jeans covering his legs. His expression was neutral and I waited for him to invite me further into the room.

The fleeting thought that this was a mistake crossed my mind when he still didn't rise to greet me. But I fought the urge to bolt.

"Parking was a bitch," I joked, but he didn't laugh. He actually didn't look happy at all.

"You're dressed up."

I glanced at my clothing. "I—"

"You went to dinner with them. With Wes."

Yes, and I totally Lewinskied the future presi-dent and the entire wait staff during appetizers. *This* was what I couldn't deal with. "Maybe I should go."

"Stay."

"So you can make me feel guilty for doing abso-lutely nothing wrong? No thanks."

I turned and he said, "Please stay. I'm not upset you went to dinner."

Pivoting, I looked at him in surprise. "You're... you're not?"

"No. Did he ask you out?"

"He gave me his card." I had no reason to lie. I wasn't going to use it.

"Before or after you told him we were involved?"

My brows lifted at his arrogance. But part of me was glad he knew I'd mention our relationship. "After."

"Did he touch you?"

"He shook my hand."

"I won't pretend that doesn't make me jealous, thinking of him even brushing his fingers to yours, but I trust you, Rayne. It's other men I don't trust."

It was almost comical, talking about something as simple as a handshake, but I couldn't resist. "It meant nothing to me."

His eyes gentled as he smiled. "I missed you."

I shook my head. "All you Davenports are nuts."

He pushed out of the chair, his body unfolding with the grace of a jaguar as he slowly stalked across the room. "He'll try again. Persistent little fuck that he is."

"I have no interest in him, Hale."

"I know." He approached and I took a small step back.

"Or Miles."

"I know that too. I was a schmuck the other night. I wanted you, plain and simple, but I let my own insecurities cloud my judgment."

My hand pressed to his chest as he leaned closer. "You need to understand that sex is a private thing for me. I've recently gone from having inadequate sex with myself to mind-blowing sex with a man I actually like. I'm not a toy for you to show off to the other boys, and if you ever make me feel like that again, I'll disappear for good. You hurt me."

He stilled, his posture drawing back as all playfulness left his expression. True regret reflected in his eyes as he bowed his head. "I'm sorry."

And there it was. His father was wrong. Hale was man enough to apologize when he hurt those he loved, because he would always be more honorable than the man who raised him.

Drawing in a deep breath, I let his apology wash over me, patching many uncertainties and building back my confidence in him. "Thank you for saying that."

He caught my hand and squeezed my fingers. "I was jealous. Scared you were pulling away."

"That side of me...it's for you, Hale. No one else."

His eyes reflected contrition, removing any further need for apology. "It wasn't my best moment. I hate that I hurt you."

"You say you want all of me...fine. But don't set unobtainable standards. You don't have to trust everyone, but you absolutely have to trust me. I'll give you whatever I can in private, but you respect that those moments *are* private. They're ours, no one else's."

"Understood."

I relaxed, rather impressed with my ability to

negotiate and communicate my feelings like an adult woman. I was growing. Maybe we both were. "Okay then."

He looked at me as if waiting for permission to move.

I shrugged. "I forgive you."

He smiled and looked into my eyes then hesitated. "I'm going to kiss you. Don't run."

"Smart ass."

Pulling me into his arms, he toppled to the couch and hugged me tight. His lips pressed into mine and all my tension faded away.

"I love you, Rayne. I don't like when we're apart."

"I love you too. And this week absolutely sucked without you."

His hold tightened around me. "This is new territory."

I nuzzled my nose into his chest and pressed a kiss to his chin. "I think we can handle it —together."

"Together," he repeated and kissed me softly.

"Hale..." It took courage to open up to another person, but I trusted him. "I've never been good at depending on others."

His fingertips brushed tenderly over my cheek. "You can depend on me, baby. I'm not going anywhere. I wasn't lying when I said I want all of you. I want the crazy. I want the sexy. I want the secrets you keep from everyone else. And I don't think I've ever wanted anything more."

The first man I'd ever wanted to love wouldn't love me back, so trusting such a promise didn't come easily. I snuggled into him, resting my ear over his steadily beating heart. "I love you." They weren't just words. "But you should know, there's more crazy than sexy."

He chuckled. "I want it all, Rayne. Every piece of your heart, even the broken ones." Tipping up my chin he brushed his lips to mine. "You don't have to hide yourself away from me."

I kissed him, my mouth moving slowly against his as the weight of all my loneliness, all the heavy emptiness, changed shape inside of me. This was forward and there would be no going back.

Hale wasn't like other guys. He was undeniably a Davenport, but he wasn't all Remington. He was determined and patient and all the things I struggled to be. Simply put, he was the other half of my puzzle, the one I'd been trying to solve for the last thirty years.

Once we made it upstairs, Hale checked on Elara. I no longer looked at his situation as a complication, but as another facet of Hale. Elara represented all of his honorability, his desire to do the right thing. She represented the unchartered distance his love braved to travel.

Hale might not always be right, but he held himself to a standard his father would never reach. And though I cared deeply for Remington, I was so grateful Hale was not a carbon copy of the man.

Resting with our heads on the pillows, our faces only inches apart, I told him, "I'm ready to meet your mother."

His smile was unguarded and genuine. He

tucked a piece of hair behind my ear and whispered, "I'll introduce you tomorrow."

As he drifted off to sleep I knew he was satisfied, content in a way he hadn't been in a long time. So was I.

489

30

All of my hopes to make a decent first impression were crushed when Hale's mom walked in on us the following morning. Thank the fucking saints we weren't doing more than sleeping. She was extremely apologetic for barging in, repeatedly apologizing for assuming Hale was alone.

"Mom," Hale grumbled, when she continued to apologize throughout breakfast. "It's fine. Let it go."

I endured the meal wearing one of Hale's dress shirts and a pair of his briefs, while my hair had its own eighties revival going on. Naomi was polite enough not to notice—or at least pretend my hair didn't resemble a bird's nest.

Elara suckled her fingers and burped as I held her in one arm. I was totally impressed by my ability to not drop her while using my other hand to eat.

Once I got over the embarrassment of being caught in Hale's bed by his mother, I came to terms with letting this woman see exactly who I was. It was much easier than I expected, being that Naomi was a fairly easygoing lady.

"So do you like working for Remmy?"

My face lit up. "You call him Remmy?" I'd asked if I could call him that and he'd said no.

"Remmy's the man I know. Remington is someone he became."

Interesting. "How did you two meet?" I could get all kinds of juicy gossip from this woman.

"In college," Naomi said, clearing the plates off the table and refilling our coffee. "I never wanted the life he has now. I couldn't handle all the politics and upper class mingling. I just wanted to be a wife."

This was the woman Remington said he never understood? She seemed pretty cut and dried to me. "Do you ever regret leaving?"

"God, no!" She laughed. "I'll always love him, but he loved himself way too much to spare what little I needed. I'd rather be alone than always coming second to whoever could do him a favor at the moment." Her smile turned, not sad, but accepting. "I learned a long time ago the one thing sadder than loneliness is feeling alone when you have a 'partner'."

And wasn't that the truth. Remington always kept a bead on those he loved, but he never put business aside. Never. I couldn't fault this woman for getting away from that sort of unsatisfying partnership. Part of me respected her for loving herself enough to leave.

After breakfast I changed into my dress and found Hale already in his office. "I have to go."

He twisted in his chair and pulled me into his lap. "Will I see you tonight?"

I nodded. "I, um, have those papers for you to sign."

He took the file from me and reached for a pen, opening to the pages Lynette had marked with Post-Its.

I caught his hand. "Wait."

He looked at me in question.

"What happens if you give her a different property, Hale? How much will she really fight you?"

He sat back and sighed. "We've been through this."

"So go through it again. I've seen you negotiate. You're no slouch."

His eyes shifted as he considered the challenges. "It'll cost me twice as much."

"What's the price of peace of mind? You don't want her that close to your family." And maybe I didn't want her that close either.

"I'll make some calls today and see what I can do, but I think it's a done deal at this point."

"Then no harm in trying one last time." Remington believed everyone had a price, it was a matter of matching it at the right moment. Speaking of Remington...

I kissed Hale's cheek and slid off his lap. "I love you. I have to go. My boss can be a real prick when I'm late."

"Don't I know it." He slapped my ass and I squeaked.

"Calm yourself. Your mother's in the house."

He arched a brow, telling me that wouldn't stop him.

Bunch of deviants, these Davenports. I kissed him one last time. "Goodbye."

When I returned to the house I hoped to change before anything pressing was thrown at me, but that was just crazy talk. The second I stepped through the door, Marta looked up and mumbled something in Spanish, before gazing away and rushing into the kitchen. That didn't sound good.

"Meyers," Remington called from the back room. "Come in here, please."

Please? His mood couldn't be that bad if he was using manners. Tossing my purse on the foyer table I went to see what he needed. "Sorry, I'm late."

He waved away my apology. "Have a seat."

Everyone else was mysteriously absent and the television was off. It usually played on a low volume throughout the day. I quickly went over my objectives from the past few days, ticking off each item wondering if there was something I overlooked.

Lowering myself to the chair, I looked at him expectantly. "Where is everyone? Why is it so quiet?"

My concern doubled when his gaze wouldn't reach my eyes. "Rayne..." He cleared his throat and my stomach knotted. Not Rayne. I was Meyers. *Meyers.*

My breath turned shaky, as he remained silent. "You're scaring me, Remington. What's going on?"

He reached beside him and held up my phone—not the bat phone, which I'd been using lately, but my actual phone. "You left this here last night. It was ringing a few minutes ago. It rang several times...so I finally answered."

I reached for it and he pulled it back. Dropping into my seat I struggled to breathe. "Who called?"

I don't know who I was expecting him to say, but I knew whoever called didn't have good news. "Your friend, Tyler. There was an accident. Your friend Elle was hurt."

My brain disconnected for a moment and I had to replay his words several times before they made sense. "What?"

Elle was in an accident? It couldn't be bad, because she was Elle. My eyes burned as I stared at him, waiting for him to explain more and how he was going to make it all better, because he was Remington and he could fix anything.

"It's not good, sweetheart. Hale said you were on your way back when I called there. He's on his way here. I've booked you a flight to go home this afternoon. Everything's taken care of. Right now she's stable, but..."

My head shook as pain tightened my chest. "What kind of accident?"

"She was run off the road by a drunk driver. They have the man in custody."

I was going to throw up. Suddenly I was on my feet, pacing. "I have to go."

"Your flight leaves in a few hours."

"That's not good enough. I have to leave now! What did Tyler say? Is she awake? Talking?"

"She woke up when they were transporting her, but nothing since. Sweetheart, take a breath and then we'll call the hospital, see if we can get an update."

"I need to call Tyler."

"The hospital will—"

Ignoring him, I grabbed my phone and speed dialed Tyler.

"Rayne?" he answered, voice distraught.

My throat was unbearably tight. "What happened?"

It was just as Remington said. Elle had been driving home from work when a drunk driver came out of nowhere and ran her off the road. Her car was totaled. She was in the ICU, but somewhat stable. However, she hadn't regained consciousness or shown any response since last night. Once off the phone with Tyler I rushed to my room and frantically tossed clothes onto my bed.

Remington followed me on his scooter. "Take a breath, Rayne."

"I need a fucking suitcase! Jesus, I can't even think!"

He sent a text out on his phone and Marta appeared, laying a suitcase on the bed. Remington scooted further into the room. "Things like this happen."

My face was damp with spent tears, but I didn't care who saw me cry. I needed to get home and it would take hours to get there. "How long does it take to fly from Florida to Oregon?"

"About six hours."

That was my breaking point. Dropping to the edge of the bed, I held my face and sobbed. Remington's hand rested lightly on my back, but there were no words that could comfort me in those agonizing moments. Even he couldn't fix this. For all his power and privilege, his wife had still died.

"What am I going to do if something happens to her?" I sobbed. "My best friend is in a fucking coma!"

A door slammed on the other end of the house as I wheezed and I tried to catch my breath. When I saw Hale I crumbled again, letting the last of my sanity go, certain he'd catch all the shattered pieces.

His father moved aside and Hale pulled me into his arms, holding me tight as his lips pressed to my temple. "Do you want me to go with you?" he whispered.

Yes... Shoulders shaking, I wiped my eyes. "You can't." He had a baby and she was too new to travel.

"I can do whatever you need, baby. If you want me to go, I'll go. Marta and my mom can take care of Elara until we get back."

I could never ask him to leave his newborn daughter. God only knew how long I'd be gone. I had to do this on my own.

"No." I shook my head, pulling myself together as much as possible. "You need to stay here."

His expression shuttered and I knew what he was going to ask, but I didn't have an answer. "How long will you be gone?"

My head pounded from too many worries. "I don't know."

He nodded. There was no sign of objection in his expression, just sad acceptance. Elle was my best friend and I would go for as long as it took. I wouldn't leave until I was certain she was safe and well.

"I'm sorry." My tears returned.

"Hey," he whispered, cupping my face. "She'll

get through this. You're going to Oregon and I'll be here waiting for you to return with good news. No apologizing. Understand?"

"I might be gone a while."

My stomach hurt when I imagined being away from him for anything more than a few days. I hated every minute wasted over the last few weeks.

What if I was gone for weeks, or *months*? We had only been together a short time. I wasn't sure our connection could survive that sort of separation.

"Who's going to take care of your dad?" It was the least of my worries, but the biggest obstacle I could manage at the moment.

"We'll figure that out."

They'd have to hire someone new if I was gone for more than a few days. Another sickening expectation to process. I didn't want to be replaced. This was my job. These were *my* Davenports.

"Hey." He tilted my face. "Look at me, baby. You're coming back. I'm sure of it. This is just an unexpected hiccup. Elle will heal and everything will be fine. Trust me."

Didn't he know cars crashed and seasickness happened? He couldn't make those sorts of guarantees, but I nodded anyway, needing to believe he could.

Hale helped me pack, insisting I leave items behind, because eventually I'd be back. Marta made me a goody bag of food for the airport and Remington insisted I take a credit card for "incidentals". No matter how much Hale promised I'd be back, when he hugged me goodbye at the gate, his fear left an imprint.

"I love you, Rayne."

The words escaped my throat like razor blades. "I love you too."

It was happening. I was already detaching, because that's what I always did when life overwhelmed me. Yet some part of me couldn't let go.

"Hale...I'm scared."

He kissed me and looked into my eyes. "If you need *anything* all you have to do is call. I can be there in a matter of hours."

Forcing my hands to release his arms, I swallowed a sob and stepped back, nodding. Everything inside of me hurt. There was so much fear, endless panic, and there would be no more Hale to ease my scattered mind.

Without Hale, without Elle, I couldn't imagine my life. It was possibly the most painful goodbye I'd ever made.

"I'll call you when I get there."

"I'll be waiting."

So many thoughts raced through my head as I turned away from him. Elle might be forever changed. Elara would grow in my absence. Remington would hire someone new. And Hale...

People always told me, true love could last forever. This trip home would be the truest test of all.

To be continued in...

Want more Calamity?
Read Calamity Rayne Back Again now!

Claim your FREE book when you subscribe to Lydia's newsletter!
Click here to sign up for Lydia Michaels' Newsletter.

Are you follow Lydia Michaels?
Stalk her on TikTok, Instagram, Facebook, Goodreads, and BookBub!
TikTok @LydiaMichaels
Instagram @lydia_michaels_books
Facebook @LydiaMichaels
Goodreads
BookBub

Show Your LOVE
If you enjoyed this book, please don't forget to leave a review.

LYDIA MICHAELS' READING ORDER

MCCULLOUGH MOUNTAIN
Almost Priest
Beautiful Distraction
Irish Rogue
British Professor
Broken Man
Controlled Chaos
Hard Fix
Intentional Risk

JASPER FALLS
Wake My Heart

THE ORDER OF VAMPIRES
<u>Original Sin</u>
<u>Dark Exodus</u>
<u>Prodigal Son</u>

STAND ALONES
<u>La Vie en Rose</u>
<u>Simple Man</u>
<u>Sugar</u>
<u>Breaking Perfect</u>
<u>Hurt</u>
<u>Protege</u>

About Lydia Michaels

Lydia Michaels is the award winning and bestselling author of more than forty titles, a certified life coach, and transformational speaker. She is the consecutive winner of the 2018 & 2019 *Author of the Year Award* from *Happenings Media,* as well as the recipient of the 2014 *Best Author Award* from the *Courier Times.* She has been featured in *USA Today, Romantic Times Magazine, Love & Lace,* and more. As the host and founder of the *East Coast Author Convention,* the *Behind the Keys Author Retreat,* and *Read Between the Wines,* she continues to celebrate her growing love for readers and romance novels around the world.

In 2021, Michaels released the groundbreaking, non-fiction series, ***Write 10K in a Day,*** to commemorate her career in the publishing industry. She looks forward to many more years of exploring both fiction and non-fiction writing, teaching about the craft, and learning from the others in the author community.

Lydia is happily married to her childhood sweetheart. Some of her favorite things include the scent of paperback books, listening to her husband play piano, escaping to her coastal home at the Jersey Shore, cheap wine, *Game of Thrones,* coffee, and kilts. She hopes to meet you soon at one of her many upcoming events.

You can follow Lydia at <u>www.Facebook.-</u>

com/LydiaMichaels or on Instagram
@lydia_michaels_books

503

<u>**Read By Mood**</u>
Billionaire Romance
<u>Falling In</u> | <u>Sacrifice Of The Pawn</u> | <u>Calamity Rayne</u> | <u>Blind</u>

Contemporary Romance
<u>Wake My Heart</u> | <u>The Best Man</u> | <u>Love Me Nots</u> | <u>Pining For You</u> |<u>Almost Priest</u>| <u>My Funny Valentine</u> | <u>Side Squeeze</u> | <u>Almost Priest</u> | <u>Beautiful Distraction</u> | <u>Irish Rogue</u> | <u>British Professor</u> | <u>Broken Man</u> (LGBTQ) | <u>Controlled Chaos</u> | <u>Hard Fix</u>|<u>Intentional Risk</u>

Emotional Favorites
<u>La Vie en Rose</u> | <u>Simple Man</u> | <u>Wake My Heart</u> | <u>Sacrifice of the Pawn</u> | <u>Crush</u>
Romantic Comedy
<u>Calamity Rayne</u>

Erotic Romance
<u>Breaking Perfect</u> | <u>Protégé</u> | <u>Falling In</u> | <u>Sugar</u>

First in Series
<u>Almost Priest</u> | <u>Falling In</u> |<u>First Comes Love</u> | <u>Wake My Heart</u> | <u>Crush</u> | <u>Original Sin</u>

Paranormal Vampire Romance
<u>Original Sin</u> | <u>Dark Exodus</u> | <u>Prodigal Son</u>

LGBTQ+ & Menage Romance
<u>Broken Man</u> (MM) | <u>Breaking Perfect</u> (MMF) | <u>Crush</u> (MMF) | <u>Hurt</u> (Non-Consensual) | <u>Protege</u>

Sexy Nerds & Second Chances
Blind | Untied
Teacher Student, Workplace, and Age-Gap Love Affairs... Oh my!
British Professor | Pining For You |Breaking Perfect | Falling In | Sacrifice of the Pawn

Single Dads & Single Moms
Simple Man | Pining For You | First Comes Love | Controlled Chaos | Intentional Risk

Dark Tortured Hero Romance
Hurt

Non-Fiction Books for Writers
Write 10K in a Day: Avoid Burnout

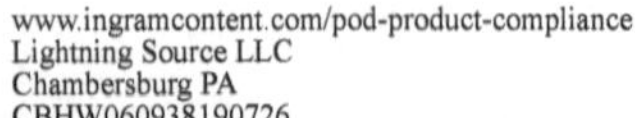
www.ingramcontent.com/pod-product-compliance
Lightning Source LLC
Chambersburg PA
CBHW060938190726
48286CB00005B/1332